VATHEK

WITH THE EPISODES OF VATHEK

VATHEK

WITH THE EPISODES OF VATHEK

William Beckford

edited by Kenneth W. Graham

translations by

Sir Frank T. Marzials and Kenneth W. Graham

broadview literary texts

National Library of Canada Cataloguing in Publication Data

Beckford, William, 1760-1844
    Vathek ; with, The episodes of Vathek

(Broadview literary texts)
Includes bibliographical references.
ISBN 1-55111-281-7

I. Graham, Kenneth W. (Kenneth Wayne). II. Marzials, Frank T. (Frank Thomas), Sir, 1840-1912. III. Title. IV. Title: Episodes of Vathek. V. Series.

PR4091.V313 2001   843'.5   C2001-930094-8

Broadview Press Ltd., is an independent, international publishing house, incorporated in 1985.

North America:
P.O. Box 1243, Peterborough, Ontario, Canada K9J 7H5
3576 California Road, Orchard Park, NY 14127
TEL: (705) 743-8990; FAX: (705) 743-8353;
E-MAIL: customerservice@broadviewpress.com

United Kingdom:
Turpin Distribution Services Ltd.,
Blackhorse Rd., Letchworth, Hertfordshire SG6 1HN
TEL: (1462) 672555; FAX (1462) 480947; E-MAIL: turpin@rsc.org

Australia:
St. Clair Press, P.O. Box 287, Rozelle, NSW 2039
TEL: (02) 818-1942; FAX: (02) 418-1923

www.broadviewpress.com

Broadview Press gratefully acknowledges the financial support of the Book Publishing Industry Development Program, Ministry of Canadian Heritage, Government of Canada.

Broadview Press is grateful to Professor Eugene Benson for advice on editorial matters for the Broadview Literary Texts series.

Text design and composition by George Kirkpatrick

PRINTED IN CANADA

William Beckford in middle age (about 40) by John Hoppner

Courtesy of the City of Salford Art Gallery

Contents

For members of the Beckford Round Table
1987, 1991, 1995, 1999

Hubertus von Amelunxen
Mirella Billi
Laurent Chatel
Dick Claesson
Stephen Clarke
Syndy Conger
Kevin Cope
Thomas Curley
John Garrett
Didier Girard
Malcolm Jack
Jürgen Klein
Guiseppe Massara
Temple Maynard
Jon Millington
Maria Laura Bettencourt Pires
Peter Sabor
Elinor Shaffer
Devendra Varma

Acknowledgements

This enterprise could not have proceeded without a great deal of help. At the top of the list are three undergraduate research assistants: Katherine Weir, Jennifer Poole, and Luke Hill. Katherine and Jennifer painstakingly deciphered and transcribed the Firouz manuscript, while Luke entered into the computer record the copy-text of *Vathek* and Marzials' translation of *The Episodes*, making careful lists of what needed to be corrected or explained. I am grateful also to Professor François Paré for making preliminary corrections of the French transcript of the Firouz *Episode*.

Two scholarly lists on the internet responded quickly and kindly to a variety of questions that rose out of the work: the Eighteenth-Century Interdisciplinary Discussion and the Society for Eighteenth-Century French Studies. I am especially grateful to the valuable contributions of Francis Assaf, Michel Baridon, Kevin Berland, Erin Blake, Adam Budd, Dick Claisson, Frederick Frank, Marie-Laure Girou-Swiderski, Victor Matthews, Karen Mulhallen, Reni Rivara, Lorna Rourke, Norbert Sclippa, Peter Sabor, Alan Sugerman, and Leon Surette.

Professor Michael Finn of Ryerson Polytechnic University is technical consultant to the project. His contributions to the preparation of the French transcript of the Firouz *Episode* and to my translation have been invaluable.

My final acknowledgment is to Katherine Weir who helped prepare the map, a number of notes, and who provided constructive comments on her readings of the whole work.

List of Illustrations

William Thomas Beckford of Fonthill: A Brief Chronology

1760 September: William Beckford born to William Beckford, Lord Mayor of London, owner of extensive estates in Jamaica and the West Indies, and Maria, daughter of the second son of the sixth Earl of Abercorn.
Childhood: Tutored at home: acquires fluency in French and a solid foundation in Latin, Greek, music, drawing.

1770 June: Father dies of rheumatic fever.

1777-78 Beckford's Grand Tour: studies law, philosophy, physics, botany in Switzerland; acquired fluency in Italian; began studies of Spanish and Portuguese; writes effusive letters and reveries.

1779-80 Tour of England; begins an affair with Louisa Beckford, wife of his cousin Peter. Meets William Courtney, then eleven, on a three-day visit to Powderham Castle. Writes a series of burlesque biographies of painters published as *Biographical Memoirs of Extraordinary Painters* (1780).

1780-81 Tour of Europe: low countries, through Germany and Austria to Italy; enjoys the social freedoms of Venice; tours the other great cities of Italy; visits his cousin, Sir William Hamilton and Lady Hamilton, British ambassador in Naples.

1781 Beckford intensifies studies of Arabic languages with someone called Zemir; celebrates his coming of age with two lavish parties in September and December, the latter a grandiose, Oriental pageant with music, elaborate sets. Both Louisa Beckford and William Courtney take part in its atmospheric delights. He meets Samuel Henley and is inspired to begin *Vathek* and other writings.

1782 Beckford at work on a volume based on his European travels, composing a musical score for an operetta, writing *Vathek*, and various fashionable dissipations of a young, single millionaire; also seeing a good deal of Courtney, then a student at Westminster school; in May embarks on a second Grand Tour, travelling in state with three carriages, physician, harpsichord-player, secretary, artist to make a pictorial record, and a variety of servants. Route passed through Low Countries, Germany, Austria, Padua, Venice, Rome and Naples. Returns to estate at Fonthill via Geneva and Paris. Through the year his activities include serious Oriental studies and translations of Arabic manuscripts.

1783 Continues work on *Vathek* and starts *The Episodes*; experiencing family disapproval for indiscretions, especially with Courtney. His travel book, *Dreams, Waking Thoughts and Incidents*, suppressed by family as too whimsical for a potential Member of Parliament. Family pressures result in an arranged marriage in May to the daughter of the Earl of Aboyne, Lady Margaret Gordon, whom Beckford learned quickly to love for her sunny disposition. They settle in Switzerland for a long honeymoon on the lake of Geneva. Beckford leaves his manuscript of *Vathek* for Henley to translate.

1784 Beckford and Lady Margaret return to England via Paris; Beckford enters Parliament as Member for Wells. Following the Beckfords' visit to Courtney's father at Powderham Castle, rumours circulate and reach the newspapers that Beckford and Courtney had been caught making love. The Beckfords in forced seclusion at Fonthill, Beckford correcting Henley's translation of *Vathek* and writing *The Episodes*.

1785 In April, Lady Margaret gives birth to a girl, Maria Margaret Elizabeth. In June the Beckfords settle in

Vevey in Switzerland where they experience no ostracism. Beckford continues work on *The Episodes* and decides that they must be published with *Vathek*.

1786 In May, Lady Margaret dies after having given birth to a second daughter, Susan Euphemia. In August or September, Beckford learns of Henley's unauthorized publication of the English version of *Vathek*, and in November he publishes the French version in Lausanne. *The Episodes*, unfinished, he never publishes.

1787 Beckford's ship takes shelter in Lisbon after a stormy beginning of a voyage to his estates in Jamaica. Beckford decides to stay and learns to love Portugal for the friendship and kindness he receives there. The visit extends to Spain.

1788-89 Beckford in Spain and Paris; with the beginnings of the French Revolution he proceeds to Germany and then to Fonthill where he engages in serious landscaping and encloses much of his estate in a six-mile stone wall, to the annoyance of fox-hunting neighbours.

1790-93 Mainly in Paris, buying books, art, and furniture from fleeing aristocrats.

1794-96 In Lausanne, he buys Edward Gibbon's library; travels to Portugal, which becomes his European home for the next two years.

1796-1822 Driven to England by European wars, he publishes two satiric novels attacking the Pitt Government and the war with France, *Modern Novel Writing* (1796) and *Azemia* (1797). Engages James Wyatt as architect for a magnificent Gothic residence, Fonthill Abbey, the only appropriate venue for his collection of art, furniture, and books. His Fonthill residence becomes the focus for his interests as a builder, landscape gardener, collector, and man of taste. In 1810, his daughter, Susan, marries Lord Douglas, later Duke of Hamilton and Brandon. In 1811, his daughter, Margaret, marries Col. James Orde.

1815-16 Lord Byron revives the fame of *Vathek* with glowing references in a number of his best-selling narrative poems. Beckford takes the time to revise and republish versions of *Vathek* in English and French.

1822 Sells his Abbey and estate at Fonthill; three years later its 300-foot tower collapses with no harm to the new owner. Beckford settles in Bath, connecting two large houses on Lansdown Crescent; in 1827 he builds Lansdown Tower on Lansdown Hill and moves there to establish a landscape garden.

1833 The literary world is delighted with the publication of a compilation of early works and letters, *Italy: with Sketches of Spain and Portugal* published by Bentley.

1834 Bentley publishes *Reminiscences of an Excursion to the Monasteries of Alcobaça and Batalha*. Beckford's fame as an author spreading. Beckford probably writes the "Firouzkah-version" of the first *Episode* around this time, but only *Vathek* is published by Bentley.

1844 Beckford dies in his 84th year.

Fonthill Abbey from the southwest
From James Storer, *A Description of Fonthill* (1812)

Introduction

Vathek is one of the most imaginative of the oriental tales originating in western Europe in the eighteenth century. It has held sway over imaginations since its unauthorized publication in 1786 and has seldom been out of print. Its creative audacity and dark vision continue to charm and trouble its readers. Its author, William Beckford, tried to counter its unauthorized first appearance and assert his pride of authorship by ensuring approved editions in French and English were published in 1815 and 1816.[1] He was never able to realize his initial ambition which was to unite *Vathek* with three or four first-person narratives of evil acts proceeding from a place of eternal punishment that he called *The Episodes*. Circumstances surrounding the first publication of *Vathek* mitigated against this larger enterprise. To accomplish that project, to combine *Vathek* with *The Episodes of Vathek*, is the purpose of this edition.

By a small miracle, the Beckford Papers at the Bodleian Library preserve a remarkable manuscript, the suppressed version of the first *Episode of Vathek*. It was suppressed because it portrays love between a young man and a boy. In the form later published, that central relationship is heterosexual. The miracle is that the manuscript exists, when Beckford's most audacious *Episodes* either did not find release from his teeming imagination or did not physically survive the nineteenth century. The differences between the two versions of *Episode* One reveal that much was lost in the suppression, but this observation seems to apply to all of Beckford's *Episodes*. Their unhappy history embraces depredation, concealment, reticence, and neglect.

This edition profits from that miracle. In uniting *Vathek* with *The Episodes of Vathek* , this volume comes as close as possible to fulfilling Beckford's original design. While Beckford's first wish was for a publication in French, the language of composition, he wrote *The Episodes* in the expectation that an English version would be published at the same time, that the

---

1   *Vathek*. Londres: Clarke, 1815; *Vathek*. Translated from the original French. Third Edition, revised and corrected. London: W. Clarke, 1816.

translation would be done by Samuel Henley, the translator of *Vathek*, and that he could collaborate in the preparation of the English version, just as he was collaborating in the preparation of the English version of *Vathek*.

Beckford's correspondence with Henley shows Beckford's developing design. That design begins with eager reports by the twenty-one-year-old of the progress of *Vathek*, apparently nearing completion in the Spring of 1782.[1]

April 29 [?], 1782: My Caliph advances in his journey to Persepolis, alias Istekar [*sic*] ...

May 1, 1782: The Tale of the Caliph Vathec goes on surprisingly.

His marriage and related concerns and activities seem to have interrupted his progress. He writes on January 13, 1783, of hoping "in a few weeks to wind up his [Vathek's] adventures."

A letter to Henley from Switzerland complaining of his silence reveals the next stage of his developing design, the translation of *Vathek* into English, and, perhaps, the creation of *The Episodes*:

November 18, 1783: We parted in peace, & you promised to write to me. You promised likewise to translate Vathek I left in your hands. Could I shew you a greater mark of confidence? ... I shall bring you some Caliphs not unworthy to succeed your beloved Vathec ...

December 29, 1783: ... I long to hear if you have finished Vathek, & when I may have an opportunity of introducing you to his other relations.

May 6, 1784: Have you finished *Vathek*? I am far gone in another episode.

---

1 Alfred Morrison, *Collection of Autograph Letters and Historical Documents*, Second Series 1882-93, Vol. I (A–B) (London: Printed for Private Circulation, 1893) I, 193-97.

The remaining record of correspondence sees the development of the enterprise to include Henley's translating the Episodes and then the whole being published as a united work, first in French and then in English.

> February 26, 1785: Your translation has all the spirit of the Caliphs & their daemons. I long for the continuation, & hope you will gratify my impatience.

> March 21, 1785: You make me proud of *Vathec*. The blaze just at present is so overpowering that I can see no faults; but you may depend upon my hunting diligently after them.
>
> Pray send the continuation, I know [not] how it happens; but the original when first born scarce gave me so much rapture as yr translation.
>
> Were I well & in spirits I should run wild amongst my rocks and forests, telling stones, trees & labourers how gloriously you have succeeded. My imagination is again on fire.
>
> I have been giving the last evenings to one episode, & sown the seeds of another which I trust will bring forth fruit in due seasons.
>
> I eagerly hope you will one day or other introduce those plants to our English soil ... I have gone on sinking my princes to Hell with active perseverance.

Beckford's next letter finds him correcting Henley's translation according to his promise: "I shall sit down immediately to revise *Vathec*, and much approve yr idea of prefacing the tale with some explanation of its costume" [9 April 1785]. The remaining record of correspondence shows the nature of the collaboration: Beckford's letters give advice on the text but freely supply information to Henley on matters of "costume." Henley's explanatory preface became an elaborate set of notes displaying considerable erudition.

Vathek with the Episodes presents Beckford at his most creative and his least inhibited. The unified work develops thematic patterns introduced in *Vathek* that reflect Beckford's relationship to his world at a wavering and insubstantial moment between his twenty-first birthday in September 1781 and the death of his wife, Lady Margaret, in 1786. To the arrogant young Beckford, the moment seemed permanent. Possessing impressive talents and fabulous wealth, he was already a published satirist,[1] much in demand as a singer, pianist, and composer, and reputed to have inherited a princely income of over £40,000 per year.[2] He was also reputed to be singular in his amorous inclinations. During the period of his writing *Vathek with the Episodes,* he remained confident of his creative talents and in his worldly ambitions: he expected eventually to take a prominent place in political and diplomatic spheres of eighteenth-century Britain.

Beckford's enterprise and confidence were shattered in consequence of a sexual singularity: he was intensely, emotionally, and indiscreetly attracted to boys. During the time he was writing *Vathek with the Episodes,* he was in love with Viscount William Courtney; Courtney was 13 in 1781, the year that Beckford came of age and started writing *Vathek.* Something transpired during a 1784 visit to Powderham Castle, the estate of Lord Courtney, William's father, that got reported as "the detestable scene lately acted in *Wiltshire,* by a pair of fashionable *male lovers.*"[3] The resulting scandal brought about a decline in Beckford's creativity and the collapse of the worldly ambitions that his wealth and social position led him to anticipate. For the rest of his long life Beckford fled that scandal, and the plan of a united edition suffered.

Soon after the incident at Powderham, Beckford retreated to

---

1 *Biographical Memoirs of Extraordinary Painters.* London: J. Robson, 1780.

2 A capital value of £10,000,000 might produce an income of £40,000. (Multiply by 60 for rough modern equivalents.) While Beckford was unquestionably wealthy (some years more than others, given fluctuating prices of the West Indian sugar on which the bulk of his income was based), the reality shows considerable difficulty in getting the income due him. See Boyd Alexander, *England's Wealthiest Son* (London: Centaur Press, 1962) 200-25. Regardless, he was the most eligible bachelor in England.

3 Timothy Mowl, *William Beckford Composing for Mozart* (London: John Murray, 1998) 127.

Switzerland. His correspondence with Samuel Henley shows at first that he preserved his confidence in the enterprise. He managed to convince himself that he was too wealthy and powerful for Powderham to have generated scandal enough to hurt him. Two letters from Switzerland reflect his determination to unite *Vathek* with *The Episodes* as a single publication and to see the French version published first.

February 9, 1786: The publication of Vathec must be postponed at least another year. I would not on any account have him precede the French edition ... The episodes to Vathec are nearly finished, & the whole work will be completed within a twelvemonth. You must be sensible that, notwithstanding my eagerness to see Vathec in print, I cannot sacrifice the French edition to my impatience.

August 1, 1786: I fear the dejection of mind into which I am plunged will prevent my finishing the other stories, & of course Vathec's making his appearance in any language this winter. I would not have him on any account come forth without his companions.

The dejection of mind delaying the enterprise resulted from the death of Lady Margaret, his loyal and loving wife, bringing into the world their second daughter.

Another event, not known to him in August 1786, affected the design more permanently. Henley published his English version of *Vathek* without Beckford's knowledge and approval.[1] Why Henley withdrew from Beckford's design is an open question. Perhaps he needed the money that the publication would bring; perhaps he wished to give the world the benefit of his notes: the proud display of a great deal of knowledge of classical and Eastern literatures; he had good cause to wonder if Beckford would ever complete his design. Perhaps he simply wished to cease his connection with Beckford, now a notori-

---

1 [Anon.] *An Arabian tale, from an unpublished manuscript: with notes critical and explanatory.* London: J. Johnson, 1786.

ous subject of scandal. His rather slippery letter to Beckford's solicitor can be read to substantiate any number of justifications, except the need for money.[1]

Henley's publication of the English *Vathek* in June, 1786, frustrated Beckford's plan for a combined edition in English. The death of Lady Margaret Beckford fostered a state of mind that discouraged further work on *The Episodes*. The Lausanne *Vathek*, which is dated 1787 but which Beckford managed to get into print by November 1786,[2] lists four episodes, one with a blank title that may indicate no more than an undeveloped idea, "Histoire du prince ... enfermé dans le palais souterrain."[3] The inescapable fact is that the Beckford Papers include manuscripts of only two completed *Episodes* (one in two versions) and the fragment of a third. We may doubt if he wrote that fourth one.[4]

Vathek united with The Episodes: thematic unity

William Beckford wrote *The Episodes of Vathek* as a series of first-person narratives of love, sin, and atrocity proceeding from an abode of eternal hatred and despair. Although *The Episodes* have since been published and attempts made to unite the frame tale of *Vathek* with *The Episodes of Vathek*, the results have never been satisfactory, chiefly because the first *Episode* gives a clumsy twist to its plot and transforms the narrative from an audacious account of love between a man and a boy into a story of sanctioned heterosexual passion. This sexual sleight-of-hand is accomplished so ineptly that readers may be forgiven if they misunderstand Beckford's reasons for writing *The Episodes* in the first place. Certainly, the first *Episode* has done no good to Beckford's reputation as a writer.

This united edition, *Vathek with the Episodes of Vathek*, should

---

1   The letter is quoted in full in Lewis Melville, ed., *The Episodes of Vathek* (London: Stephen Swift and Co., 1912) xxiii-xxv.

2   It is reviewed in the *Journal de Lausanne* 1 (2 Decembre, 1786): 1-2.

3   "The History of Prince ... confined in the palace of subterraneous fire." [Beckford's translation]

4   André Parreaux has written the most thorough study of *The Episodes* yet published. See *William Beckford Auteur de "Vathek"* (Paris: A.G. Nizet, 1960) 411-50.

counteract the malign influence of the only published version of the first *Episode*. It installs the suppressed version, the "Firouz" version, in its proper place as the first *Episode*. The manuscript has lain among the Beckford Papers for a century and a half, but no previous edition publishes or even mentions it. This story depicts no alteration in sex: it describes a love relationship between a young man and a boy. Years later, Beckford reinscribed the relationship as heterosexual, violated the motivation, and undermined the enterprise for uniting *Vathek* with *The Episodes*. It appears that the same pressures that provoked Beckford's revision prompted Lewis Melville to publish the inferior version in 1912, almost sixty years after Beckford's death, and a significant number of Beckford scholars to remain silent about the original *Episode*.[1] Obviously the original version was suppressed in an attempt to protect Beckford's reputation by concealing a story that might arouse memories of the Powderham scandal. The miracle is that it survived Beckford's own self-defensive culling of his manuscripts[2] and the depredations of his daughter, the Duchess of Hamilton, in the next generation.

The contrasting "Firouz" and "Firouzkah" versions provide keys to the understanding of Beckford's enterprise and of his inability to bring it to completion. The Firouzkah version tells how the twenty-year-old king of Kharezme, Alasi, takes under his protection a young prince from a neighbouring kingdom, Prince Firouz, a boy of thirteen. Alasi becomes increasingly attracted to the boy and experiences considerable tumult and confusion as he tries to come to terms with his affection. Fortunately the smitten Alasi does not have to remain too long in this disturbed state. There is a battle and Firouz is wounded. To stanch the bleeding, Alasi strips away his shirt to discover "a

---

1 Malcolm Jack reminds us that the subject matter of *The Episodes* "put them beyond the pale until modern times." "Introduction," *The Episodes of Vathek* (London: Dedalus, 1994) 12.

2 In dealing with Beckford's manuscripts, one feels inclined to join Timothy Mowl in condemning Beckford's practice of rewriting his own biography by tampering with manuscripts. See Mowl, 301. "Where is the original letter?" is Mowl's repeated and justified question. That Beckford (and his daughter) left alone the Firouz-version is indeed a miracle.

breast which the houris might have envied."[1] The remainder of the story recounts a series of malicious acts intended to please and placate the powers of fire in order to win for Alasi and Firouzkah an eternity of love. The outcome brings them to the Hall of Eblis and the interlude in the small chamber. The inescapable problem of the Firouzkah version is that a sanctioned heterosexual love does not need extraordinary measures to be requited. The culture abets their fidelity to one another, if not for eternity, at least for a very, very long time. The Firouzkah version supplies weak motivations for rebellion and atrocity.

In the Firouz version, their awareness that same-sex love lacks a cultural sanction provokes the rebellion of the alienated couple. The very existence of the story demonstrates how one sensitive and witty man represented love between a man and a boy in 1784 or 1785 and how he modulated that love story into a credible depiction of evil without derogating the love associated with it. Compared to the version hitherto published, the suppressed *Episode* is more coherent, more credible, more full of telling incident, and more audaciously in the spirit of *Vathek* and a young, self-confident William Beckford. It is also much more profound in its explorations of alienation in a culture whose repressive power Beckford was beginning to comprehend.[2] In including the Firouz-version, this edition comes as close as possible to fulfilling Beckford's original design of uniting *Vathek* and *The Episodes* in the English language.

An edition of *Vathek with the Episodes* that includes among the four plots the suppressed Firouz *Episode* forces a revision of our understanding of Beckford's purposes and abilities. *Vathek* becomes the originating narrative of a long work of complex meanings within a thematic unity. The stories are introduced

---

1   Beckford may have borrowed the transformation scene from M.G. Lewis's *The Monk* (1795). The monk, Ambrosio, experiences a similarly disturbing homoerotic attraction to his novice, Rosario. When Rosario confesses to being a woman, their relationship is eagerly consummated.

2   George E. Haggerty discusses Beckford in a context of a growing social opprobrium directed against male-male love. See the chapter on Beckford in *Men in Love: Masculinity and Sexuality in the Eighteenth Century* (New York: Columbia University Press, 1999).

near the end of the framing narrative when Vathek and Nouronihar have encountered the transcendent horror of the Hall of Eblis where dedicated love turns to aversion and self-confident egoism into a selfish, lonely agony. Ambitions for power and knowledge dispelled, they withdraw to a small chamber to await their fate; there they meet four young men and a young woman morosely anticipating the same future. They agree to pass the hours remaining to them recounting the adventures that brought about their dismal destiny. *Vathek* and *The Episodes* are bound together by variations on a theme of otherness based on the depth and intensity of the characters' passions. The Firouz *Episode* continues a pattern of sexual extremism foreshadowed in *Vathek*. Homosexuality, libertinism, necrophilia, and incest, present in *Vathek*,[1] flourish in *Episodes* One, Two, and Three. Unsanctified passions, metaphors for the unattainable, make the Hall of Eblis the site for the legitimation of singularities in desires and ambitions.

Vathek: Sensuality and Curiosity

Vathek with the Episodes is about singularity and rebellion, both of which take sexual and intellectual forms. The Firouz version is close in spirit to *Vathek* in presenting singular and defiant individuals of culturally-shady sexuality whose fate it is to be damned. Vathek rebels against a benign but restrictive Islam in order to embrace sensuality and forbidden knowledge: he exercises a libertine sensuality that, under the influence of his obsessive curiosity, knows no bounds. His palaces of the senses almost dignify his commitment to voluptuous pleasures by associating them with what might be a Lockean epistemology based on sense experience. They are both museums and sites of hedonistic experience. Interestingly, even though his licentious practices contradict the teachings and example of Omar Ben Abdalaziz, Islam's most pious caliph, Vathek does not attract the

---

1 The luscious descriptions of Gulchenrouz, Vathek's courtship of Nouronihar, the incident of Carathis and the ghouls, and the Nouronihar-Gulchenrouz relationship are examples in *Vathek* suggesting male homosexuality, libertinism, necrophilia, and incest.

reproach of Mahomet.[1] That condemnation arises from his impious tower, a site of intellectual rebellion and symbol of impertinent curiosity.

The mad and zany influence of the Giaour,[2] the first of an array of grotesques in the united work, drives Vathek beyond all bounds of decency. Vathek commits repeated atrocities to attain forbidden knowledge and eternal sensual repletion in the arms of the enchanting Nouronihar. It is not a determined hetero-sexuality that has Vathek prefer Nouronihar. He also notices the effeminate charms of her male companion, Gulchenrouz. But Nouronihar's mischievous allure dazzles him, and a man of his power, unable to brook any kind of sensual restraint, takes her from her reluctant father. Vathek's path to Istakhar and damnation is strewn with victims whose piety makes them vul-nerable to what they cannot conceive of – the extent of Vathek's evil.

"The Story of the Princes and Friends Alasi and Firouz": rebellion and atrocity

The Firouz version continues this pattern of rebellion and atrocity, but with variations. A series of scenes, absent from the Firouzkah version, highlights the passionate uniqueness of the central characters. The first scene, the prince Alasi at the death-bed of his father, introduces Alasi's alienation from the mildly coercive forces of his culture, an alienation occasioned by his self-acknowledged singularity. The advice of his dying father underscores this cultural tension: the father's concern is that Alasi's artistic sensitivities may draw him "towards frivolous designs"[3] that do not conform with the demands that practical politics place on a king. Recognizing Alasi's otherness, the father has arranged to match Alasi with the Princess Roud-

---

1   Beckford's spelling of Muhammed.

2   In *Vathek*, Beckford withholds the second signification of that word. A giaour gen-erally is an unbeliever, but specifically a follower of Zoroaster. In *The Episodes*, he amplifies the significance of the religion of Zoroaster as a spiritual authority to rival Islam.

3   All quotations from the Firouz version come from my translation of *Beckford Papers*. Ms d 13.

abah, the lovely, competent, and wise daughter of a neighbouring king.

The father and Roudabah represent the roles that society expects Alasi to play: Alasi's narrative does not demean those roles, although it introduces a number of greybeards, as *Vathek* does, the subjects of irony for unquestioning or hypocritical conformity to various social and religious constraints. Alasi is conscious of not belonging. He admits to tastes for the voluptuous and the exquisite. He insists that he made a sympathetic king because he balanced his civic activities with therapeutic interludes of dreamy solitude, indulging tender melancholy through poetry and music in four pastoral pavilions erected in the forest beside a stream of crystalline waters, pavilions whose interiors he designed with the care and earnestness of an interior decorator.[1]

In that setting, Alasi, a man of feeling, eighteen years old in this version, highly susceptible to refined and ardent stimulations, receives into his protection the son of a neighbouring king.[2] "A young boy, more beautiful than the morning star" is delivered into his arms. "We held one another, embracing with ... tenderness." Alasi is staggered by the ardour of his own emotional response.

Alasi insists at the outset that, while love brought him to his fate, it entered his heart through "the soft sentiments of friendship" and undermined a spirit armed against unruly passion. As the relationship develops, Alasi becomes increasingly enchanted and Firouz reveals, increasingly, a vicious nature. A series of incidents, varying from the published version, shows how the relationship intensifies and becomes evil, but evil not because of paederasty, if we can use that term to refer to eighteen- and thirteen-year-old minors, but from alienation from the values and expectations of their own culture. Alasi is not more than

---

1 Andrew Elfenbein connects Beckford's passion for collecting with his paedophilia. He might have seen foreshadowed in Alasi's pavilion the carefully arranged interiors of Fonthill Abbey. Andrew Elfenbein, *Romantic Genius: the Prehistory of a Homosexual Role* (New York: Columbia University Press, 1999) 45.

2 Both versions, straight and gay, present the same developing relationship, but if we cannot anticipate a serendipitous change in sex suggested in the title about Prince Alasi and *Princess* Firouzkah, we read the developing relationship quite differently.

mildly alienated from his culture until Firouz connives to give him direction.

Like Alasi, Firouz is acted upon by love and, unlike Alasi, by religion. His love makes him intensely, even insanely, jealous. The primary focus of his jealousy is the Princess Roudabah and heterosexual love. Two incidents, exclusive to the Firouz text, take revenge on conventional power given women over love and marriage. As the last act of a concerted campaign against Roudabah, he smears an ointment on the sleeping princess that renders her hideous. He then proclaims his victory, "I have taken from her her lover and her beauty. What more can one do to a woman!" In a second campaign against conventional heterosexuality, Firouz compels two lovers to murder each other on the eve of their wedding so that he can boast the superiority of male-male love: "As for women, there is not one of them who would not hurry to drown her lover, or her husband, to save her own life ..." Misogyny plays an important role in Firouz's motivations.

Firouz's other campaign is against Islam. His religion is Zoroastrianism, in Beckford's fantastical construction a demonic cult that encourages the most malign acts in its opposition to Islam. Before encountering Alasi, Firouz has already been conditioned by his guardian, the Magus, to reject Islam for Zoroaster. With the continuing encouragement of the Magus, Firouz makes victims of representative figures of Islamic teachers and pastors, assailed by Firouz for self-indulgence and hypocrisy. On behalf of Zoroaster, Alasi and Firouz perpetrate a holocaust against the mass of believers for unreflecting acquiescence to religious practices prescribed by the leaders of Islam.

Both Alasi and Firouz recognize that their passionate friendship runs counter to their culture's expectations. The intensity of their Zoroastrianism and their same-sex love drives them to take revenge on the tyrannies of society's universalizing models in sexual love and religion. Firouz draws Alasi into complicity, acting out his alterity through impetuous, violent, and vengeful acts which he describes to Alasi in a manner so charming to him that his dissent is disarmed. Alasi cooperates with Firouz in the hope that their evil acts are gratifying the powers that will endorse their relationship and give it eternal refuge. As happens so often in Beckford's works, his narrative distance permits him to give weight to opposing perspectives. In the story Alasi tells, their alienation from their culture's values and expectations opens their minds to counter-cultures that draw them into acts of betrayal and revenge. That their singularity finds no refuge in their world makes the Hall of Eblis so attractive a goal. Beckford lets the outcome in damnation express a contrasting perspective.

"The Story of Prince Barkiarokh": picaro meets apprentice

The second *Episode* is shaped by two narrative forms, the picaresque and the *Bildungsroman*. The narrative of Prince Barkiarokh takes a picaresque form — the adventures of a rogue moving from incident to incident with no meaningful direction or character-development. The *Bildungsroman* describes an apprenticeship to life; in this case, the apprentice is the Peri Homaïouna. Since she is a peri,[1] and not human, and since she chooses to involve herself in human affairs, she must learn about human mendacity and human inconsistency. Her greatest instrument for the development of understanding is Barkiarokh, the rogue with whom she has fallen in love. Their two narratives come together, separate, and again meet at the threshold of the Hall of Eblis.

This *Episode* supplies an overreaching libertine to personify singularity and rebellion. In the first *Episode*, the tension between nature and nurture has its outcome in an uneasy compromise as Alasi's sensitive uniqueness falls into harmony with Firouz's evil nurture under the tutelage of the Zoroastrian Magus. Barkiarokh acknowledges his evil nature from the outset with a sardonic frankness that characterizes his narrative just as Alasi's regretful resignation characterizes his.

---

1 According to a book owned by Beckford, peris are formed from fire: "they live long, but are subject to death; and though possessed of superhuman powers, have in many respects the sentiments and passions of mankind." John Richardson, *A Dissertation on the Languages, Literatures and Manners of Eastern Nations* (Oxford: Clarendon Press, 1777) 144.

Barkiarokh's wicked audacity carries him to atrocious extremes and evil company. He is a likeable rogue with good looks, impudence, and luck. He lacks a dominating purpose and merely stumbles from opportunity to disaster through a world apparently populated by fools and knaves, relating his adventures with a mordant wit, frank villainy, and a zest for simile. He narrates his criminal and libertine life as a catalogue of hypocrisy, duplicity, murder (including an eager parricide), adultery, seduction, a form of necrophilia (sex acts upon the unconscious body of his wife Gazahidé), and the attempted corruption of his kingdom with an anti-Islamic religion of "unbridled enjoyment and illicit pleasure." His final licentious campaign is the seduction of his daughter, an unsuspecting girl of about twelve.

Barkiarokh's picaresque account of ambitious evil is balanced against Homaïouna's apprenticeship-narrative of redemptive goodness. The peri expands Roudabah's function as an agent of righteousness. Her long narrative illustrates the credulousness of virtue and the guile of vice. It is a narrative of character-development leading to deliverance in contrast to Barkiarokh's of wilful guile leading to inexorable damnation. Before encountering Barkiarokh, Homaïouna has already experienced the worst of human perversity in various forms of hypocrisy, malice, lust, and betrayal. She proves herself vulnerable to human duplicity and demonstrates that vulnerability again when she falls in love with Barkiarokh. She intervenes but cannot always prevent the worst of crimes. Her final statement expresses the moral of all of Beckford's stories in *Vathek with the Episodes*: resistance to the wand of remorse will result in the rod of despair.

"The Story of Princess Zulkaïs and the Prince Kalilah": ambition and incest

The headstrong and passionate narrator of the third *Episode*, the Princess Zulkaïs, attributes her doom to her father's ambition. Of all the stories in the collection, this one offers the most extreme representation of a tension between the individual and the culture. The initiating conflict between the interests and ambitions of her father and the pious constraints of a reactionary Islam gives rise to a nurture that the Princess blames for the extraordinary actions of her and her brother, Kalilah. Their father, Emir of the Islamic province of Masre (Egypt), has the impious desire to know and control the future, a desire he manifests in regulating the Nile's flooding, encouraging commerce, and studying the occult arts of ancient Egypt. Various representatives of Islam find his interest in the future "unpardonable" and "blasphemous," a seeking to forestall Providence. The ambivalent narrative recommends neither side: flood control that resulted in luxurious vegetation exhausts the soil; the apparent success of sea commerce masks a considerable loss of ships; the sages engaged in ancient studies are never in agreement. Ambitions are partly fulfilled, but partly frustrated.

The ambitions of the chief representative of Islam, the holy Iman Abzenderoud, are similarly frustrated when the religiously-indifferent Emir conceives a passion for his lovely daughter. The Iman's attempt to wrest appropriately-pious marriage conditions from the Emir is thwarted by his daughter's lack of co-operation. She simply will not resist the urgent ardour of the emir and the relationship is consummated before the Emir can contract stipulations. The acts of both progressive and reactionary are thwarted by human fallibility and absurdity operating within the inexorable and inscrutable operations of destiny. The Iman dies of disappointment and his daughter becomes pregnant with the twins, Zulkaïs and Kalilah.

The singular pair is born in the midst of this conflict between the Emir's ambitions and the admonitions of Islam. Like most early alchemists, the Emir does not distinguish between pursuits in science and commerce that Beckford's world might regard as commendable, and excursions into occult knowledge that the European enlightenment would view as retrograde. Beckford's Emir seeks in the pyramids and their hieroglyphic messages admittance to an ancient time when human beings had access to fragments of divine wisdom.[1] Such interests, of course, infuriate the leaders of Islam, excruciatingly conscious of the Emir's general laxness in the practices of Islamic faith. In this story, Islamic culture is actively coercive. The representatives that succeed the Iman, like the Hermit of the Great Sandy Desert, announce sweeping condemnations of all science. Indeed, the Hermit enrages the household by encouraging the Sultana, daughter of the late Iman, to die rather than give birth to rebellious, presumptuous creatures. The household rises up in a mad outburst on behalf of the terrified Sultana and kills the hermit: in this atmosphere of fury and remorse the Sultana indeed dies, giving birth to the girl, Zulkaïs, and the boy, Kalilah.

The twins attribute their extraordinary natures to their nurture. From birth, they are placed in the care of the Emir's sages; under their influence they become proud, wilful, vicious, rebellious, contemptuous of the Koran, and passionately sensitive, especially to one another. The narrative recounts the growth of their mutual tenderness, a tenderness that intensifies to active desire as they approach puberty. Despite the Emir's efforts to occupy Kalilah with robust, manly pursuits, at every opportunity he returns to Zulkaïs in response to the supernatural bond uniting them, a passionate need for one another's company.

A separation-reunion plot results from these growing incestuous desires: the Emir tries to discourage the association by sending Zulkaïs on a thirty-day Nile journey to the Isle of Palms and to his most grotesque sage, the heavy-drinking, anti-Islamic Palm-tree Climber. A secret subject of the fallen angel, Eblis, the Climber encourages Zulkaïs's fiery passion for her brother. Promising reunion with Kalilah in an environment that will sanction their yearnings, he leads her into the most vividly-psychological of Beckford's settings, a Gothic labyrinth bordered by wells inhabited by "reptiles with human faces" and leading to a chamber, a "place of terror," paved with flesh-coloured marble "marked as with the veins and arteries of the human body." In this womb-like setting, with Zulkaïs about to

---

1   Magic, *sihr*, in Islamic teachings, represents fragments of a celestial knowledge, transmitted to humankind by fallen angels. Black magic influences nature to do harm and is prohibited by Islam. [*Islam2* IX, 569]

start on a ghastly quest that will re-unite her with her twin, her womb-companion, the *Episode* breaks off.

Samuel Rogers, a man of letters prominent at the time, described how in 1818 Beckford read him the *Episodes*. John Mitford made notes of Rogers' account of the story's continuation: "1st Prince –Had carnal connection with his sister, in the centre of the great Pyramid."[1] While the story seems to be leading to this act of incest, we have to wonder if Beckford wrote down the continuation or summarized a continuation he intended to write. The two manuscript versions of the third *Episode* both stop at precisely the same point. It seems doubtful if the continuation was ever inscribed.

Conclusion: Beckford's Oriental Vision

Orientalism unleashed the *agent-provocateur* in the youthful Beckford, uncomfortably and ambivalently situated at the centre yet on the periphery of his culture. His wealth and political connections established him at the favoured heart of his society, with power, influence, and status, but his paederasty thrust him to the frontier of his culture's fragile tolerance. This ambivalence generated an ironic vision in the combined stories that translates into ambiguously subversive polarities. The central polarities surround his constructions of a repressive Islam and a transgressive, liberating Zoroastrianism. That ambivalent and subversive contrast provokes other subversions: a carnival impulse that undermines human dignity and carries ambitions to absurd or inhuman lengths; an art that adapts joyfully the confident artifice of the *Arabian Nights* and the *Shah-nama* and their techniques of grotesquerie, fragmentation, and deferral to his own purposes of engaging the limiting prohibitions of his own world; and the deconstruction of the quest motif, traditionally Christian in western literatures, into a series of pilgrimages, often zany and usually vicious, through various Oriental landscapes, benign or malign, lush or parched, civilized or wild, but resonant of an ancient and mysterious past. The quest

---

1   Quoted in André Parreaux, *William Beckford Auteur de Vathek*, 413.

ends at the gates of Hell itself, a strange, Oriental hell that nevertheless recalls and echoes the hopelessness of Dante's Inferno. Beckford constructed his Orientalism to comprehend Western literary traditions: the Satan of Milton's *Paradise Lost* echoes through the presentation of Eblis just as the Hall of Eblis reminds us of Dante's Inferno. We must not dismiss Beckford's Orientalism as merely a fabrication based on his own European experience because that view does not give sufficient weight to the thorough knowledge of customs, literatures, languages, and legends of Persia and Arabia that forms his unique vision. Beckford fabricated a rich and exotic setting to impose a comprehensive ambience on the united work and engage the cultural and moral antitheses of his own experience with telling ironies.

Oriental and Occidental, benign and malevolent, funny and appalling, the complex contradictions of *Vathek with the Episodes* explore chaos as a problematic of the human condition. Beckford's work manages to accomplish closure and yet defer it in the very concepts of eternity and futurity, refusing a resolution at the same time that it provides one. Its ending, however, makes explicit an all-embracing divine scheme that subjects fallible and confident human protagonists to an ironic scrutiny. Controlling and often abetting ironies is the sometimes vivid, sometimes shadowy world of the non-human, the world of djinns, peris, angels, and even the Prophet himself. Under their often baffled scrutiny, the chaotic world of human agony and absurdity sometimes rises to nobility and self-sacrifice but more often sinks to foolishness and savagery. Presiding over the variety of character and incident is a mythic frame that comprehends many of the work's polarities and subversions in a perspective that encompasses the beginnings of human time.

Beckford's organizing myth begins with Gian ben Gian, one of seventy-two sultans who governed the world and its rational inhabitants, the djinn, for 7000 years until the creation of Adam. In the later ages of these pre-Adamite kings, the djinn grew rebellious, and God sent his angel, Eblis, to chastise them. Eblis defeated Gian ben Gian in battle and began to govern the earth in his place. When God created Adam and ordered the earth to obey him, Eblis scorned the directive. "Why should I, composed of the element of fire, submit to a creature formed of clay?" He rebelled against the Divine will and was joined in his revolt by the djinn. They were defeated, of course, and banished to the place furthest from God's throne.[1] The Persian poet Esfahani comments on Eblis: "The fire that is the origin of his nature and pride, will be endlessly the instrument of his punishment."[2]

Eblis is Beckford's instrument of authorial control in the united work. Beckford's sense of his own uniqueness drew him to the character of Eblis, described with such passionate sublimity near the end of *Vathek*. Perhaps early disaffections with his world linked him to Eblis's alterity: each experienced alienation from a culture whose prohibitions seemed irrelevant and incomprehensible to his nature. Among the correspondence of his godfather, the Earl of Chatham, we can glimpse Beckford's uniqueness at an early age encountering firm and insensitive social control. In 1773, Chatham, wrote his son, William Pitt, Britain's future prime minister:

> Little Beckford was really disappointed at not being in time to see you—a good mark for my young *vivid* friend. He is just as much compounded of the elements of *air* and *fire* as he was. A due proportion of *terrestrial* solidity will, I trust, come and make him perfect.[3]

In the interests of bringing him down to earth, Chatham appointed a new tutor for the thirteen-year-old Beckford. The Reverend John Lettice reported on Beckford's response to the new regime:

---

1 John Richardson, *Dissertation on the Languages, Literature and Manners of Eastern Nations*, 142-43.
2 Quoted in *Barthélemy d'Herbelot's Bibliothèque Orientale* (Paris, 1697) in the entry for Eblis [editor's translation].
3 W.S. Taylor and J.H. Pringle, *Correspondence of William Pitt, Earl of Chatham*, 4 vols. (London: J. Murray, 1838-40) IV, 313 [letter of 19 October, 1773].

... I shall give your Lordship an advantageous account of our proceedings, as I am greatly indebted for it to the good effect of your own advice.... these closer studies, you were pleased to recommend to my pupil ... It was likely that our first setting out in this thorny path should prove rather irksome to so warm an imagination; and so, indeed, it happened ... he has lately applied himself ... [Lettice supplies a reading list that includes Locke's *Essay on Human Understanding*, and Homer, Livy, Cicero, and Horace in their original languages.]

... it will give your Lordship pleasure to be informed that, about a month ago, that splendid heap of oriental drawings, &c. which filled a large table at Burton [Chatham's estate], has been sacrificed at the shrine of good taste. Mr. Beckford had firmness enough to burn them with his own hand ... as his judgment grows maturer, it will give me an opportunity of acquainting your Lordship with other sacrifices to the same power.[1]

However insistent on the virtues of sacrifice, neither Chatham nor Lettice succeeded in extinguishing Beckford's fire, though they might have sown seeds to make Beckford see in Eblis a commentary on his own rebellion against bewildering and eccentric restrictions. Lettice remained Beckford's tutor and companion until his coming of age, but he was never able to constrict the element of air, extinguish the element of fire, nor reduce to cinders his fascination with the Orient. The Orient supplied the vehicle for Beckford's own protest against the oppressions of his earth-bound compatriots. His Orient is a metaphor for the untrammeled imagination: there everything is possible.

While only *Vathek* was published in Beckford's lifetime, the four narratives of his original enterprise, now united in *Vathek with the Episodes,* communicate his uncomfortable associations with his own cultural environments. He voiced his discomfort

---

1 *Correspondence of ... Chatham* IV, 313 [letter of 11 December, 1773].

as well in many letters and reveries in which he acknowledges that his own singularities are at odds with the expectations and forbearance of the society in which he must find his place. His youthful imagination returns repeatedly to a grotto retreat "sunk deep in the centre of the Earth," a providential site for easing the tensions acquired from opposing the current of the world. In one reverie an "Angelic Shadow issued suddenly ... leading in its hand the one I love—he flew to me. I sprang forward to catch him in my arms. Rest happy said a thrilling voice—no one shall disturb you for ages."[1] Magically sequestered from his world and his time, Beckford in his dream-vision may fulfill his longings. The journey underground and escape from time[2] is a pattern repeated through *Vathek with the Episodes* but with an ironic twist that makes the sequestered destination the site of eternal punishment. Beckford's collection of stories rejects any hope for providential outcomes. In sites presided over by Eblis, expectations are fulfilled only ironically.

Beckford's narratives display some of Eblis's duplicity in portrayals of worldly confusion where villainy does not seem qualitatively inferior to stupidity, hypocrisy, and weakness. The outcome disappoints their heroes' expectations, damns their transgressions, and, surprisingly, asserts the culture's prohibitions. Yet the duplicitous skills of narrative subtly affirm values the stories explicitly censure: the tales do full aesthetic justice to antagonistic ideas and practices before they are sublimely punished. Zulkaïs brands "the yearnings of my heart" as "criminal avowals," but she pledges herself to that incestuous covenant. The phantom Roudabah voices inflammatory feminist views that strike at the roots of marriage and inheritance:

---

1 Guy Chapman, *Beckford* (London: Jonathan Cape, 1937) 57.

2 "All the princes in *Vathek* and *The Episodes* seek just such a sanctuary, one which we may presume had a powerful appeal for the author himself." Temple Maynard, "The Movement Underground and the Escape from Time in Beckford's Fiction," *Vathek and the Escape from Time*, ed. Kenneth W. Graham (New York, AMS Press, 1990) 15.

"The [man] destined to be [my husband] loves only his Firouz ... I am Alasi's equal. I may be permitted as well to have a favourite. If all women thought like me, men would have to change the unjust laws that they have passed, or we would stop nourishing with our milk the tyrants who subjugate us."

The context condemns such statements while the text inscribes them.

These physically attractive and socially eminent people[1] are variations on Beckford's own prominence and defiance during his early twenties. The four narratives of the combined work concern high-born individuals whose dispositions put them at odds with their cultural environments. Their ambitions and passions, unbounded by mundane considerations, embrace occult undertakings, libertine passions, male-male love, father-daughter incest, and sister-brother incest. Their estrangements drive them to acts of viciousness in their quest for fulfillments not countenanced by their, or, indeed, by most cultures. Notwithstanding the power, beauty, and arrogance of the protagonists, the unmistakable conclusion of *Vathek with the Episodes* is that the Hall of Eblis is Hell, and its inhabitants are there as punishment for their monstrous sins.

Like Beckford, his damned heroes are creatures of air and fire, imagination and passion. Their imaginations are lethal and their passions predatory; they dare to desire what society and morality forbid and draw others with them toward the abyss. Their twilight world of self-centeredness leaves them indifferent to the pain they cause others. These companions in perversity follow the same selfish paths, daring to contest prohibition, and presuming to expect to find a secure retreat in which to

---

1   In discussing *Vathek*, Andrew Elfenbein sees the ambivalence in Beckford's narrative that creates a "fantasy space in which he can both display and keep a critical distance on the enchantments of consumption, to which he seemed to have succumbed in life." *Vathek with the Episodes* shows Beckford simultaneously revealing enchantments and keeping a critical distance from them in much larger contexts. See Elfenbein, *Romantic Genius*, 50.

enjoy their perversities. They sacrifice their souls to fulfill their selves.[1]

Eblis offers a salutary perspective on these intrepid transgressors. He addresses Vathek and Nouronihar as "creatures of clay" to distinguish them from angelic beings like himself, created from fire. Eblis proudly asserts his distinction from human beings, but his presence in Hell affirms a bond with human creatures who, in their audacious and selfish aspirations, have separated themselves from other creatures of clay. Beckford's ambivalent vision for his perverse protagonists shows that unsanctioned desire brings bliss and corruption. In pallid contrast to these vital sinners are Gulchenrouz and other representatives of Beckford's ideal of childish love uncorrupted by desire. Their providential retreat represents an insubstantial and fleeting song of innocence that concludes *Vathek* "in the pure happiness of childhood." The romantic irony in these contrasting fates is the final expression of ambivalence in *Vathek* and its suite of tales.

Eblis provides the overarching irony in this version of Dante's Inferno. Beckford's vital sinners are victims of a titanic plot that explains why the stories' demonic version of Zoroastrianism is so counter to what history tells us of the benevolent and monotheistic religion that taught justice to Persian kings in the pre-Islamic era. What Beckford's sinners encounter is Zoroastrianism as created by Eblis, an instrument to revenge himself on humankind. His representatives, deluded humans like the Magus, or un-human malcontents like the Giaour, serve his endless vengeance. Creatures of clay had displaced him from the Divine countenance and provoked his rebellion and alienation from God. He turns his vengeance on Beckford's selfish, passionate, vulnerable characters, whose egoism insists, against all evidence, that there must be an opposed

---

1   "... the Vathekian character, like Ambrosio in Lewis's *The Monk*, inevitably loses his soul in a struggle to realize a fundamental self." Robert J. Gemmett, ed., Introduction to *The Episodes of Vathek by William Beckford* (London: Associated University Presses, 1975) xlv.

power equal to the power of God, a power who can reward their service with a secure outlet for their lethal sensibilities.[1] The function of the shepherd-genie in *Vathek*, Roudabah in the first *Episode*, and the Peri Homaïouna in the second, is to warn the heroic transgressors of the terrible fate threatening them. They cannot or will not accept the warnings and proceed to the non-closure of their lives, an escape from time, trapped in an underground labyrinth with no terminus,[2] suspended in an endless agony both appalling and sublime.

---

1   Remember Alasi's shock when he discovers that a power stronger than Zoroaster protects Roudabah from Firouz's malice.

2   "Dante's Hell magnifies the notion of a jail, and Beckford's, the tunnels of a nightmare ..." Jorge Luis Borges, "About William Beckford's *Vathek*," *Other Inquisitions 1937-1952*, trans. Ruth L.C. Simms (Austin: University of Texan Press, 1964) 140.

Bibliography

Alexander, Boyd. *England's Wealthiest Son.* London: Centaur Press, 1962.

Chapman, Guy. *Beckford.* London: Jonathan Cape, 1937.

Fothergill, Brian. *Beckford of Fonthill.* London: Faber & Faber, 1979.

Jack, Malcolm. *William Beckford: An English Fidalgo.* New York: AMS Press, 1996.

Mowl, Tim. *William Beckford: composing for Mozart.* London: J. Murray, 1998.

Oliver, J.W. *The Life of William Beckford.* London: Oxford University Press, 1932.

VATHEK

VATHEK[1], ninth Caliph[2] of the race of the Abassides,[3] was the son of Motassem,[4] and the grandson of Haroun al Raschid.[5] From an early accession to the throne, and the talents he possessed to adorn it, his subjects were induced to expect that his reign would be long and happy. His figure was pleasing and majestic; but when he was angry, one of his eyes became so terrible, that no person could bear to behold it; and the wretch upon whom it was fixed, instantly fell backward, and sometimes expired. For fear, however, of depopulating his dominions and making his palace desolate, he but rarely gave way to his anger.

Being much addicted to women and the pleasures of the table, he sought by his affability, to procure agreeable companions; and he succeeded the better as his generosity was unbounded and his indulgencies unrestrained: for he did not think, with the Caliph Omar Ben Abdalaziz[6] that it was

1   Vathek, al-Wathik Bi'llah (ruled AD 842-47) : Beckford's introduction echoes D'Herbelot, whose account of Vathek recounts his fondness for the study of the sciences, for men of letters, and for astrology. D'Herbelot reveals that Vathek ate and drank to excess, enjoyed women to excess, and had so terrible an eye that one of his servants fell back against another servant close behind. Vathek died that very instant of dropsy, at the age of 36, although his astrologers foretold a life of fifty years.

2   Caliph: formerly, the head of the Islamic community. By Vathek's time, the Caliph is the sovereign of the Arabian empire claiming absolute power and independent authority over everything concerning religion and government. [Islam2, D'Herbelot]

3   Abassides, Abbāsids: the dynasty that succeeded the Umayyad dynasty and held the caliphate from 750 to 1258.

4   Motassem, Mu'tasim Bi'llah (AD 833-42): son of Harun al-Rashid and leader of successful military campaigns. [Islam2 VII, 776]

5   Haroun al Raschid, Harun al-Rashid (AD 786-809): legendary Caliph, whom the Arabian Nights shows presiding benevolently over a golden age, but who actually had to contend with a troubled reign full of disturbances. Despite instabilities, commerce flourished during his reign, and his court was the centre of arts and learning. [Islam2 III, 232]

6   Omar Ben Abdalaziz, Omar ben Abd al-Aziz ben Marwan (ruled AD717-?): the 8th Umayyad caliph and reputed to be the most pious of their dynasty. [Islam1 VIII, 998, 1002]

necessary to make a hell of this world to enjoy paradise in the next.

He surpassed in magnificence all his predecessors. The palace of Alkoremi,[1] which his father, Motassem, had erected on the hill of Pied Horses,[2] and which commanded the whole city of Samarah,[3] was, in his idea far too scanty: he added, therefore, five wings, or rather other palaces, which he destined for the particular gratification of each of the senses.

In the first of these were tables continually covered with the most exquisite dainties; which were supplied both by night and by day, according to their constant consumption; whilst the most delicious wines and the choicest cordials flowed forth from a hundred fountains that were never exhausted. This palace was called *The Eternal or unsatiating Banquet*.

The second was styled, *The Temple of Melody*, or *The Nectar of the Soul*. It was inhabited by the most skilful musicians and admired poets of the time; who not only displayed their talents within, but dispersing in bands without, caused every surrounding scene to reverberate their songs; which were continually varied in the most delightful succession.

The palace named *The Delight of the Eyes*, or *The Support of Memory*, was one entire enchantment. Rarities, collected from every corner of the earth were there found in such profusion as to dazzle and confound, but for the order in which they were arranged. One gallery exhibited the pictures of the celebrated Mani,[4] and statues, that seemed to be alive. Here a well-managed perspective attracted the sight; there the magic of optics agreeably deceived it: whilst the naturalist on his part, exhibited

---

1 Alkoremi: Perhaps the palace commemorates the victory of Vathek's father, Motassem, over the Persian rebel Babak Alkorremi, who fomented risings against the Arab Caliphate. The second *Episode* alludes to this figure.

2 hill of Pied Horses: Motassem built his palace on an elevation created when each of his 130,000 horses carried a sack of earth to the site. [*Lonsdale*, 124]

3 Samarah, *Samarra*: a city located on the plain of Catoul in Irak where Vathek's father established his military and administrative centre. The city was just north of Baghdad, which Motassem left because of frequent insurrections there. [*Islam2* VII, 776] The Tower of Babel, from the time of Nimrod, was reputed to have been built in the same place.

4 Mani: famous painter and sculptor from China. [*Inatulla* I, 81]

in their several classes the various gifts that Heaven had bestowed on our globe. In a word, Vathek omitted nothing in this palace, that might gratify the curiosity of those who resorted to it, although he was not able to satisfy his own; for, of all men, he was the most curious.

The Palace of Perfumes, which was termed likewise *The Incentive to Pleasure*, consisted of various halls, where the different perfumes which the earth produces were kept perpetually burning in censers of gold. Flambeaux and aromatic lamps were here lighted in open day. But the too powerful effects of this agreeable delirium might be alleviated by descending into an immense garden, where an assemblage of every fragrant flower diffused through the air the purest odours.

The fifth palace, denominated *The Retreat of Mirth*, or *The Dangerous*, was frequented by troops of young females beautiful as the Houris,[1] and not less seducing; who never failed to receive with caresses, all whom the Caliph allowed to approach them, and enjoy a few hours of their company.

Notwithstanding the sensuality in which Vathek indulged, he experienced no abatement in the love of his people, who thought that a sovereign giving himself up to pleasure, was as able to govern, as one who declared himself an enemy to it. But the unquiet and impetuous disposition of the Caliph would not allow him to rest there. He had studied so much for his amusement in the life-time of his father, as to acquire a great deal of knowledge, though not a sufficiency to satisfy himself; for he wished to know every thing; even sciences that did not exist. He was fond of engaging in disputes with the learned, but did not allow them to push their opposition with warmth. He stopped with presents the mouths of those whose mouths could be stopped; whilst others, whom his liberality was unable to subdue, he sent to prison to cool their blood; a remedy that often succeeded.

Vathek discovered also a predilection for theological controversy; but it was not with the orthodox that he usually held. By

---

1 Houris, *hur*: unfading virgins of Paradise and solace to the spirits of the faithful. [*Sale* 101; *Islam2* III, 581]

this means he induced the zealots to oppose him, and then persecuted them in return; for he resolved, at any rate, to have reason on his side.

The great prophet, Mahomet,[1] whose vicars the caliphs are, beheld with the indignation from his abode in the seventh heaven,[2] the irreligious conduct of such a vicegerent. "Let us leave him to himself," said he to the Genii,[3] who are always ready to receive his commands: "let us see to what lengths his folly and impiety will carry him: if he run into excess, we shall know how to chastise him. Assist him, therefore, to complete the tower, which, in imitation of Nimrod,[4] he hath begun; not, like that great warrior, to escape being drowned, but from the insolent curiosity of penetrating the secrets of heaven: – he will not divine the fate that awaits him."

The Genii obeyed; and, when the workmen had raised their structure a cubit in the day time, two cubits more were added in the night. The expedition, with which the fabric arose, was not a little flattering to the vanity of Vathek: he fancied, that even insensible matter shewed a forwardness to subserve his designs; not considering, that the successes of the foolish and wicked form the first rod of their chastisement.

His pride arrived at its height, when having ascended, for the first time, the fifteen hundred stairs of his tower, he cast his eyes below, and beheld men not larger than pismires;[5] mountains,

---

1   Mahomet, *Muhammed*: the founder of the religion of Islam.
2   seventh heaven: the part of Paradise nearest God's throne and occupied by the most righteous.
3   Genii, *djinn*: What the Persians call *dives*, Genii are demons or giants. They were created by God before Adam and governed the world for 7000 years. "Besides angels and devils, the Mohammedans are taught by the Koran to believe an intermediate order of creatures, which they call Jin or Genii, created also of fire, but of a grosser fabric than angels; since they eat and drink, and propagate their species, and are subject to death ... They also make different ranks and degrees among these beings ... some being called absolutely *Jin*, some *Peri* or *fairies*, some *Div* or *giants*, others *Tacwins* or *fates* ..." [*Sale* 72-73]
4   Nimrod is credited with trying to reach Heaven by building the Tower of Babel. God confounded his ambitions by making his workers speak a babble of languages incomprehensible to one another. [Genesis 10:8-10 and 11:1-9] In Islamic and Jewish tradition, Nimrod persecuted Abraham. [Thomas Patrick Hughes, *A Dictionary of Islam*. (London, W.H. Allen and Co., 1895) 434.]
5   pismires: ants.

than shells; and cities, than bee-hives. The idea, which such an elevation inspired of his own grandeur, completely bewildered him: he was almost ready to adore himself; till, lifting his eyes upward, he saw the stars as high above him as they appeared when he stood on the surface of the earth. He consoled himself, however, for this intruding and unwelcome perception of his littleness, with the thought of being great in the eyes of others; and flattered himself that the light of his mind would extend beyond the reach of his sight, and extort from the stars the decrees of his destiny.

With this view, the inquisitive Prince passed most of his nights on the summit of his tower, till becoming an adept in the mysteries of astrology, he imagined that the planets had disclosed to him the most marvellous adventures, which were to be accomplished by an extraordinary personage, from a country altogether unknown. Prompted by motives of curiosity, he had always been courteous to strangers; but, from this instant, he redoubled his attention, and ordered it to be announced, by sound of trumpet through all the streets of Samarah, that no one of his subjects, on peril of his displeasure, should either lodge or detain a traveller, but forthwith bring him to the palace.

Not long after this proclamation, arrived in his metropolis a man so abominably hideous that the very guards, who arrested him, were forced to shut their eyes, as they led him along: the Caliph himself appeared startled at so horrible a visage; but joy succeeded to this emotion of terror, when the stranger displayed to his view such rarities as he had never before seen, and of which he had no conception.

In reality, nothing was ever so extraordinary as the merchandize this stranger produced: most of his curiosities, which were not less admirable for their workmanship than splendour, had, besides, their several virtues described on a parchment fastened to each. There were slippers, which, by spontaneous springs, enabled the feet to walk; knives, that cut without motion of the hand; sabres, that dealt the blow at the person they were wished to strike; and the whole enriched with gems, that were hitherto unknown.

The sabres, especially, the blades of which, emitted a dazzling radiance, fixed, more than all the rest, the Caliph's attention; who promised himself to decipher, at his leisure, the uncouth characters engraven on their sides. Without, therefore, demanding their price, he ordered all the coined gold to be brought from his treasury, and commanded the merchant to take what he pleased. The stranger obeyed, took little, and remained silent.

Vathek, imagining that the merchant's taciturnity was occasioned by the awe which his presence inspired, encouraged him to advance; and asked him, with an air of condescension, who he was? whence he came? and where he obtained such beautiful commodities? The man, or rather monster, instead of making a reply, thrice rubbed his forehead, which, as well as his body, was blacker than ebony; four times clapped his paunch, the projection of which was enormous; opened wide his huge eyes, which glowed like firebrands; began to laugh with a hideous noise, and discovered his long amber-coloured teeth, bestreaked with green.

The Caliph, though a little startled, renewed his inquiries, but without being able to procure a reply. At which, beginning to be ruffled, he exclaimed: "Knowest thou, wretch, who I am, and at whom thou art aiming thy gibes?" – Then, addressing his guards, – "Have ye heard him speak? – is he dumb?" – "He hath spoken," they replied, "but to no purpose." "Let him speak then again," said Vathek, "and tell me who he is, from whence he came, and where he procured these singular curiosities; or I swear, by the ass of Balaam, that I will make him rue his pertinacity."

This menace was accompanied by one of the Caliph's angry and perilous glances, which the stranger sustained without the slightest emotion; although his eyes were fixed on the terrible eye of the Prince.

No words can describe the amazement of the courtiers, when they beheld this rude merchant withstand the encounter unshocked. They all fell prostrate with their faces on the ground, to avoid the risk of their lives; and would have continued in the same abject posture, had not the Caliph exclaimed in a furious tone – "Up, cowards! seize the miscreant! see that he be committed to prison, and guarded by the best of my soldiers! Let him, however, retain the money I gave him; it is not my intent to take from him his property; I only want him to speak."

No sooner had he uttered these words, than the stranger was surrounded, pinioned and bound with strong fetters, and hurried away to the prison of the great tower; which was encompassed by seven empalements of iron bars, and armed with spikes in every direction, longer and sharper than spits. The Caliph, nevertheless, remained in the most violent agitation. He sat down indeed to eat; but, of the three hundred dishes that were daily placed before him, he could taste of no more than thirty-two.

A diet, to which he had been so little accustomed, was sufficient of itself to prevent him from sleeping; what then must be its effect when joined to the anxiety that preyed upon his spirits? At the first glimpse of dawn he hastened to the prison, again to importune this intractable stranger; but the rage of Vathek exceeded all bounds on finding the prison empty; the grates burst asunder, and his guards lying lifeless around him. In the paroxism of his passion he fell furiously on the poor carcases, and kicked them till evening without intermission. His courtiers and vizirs[1] exerted their efforts to soothe his extravagance; but, finding every expedient ineffectual, they all united in one vociferation – "The Caliph is gone mad! the Caliph is out of his senses!"

This outcry, which soon resounded through the streets of Samarah, at length reached the ears of Carathis, his mother, who flew in the utmost consternation to try her ascendancy on the mind of her son. Her tears and caresses called off his attention; and he was prevailed upon, by her intreaties, to be brought back to the palace.

Carathis, apprehensive of leaving Vathek to himself, had him put to bed; and, seating herself by him, endeavoured by her conversation to appease and compose him. Nor could any one

---

1   vizir, *wazir.* director of the central bureaucracy.

have attempted it with better success; for the Caliph not only loved her as a mother, but respected her as a person of superior genius. It was she who had induced him, being a Greek herself, to adopt the sciences and systems of her country which all good Mussulmans hold in such thorough abhorrence.

Judiciary astrology[1] was one of those sciences, in which Carathis was a perfect adept. She began, therefore, with reminding her son of the promise which the stars had made him; and intimated an intention of consulting them again. "Alas!" said the Caliph as soon as he could speak, "what a fool I have been! not for having bestowed forty thousand kicks on my guards, who so tamely submitted to death; but for never considering that this extraordinary man was the same that the planets had foretold; whom, instead of ill-treating, I should have conciliated by all the arts of persuasion."

"The past," said Carathis, "cannot be recalled; but it behoves us to think of the future: perhaps, you may again see the object you so much regret: it is possible the inscriptions on the sabres will afford information. Eat, therefore, and take thy repose, my dear son. We will consider, to-morrow, in what manner to act."

Vathek yielded to her counsel as well as he could, and arose in the morning with a mind more at ease. The sabres he commanded to be instantly brought; and, poring upon them, through a coloured glass, that their glittering might not dazzle, he set himself in earnest to decipher the inscriptions; but his reiterated attempts were all of them nugatory: in vain did he

---

1   judicial astrology: the use of stars and planets to determine human destiny. D'Herbelot mentions Vathek's interest in the subject, but in the Abbasid period, the astrologer was a permanent functionary in the Caliph's court. Beckford depicts a tension between Islam and Western beliefs over the use of astrology, but at the time of Vathek and well into the seventeenth century, both Islam and the West cast horoscopes and considered planetary "influences" even in matters of state. Beckford may have in mind Richardson's discussion of Judicial Astrology as the forerunner of advances in navigation, although the Europe contemporary with *Vathek* does not seem especially advanced in these matters. Medieval Europe's astrolabes were made from Islamic models. [*Islam2* I, 722; VIII, 107; *Richardson, 32*]

   For Beckford's use of Occident-Orient tensions, see John Garrett, "Ending in Infinity: William Beckford's Arabian Tale," *Eighteenth-Century Fiction* 5 (October 1992): 26.

beat his head, and bite his nails; not a letter of the whole was he able to ascertain. So unlucky a disappointment would have undone him again, had not Carathis, by good fortune, entered the apartment.

"Have patience, my son!" said she: – "you certainly are possessed of every important science; but the knowledge of languages is a trifle at best; and the accomplishment of none but a pedant. Issue a proclamation, that you will confer such rewards as become your greatness, upon any one that shall interpret what you do not understand, and what is beneath you to learn; you will soon find your curiosity gratified."

"That may be," said the Caliph; "but, in the mean time, I shall be horribly disgusted by a crowd of smatterers, who will come to the trial as much for the pleasure of retailing their jargon, as from the hope of gaining the reward. To avoid this evil, it will be proper to add, that I will put every candidate to death, who shall fail to give satisfaction: for, thank Heaven! I have skill enough to distinguish, whether one translates or invents."

"Of that I have no doubt," replied Carathis; "but, to put the ignorant to death is somewhat severe, and may be productive of dangerous effects. Content yourself with commanding their beards to be burnt:[1] – beards in a state, are not quite so essential as men."

The Caliph submitted to the reasons of his mother; and, sending for Morakanabad, his prime vizir, said, – "Let the common criers proclaim, not only in Samarah, but throughout every city in my empire, that whosoever will repair hither and decipher certain characters which appear to be inexplicable, shall experience the liberality for which I am renowned; but, that all who fail upon trail shall have their beards burnt off to the last hair. Let them add, also, that I will bestow fifty beautiful slaves, and as many jars of apricots from the Isle of Kirmith, upon any man that shall bring me intelligence of the stranger."

---

1 beards to be burnt: A beard was held sacred, and heavy fines protected beards from abuse. Molesting beards signals for Beckford a departure from values of Islam. This motif takes on diabolical significance in the first *Episode*.

The subjects of the Caliph, like their sovereign, being great admirers of women and apricots from Kirmith, felt their mouths water at these promises, but were totally unable to gratify their hankering; for no one knew what had become of the stranger.

As to the Caliph's other requisition, the result was different. The learned, the half learned, and those who were neither, but fancied themselves equal to both, came boldly to hazard their beards, and all shamefully lost them. The exaction of these forfeitures, which found sufficient employment for the eunuchs, gave them such a smell of singed hair, as greatly to disgust the ladies of the seraglio, and to make it necessary that this new occupation of their guardians should be transferred to other hands.

At length, however, an old man presented himself, whose beard was a cubit and a half longer than any that had appeared before him. The officers of the palace whispered to each other, as they ushered him in – "What a pity, oh! what a great pity that such a beard should be burnt!" Even the Caliph, when he saw it, concurred with them in opinion; but his concern was entirely needless. This venerable personage read the characters with facility, and explained them verbatim as follows: "We were made where every thing is well made: we are the least of the wonders of a place where all is wonderful and deserving the sight of the first potentate on earth."

"You translate admirably!" cried Vathek; "I know to what these marvellous characters allude. Let him receive as many robes of honour and thousands of sequins of gold[1] as he hath spoken words. I am in some measure relieved from the perplexity that embarrassed me!" Vathek invited the old man to dine, and even to remain some days in the palace.

Unluckily for him, he accepted the offer; for the Caliph having ordered him next morning to be called, said – "Read again to me what you have read already; I cannot hear too often the promise that is made me – the completion of which I languish to obtain." The old man forthwith put on his green spectacles,

---

1 sequin: a gold coin.

but they instantly dropped from his nose, on perceiving that the characters he had read the day preceding, had given place to others of different import. "What ails you?" asked the Caliph; "and why these symptoms of wonder?" – "Sovereign of the world!" replied the old man, "these sabres hold another language today from that they yesterday held." – "How say you?" returned Vathek: – "but it matters not; tell me, if you can, what they mean." – "It is this, my lord," rejoined the old man: "Woe to the rash mortal who seeks to know that of which he should remain ignorant; and to undertake that which surpasseth his power!" – "And woe to thee!" cried the Caliph, in a burst of indignation, "to-day thou art void of understanding: begone from my presence, they shall burn but the half of thy beard, because thou wert yesterday fortunate in guessing: – my gifts I never resume." The old man, wise enough to perceive he had luckily escaped, considering the folly of disclosing so disgusting a truth, immediately withdrew and appeared not again.

But it was not long before Vathek discovered abundant reason to regret his precipitation; for, though he could not decipher the characters himself, yet, by constantly poring upon them, he plainly perceived that they every day changed; and, unfortunately, no other candidate offered to explain them. This perplexing occupation inflamed his blood, dazzled his sight, and brought on such a giddiness and debility that he could hardly support himself. He failed not, however, though in so reduced a condition, to be often carried to his tower, as he flattered himself that he might there read in the stars, which he went to consult, something more congruous to his wishes; but in this his hopes were deluded: for his eyes, dimmed by the vapours of his head, began to subserve his curiosity so ill, that he beheld nothing but a thick, dun cloud, which he took for the most direful of omens.

Agitated with so much anxiety, Vathek entirely lost all firmness; a fever seized him, and his appetite failed. Instead of being one of the greatest eaters, he became as distinguished for drinking. So insatiable was the thirst which tormented him, that his mouth, like a funnel, was always open to receive the various liquors that might be poured into it, and especially cold water, which calmed him more than any other.

This unhappy prince, being thus incapacitated for the enjoyment of any pleasure, commanded the palaces of the five senses to be shut up; forebore to appear in public, either to display his magnificence, or administer justice, and retired to the inmost apartment of his harem. As he had ever been an excellent husband, his wives, overwhelmed with grief at his deplorable situation, incessantly supplied him with prayers for his health, and water for his thirst.

In the mean time the Princess Carathis, whose affliction no words can describe, instead of confining herself to sobbing and tears, was closetted daily with the vizir Morakanabad, to find out some cure, or mitigation, of the Caliph's disease. Under the persuasion that it was caused by enchantment, they turned over together, leaf by leaf, all the books of magic that might point out a remedy; and caused the horrible stranger, whom they accused as the enchanter, to be every where sought for, with the strictest diligence.

At the distance of a few miles from Samarah stood a high mountain, whose sides were swarded with wild thyme and basil, and its summit overspread with so delightful a plain, that it might have been taken for the Paradise[1] destined for the faithful. Upon it grew a hundred thickets of eglantine and other fragrant shrubs; a hundred arbours of roses, entwined with jessamine and honey-suckle; as many clumps of orange trees, cedar, and citron; whose branches, interwoven with the palm, the pomegranate, and the vine, presented every luxury that could regale the eye or the taste. The ground was strewed with violets, hare-bells, and pansies; in the midst of which numerous tufts of jonquils, hyacinths, and carnations perfumed the air. Four fountains, not less clear than deep, and so abundant as to slake the thirst of ten armies, seemed purposely placed here, to make the scene more resemble the garden of Eden

---

1 Paradise, *djanna:* Many of Beckfords's lavish descriptions of fountains, pavilions, fruits, scents, exquisite banquets served by beautiful youths, scented wines, couches inlaid with gold and precious stones, are in harmony with the descriptions of paradise in the Koran. [*Islam2* II, 447]

watered by four sacred rivers.[1] Here, the nightingale[2] sang the birth of the rose, her well-beloved, and, at the same time, lamented its short-lived beauty: whilst the dove deplored the loss of more substantial pleasures; and the wakeful lark hailed the rising light that re-animates the whole creation. Here, more than any where, the mingled melodies of birds expressed the various passions which inspired them; and the exquisite fruits, which they pecked at pleasure, seemed to have given them a double energy.

To this mountain Vathek was sometimes brought, for the sake of breathing a purer air; and, especially, to drink at will of the four fountains. His attendants were his mother, his wives, and some eunuchs, who assiduously employed themselves in filling capacious bowls of rock crystal, and emulously presenting them to him. But it frequently happened, that his avidity exceeded their zeal, insomuch, that he would prostrate himself upon the ground to lap the water, of which he could never have enough.

One day, when this unhappy Prince had been long lying in so debasing a posture, a voice, hoarse but strong, thus addressed him: "Why dost thou assimilate thyself to a dog, O Caliph, proud as thou art of thy dignity and power?" At this apostrophe, he raised his head, and beheld the stranger that had caused him so much affliction. Inflamed with anger at the sight, he exclaimed: – "Accursed Giaour![3] what comest thou hither to do? – is it not enough to have transformed a prince, remarkable for his agility, into a water budget? Perceivest thou not, that I may perish by drinking to excess, as well as by thirst?"

"Drink then this draught," said the stranger, as he presented to him a phial of a red and yellow mixture: "and, to satiate the thirst of thy soul, as well as of thy body, know, that I am an Indian; but, from a region of India, which is wholly unknown."

---

1 four sacred rivers: a commentator, Muhammed Tāhir, identifies the four rivers of Paradise as the Jaxartes, the Jihen, the Euphrates, and the Nile. They rose in Eden originally, before flowing into our earth. [Thomas Patrick Hughes, *A Dictionary of Islam*. (London: W.H. Allen and Co., 1895), 106.]

2 nightingale: A favourite subject in Persian and Turkish poetry is the nightingale's love of the rose. In high summer it fills the nights with laments at the rose's death.

3 Giaour, *gabr, gebir, kafir:* Zoroastrian fire-worshipper; unbeliever. [*Islam2* II, 970]

The Caliph, delighted to see his desires accomplished in part, and flattering himself with the hope of obtaining their entire fulfilment, without a moment's hesitation swallowed the potion, and instantaneously found his health restored, his thirst appeased, and his limbs as agile as ever. In the transports of his joy, Vathek leaped upon the neck of the frightful Indian, and kissed his horrid mouth and hollow cheeks, as though they had been the coral lips and lilies and roses of his most beautiful wives.

Nor would these transports have ceased, had not the eloquence of Carathis repressed them. Having prevailed upon him to return to Samarah, she caused a herald to proclaim as loudly as possible – "The wonderful stranger hath appeared again; he hath healed the Caliph; – he hath spoken! he hath spoken!"

Forthwith, all the inhabitants of this vast city quitted their habitations, and ran together in crowds to see the procession of Vathek and the Indian, whom they now blessed as much as they had before execrated, incessantly shouting – "He hath healed our sovereign; – he hath spoken! he hath spoken!" Nor were these words forgotten in the public festivals, which were celebrated the same evening, to testify the general joy; for the poets applied them as a chorus to all the songs they composed on this interesting subject.

The Caliph, in the meanwhile, caused the palaces of the senses to be again set open; and, as he found himself naturally prompted to visit that of Taste in preference to the rest, immediately ordered a splendid entertainment, to which his great officers and favourite courtiers were all invited. The Indian, who was placed near the Prince, seemed to think that, as a proper acknowledgment of so distinguished a privilege, he could neither eat, drink, nor talk too much. The various dainties were no sooner served up than they vanished, to the great mortification of Vathek, who piqued himself on being the greatest eater alive; and, at this time in particular, was blessed with an excellent appetite.

The rest of the company looked round at each other in amazement; but the Indian, without appearing to observe it, quaffed large bumpers to the health of each of them; sung in a style altogether extravagant; related stories, at which he laughed immoderately; and poured forth extemporaneous verses, which would not have been thought bad, but for the strange grimaces with which they were uttered. In a word, his loquacity was equal to that of a hundred astrologers; he ate as much as a hundred porters, and caroused in proportion.

The Caliph, notwithstanding the table had been thirty-two times covered, found himself incommoded by the voraciousness of his guest, who was now considerably declined in the Prince's esteem. Vathek, however, being unwilling to betray the chagrin he could hardly disguise, said in a whisper to Bababalouk, the chief of his eunuchs, "You see how enormous his performances are in every way; what would be the consequence should he get at my wives! – Go! redouble your vigilance, and be sure look well to my Circassians,[1] who would be more to his taste than all of the rest."

The bird of the morning had thrice renewed his song, when the hour of the Divan[2] was announced. Vathek, in gratitude to his subjects, having promised to attend, immediately arose from table, and repaired thither, leaning upon his vizir who could scarcely support him: so disordered was the poor Prince by the wine he had drunk, and still more by the extravagant vagaries of his boisterous guest.

The vizirs, the officers of the crown and of the law, arranged themselves in a semicircle about their sovereign, and preserved a respectful silence; whilst the Indian, who looked as cool as if he had been fasting, sat down without ceremony on one of the steps of the throne, laughing in his sleeve at the indignation with which his temerity had filled the spectators.

The Caliph, however, whose ideas were confused, and whose head was embarrassed, went on administering justice at hap-hazard; till at length the prime vizir, perceiving his situation, hit upon a sudden expedient to interrupt the audience and rescue the honour of his master, to whom he said in a whisper: – "My lord, the Princess Carathis, who hath passed the

---

1 Circassians: a people who lived on the shores of the Black Sea.
2 Divan, *diwan*: a chamber of council, justice, police, and finance presided over by the caliph. [*Islam2* II, 323]

night in consulting the planets, informs you, that they portend you evil, and the danger is urgent. Beware, lest this stranger, whom you have so lavishly recompensed for his magical gew-gaws, should make some attempt on your life: his liquor, which at first had the appearance of effecting your cure, may be no more than a poison, the operation of which will be sudden. – Slight not this surmise; ask him, at least, of what it was com-pounded, whence he poured it; and mention the sabres, which you seem to have forgotten."

Vathek, to whom the insolent airs of the stranger became every moment less supportable, intimated to his vizir, by a wink of acquiescence, that he would adopt his advice; and, at once turning towards the Indian, said – "Get up, and declare in full Divan of what drugs was compounded the liquor you enjoined me to take, for it is suspected to be poison: give also, that expla-nation I have so earnestly desired, concerning the sabres you sold me, and thus shew your gratitude for the favours heaped upon you."

Having pronounced these words, in as moderate a tone as he well could, he waited in silent expectation for an answer. But the Indian, still keeping his seat, began to renew his loud shouts of laughter, and exhibit the same horrid grimaces he had shewn them before, without vouchsafing a word in reply. Vathek, no longer able to brook such insolence, immediately kicked him from the steps; instantly descending, repeated his blow; and persisted, with such assiduity, as incited all who were pre-sent to follow his example. Every foot was up and aimed at the Indian, and no sooner had any one given him a kick, than he felt himself constrained to reiterate the stroke.

The stranger afforded them no small entertainment: for, being both short and plump, he collected himself into a ball, and rolled round on all sides, at the blows of his assailants, who pressed after him, wherever he turned, with an eagerness beyond conception, whilst their numbers were every moment increasing. The ball indeed, in passing from one apartment to another, drew every person after it that came in its way; inso-much, that the whole palace was thrown into confusion and resounded with a tremendous clamour. The women of the harem, amazed at the uproar, flew to their blinds to discover the cause; but, no sooner did they catch a glimpse of the ball, than, feeling themselves unable to refrain, they broke from the clutches of their eunuchs,[1] who, to stop their flight, pinched them till they bled; but, in vain: whilst themselves, though trembling with terror at the escape of their charge, were as incapable of resisting the attraction.

After having traversed the halls, galleries, chambers, kitchens, gardens, and stables of the palace, the Indian at last took his course through the courts; whilst the Caliph, pursuing him closer than the rest, bestowed as many kicks as he possibly could; yet, not without receiving now and then a few which his competitors, in their eagerness, designed for the ball.

Carathis, Morakanabad, and two or three old vizirs, whose wisdom had hitherto withstood the attraction, wishing to prevent Vathek from exposing himself in the presence of his subjects, fell down in his way to impede the pursuit: but he, regardless of their obstruction, leaped over their heads, and went on as before. They then ordered the Muezins[2] to call the people to prayers; both for the sake of getting them out of the way, and of endeavouring, by their petitions, to avert the calamity; but neither of these expedients was a whit more successful. The sight of this fatal ball was alone sufficient to draw after it every beholder. The Muezins themselves, though they saw it but at a distance, hastened down from their minarets,[3] and mixed with the crowd; which continued to increase in so surprising a man-

---

1   eunuch, *Khasi*: men who have been emasculated (usually before puberty) by either of two methods: by cutting away the penis and testicles or, more commonly, by incising the scrotum with a red-hot blade and removing the testicles, but leaving the penis. Eunuchs were the most valuable slaves, acting often as intermediaries in the harem between the master and his wives and concubines. Their freedom of movement permitted them to become accomplices in plots, informants, and participants in the state politics. Some achieved high political or administrative office. A eunuch, if operated on before puberty, grows no beard, does not experience baldness, has soft skin, and a distinctive voice. In Beckford's time, eunuchs, or *castrati*, with powerful voices that ranged into the soprano register, dominated European opera. [*Islam2* IV, 1087]

2   Muezins, *mu'adhdhin*: criers who call faithful Muslims to divine service. [*D'Herbelot*, 576; *Islam2* I, 187]

3   minarets: towers on mosques from which the Muezins call the faithful. [*D'Herbelot*, 576; *Islam2* I, 187]

ner, that scarce an inhabitant was left in Samarah, except the aged; the sick, confined to their beds; and infants at the breast, whose nurses could run more nimbly without them. Even Carathis, Morakanabad, and the rest, were all become of the party. The shrill screams of the females, who had broken from their apartments, and were unable to extricate themselves from the pressure of the crowd, together with those of the eunuchs jostling after them, and terrified lest their charge should escape from their sight; the execrations of husbands, urging forward and menacing each other; kicks given and received; stumblings and overthrows at every step; in a word, the confusion that universally prevailed, rendered Samarah like a city taken by storm, and devoted to absolute plunder. At last, the cursed Indian, who still preserved his rotundity of figure, after passing through all the streets and public places, and leaving them empty, rolled onwards to the plain of Catoul, and entered the valley at the foot of the mountain of the four fountains.

As a continual fall of water had excavated an immense gulph in the valley whose opposite side was closed in by a steep acclivity, the Caliph and his attendants were apprehensive, lest the ball should bound into the chasm, and, to prevent it, redoubled their efforts, but in vain. The Indian persevered in his onward direction; and, as had been apprehended, glancing from the precipice with the rapidity of lightning, was lost in the gulph below.

Vathek would have followed the perfidious Giaour, had not an invisible agency arrested his progress. The multitude that pressed after him were at once checked in the same manner, and a calm instantaneously ensued. They all gazed at each other with an air of astonishment, and notwithstanding that the loss of veils and turbans, together with torn habits, and dust blended with sweat, presented a most laughable spectacle, yet there was not one smile to be seen. On the contrary, all with looks of confusion and sadness returned in silence to Samarah, and retired to their inmost apartments, without ever reflecting, that they had been impelled by an invisible power into the extravagance, for which they reproached themselves: for it is but just that men, who so often arrogate to their own merit the good of which they are but instruments, should also attribute to themselves absurdities which they could not prevent.

The Caliph was the only person who refused to leave the valley. He commanded his tents to be pitched there, and stationed himself on the very edge of the precipice, in spite of the representations of Carathis and Morakanabad, who pointed out the hazard of its brink giving way, and the vicinity to the magician, that had so cruelly tormented him. Vathek derided all their remonstrances; and, having ordered a thousand flambeaux to be lighted, and directed his attendants to proceed in lighting more, lay down on the slippery margin, and attempted, by the help of this artificial splendour, to look through that gloom, which all the fires of the empyrean had been insufficient to pervade. One while he fancied to himself voices arising from the depth of the gulph; at another, he seemed to distinguish the accents of the Indian; but all was no more than the hollow murmur of waters, and the din of the cataracts that rushed from steep to steep down the sides of the mountain.

Having passed the night in this cruel perturbation, the Caliph, at day-break, retired to his tent; where, without taking the least sustenance, he continued to doze till the dusk of evening began again to come on. He then resumed his vigils as before, and persevered in observing them for many nights together. At length, fatigued with so fruitless an employment, he sought relief from change. To this end, he sometimes paced with hasty strides across the plain; and, as he wildly gazed at the stars, reproached them with having deceived him; but, lo! on a sudden, the clear blue sky appeared streaked over with streams of blood, which reached from the valley even to the city of Samarah. As this awful phenomenon seemed to touch his tower, Vathek at first thought of repairing thither to view it more distinctly; but, feeling himself unable to advance, and being overcome with apprehension, he muffled up his face in the folds of his robe.

Terrifying as these prodigies were, this impression upon him was no more than momentary, and served only to stimulate his love of the marvellous. Instead, therefore, of returning to his palace, he persisted in the resolution of abiding where the

Indian had vanished from his view. One night, however, while he was walking as usual on the plain, the moon and stars were eclipsed at once, and a total darkness ensued. The earth trembled beneath him, and a voice came forth, the voice of the Giaour, who, in accents more sonorous than thunder, thus addressed him: "Wouldest thou devote thyself to me, adore the terrestrial influences, and abjure Mahomet? On these conditions I will bring thee to the Palace of Subterranean Fire. There shalt thou behold, in immense depositories, the treasures which the stars have promised thee; and which will be conferred by those intelligences,[1] whom thou shalt thus render propitious. It was from thence I brought my sabres, and it is there that Soliman Ben Daoud[2] reposes, surrounded by the talismans that control the world."

The astonished Caliph trembled as he answered, yet he answered in a style that shewed him to be no novice in preternatural adventures: "Where art thou? be present to my eyes; dissipate the gloom that perplexes me, and of which I deem thee the cause. After the many flambeaux I have burnt to discover thee, thou mayest, at least, grant a glimpse of thy horrible visage." – "Abjure then Mahomet!" replied the Indian, "and promise me full proofs of thy sincerity: otherwise, thou shalt never behold me again."

The unhappy Caliph, instigated by insatiable curiosity, lavished his promises in the utmost profusion. The sky immediately brightened; and, by the light of the planets, which seemed almost to blaze, Vathek beheld the earth open; and, at the extremity of a vast black chasm, a portal of ebony, before which

---

1 Intelligences; *Ruh*, breath: a special angel messenger; a special divine quality. The term is applied to the human spirit, angels, and djinn.

2 Soliman Ben Daoud, *Sulayman ben Dawud*: the wise Solomon of the Bible, son of David. Islamic legends emphasize his wisdom and justice, although tradition multiplies tales of his powers of magic and his wealth. According to such accounts, he commanded the djinn to build shrines, statues, and temples, including the temple at Jerusalem. He wove a magic carpet for aerial transportation, and he accumulated untold wealth in gold, silver, and precious stones. His marvels are related in stories so countless that the tongue of a man would grow hair before he could tell them. Beckford departs from the Koran, where Solomon is favoured of God, a great and respected prophet. [*Islam2* IX, 822]

stood the Indian, holding in his hand a golden key, which he sounded against the lock.

"How," cried Vathek, "can I descend to thee? – Come, take me, and instantly open the portal." – "Not so fast," replied the Indian, "impatient Caliph! – Know that I am parched with thirst, and cannot open this door, till my thirst be thoroughly appeased; I require the blood of fifty children. Take them from among the most beautiful sons of thy vizirs and great men; or, neither can my thirst nor thy curiosity be satisfied. Return to Samarah; procure for me this necessary libation; come back hither; throw it thyself into this chasm, and then shalt thou see!"

Having thus spoken, the Indian turned his back on the Caliph, who, incited by the suggestions of demons, resolved on the direful sacrifice. – He now pretended to have regained his tranquillity, and set out for Samarah amidst the acclamations of a people who still loved him, and forebore not to rejoice, when they believed him to have recovered his reason. So successfully did he conceal the emotion of his heart, that even Carathis and Morakanabad were equally deceived with the rest. Nothing was heard of but festivals and rejoicings. The fatal ball, which no tongue had hitherto ventured to mention, was brought on the tapis.[1] A general laugh went round, though many, still smarting under the hands of the surgeon, from the hurts received in that memorable adventure, had no great reason for mirth.

The prevalence of this gay humour was not a little grateful to Vathek, who perceived how much it conduced to his project. He put on the appearance of affability to every one; but especially to his vizirs, and the grandees[2] of his court, whom he failed not to regale with a sumptuous banquet; during which, he insensibly directed the conversation to the children of his guests. Having asked, with a good-natured air, which of them were blessed with the handsomest boys, every father at once asserted the pretensions of his own; and the contest impercepti-

---

1   tapis, Fr. *carpet*: to lay on the table for discussion.
2   grandees: persons of high rank.

bly grew so warm, that nothing could have withholden them from coming to blows, but their profound reverence for the person of the Caliph. Under the pretence, therefore, of reconciling the disputants, Vathek took upon him to decide; and, with this view, commanded the boys to be brought.

It was not long before a troop of these poor children made their appearance, all equipped by their fond mothers with such ornaments, as might give the greatest relief to their beauty, or most advantageously display the graces of their age. But, whilst this brilliant assemblage attracted the eyes and hearts of every one besides, the Caliph scrutinized each, in his turn, with a malignant avidity that passed for attention, and selected from their number the fifty whom he judged the Giaour would prefer.

With an equal shew of kindness as before, he proposed to celebrate a festival on the plain, for the entertainment of his young favourites, who, he said, ought to rejoice still more than all, at the restoration of his health, on account of the favours he intended for them.

The Caliph's proposal was received with the greatest delight, and soon published through Samarah. Litters, camels, and horses were prepared. Women and children, old men and young, every one placed himself as he chose. The cavalcade set forward, attended by all the confectioners in the city and its precincts; the populace, following on foot, composed an amazing crowd, and occasioned no little noise. All was joy; nor did any one call to mind, what most of them had suffered, when they lately travelled the road they were now passing so gaily.

The evening was serene, the air refreshing, the sky clear, and the flowers exhaled their fragrance. The beams of the declining sun, whose mild splendour reposed on the summit of the mountain, shed a glow of ruddy light over its green declivity, and the white flocks sporting upon it. No sounds were heard, save the murmurs of the four fountains; and the reeds and voices of shepherds calling to each other from different eminences.

The lovely innocents destined for the sacrifice, added not a little to the hilarity of the scene. They approached the plain full of sportiveness, some coursing butterflies, others culling flowers, or picking up the shining little pebbles that attracted their notice. At intervals they nimbly started from each other for the sake of being caught again, and mutually imparting a thousand caresses.

The dreadful chasm, at whose bottom the portal of ebony was placed, began to appear at a distance. It looked like a black streak that divided the plain. Morakanabad and his companions, took it for some work which the Caliph had ordered. Unhappy men! little did they surmise for what it was destined. Vathek unwilling that they should examine it too nearly, stopped the procession, and ordered a spacious circle to be formed on this side, at some distance from the accursed chasm. The body-guard of eunuchs was detached, to measure out the lists intended for the games; and prepare the rings for the arrows of the young archers. The fifty competitors were soon stripped, and presented to the admiration of the spectators the suppleness and grace of their delicate limbs. Their eyes sparkled with a joy, which those of their fond parents reflected. Every one offered wishes for the little candidate nearest his heart, and doubted not of his being victorious. A breathless suspence awaited the contests of these amiable and innocent victims.

The Caliph, availing himself of the first moment to retire from the crowd, advanced towards the chasm; and there heard, yet not without shuddering, the voice of the Indian; who, gnashing his teeth, eagerly demanded: "Where are they? – Where are they? – perceivest thou not how my mouth waters?" – "Relentless Giaour!" answered Vathek, with emotion; "can nothing content thee but the massacre of these lovely victims? Ah! wert thou to behold their beauty, it must certainly move thy compassion." – "Perdition on thy compassion, babbler!" cried the Indian: "give them me; instantly give them, or, my portal shall be closed against thee for ever!" – "Not so loudly," replied the Caliph, blushing. – "I understand thee," returned the Giaour with the grin of an Ogre;[1] "thou wantest no presence of mind: I will, for a moment, forbear."

During this exquisite dialogue, the games went forward with

---

1 ogre: ghoul or a demon who lurks in remote places and attacks and devours travellers.

all alacrity, and at length concluded, just as the twilight began to overcast the mountains. Vathek, who was still standing on the edge of the chasm, called out, with all his might: – "Let my fifty little favourites approach me, separately: and let them come in the order of their success. To the first, I will give my diamond bracelet; to the second, my collar of emeralds; to the third, my aigret[1] of rubies; to the fourth, my girdle of topazes; and to the rest, each a part of my dress, even down to my slippers."

This declaration was received with reiterated acclamations; and all extolled the liberality of a prince, who would thus strip himself, for the amusement of his subjects, and the encouragement of the rising generation. The Caliph, in the meanwhile, undressed himself by degrees; and, raising his arm as high as he was able, made each of the prizes glitter in the air; but, whilst he delivered it, with one hand, to the child, who sprung forward to receive it; he, with the other, pushed the poor innocent into the gulph; where the Giaour, with sullen muttering, incessantly repeated; "more! more!"

This dreadful device was executed with so much dexterity, that the boy who was approaching him, remained unconscious of the fate of his forerunner; and, as to the spectators, the shades of evening, together with their distance, precluded them from perceiving any object distinctly. Vathek, having in this manner thrown in the last of the fifty; and, expecting that the Giaour, on receiving him, would have presented the key; already fancied himself, as great as Soliman, and, consequently, above being amenable for what he had done: – when, to his utter amazement, the chasm closed, and the ground became as entire as the rest of the plain.

No language could express his rage and despair. He execrated the perfidy of the Indian; loaded him with the most infamous invectives; and stamped with his foot, as resolving to be heard. He persisted in this till his strength failed him; and, then, fell on the earth like one void of sense. His vizirs and grandees, who were nearer than the rest, supposed him, at first, to be sitting on the grass, at play with their amiable children; but, at

---

1   aigret: a spray of gems worn on a headpiece or, sometimes, the jeweled headpiece itself.

length, prompted by doubt, they advanced towards the spot, and found the Caliph alone, who wildly demanded what they wanted? "Our children! our children!" cried they. "It is, assuredly, pleasant," said he, "to make me accountable for accidents. Your children, while at play, fell from the precipice, and I should have experienced their fate, had I not suddenly started back."

At these words, the fathers of the fifty boys cried out aloud; the mothers repeated their exclamations an octave higher; whilst the rest, without knowing the cause, soon drowned the voices of both, with still louder lamentations of their own. "Our Caliph," said they, and the report soon circulated, "our Caliph has played us this trick, to gratify his accursed Giaour. Let us punish him for perfidy! let us avenge ourselves! let us avenge the blood of the innocent! let us throw this cruel prince into the gulph that is near, and let his name be mentioned no more!"

At this rumour and these menaces, Carathis, full of consternation, hastened to Morakanabad, and said: "Vizir, you have lost two beautiful boys, and must necessarily be the most afflicted of fathers; but you are virtuous; save your master." – "I will brave every hazard," replied the vizir, "to rescue him from his present danger; but, afterwards, will abandon him to his fate. Bababalouk," continued he, "put yourself at the head of your eunuchs: disperse the mob, and, if possible, bring this unhappy prince to his palace." Bababalouk and his fraternity, felicitating each other in a low voice on their having been spared the cares as well as honour of paternity, obeyed the mandate of the vizir; who, seconding their exertions, to the utmost of his power, at length, accomplished his generous enterprize; and retired, as he resolved, to lament at his leisure.

No sooner had the Caliph re-entered his palace, than Carathis commanded the doors to be fastened; but perceiving the tumult to be still violent, and hearing the imprecations which resounded from all quarters, she said to her son: "Whether the populace be right or wrong, it behoves you to provide for your safety; let us retire to your own apartment, and, from thence, through the subterranean passage, known only to ourselves, into your tower: there, with the assistance of the mutes[1] who never leave it, we may be able to make a powerful resistance. Bababalouk, supposing us to be still in the palace, will guard its avenues, for his own sake; and we shall soon find, without the counsels of that blubberer Morakanabad, what expedient may be the best to adopt."

Vathek, without making the least reply, acquiesced in his mother's proposal, and repeated as he went: "Nefarious Giaour! where art thou? hast thou not yet devoured those poor children? where are thy sabres? thy golden key? thy talismans?" – Carathis, who guessed from these interrogations a part of the truth, had no difficulty to apprehend, in getting at the whole as soon as he should be a little composed in his tower. This Princess was so far from being influenced by scruples, that she was as wicked, as woman could be; which is not saying a little; for the sex pique themselves on their superiority, in every competition. The recital of the Caliph, therefore, occasioned neither terror nor surprise to his mother: she felt no emotion but from the promises of the Giaour, and said to her son: "This Giaour, it must be confessed, is somewhat sanguinary in his taste; but, the terrestrial powers are always terrible; nevertheless, what the one hath promised, and the others can confer, will prove a sufficient indemnification. No crimes should be thought too dear for such a reward: forbear, then, to revile the Indian; you have not fulfilled the conditions to which his services are annexed: for instance; is not a sacrifice to the subterranean Genii required? and should we not be prepared to offer it as soon as the tumult is subsided? This charge I will take on myself, and have no doubt of succeeding, by means of your treasures, which as there are now so many others in store, may, without fear, be exhausted." Accordingly, the Princess, who possessed the most consummate skill in the art of persuasion, went immediately back through the subterranean passage; and, presenting herself to the populace, from a window of the palace, began to harangue them with all the address of which she was mistress; whilst Bababalouk, showered money from

---

1 mute: one who is unable to speak. Mutes were valued for their capacities for silent
   communication and silent execution with the garotte. [*Habesci*, 164]

both hands amongst the crowd, who by these united means were soon appeased. Every person retired to his home, and Carathis returned to the tower.

Prayer at break of day was announced, when Carathis and Vathek ascended the steps, which led to the summit of the tower; where they remained for some time though the weather was lowering and wet. This impending gloom corresponded with their malignant dispositions; but when the sun began to break through the clouds, they ordered a pavilion to be raised, as a screen against the intrusion of his beams. The Caliph, overcome with fatigue, sought refreshment from repose; at the same time, hoping that significant dreams might attend on his slumbers; whilst the indefatigable Carathis, followed by a party of her mutes, descended to prepare whatever she judged proper, for the oblation of the approaching night.

By secret stairs, contrived within the thickness of the wall, and known only to herself and her son, she first repaired to the mysterious recesses in which were deposited the mummies[1] that had been wrested from the catacombs of the ancient Pharaohs. Of these she ordered several to be taken. From thence, she resorted to a gallery; where, under the guard of fifty female negroes mute and blind of the right eye, were preserved the oil of the most venomous serpents; rhinoceros' horns; and woods of a subtile and penetrating odour, procured from the interior of the Indies, together with a thousand other horrible rarities. This collection had been formed for a purpose like the present, by Carathis herself; from a presentiment, that she might one day, enjoy some intercourse with the infernal powers: to whom she had ever been passionately attached, and to whose taste she was no stranger.

To familiarize herself the better with the horrors in view, the Princess remained in the company of her negresses, who squinted in the most amiable manner from the only eye they had; and leered with exquisite delight, at the sculls and skele-

---

1   mummies, *mumiya'*: bodies which have become petrified after being interred in dry, hot land [Chardin]. Bitumen or mineral tar as well as the bituminous substance from Egyptian mummies were both used in ancient medicine. [*Islam2* VII, 556]

tons which Carathis had drawn forth from her cabinets; all of them making the most frightful contortions and uttering such shrill chatterings, that the Princess stunned by them and suffocated by the potency of the exhalations, was forced to quit the gallery, after stripping it of a part of its abominable treasures.

Whilst she was thus occupied, the Caliph, who instead of the visions he expected, had acquired in these unsubstantial regions a voracious appetite, was greatly provoked at the mutes. For having totally forgotten their deafness, he had impatiently asked them for food; and seeing them regardless of his demand, he began to cuff, pinch, and bite them, till Carathis arrived to terminate a scene so indecent, to the great content of these miserable creatures: "Son! what means all this?" said she, panting for breath. "I thought I heard as I came up, the shrieks of a thousand bats, torn from their crannies in the recesses of a cavern; and it was the outcry only of these poor mutes, whom you were so unmercifully abusing. In truth, you but ill deserve the admirable provision I have brought you." – "Give it me instantly," exclaimed the Caliph; "I am perishing for hunger!" – "As to that," answered she, "you must have an excellent stomach if it can digest what I have brought." – "Be quick," replied the Caliph; – "but, oh heavens! what horrors! what do you intend?" "Come; come;" returned Carathis, "be not so squeamish; but help me to arrange every thing properly; and you shall see that, what you reject with such symptoms of disgust, will soon complete your felicity. Let us get ready the pile, for the sacrifice of to-night; and think not of eating, till that is performed: know you not, that all solemn rites ought to be preceded by a rigorous abstinence?"

The Caliph, not daring to object, abandoned himself to grief and the wind that ravaged his entrails, whilst his mother went forward with the requisite operations. Phials of serpents' oil, mummies, and bones, were soon set in order on the balustrade[1] of the tower. The pile began to rise; and in three hours was twenty cubits high. At length darkness approached, and Carathis, having stripped herself to her inmost garment,

---

1   balustrade: a row of columns surmounted by a rail forming an ornamental barrier along the edge of a balcony or terrace.

clapped her hands in an impulse of ecstacy; the mutes followed her example; but Vathek, extenuated with hunger and impatience, was unable to support himself, and fell down in a swoon. The sparks had already kindled the dry wood; the venomous oil burst into a thousand blue flames; the mummies, dissolving, emitted a thick dun vapour; and the rhinoceros' horns, beginning to consume; all together diffused such a stench, that the Caliph, recovering, started from his trance, and gazed wildly on the scene in full blaze around him. The oil gushed forth in a plenitude of streams; and the negresses, who supplied it without intermission, united their cries to those of the Princess. At last, the fire became so violent, and the flames reflected from the polished marble so dazzling, that the Caliph, unable to withstand the heat and the blaze, effected his escape; and took shelter under the imperial standard.

In the mean time, the inhabitants of Samarah, scared at the light which shone over the city, arose in haste; ascended their roofs; beheld the tower on fire, and hurried, half naked to the square. Their love for their sovereign immediately awoke; and, apprehending him in danger of perishing in his tower, their whole thoughts were occupied with the means of his safety. Morakanabad flew from his retirement, wiped away his tears, and cried out for water like the rest. Bababalouk, whose olfactory nerves were more familiarized to magical odours, readily conjecturing, that Carathis was engaged in her favourite amusements, strenuously exhorted them not to be alarmed. Him, however, they treated as an old poltroon, and styled him a rascally traitor. The camels and dromedaries were advancing with water; but, no one knew by which way to enter the tower. Whilst the populace was obstinate in forcing the doors, a violent north-east wind drove an immense volume of flame against them. At first, they recoiled, but soon came back with redoubled zeal. At the same time, the stench of the horns and mummies increasing, most of the crowd fell backward in a state of suffocation. Those that kept their feet, mutually wondered at the cause of the smell; and admonished each other to retire. Morakanabad, more sick than the rest, remained in a piteous condition. Holding his nose with one hand, every one persisted in his efforts with the other to burst open the doors and obtain admission. A hundred and forty of the strongest and most resolute, at length accomplished their purpose. Having gained the stair-case, by their violent exertions, they attained a great height in a quarter of an hour.

Carathis, alarmed at the signs of her mutes, advanced to the stair-case; went down a few steps, and heard several voices calling out from below: "You shall, in a moment have water!" Being rather alert, considering her age, she presently regained the top of the tower; and bade her son suspend the sacrifice for some minutes; adding, – "We shall soon be enabled to render it more grateful. Certain dolts of your subjects, imagining no doubt that we were on fire, have been rash enough to break through those doors, which had hitherto remained inviolate; for the sake of bringing up water. They are very kind, you must allow, so soon to forget the wrongs you have done them; but that is of little moment. Let us offer them to the Giaour, – let them come up; our mutes, who neither want strength nor experience, will soon dispatch them; exhausted as they are, with fatigue." – "Be it so," answered the Caliph, "provided we finish, and I dine." In fact, these good people, out of breath from ascending fifteen hundred stairs in such haste; and chagrined, at having spilt by the way, the water they had taken, were no sooner arrived at the top, than the blaze of the flames, and the fumes of the mummies, at once overpowered their senses. It was a pity! for they beheld not the agreeable smile, with which the mutes and negresses adjusted the cord to their necks: these amiable personages rejoiced, however, no less at the scene. Never before had the ceremony of strangling been performed with so much facility. They all fell, without the least resistance or struggle: so that Vathek, in the space of a few moments, found himself surrounded by the dead bodies of the most faithful of his subjects; all which were thrown on the top of the pile. Carathis, whose presence of mind never forsook her, perceiving that she had carcasses sufficient to complete her oblation, commanded the chains to be stretched across the stair-case, and the iron doors barricaded, that no more might come up.

No sooner were these orders obeyed, than the tower shook;

the dead bodies vanished in the flames; which, at once, changed from a swarthy crimson, to a bright rose colour: an ambient vapour emitted the most exquisite fragrance; the marble columns rang with harmonious sounds, and the liquified horns diffused a delicious perfume. Carathis, in transports, anticipated the success of her enterprize; whilst her mutes and negresses, to whom these sweets had given the cholic, retired grumbling to their cells.

Scarcely were they gone, when, instead of the pile, horns, mummies and ashes, the Caliph both saw and felt, with a degree of pleasure which he could not express, a table, covered with the most magnificent repast: flaggons of wine, and vases of exquisite sherbet reposing on snow. He availed himself, without scruple, of such an entertainment; and had already laid hands on a lamb stuffed with pistachios, whilst Carathis was privately drawing from a fillagreen[1] urn, a parchment that seemed to be endless; and which had escaped the notice of her son. Totally occupied in gratifying an importunate appetite, he left her to peruse it without interruption; which having finished, she said to him, in an authoritative tone, "Put an end to your gluttony, and hear the splendid promises with which you are favoured!" She then read, as follows: "Vathek, my well-beloved, thou hast surpassed my hopes: my nostrils have been regaled by the savour of thy mummies, thy horns; and, still more by the lives, devoted on the pile. At the full of the moon, cause the hands of thy musicians, and thy tymbals, to be heard; depart from thy palace, surrounded by all the pageants of majesty; thy most faithful slaves; thy best beloved wives; thy most magnificent litters; thy richest loaden camels; and set forward on thy way to Istakhar.[2] There, I await thy coming: that is

---

1 fillagreen; filigree: delicate ornamental work done with jewels and gold and silver thread.

2 Istakhar, Istakar, Istakhr: Beckford conflates the city of Istakhar with the city of Persepolis which was located a short distance to the south; Chardin, Beckford's source, seems to have confused the two. Capital of the district of Fars, Istakhr was founded soon after Alexander's sack of Persepolis, the ruins of which formed a quarry for the stone of Istakhr's buildings. It was a centre of fire worship and fiercely resisted the Muslims. At least two ruins in the complex are believed to be former fire temples, one of which is called the Ka'aba of Zoroaster. Istakhar declined as a city when Shiraz was made capital of Fars.

the region of wonders: there shalt thou receive the diadem of Gian Ben Gian;[1] the talismans of Soliman;[2] and the treasures of the pre-adamite sultans:[3] there shalt thou be solaced with all kinds of delight. – But beware how thou enterest any dwelling on thy route; or thou shalt feel the effects of my anger."

The Caliph, notwithstanding his habitual luxury, had never before dined with so much satisfaction. He gave full scope to the joy of these golden tidings; and betook himself to drinking anew. Carathis, whose antipathy to wine was by no means insuperable, failed not to pledge him at every bumper he ironically quaffed to the health of Mahomet. This infernal liquor completed their impious temerity, and prompted them to utter a profusion of blasphemies. They gave a loose to their wit, at the expense of the ass of Balaam, the dog of the seven sleepers,[4] and the other animals admitted into the paradise of Mahomet. In this sprightly humour, they descended the fifteen hundred stairs, diverting themselves as they went, at the anxious faces they saw on the square, through the barbacans and loopholes of the tower; and, at length, arrived at the royal apartments, by the subterranean passage. Bababalouk was parading to and fro, and issuing his mandates, with great pomp to the eunuchs; who were snuffing the lights and painting the eyes of the Circassians. No sooner did he catch sight of the Caliph and his mother, than he exclaimed, "Hah! you have, then, I perceive, escaped from the flames: I was not, however, altogether out of doubt." – "Of what moment is it to us what you thought, or think?"

The construction of Persepolis, while ascribed to the legendary hero and king, Djamshid, was begun under Darius I (522–486 BC) who made it the ceremonial capital of Persia. Alexander the Great sacked it in 330 BC. The ruins still show an extensive terrace extending to the mountains on which huge buildings had been erected. Many of the columns are still visible. [*Islam2* IV, 219]

1 Gian Ben Gian: King of the *djinn*, governed the world just before the creation of Adam.

2 talismans of Soliman: A ring, engraved with the secret name of God, gave Solomon command over the *djinn* and all other created beings. [*Richardson* 271; *D'Herbelot* 820; *Islam2* IX, 822]

3 preadamite sultans: the forty (sometimes 72) kings of the *djinn* before the creation of Adam; each was named Solomon. [*Islam2* IX, 823]

4 dog of the seven sleepers: According to the Koran there are animals in Paradise. Beckford speculates that the dog of the seven sleepers and the ass of Balaam would be among them. [Sale's *Koran*, ch xviii].

cried Carathis: "go; speed; tell Morakanabad that we immediately want him: and take care, not to stop by the way, to make your insipid reflections."

Morakanabad delayed not to obey the summons; and was received by Vathek and his mother, with great solemnity. They told him, with an air of composure and commiseration, that the fire at the top of the tower was extinguished; but that it had cost the lives of the brave people who sought to assist them.

"Still more misfortunes!" cried Morakanabad, with a sigh. "Ah, commander of the faithful, our holy prophet is certainly irritated against us! it behoves you to appease him." – "We will appease him, hereafter!" replied the Caliph, with a smile that augured nothing good. "You will have leisure sufficient for your supplications, during my absence: for this country is the bane of my health. I am disgusted with the mountain of the four fountains, and am resolved to go and drink of the stream of Rocnabad.[1] I long to refresh myself, in the delightful valleys which it waters. Do you, with the advice of my mother, govern my dominions, and take care to supply whatever her experiments may demand; for, you well know, that our tower abounds in materials for the advancement of science."

The tower but ill suited Morakanabad's taste. Immense treasures had been lavished upon it; and nothing had he ever seen carried thither but female negroes, mutes and abominable drugs. Nor did he know well what to think of Carathis, who, like a cameleon, could assume all possible colours. Her cursed eloquence had often driven the poor Mussulman to his last shifts. He considered, however, that if she possessed but few good qualities, her son had still fewer; and that the alternative, on the whole, would be in her favour. Consoled, therefore, with this reflection; he went, in good spirits, to soothe the populace, and make the proper arrangements for his master's journey.

Vathek, to conciliate the Spirits of the subterranean palace, resolved that his expedition should be uncommonly splendid.

---

1 Rocnabad: a brook that flows close to the city of Shiraz in the province of Fars. Its water is pure and clear; its verdure pleasant. An oratory was founded there for pious contemplation.

With this in view he confiscated, on all sides, the property of his subjects; whilst his worthy mother stripped the seraglios she visited, of the gems they contained. She collected all the sempstresses and embroiderers of Samarah and other cities, to the distance of sixty leagues; to prepare pavilions, palanquins,[1] sofas, canopies, and litters for the train of the monarch. There was not left, in Masulipatan, a single piece of chintz; and so much muslin had been brought up to dress out Bababalouk and the other black eunuchs, that there remained not an ell[2] of it in the whole Irak of Babylon.

During these preparations, Carathis, who never lost sight of her great object, which was to obtain favour with the powers of darkness, made select parties of the fairest and most delicate ladies of the city: but in the midst of their gaiety, she contrived to introduce vipers amongst them, and to break pots of scorpions under the table. They all bit to a wonder, and Carathis would have left her friends to die, were it not that, to fill up the time, she now and then amused herself in curing their wounds, with an excellent anodyne of her own invention: for this good Princess abhorred being indolent.

Vathek, who was not altogether as active as his mother, devoted his time to the sole gratification of his senses, in the palaces which were severally dedicated to them. He disgusted himself no more with the divan, or the mosque. One half of Samarah followed his example, whilst the other lamented the progress of corruption.

In the midst of these transactions, the embassy returned, which had been sent, in pious times, to Mecca.[3] It consisted of the most reverend Moullahs[4] who had fulfilled their commission, and brought back one of those precious besoms[5] which

---

1 palanquin: a couch or litter borne by four or six men on their shoulders.
2 ell: a cloth measure, now 45 inches.
3 Mecca: the most sacred city of Islam where the Ka'aba is situated and the Prophet Muhammed was born. [*Islam2* VI, 144]
4 Moullah, *molla*: general title of respect, normally applied to clergy and learned men. [*Islam2* VII, 221]
5 besom: broom made of twigs bound around a handle, or, figuratively, anything that sweeps away impurity.

are used to sweep the sacred Cahaba:[1] a present truly worthy of the greatest potentate on earth!

The Caliph happened at this instant to be engaged in an apartment by no means adapted to the reception of embassies. He heard the voice of Bababalouk, calling from between the door and the tapestry that hung before it: "Here are the excellent Edris al Shafei,[2] and the seraphic Al Mouhateddin, who have brought the besom from Mecca, and, with tears of joy, entreat they may present it to your majesty in person." – "Let them bring the besom hither, it may be of use," said Vathek. "How!" answered Bababalouk, half aloud and amazed. "Obey," replied the Caliph, "for it is my sovereign will; go instantly, vanish! for here will I receive the good folk who have thus filled thee with joy."

The eunuch departed muttering, and bade the venerable train attend him. A sacred rapture was diffused amongst these reverend old men. Though fatigued with the length of their expedition, they followed Bababalouk with an alertness almost miraculous, and felt themselves highly flattered, as they swept along the stately porticos, that the Caliph would not receive them like ambassadors in ordinary in his hall of audience. Soon reaching the interior of the harem (where, through blinds of Persian,[3] they perceived large soft eyes, dark and blue, that came and went like lightning) penetrated with respect and wonder, and full of their celestial mission, they advanced in procession towards the small corridors that appeared to terminate in nothing, but, nevertheless, led to the cell where the Caliph expected their coming.

"What! is the commander of the faithful sick?" said Edris al Shafei, in a low voice to his companion? – "I rather think he is in his oratory,"[4] answered Al Mouhateddin. Vathek, who heard

---

1   Cahaba, Ka'aba: "In the middle of Mecca is the temple and in the middle of the temple a square stone building, called the Caaba ... the house of God ... being peculiarly hallowed and set apart for his worship." [Sale 114] It is toward this temple that the devout, anywhere in the world, turn when they pray. [D'Herbelot; Islam2 IV, 317]

2   Edris al Shafei, al-Imam Abu 'Abd Allah Muhammad al-Shafi'i ben Idris: famous theologian and teacher who commented on and codified Islamic law. [Islam2 IX 183]

3   blinds of Persian: like a Venetian blind.

4   oratory: a small chapel, especially one for private devotions.

the dialogue, cried out: – "What imports it you, how I am employed? approach without delay." They advanced, whilst the Caliph, without shewing himself, put forth his hand from behind the tapestry that hung before the door, and demanded of them the besom. Having prostrated themselves as well as the corridor would permit, and, even in a tolerable semicircle, the venerable Al Shafei, drawing forth the besom from the embroidered and perfumed scarves, in which it had been enveloped, and secured from the profane gaze of vulgar eyes, arose from his associates, and advanced, with an air of the most awful solemnity towards the supposed oratory; but, with what astonishment! with what horror was he seized! – Vathek, bursting out into a villainous laugh, snatched the besom from his trembling hand, and, fixing upon some cobwebs, that hung from the ceiling, gravely brushed them away till not a single one remained. The old men, overpowered with amazement, were unable to lift their beards from the ground: for, as Vathek had carelessly left the tapestry between them half drawn, they were witnesses of the whole transaction. Their tears bedewed the marble. Al Mouhateddin swooned through mortification and fatigue, whilst the Caliph, throwing himself backward on his seat, shouted, and clapped his hands without mercy. At last, addressing himself to Bababalouk! – "My dear black," said he, "go, regale these pious poor souls, with my good wine from Shiraz,[1] since they can boast of having seen more of my palace than any one besides." Having said this, he threw the besom in their face, and went to enjoy the laugh with Carathis. Bababalouk did all in his power to console the ambassadors; but the two most infirm expired on the spot: the rest were carried to their beds, from whence, being heart-broken with sorrow and shame, they never arose.

The succeeding night, Vathek, attended by his mother, ascended the tower to see if every thing were ready for his journey: for, he had great faith in the influence of the stars. The planets appeared in their most favourable aspects. The Caliph,

---

1 Shiraz, *Shiraz*: the capital of the province of Fars in Persia, not far from Istakhar, which has lovely gardens served by springs. Vathek is being insulting since devout Muslims refuse wine.

to enjoy so flattering a sight, supped gaily on the roof; and fancied that he heard, during his repast, loud shouts of laughter resound through the sky, in a manner, that inspired the fullest assurance.

All was in motion at the palace; lights were kept burning through the whole of the night: the sound of implements, and of artizans finishing their work; the voices of women, and their guardians, who sung at their embroidery: all conspired to interrupt the stillness of nature, and infinitely delighted the heart of Vathek who imagined himself going in triumph to sit upon the throne of Soliman. The people were not less satisfied than himself: all assisted to accelerate the moment, which should rescue them from the wayward caprices of so extravagant a master.

The day preceding the departure of this infatuated Prince, was employed by Carathis, in repeating to him the decrees of the mysterious parchment; which she had thoroughly gotten by heart; and, in recommending him, not to enter the habitation of any one by the way: "for, well thou knowest," added she, "how liquorish thy taste is after good dishes and young damsels; let me, therefore, enjoin thee, to be content with thy old cooks, who are the best in the world: and not to forget that, in thy ambulatory seraglio, there are at least three dozen of pretty faces which Bababalouk hath not yet unveiled. I myself have a great desire to watch over thy conduct, and visit the subterranean palace, which, no doubt, contains whatever can interest persons, like us. There is nothing so pleasing as retiring to caverns: my taste for dead bodies, and every thing like mummy is decided: and, I am confident, thou wilt see the most exquisite of their kind. Forget me not then, but the moment thou art in possession of the talismans which are to open the way to the mineral kingdoms and the centre of the earth itself, fail not to dispatch some trusty genius[1] to take me and my cabinet: for the oil of the serpents I have pinched to death will be a pretty present to the Giaour who cannot but be charmed with such dainties."

---

1   genius: the singular form of genii, *djinn:* what the Persians call *dives.*

Scarcely had Carathis ended this edifying discourse, when the sun, setting behind the mountain of the four fountains, gave place to the rising moon. This planet, being that evening at full, appeared of unusual beauty and magnitude, in the eyes of the women, the eunuchs and the pages who were all impatient to set forward. The city re-echoed with shouts of joy, and flourishing of trumpets. Nothing was visible, but plumes, nodding on pavilions, and aigrets shining in the mild lustre of the moon. The spacious square resembled an immense parterre[1] variegated with the most stately tulips of the east.

Arrayed in the robes which were only worn at the most distinguished ceremonials, and supported by his vizir and Bababalouk, the Caliph descended the great staircase of the tower in the sight of all his people. He could not forbear pausing, at intervals, to admire the superb appearance which every where courted his view: whilst the whole multitude, even to the camels with their sumptuous burdens, knelt down before him. For some time a general stillness prevailed, which nothing happened to disturb, but the shrill screams of some eunuchs in the rear. These vigilant guards, having remarked certain cages of the ladies swagging somewhat awry, and discovered that a few adventurous gallants had contrived to get in, soon dislodged the enraptured culprits and consigned them, with good commendations, to the surgeons of the serail.[2] The majesty of so magnificent a spectacle, was not, however, violated by incidents like these. Vathek, meanwhile, saluted the moon with an idolatrous air, that neither pleased Morakanabad, nor the doctors of the law, any more than the vizirs and grandees of his court, who were all assembled to enjoy the last view of their sovereign.

At length, the clarions and trumpets from the top of the tower, announced the prelude of departure. Though the instruments were in unison with each other, yet a singular dissonance was blended with their sounds. This proceeded from Carathis who was singing her direful orisons to the Giaour, whilst the negresses and mutes supplied thorough base, without articulating a word. The good Mussulmans fancied that they heard the

---

1 parterre: an ornamental arrangement of flower-beds, with intervening walks.
2 serail: apartments reserved for women, also referred to as the *harem* or *seraglio*.

sullen hum of those nocturnal insects, which presage evil; and importuned Vathek to beware how he ventured his sacred person.

On a given signal, the great standard of the Califat was displayed; twenty thousand lances shone around it; and the Caliph, treading royally on the cloth of gold, which had been spread for his feet, ascended his litter, amidst the general acclamations of his subjects.

The expedition commenced with the utmost order and so entire a silence, that, even the locusts were heard from the thickets on the plain of Catoul. Gaiety and good humour prevailing, they made full six leagues before the dawn; and the morning star was still glittering in the firmament, when the whole of this numerous train had halted on the banks of the Tigris,[1] where they encamped to repose for the rest of the day.

The three days that followed were spent in the same manner; but, on the fourth, the heavens looked angry; lightnings broke forth, in frequent flashes; re-echoing peals of thunder succeeded; and the trembling Circassians clung with all their might, to their ugly guardians. The Caliph himself, was greatly inclined to take shelter in the large town of Ghulchissar, the governor of which, came forth to meet him, and tendered every kind of refreshment the place could supply. But, having examined his tablets, he suffered the rain to soak him, almost to the bone, notwithstanding the importunity of his first favourites. Though he began to regret the palace of the senses; yet, he lost not sight of his enterprize, and his sanguine expectation confirmed his resolution. His geographers were ordered to attend him; but, the weather proved so terrible that these poor people exhibited a lamentable appearance: and their maps of the different countries spoiled by the rain, were in a still worse plight than themselves. As no long journey had been undertaken since the time of Haroun al Raschid, every one was ignorant which way to turn; and Vathek, though well versed in the course of the heavens, no longer knew his situation on earth. He thundered even louder than the elements; and mut-

---

1 the Tigris: a river that rises in Turkey, flows through Arabia and past Samarra, and empties into the Persian Gulf.

tered forth certain hints of the bow-string[1] which were not very soothing to literary ears. Disgusted at the toilsome weariness of the way, he determined to cross over the craggy heights and follow the guidance of a peasant, who undertook to bring him, in four days, to Rocnabad. Remonstrances were all to no purpose; his resolution was fixed.

The females and eunuchs uttered shrill wailings at the sight of the precipices below them and the dreary prospects that opened, in the vast gorges of the mountains. Before they could reach the ascent of the steepest rock, night overtook them, and a boisterous tempest arose, which, having rent the awnings of the palanquins and cages, exposed to the raw gusts the poor ladies within, who had never before felt so piercing a cold. The dark clouds that overcast the face of the sky deepened the horrors of this disastrous night, insomuch that nothing could be heard distinctly, but the mewling of pages and lamentations of sultanas.

To increase the general misfortune, the frightful uproar of wild beasts resounded at a distance; and there were soon perceived in the forest they were skirting, the glaring eyes, which could belong only to devils or tigers. The pioneers, who, as well as they could, had marked out a track; and a part of the advanced guard, were devoured, before they had been in the least apprized of their danger. The confusion that prevailed was extreme. Wolves, tigers, and other carnivorous animals, invited by the howling of their companions, flocked together from every quarter. The crashing of bones was heard on all sides, and a fearful rush of wings over head; for now vultures also began to be of the party.

The terror at length reached the main body of the troops which surrounded the monarch and his harem at the distance of two leagues from the scene. Vathek (voluptuously reposed in his capacious litter upon cushions of silk, with two little pages beside him of complexions more fair than the enamel of Franguistan,[2] who were occupied in keeping off flies) was soundly

---

1 hints of the bow-string: the bow-string was effective in executions by strangulation.
2 Franguistan, *Firangistan*: land of the Franks; western Europe generally. [*Islam2* III, 1044]

asleep, and contemplating in his dreams the treasures of Soliman. The shrieks however of his wives, awoke him with a start; and, instead of the Giaour with his key of gold, he beheld Bababalouk full of consternation. "Sire," exclaimed this good servant of the most potent of monarchs, "misfortune is arrived at its height, wild beasts, who entertain no more reverence for your sacred person, than for a dead ass, have beset your camels and their drivers; thirty of the most richly laden are already become their prey, as well as your confectioners, your cooks, and purveyors: and, unless our holy Prophet should protect us, we shall have all eaten our last meal." At the mention of eating, the Caliph lost all patience. He began to bellow, and even beat himself (for there was no seeing in the dark). The rumour every instant increased; and Bababalouk, finding no good could be done with his master, stopped both his ears against the hurlyburly of the harem, and called out loud: "Come, ladies, and brothers! all hands to work: strike light in a moment! never shall it be said, that the commander of the faithful served to regale these infidel brutes." Though there wanted not in this bevy of beauties, a sufficient number of capricious and wayward; yet, on the present occasion, they were all compliance. Fires were visible, in a twinkling, in all their cages. Ten thousand torches were lighted at once. The Caliph, himself, seized a large one of wax: every person followed his example; and, by kindling ropes ends, dipped in oil and fastened on poles, an amazing blaze was spread. The rocks were covered with the splendour of sun-shine. The trails of sparks, wafted by the wind, communicated to the dry fern, of which there was plenty. Serpents were observed to crawl forth from their retreats, with amazement and hissings; whilst the horses snorted, stamped the ground, tossed their noses in the air, and plunged about, without mercy.

One of the forests of cedar that bordered their way, took fire; and the branches that overhung the path, extending their flames to the muslins and chintzes, which covered the cages of the ladies obliged them to jump out, at the peril of their necks. Vathek, who vented on the occasion a thousand blasphemies, was himself compelled to touch, with his sacred feet, the naked earth.

Never had such an incident happened before. Full of mortification, shame, and despondence, and not knowing how to walk, the ladies fell into the dirt. "Must I go on foot!" said one: "Must I wet my feet!" cried another: "Must I soil my dress!" asked a third: "Execrable Bababalouk!" exclaimed all: "Outcast of hell! what hast thou to do with torches! Better were it to be eaten by tigers, than to fall into our present condition! we are for ever undone! Not a porter is there in the army nor a currier of camels; but hath seen some part of our bodies; and, what is worse, our very faces!" On saying this, the most bashful amongst them hid their foreheads on the ground, whilst such as had more boldness flew at Bababalouk; but he, well apprized of their humour and not wanting in shrewdness, betook himself to his heels along with his comrades, all dropping their torches and striking their tymbals.

It was not less light than in the brightest of the dog-days, and the weather was hot in proportion; but how degrading was the spectacle, to behold the Caliph bespattered, like an ordinary mortal! As the exercise of his faculties seemed to be suspended, one of his Ethiopian wives (for he delighted in variety) clasped him in her arms; threw him upon her shoulder, like a sack of dates, and, finding that the fire was hemming them in, set off, with no small expedition, considering the weight of her burden. The other ladies, who had just learnt the use of their feet, followed her; their guards galloped after; and the camel-drivers brought up the rear, as fast as their charge would permit.

They soon reached the spot, where the wild beasts had commenced the carnage, but which they had too much good sense not to leave at the approaching of the tumult, having made besides a most luxurious supper. Bababalouk, nevertheless, seized on a few of the plumpest, which were unable to budge from the place, and began to flea them with admirable adroitness. The cavalcade having proceeded so far from the conflagration, that the heat felt rather grateful than violent, it was, immediately, resolved on to halt. The tattered chintzes were picked up; the scraps, left by the wolves and tigers, interred; and vengeance was taken on some dozens of vultures, that were too much glutted to rise on the wing. The camels, which had been left unmolested to make sal ammoniac,[1] being numbered; and the ladies once more inclosed in their cages; the imperial tent was pitched on the levellest ground they could find.

Vathek, reposing upon a mattress of down, and tolerably recovered from the jolting of the Ethiopian, who, to his feelings, seemed the roughest trotting jade he had hitherto mounted, called out for something to eat. But, alas! those delicate cakes, which had been baked in silver ovens, for his royal mouth; those rich manchets;[2] amber comfits;[3] flaggons of Shiraz wine; porcelain vases of snow; and grapes from the banks of the Tigris; were all irremediably lost! − And nothing had Bababalouk to present in their stead, but a roasted wolf; vultures à la daube;[4] aromatic herbs of the most acrid poignancy; rotten truffles; boiled thistles: and such other wild plants, as must ulcerate the throat and parch up the tongue. Nor was he better provided, in the article of drink: for he could procure nothing to accompany these irritating viands, but a few phials of abominable brandy which had been secreted by the scullions in their slippers. Vathek made wry faces at so savage a repast; and Bababalouk answered them, with shrugs and contortions. The Caliph, however, eat with tolerable appetite; and fell into a nap, that lasted six hours.

The splendour of the sun, reflected from the white cliffs of the mountains, in spit of the curtains that inclosed Vathek, at length disturbed his repose. He awoke, terrified; and stung to the quick by wormwood-colour flies, which emitted from their wings a suffocating stench. The miserable monarch was perplexed how to act; though his wits were not idle, in seeking expedients, whilst Bababalouk lay snoring, amidst a swarm of those insects that busily thronged, to pay court to his nose. The little pages, famished with hunger, had dropped their fans on the ground; and exerted their dying voices, in bitter reproaches

---

1   sal ammoniac; ammonium chloride: urine in this context.
2   manchets: the finest kind of wheaten bread baked in small loaves.
3   comfits: fruit preserved in sugar.
4   vulture à la daube: vulture stew or vulture casserole.

on the Caliph; who now, for the first time, heard the language of truth.

Thus stimulated, he renewed his imprecations against the Giaour; and bestowed upon Mahomet some soothing expressions. "Where am I?" cried he: "What are these dreadful rocks? these valleys of darkness! are we arrived at the horrible Kaf![1] is the Simurgh[2] coming to pluck out my eyes, as a punishment for undertaking this impious enterprize!" Having said this he turned himself towards an outlet in the side of the pavilion, but, alas! what objects occurred to his view? on one side, a plain of black sand that appeared to be unbounded; and, on the other, perpendicular crags, bristled over with those abominable thistles, which had, so severely, lacerated his tongue. He fancied, however, that he perceived, amongst the brambles and briars, some gigantic flowers but was mistaken: for, these were only the dangling palampores[3] and variegated tatters of his gay retinue. As there were several clefts in the rock from whence water seemed to have flowed, Vathek applied his ear with the hope of catching the sound of some latent torrent; but could only distinguish the low murmurs of his people who were repining at their journey, and complaining for the want of water. "To what purpose," asked they, "have we been brought hither? hath our Caliph another tower to build? or have the relentless afrits,[4] whom Carathis so much loves, fixed their abode in this place?"

At the name of Carathis, Vathek recollected the tablets he had received from his mother; who assured him, they were fraught with preternatural qualities, and advised him to consult them, as emergencies might require. Whilst he was engaged in

---

1   Kaf: the mountain-boundary of the earth, surrounding the earth as a ring does the finger. [*Richardson* 143]. In mythologies, these mountains, inaccessible to humans, are the home of the genii (djinn) and the haunt of the fabulous bird, Simorg. [*Islam1*] Kaf is the earth's primary mountain. When God sets it to tremble, it causes earthquakes wherever a people needs to be punished. [*Islam2* IV, 400]
2   Simurgh, *Simurghor, Simorg*: Persian word for a rational, articulate, gigantic, mythological bird, in appearance like the gryphon. Its habitat is Kaf. [*Richardson*141]
3   palampore: A chinz bed-cover, probably named for the cotton cloth that comes from Palanpur, a princely state of India. [*Islam2* VIII, 244]
4   afrit, *ifrit*: to the Arabs, the most terrible, cruel, and cunning monster of the race of Genii, or djinn. [*Islam2* III, 1050]

turning them over, he heard a shout of joy, and a loud clapping of hands. The curtains of his pavilion were soon drawn back and he beheld Bababalouk, followed by a troop of his favourites, conducted by two dwarfs each a cubit high; who brought between them a large basket of melons, oranges, and pomegranates. They were singing in the sweetest tones the words that follow: "We dwell on the top of these rocks, in a cabin of rushes and canes; the eagles envy us our nest: a small spring supplies us with water for the Abdest,[1] and we daily repeat prayers, which the Prophet approves. We love you, O commander of the faithful! our master, the good Emir[2] Fakreddin, loves you also: he reveres, in your person, the vicegerent of Mahomet. Little as we are, in us he confides: he knows our hearts to be as good, as our bodies are contemptible; and hath placed us here to aid those who are bewildered on these dreary mountains. Last night, whilst we were occupied within our cell in reading the holy Koran,[3] a sudden hurricane blew out our lights, and rocked our habitation. For two whole hours, a palpable darkness prevailed; but we heard sounds at a distance, which we conjectured to proceed from the bells of Cafila,[4] passing over the rocks. Our ears were soon filled with deplorable shrieks, frightful roarings, and the sound of tymbals. Chilled with terror, we concluded that the Deggial,[5] with his exterminating angels, had sent forth his plagues on the earth. In the midst of these melancholy reflections, we perceived flames of the deepest red, glow in the horizon; and found ourselves, in a few moments, covered with flakes of fire. Amazed at so strange an appearance, we took up the volume dictated by the blessed intelligence, and, kneeling, by the light of the fire that surrounded us, we recited the verse which says: 'Put no trust in any thing but the mercy of Heaven: there is no help, save in the holy Prophet: the mountain of Kaf, itself, may trem-

---

1 Abdest: the water used in ritual washing.
2 emir, *amir*: commandant, chief, prince; title give to commanders of armies and sovereigns of territories under the caliph. [*Islam2* I, 438]
3 Koran: the Holy Book of Islam, written by the inspired prophet, Muhammed.
4 cafila: caravans.
5 Deggial: the Muslim Antichrist. [*D'Herbelot; Sale* 80]

ble; it is the power of Alla only, that cannot be moved.' After having pronounced these words, we felt consolation, and our minds were hushed into a sacred repose. Silence ensued, and our ears clearly distinguished a voice in the air, saying: 'Servants of my faithful servant! go down to the happy valley of Fakreddin: tell him that an illustrious opportunity now offers to satiate the thirst of his hospitable heart. The commander of true believers is, this day, bewildered amongst these mountains and stands in need of thy aid.' – We obeyed, with joy, the angelic mission; and our master, filled with pious zeal, hath culled, with his own hands, these melons, oranges, and pomegranates. He is following us with a hundred dromedaries, laden with the purest waters of his fountains; and is coming to kiss the fringe of your consecrated robe, and to implore you to enter his humble habitation which, placed amidst these barren wilds, resembles an emerald set in lead." The dwarfs, having ended their address, remained still standing, and, with hands crossed upon their bosoms, preserved a respectful silence.

Vathek, in the midst of this curious harangue, seized the basket; and, long before it was finished, the fruits had dissolved in his mouth. As he continued to eat, his piety increased; and, in the same breath, he recited his prayers and called for the Koran and sugar.

Such was the state of his mind, when the tablets, which were thrown by, at the approach of the dwarfs, again attracted his eye. He took them up; but was ready to drop on the ground, when he beheld in large red characters inscribed by Carathis, these words; which were, indeed, enough to make him tremble; "Beware of old doctors and their puny messengers of but one cubit high: distrust their pious frauds; and, instead of eating their melons, empale on a spit the bearers of them. Shouldest thou be such a fool as to visit them, the portal of the subterranean palace will shut in thy face with such force, as shall shake thee asunder: thy body shall be spit upon, and bats will nestle in thy belly."

"To what tends this ominous rhapsody?" cries the Caliph: "and must I then perish in these deserts, with thirst; whilst I may refresh myself in the delicious valley of melons and cucumbers? – Accursed be the Giaour with his portal of ebony! he hath made me dance attendance, too long already. Besides, who shall prescribe laws to me? – I, forsooth, must not enter any one's habitation! Be it so: but, what one can I enter, that is not my own!" Bababalouk, who lost not a syllable of this soliloquy, applauded it with all his heart; and the ladies, for the first time, agreed with him in opinion.

The dwarfs were entertained, caressed, and seated, with great ceremony, on little cushions of satin. The symmetry of their persons was a subject of admiration; not an inch of them was suffered to pass unexamined. Knick-knacks and dainties were offered in profusion; but all were declined, with respectful gravity. They climbed up the sides of the Caliph's seat; and, placing themselves each on one of his shoulders, began to whisper prayers in his ears. Their tongues quivered, like aspen leaves; and the patience of Vathek was almost exhausted, when the acclamations of the troops announced the approach of Fakreddin, who was come with a hundred old grey-beards, and as many Korans and dromedaries. They instantly set about their ablutions, and began to repeat the Bismillah.[1] Vathek, to get rid of these officious monitors, followed their example; for his hands were burning.

The good emir, who was punctiliously religious, and likewise a great dealer in compliments, made an harangue five times more prolix and insipid than his little harbingers had already delivered. The Caliph, unable any longer to refrain, exclaimed: "For the love of Mahomet, my dear Fakreddin, have done! let us proceed to your valley, and enjoy the fruits that Heaven hath vouchsafed you." The hint of proceeding, put all into motion. The venerable attendants of the emir set forward, somewhat slowly; but Vathek, having ordered his little pages, in private, to goad on the dromedaries, loud fits of laughter broke forth from the cages; for, the unwieldy curvetting of these poor beasts, and the ridiculous distress of their superannuated riders, afforded the ladies no small entertainment.

They descended, however, unhurt into the valley, by the easy

---

1   Bismillah: "In the name of the most merciful God"– A preface to prayer.

slopes which the emir had ordered to be cut in the rock; and already, the murmuring of the streams and the rustling of the leaves began to catch their attention. The cavalcade soon entered a path, which was skirted by flowering shrubs, and extended to a vast wood of palm trees, whose branches overspread a vast building of free stone. This edifice was crowned with nine domes, and adorned with as many portals of bronze, on which was engraven the following inscription: "This is the asylum of pilgrims, the refuge of travellers, and the depository of secrets from all parts of the world."

Nine pages, beautiful as the day, and decently clothed in robes of Egyptian linen, were standing at each door. They received the whole retinue with an easy and inviting air. Four of the most amiable placed the Caliph on a magnificent tecthtrevan:[1] four others, somewhat less graceful, took charge of Bababalouk, who capered for joy at the snug little cabin that fell to his share; the pages that remained waited on the rest of the train.

Every man being gone out of sight, the gate of a large inclosure, on the right, turned on its harmonious hinges; and a young female, of a slender form, came forth. Her light brown hair floated in the hazy breeze of the twilight. A troop of young maidens, like the Pleiades,[2] attended her on tip-toe. They hastened to the pavilions that contained the sultanas: and the young lady, gracefully bending, said to them: "Charming princesses, every thing is ready: we have prepared beds for your repose, and strewed your apartments with jasmine: no insects will keep off slumber from visiting your eye-lids; we will dispel them with a thousand plumes. Come then, amiable ladies, refresh your delicate feet, and your ivory limbs, in baths of rose water; and, by the light of perfumed lamps, your servants will amuse you with tales." The sultanas accepted, with pleasure, these obliging offers; and followed the young lady to the emir's harem; where we must, for a moment, leave them, and return to the Caliph.

---

1 tecthtrevan: a moving throne.
2 Pleiades: the seven daughters of Atlas.

Vathek found himself beneath a vast dome, illuminated by a thousand lamps of rock crystal: as many vases of the same material, filled with excellent sherbet, sparkled on a large table, where a profusion of viands were spread. Amongst others, were rice boiled in milk of almonds, saffron soups, and lamb à la creme; of all which the Caliph was amazingly fond. He took of each, as much as he was able, testified his sense of the emir's friendship, by the gaiety of his heart; and made the dwarfs dance, against their will: for these little devotees durst not refuse the commander of the faithful. At last, he spread himself on the sofa, and slept sounder than he ever had before.

Beneath this dome, a general silence prevailed; for there was nothing to disturb it but the jaws of Bababalouk, who had untrussed himself to eat with greater advantage; being anxious to make amends for his fast, in the mountains. As his spirits were too high to admit of his sleeping; and hating to be idle, he proposed with himself to visit the harem and repair to his charge of the ladies: to examine if they had been properly lubricated with the balm of Mecca; if their eye-brows, and tresses, were in order; and, in a word, to perform all the little offices they might need. He sought for a long time together but without being able to find out the door. He durst not speak aloud for fear of disturbing the Caliph; and not a soul was stirring in the precincts of the palace. He almost despaired of effecting his purpose, when a low whispering just reached his ear. It came from the dwarfs, who were returned to their old occupation, and, for the nine hundred and ninety-ninth time in their lives, were reading over the Koran. They very politely invited Bababalouk to be of their party; but his head was full of other concerns. The dwarfs, though not a little scandalized at his dissolute morals, directed him to the apartments he wanted to find. His way thither lay through a hundred dark corridors, along which he groped as he went; and at last, began to catch, from the extremity of a passage, the charming gossiping of the women which not a little delighted his heart. "Ah, ha! what not yet asleep?" cried he; and, taking long strides as he spoke, "did you not suspect me of abjuring my charge?" Two of the black eunuchs, on hearing a voice so loud, left their party in haste, sabre in hand, to discover the cause: but, presently, was repeated on all sides: "'Tis only Bababalouk! no one but Bababalouk!" This circumspect guardian, having gone up to a thin veil of carnation-colour silk that hung before the door-way, distinguished, by means of the softened splendour that shone through it, an oval bath of dark porphyry surrounded by curtains, festooned in large folds. Through the apertures between them, as they were not drawn close, groups of young slaves were visible; amongst whom, Bababalouk perceived his pupils, indulgingly expanding their arms, as if to embrace the perfumed water, and refresh themselves after their fatigues. The looks of tender languor; their confidential whispers; and the enchanting smiles with which they were imparted; the exquisite fragrance of the roses: all combined to inspire a voluptuousness, which even Bababalouk himself was scarce able to withstand.

He summoned up, however, his usual solemnity, and in this peremptory tone of authority, commanded the ladies, instantly, to leave the bath. Whilst he was issuing these mandates, the young Nouronihar, daughter of the emir, who was as sprightly as an antelope, and full of wanton gaiety, beckoned one of her slaves to let down the great swing which was suspended to the ceiling by cords of silk: and whilst this was doing, winked to her companions in the bath: who, chagrined to be forced from so soothing a state of indolence, began to twist and entangle their hair to plague and detain Bababalouk; and teased him besides with a thousand vagaries.

Nouronihar perceiving that he was nearly out of patience accosted him, with an arch air of respectful concern, and said: "My lord! it is not, by any means decent, that the chief eunuch of the Caliph our sovereign should thus continue standing: deign but to recline your graceful person upon this sofa which will burst with vexation, if it have not the honour to receive you." Caught by these flattering accents, Bababalouk gallantly replied: "Delight of the apple of my eye! I accept the invitation of your honied lips; and, to say truth, my senses are dazzled with the radiance that beams from your charms." – "Repose, then, at your ease," replied the beauty; as she placed him on the pretended sofa which, quicker than lightning, flew up all at once. The rest of the women, having aptly conceived her design, sprang naked from the bath, and plied the swing, with such unmerciful jerks, that it swept through the whole compass of a very lofty dome, and took from the poor victim all power of respiration. Sometimes, his feet rased the surface of the water; and, at others, the skylight almost flattened his nose. In vain did he fill the air with the cries of a voice that resembled the ringing of a cracked jar; their peals of laughter were still predominant.

Nouronihar, in the inebriety of youthful spirits, being used only to eunuchs of ordinary harems; and having never seen any thing so eminently disgusting, was far more diverted than all of the rest. She began to parody some Persian verses and sang with an accent most demurely piquant: "Oh gentle white dove, as thou soar'st through the air, vouchsafe one kind glance on the mate of thy love: melodious Philomel,[1] I am thy rose; warble some couplet to ravish my heart!"

The sultanas and their slaves, stimulated by these pleasantries, persevered at the swing, with such unremitted assiduity, that at length, the cord which had secured it, snapt suddenly asunder; and Bababalouk fell, floundering like a turtle, to the bottom of the bath. This accident occasioned an universal shout. Twelve little doors, till now unobserved, flew open at once; and the ladies, in an instant, made their escape; but not before having heaped all the towels on his head and put out the lights that remained.

The deplorable animal, in water to the chin, overwhelmed with darkness, and unable to extricate himself from the wrappers that embarrassed him, was still doomed to hear, for his further consolation, the fresh bursts of merriment his disaster occasioned. He bustled, but in vain, to get from the bath; for, the margin was become so slippery, with the oil spilt in break-

---

1   Philomel: the nightingale.

ing the lamps, that, at every effort, he slid back with a plunge which resounded aloud through the hollow of the dome. These cursed peals of laughter, were redoubled at every relapse, and he, who thought the place infested rather with devils than women, resolved to cease groping, and abide in the bath; where he amused himself with soliloquies, interspersed with imprecations, of which his malicious neighbours, reclining on down, suffered not an accent to escape. In this delectable plight, the morning surprised him. The Caliph, wondering at his absence, had caused him to be sought for every where. At last, he was drawn forth almost smothered from under the wisp of linen, and wet even to the marrow. Limping, and his teeth chattering with cold, he approached his master; who inquired what was the matter, and how he came soused in so strange a pickle? – And why did you enter this cursed lodge?" answered Bababalouk, gruffly. – "Ought a monarch like you to visit with his harem, the abode of a grey-bearded emir, who knows nothing of life? – And, with what gracious damsels doth the place too abound! Fancy to yourself how they have soaked me like a burnt crust; and made me dance like a jack-pudding, the livelong night through, on their damnable swing. What an excellent lesson for your sultanas, into whom I had instilled such reserve and decorum!" Vathek, comprehending not a syllable of all this invective, obliged him to relate minutely the transaction: but, instead of sympathizing with the miserable sufferer, he laughed immoderately at the device of the swing and the figure of Bababalouk, mounted upon it. The stung eunuch could scarcely preserve the semblance of respect. "Aye, laugh, my Lord! laugh," said he; "but I wish this Nouronihar would play some trick on you; she is too wicked to spare even majesty itself." These words made, for the present, but a slight impression on the Caliph: but they, not long after, recurred to his mind.

This conversation was cut short by Fakreddin, who came to request that Vathek would join in the prayers and ablutions, to be solemnized on a spacious meadow watered by innumerable streams. The Caliph found the waters refreshing, but the prayers abominably irksome. He diverted himself, however, with the multitude of calenders,[1] santons,[2] and derviches,[3] who were continually coming and going; but especially with the bramins,[4] faquirs,[5] and other enthusiasts, who had travelled from the heart of India, and halted on their way with the emir. These latter had each of them some mummery peculiar to himself. One dragged a huge chain wherever he went; another an ouran-outang; whilst a third, was furnished with scourges; and all performed to a charm. Some would climb trees, holding one foot in the air; others poise themselves over a fire, and, without mercy, fillip[6] their noses. There were some amongst them that had cherished vermin, which were not ungrateful in requiting their caresses. These rambling fanatics revolted the hearts of the derviches, the calenders, and santons; however, the vehemence of their aversion soon subsided, under the hope that the presence of the Caliph would cure their folly, and convert them to the Mussulman faith. But, alas! how great was their disappointment! for Vathek, instead of preaching to them, treated them as buffoons, bade them present his compliments to Visnow[7] and Ixhora,[8] and discovered a predilection for a squat old man from the Isle of Serendib,[9] who was more ridiculous than any of the rest. "Come!" said he, "for the love of your gods, bestow a few slaps on your chops to amuse me."

---

1 calender, *kalandar*: a type of dervish in the Islamic world who is unconventional in dress and behaviour, has renounced worldly things, and wanders the world like a vagabond. [*Islam2* IV, 472]

2 santon: European designation for a Muslim monk or hermit.

3 derviche, *darwish*: Persian term for a *fakir*, a religious mendicant. [*Islam2* II, 164]

4 bramin; *brahman*: Hindu priest.

5 faquir, *fakir*: one who lives a religious life of great austerity, rejecting private property and resigning himself to the will of God. [*Islam2* II, 757]

6 fillip: to flick; to strike with the nail of the finger by a sudden jerk from under the thumb.

7 Visnow, *Visnu*: a major Hindu deity, protector and preserver of the world, benevolent, active for the good of the community.

8 Ixhora: By Ixhora, Beckford may mean Siva, who represents Visnu's opposite, untamed wildness and destructiveness.

9 Isle of Serendib: Arabic name for Ceylon. Beckford may be acknowledging Horace Walpole's Persian fairy tale, "The Three Princes of Serendip," in which the word, *serendipity*, is invented to denote fortuitous chance discoveries. Vathek is, after all, about to encounter and fall in love with Nouronihar.

The old fellow, offended at such an address, began loudly to weep; but, as he betrayed a villainous drivelling in shedding tears, the Caliph turned his back and listened to Bababalouk, who whispered, whilst he held the umbrella over him: "Your majesty should be cautious of this odd assembly; which hath been collected, I know not for what. Is it necessary to exhibit such spectacles to a mighty potentate, with interludes of talapoins[1] more mangy than dogs? Were I you, I would command a fire to be kindled, and at once rid the estates of the emir, of his harem, and all his menagerie." – "Tush, dolt," answered Vathek; "and know, that all this infinitely charms me. Nor shall I leave the meadow, till I have visited every hive of these pious mendicants."

Wherever the Caliph directed his course, objects of pity were sure to swarm round him; the blind, the purblind,[2] smarts without noses, damsels without ears, each to extol the munificence of Fakreddin, who as well as his attendant grey-beards, dealt about, gratis, plasters and cataplasms[3] to all that applied. At noon, a superb corps of cripples made its appearance; and soon after advanced, by platoons, on the plain, the completest association of invalids that had ever been embodied till then. The blind went groping with the blind, the lame limped on together, and the maimed made gestures to each other with the only arm that remained. The sides of a considerable water-fall were crowded by the deaf; amongst whom were some from Pegû, with ears uncommonly handsome and large, but who were still less able to hear than the rest. Nor were there wanting others in abundance with hump-backs; wenny necks; and even horns of an exquisite polish.

The emir, to aggrandize the solemnity of the festival, in honour of his illustrious visitant, ordered the turf to be spread, on all sides, with skins and table-cloths; upon which were served up for the good Mussulmans, pilaus[4] of every hue, with other orthodox dishes; and, by the express order of Vathek, who was

---

1 talapoin: Buddhist monk, originally from Pegû in southern Burma.
2 purblind: partially blind; near-sighted or dim-sighted.
3 cataplasm: a bandage or poultice for a wound.
4 pilau, *pilaw*: oriental dish consisting of rice boiled with meat, raisins and spices.

shamefully tolerant, small plates of abominations[1] were prepared, to the great scandal of the faithful. The holy assembly began to fall to. The Caliph, in spite of every remonstrance from the chief of his eunuchs, resolved to have a dinner dressed on the spot. The complaisant emir immediately gave orders for a table to be placed in the shade of the willows. The first service consisted of fish, which they drew from the river, flowing over sands of gold at the foot of a lofty hill. These were broiled as fast as taken, and served up with a sauce of vinegar, and small herbs that grew on mount Sinai:[2] for ever thing with the emir was excellent and pious.

The desert was not quite set on, when the sound of lutes, from the hill, was repeated by the echoes of the neighbouring mountains. The Caliph, with an emotion of pleasure and surprise, had no sooner raised up his head, than a handful of jasmine dropped on his face. An abundance of tittering succeeded the frolic, and instantly appeared, through the bushes, the elegant forms of several young females, skipping and bounding like roes. The fragrance diffused from their hair, struck the sense of Vathek, who, in an ecstacy, suspending his repast, said to Bababalouk:"Are the peries[3] come down from their spheres? Note her, in particular, whose form is so perfect; venturously running on the brink of the precipice, and turning back her head, as regardless of nothing but the graceful flow of her robe. With what captivating impatience doth she contend with the bushes for her veil? could it be her who threw the jasmine at me!" – "Aye! she it was; and you too would she throw, from the top of the rock," answered Bababalouk; "for that is my good friend Nouronihar, who so kindly lent me her swing. My dear lord and master," added he, wresting a twig from a willow, "let

---

1 abominations: foods not complying with the Koran's dietary laws.
2 Sinai, *Sina*: peninsula bordered by the Mediterranean to the north, the Gulf of Suez on the west, and the Gulf of Aqaba on the east. Mount Sinai was, according to the Bible, the site of God's appearance to Moses. It is sacred in Hebrew, Christian, and Islamic tradition.
3 perie, *pari*: a beautiful and benevolent creature of the nation of djinn, a species neither angel nor human. They live in Ginnistan and surpass in beauty all creatures in Ginnistan. The daughter of the king of the peries is a leading character in many stories, as it is in Beckford's second Episode. [*D'Herbelot; Richardson* 144]

me correct her for her want of respect: the emir will have no reason to complain; since (bating what I owe to his piety) he is much to be blamed for keeping a troop of girls on the mountains, where the sharpness of the air gives their blood too brisk a circulation."

"Peace! blasphemer," said the Caliph; "speak not thus of her, who, over these mountains, leads my heart a willing captive. Contrive, rather, that my eyes may be fixed upon her's: that I may respire her sweat breath as she bounds panting along these delightful wilds!" On saying these words, Vathek extended his arms towards the hill, and directing his eyes, with an anxiety unknown to him before, endeavoured to keep within view the object that enthralled his soul: but her course was as difficult to follow, as the flight of one of those beautiful blue butterflies of Cachemire,[1] which are, at once, so volatile and rare.

The Caliph, not satisfied with seeing, wished also to hear Nouronihar, and eagerly turned to catch the sound of her voice. At last, he distinguished her whispering to one of her companions behind the thicket from whence she had thrown the jasmine: "A Caliph, it must be owned, is a fine thing to see; but my little Gulchenrouz is much more amiable: one lock of his hair is of more value to me than the richest embroidery of the Indies. I had rather that his teeth should mischievously press my finger, than the richest ring of the imperial treasure. Where have you left him, Sutlememe? and why is he not here?"

The agitated Caliph still wished to hear more; but she immediately retired with all her attendants. The fond monarch pursued her with his eyes till she was gone out of sight; and then continued like a bewildered and benighted traveller, from whom the clouds had obscured the constellation that guided his way. The curtain of night seemed dropped before him: every thing appeared discoloured. The falling waters filled his soul with dejection, and his tears trickled down the jasmines he

---

1   Cachemire, *Kashmir*: a territory in the western Himalayas. Beckford, in a letter to Henley: "The butterflies of Cachemere are celebrated in a poem of Mesihi I slaved at with Zemir, the old Mahometan who assisted me in translating W. Montague's M.S., but they are hardly worth a note."

had caught from Nouronihar, and placed in his inflamed bosom. He snatched up a few shining pebbles, to remind him of the scene where he felt the first tumults of love. Two hours were elapsed, and evening drew on, before he could resolve to depart from the place. He often, but in vain, attempted to go: a soft languor enervated the powers of his mind. Extending himself on the brink of the stream, he turned his eyes towards the blue summits of the mountain, and exclaimed, "What concealest thou behind thee, pitiless rock? what is passing in thy solitudes? Whither is she gone? O heaven! perhaps she is now wandering in thy grottoes with her happy Gulchenrouz!"

In the mean time, the damps began to descend; and the emir; solicitous for the health of the Caliph, ordered the imperial litter to be brought. Vathek, absorbed in his reveries, was imperceptibly removed and conveyed back to the saloon, that received him the evening before. But, let us leave the Caliph immersed in his new passion: and attend Nouronihar beyond the rocks where she had again joined her beloved Gulchenrouz.

This Gulchenrouz was the son of Ali Hassan, brother to the emir: and the most delicate and lovely creature in the world. Ali Hassan, who had been absent ten years on a voyage to the unknown seas, committed, at his departure, this child, the only survivor of many, to the care and protection of his brother. Gulchenrouz could write in various characters with precision, and paint upon vellum the most elegant arabesques that fancy could devise. His sweet voice accompanied the lute in the most enchanting manner; and, when he sang the loves of Megnoun and Leilah,[1] or some unfortunate lovers of ancient days, tears insensibly overflowed the cheeks of his auditors. The verses he composed (for, like Megnoun, he, too, was a poet) inspired that unresisting languor, so frequently fatal to the female heart. The women all doated upon him; and, though he had passed his thirteenth year, they still detained him in the harem. His dancing was light as the gossamer waved by the zephyrs[2] of spring;

---

1 Megnoun and Leilah: Models of perfect lovers, their love is the subject of poems and stories in the Arab, Persian, and Turkish traditions. [D'Herbelot]
2 zephyrs: gentle breezes, usually from the west.

but his arms, which twined so gracefully with those of the young girls in the dance, could neither dart the lance in the chase, nor curb the steeds that pastured in his uncle's domains. The bow, however, he drew with a certain aim, and would have excelled his competitors in the race, could he have broken the ties that bound him to Nouronihar.

The two brothers had mutually engaged their children to each other; and Nouronihar loved her cousin, more than her own beautiful eyes. Both had the same tastes and amusements; the same long, languishing looks; the same tresses; the same fair complexions; and, when Gulchenrouz appeared in the dress of his cousin, he seemed to be more feminine than even herself. If, at any time, he left the harem, to visit Fakreddin; it was with all the bashfulness of a fawn, that consciously ventures forth from the lair of its dam: he was, however, wanton enough to mock the solemn old grey-beards, though sure to be rated without mercy in return. Whenever this happened, he would hastily plunge into the recesses of the harem; and, sobbing, take refuge in the fond arms of Nouronihar who loved even his faults beyond the virtues of others.

It fell out this evening, that, after leaving the Caliph in the meadow, she ran with Gulchenrouz over the green sward of the mountain, that sheltered the vale where Fakreddin had chosen to reside. The sun was dilated on the edge of the horizon; and the young people, whose fancies were lively and inventive, imagined they beheld, in the gorgeous clouds of the west, the domes of Shaddukian[1] and Ambreabad,[2] where the Peries have fixed their abode. Nouronihar, sitting on the slope of the hill, supported on her knees the perfumed head of Gulchenrouz. The unexpected arrival of the Caliph and the splendour that marked his appearance, had already filled with emotion the ardent soul of Nouronihar. Her vanity irresistibly prompted her to pique the prince's attention; and this, she before took good care to effect, whilst he picked up the jasmine she had thrown upon him. But, when Gulchenrouz asked after the flowers he

---

1 Shadukian: city of "pleasure and desire" of the Peries in Ginnistan [*Richardson* 144]; called Shaduka in *Episode 2*.
2 Ambreabad: Peri "city of ambergris" in Ginnistan. [*Richardson* 144]

had culled for her bosom, Nouronihar was all in confusion. She hastily kissed his forehead; arose in a flutter; and walked, with unequal steps, on the border of the precipice. Night advanced, and the pure gold of the setting sun had yielded to a sanguine red; the glow of which, like the reflection of a burning furnace, flushed Nouronihar's animated countenance. Gulchenrouz, alarmed at the agitation of his cousin, said to her, with a supplicating accent – "Let us begone; the sky looks portentous; the tamarisks[1] tremble more than common; and the raw wind chills my very heart. Come! let us begone; 'tis a melancholy night!" Then, taking hold of her hand, he drew it towards the path he besought her to go. Nouronihar, unconsciously followed the attraction; for, a thousand strange imaginations occupied her spirits. She passed the large round of honey-suckles, her favourite resort, without ever vouchsafing it a glance; yet Gulchenrouz could not help snatching off a few shoots in his way, though he ran as if a wild beast were behind.

The young females seeing them approach in such haste, and, according to custom, expecting a dance, instantly assembled in a circle and took each other by the hand: but, Gulchenrouz coming up out of breath, fell down at once on the grass. This accident struck with consternation the whole of this frolicsome party; whilst Nouronihar, half distracted and overcome, both by the violence of her exercise, and the tumult of her thoughts, sunk feebly down at his side; cherished his cold hands in her bosom, and chafed his temples with a fragrant perfume. At length, he came to himself; and, wrapping up his head in the robe of his cousin, intreated that she would not return to the harem. He was afraid of being snapped at by Shaban his tutor; a wrinkled old eunuch of a surly disposition; for, having interrupted the wonted walk of Nouronihar, he dreaded lest the churl should take it amiss. The whole of this sprightly group, sitting round upon a mossy knoll, began to entertain themselves with various pastimes; whilst their superintendants, the eunuchs, were gravely conversing at a distance. The nurse of the emir's daughter, observing her pupil sit ruminating with

---

1   tamarisks: shrubs or small trees with scalelike leaves and pink flowers in clusters.

her eyes on the ground, endeavoured to amuse her with diverting tales; to which Gulchenrouz, who had already forgotten his inquietudes, listened with a breathless attention. He laughed; he clapped his hands; and passed a hundred little tricks on the whole of the company, without omitting the eunuchs whom he provoked to run after him, in spite of their age and decrepitude.

During these occurrences, the moon arose, the wind subsided, and the evening became so serene and inviting, that a resolution was taken to sup on the spot. One of the eunuchs ran to fetch melons whilst others were employed in showering down almonds from the branches that overhung this amiable party. Sutlememe, who excelled in dressing a salad, having filled large bowls of porcelain with eggs of small birds, curds turned with citron juice, slices of cucumber, and the inmost leaves of delicate herbs, handed it round from one to another and gave each their shares with a large spoon of cocknos.[1] Gulchenrouz, nestling, as usual, in the bosom of Nouronihar, pouted out his vermillion little lips against the offer of Sutlememe; and would take it, only, from the hand of his cousin, on whose mouth he hung, like a bee inebriated with the nectar of flowers.

In the midst of this festive scene, there appeared a light on the top of the highest mountain, which attracted the notice of every eye. This light was not less bright than the moon when at full, and might have been taken for her, had not the moon already risen. The phenomenon occasioned a general surprise and no one could conjecture the cause. It could not be a fire, for the light was clear and bluish: nor had meteors ever been seen of that magnitude or splendour. This strange light faded, for a moment; and immediately renewed its brightness. It first appeared motionless, at the foot of the rock; whence it darted in an instant, to sparkle in a thicket of palm-trees: from thence it glided along the torrent; and at last fixed in a glen that was narrow and dark. The moment it had taken its direction, Gulchenrouz, whose heart always trembled at any thing sudden or rare, drew Nouronihar by the robe and anxiously requested

---

1 cocknos: a beautiful bird whose polished beak is used as a spoon. [Petis de la Croix, *Contes Persanes* (Paris, 1710-12), III. 36-158]

her to return to the harem. The women were importunate in seconding the intreaty; but the curiosity of the emir's daughter prevailed. She not only refused to go back, but resolved, at all hazards, to pursue the appearance.

Whilst they were debating what was best to be done, the light shot forth so dazzling a blaze that they all fled away shrieking. Nouronihar followed them a few steps; but, coming to the turn of a little bye path, stopped, and went back alone. As she ran with an alertness peculiar to herself, it was not long before she came to the place, where they had just been supping. The globe of fire now appeared stationary in the glen, and burned in majestic stillness. Nouronihar, pressing her hands in her bosom, hesitated, for some moments to advance. The solitude of her situation was new; the silence of the night, awful; and every object inspired sensations, which, till then, she never had felt. The affright of Gulchenrouz recurred to her mind, and she, a thousand times turned to go back; but this luminous appearance was always before her. Urged on by an irresistible impulse, she continued to approach it, in defiance of every obstacle that opposed her progress.

At length she arrived at the opening of the glen; but, instead of coming up to the light, she found herself surrounded by darkness; excepting that, at a considerable distance, a faint spark glimmered by fits. She stopped, a second time: the sound of water-falls mingling their murmurs; the hollow rustlings among the palm-branches; and the funereal screams of the birds from their rifted trunks: all conspired to fill her soul with terror. She imagined, every moment, that she trod on some venomous reptile. All the stories of malignant Dives[1] and dismal Goules[2] thronged into her memory: but, her curiosity was, notwithstanding, more predominant than her fears, She, therefore, firmly entered a winding track that led towards the spark; but, being a stranger to the path, she had not gone far, till she

---

1 Dives, *diw*: Persian name for spirits of evil and darkness, creatures of Ahriman, the personification of sin. [*Islam2* II, 322]

2 Goules, *ghul*: terrifying monsters that inhabit deserted places, lead travellers astray, kill, and devour them. The word also denotes a kind of vampire that digs up bodies at night to feed upon them. [*Islam2* II, 1079; *Richardson*, 174, 274]

began to repent of her rashness. "Alas!" said she, "that I were but in those secure and illuminated apartments, where my evenings glided on with Gulchenrouz! Dear child! how would thy heart flutter with terror, wert thou wandering in these wild solitudes, like me!" Thus speaking, she advanced, and, coming up to steps hewn in the rock, ascended them undismayed. The light, which was now gradually enlarging, appeared above her on the summit of the mountain, and as if proceeding from a cavern. At length, she distinguished a plaintive and melodious union of voices, that resembled the dirges which are sung over tombs. A sound, like that which arises from the filling of baths, struck her ear at the same time. She continued ascending, and discovered large wax torches in full blaze, planted here and there in the fissures of the rock. This appearance filled her with fear, whilst the subtile and potent odour, which the torches exhaled, caused her to sink, almost lifeless, at the entrance of the grot.

Casting her eyes within, in this kind of trance, she beheld a large cistern of gold, filled with water, the vapour of which distilled on her face a dew of the essence of roses. A soft symphony resounded through the grot. On the sides of the cistern, she noticed appendages of royalty, diadems and feathers of the heron, all sparkling with carbuncles.[1] Whilst her attention was fixed on this display of magnificence, the music ceased, and a voice instantly demanded: "For what monarch are these torches kindled, this bath prepared, and these habiliments which belong, not only to the sovereigns of the earth, but even to the talismanick powers!" To which a second voice answered: "They are for the charming daughter of the emir Fakreddin." – "What," replied the first, "for that trifler, who consumes her time with a giddy child, immersed in softness, and who, at best, can make but a pitiful husband?" – "And can she," rejoined the other voice, "be amused with such empty toys, whilst the Caliph, the sovereign of the world, he who is destined to enjoy the treasures of the pre-adamite sultans; a prince six feet high; and whose eyes pervade the inmost soul of a female, is inflamed

---

1 carbuncle: fiery red precious stone, a ruby or sapphire; the mythical carbuncle of Giamshid is reputed to glow in the dark. See Byron's note to *The Giaour*, l. 479.

with love for her. No! she will be wise enough to answer that passion alone, that can aggrandize her glory. No doubt she will; and despise the puppet of her fancy. Then all the riches this place contains, as well as the carbuncle of Giamschid,[1] shall be her's." – "You judge right," returned the first voice; "and I haste to Istakhar, to prepare the palace of subterranean fire for the reception of the bridal pair."

The voices ceased; the torches were extinguished, the most entire darkness succeeded; and Nouronihar recovering, with a start, found herself reclined on a sofa, in the harem of her father. She clapped her hands, and immediately came together, Gulchenrouz and her women; who, in despair at having lost her, had dispatched eunuchs to seek her, in every direction. Shaban appeared with the rest, and began to reprimand her, with an air of consequence: "Little impertinent," said he, "have you false keys, or are you beloved of some genius, that hath given you a picklock? I will try the extent of your power: come to the dark chamber, and expect not the company of Gulchenrouz: – be expeditious! I will shut you up, and turn the key twice upon you!" At these menaces, Nouronihar indignantly raised her head, opened on Shaban her black eyes, which, since the important dialogue of the enchanted grot, were considerably enlarged, and said: "Go, speak thus to slaves; but learn to reverence her who is born to give laws and subject all to her power."

Proceeding in the same style, she was interrupted by a sudden exclamation of, "The Caliph! the Caliph!" All the curtains were thrown open, the slaves prostrated themselves in double rows, and poor little Gulchenrouz went to hide beneath the couch of a sofa. At first appeared a file of black eunuchs trailing after them long trains of muslin embroidered with gold, and holding in their hands censers, which dispensed, as they passed,

---

1 Giamschid, *Djamshid, Jamshid*: according to legend, fourth king of ancient Persia whose beauty dazzled or blinded any who stared at him. He owned a magic cup in which he could see the whole universe. Legends confuse and identify Djamshid with Solomon. Djamshid controlled the *diws* (as Solomon did the *djinn*) and both are credited with building Persepolis. It seems to have suited Beckford's purpose to accept the identification and attribute Persepolis and Istakhar to Solomon. [*D'Herbelot*; *Islam2* II, 322, 438]

the grateful perfume of the wood of aloes. Next marched Bababalouk with a solemn strut, and tossing his head, as not overpleased at the visit. Vathek came close after, superbly robed: his gait was unembarassed and noble; and his presence would have engaged admiration, though he had not been the sovereign of the world. He approached Nouronihar with a throbbing heart, and seemed enraptured at the full effulgence of her radiant eyes, of which he had before caught but a few glimpses: but she instantly depressed them, and her confusion augmented her beauty.

Bababalouk, who was a thorough adept in coincidences of this nature, and knew that the worst game should be played with the best face, immediately made a signal for all to retire; and so sooner did he perceive beneath the sofa the little one's feet, than he drew him forth without ceremony, set him upon his shoulders, and lavished on him, as he went off, a thousand unwelcome caresses. Gulchenrouz cried out, and resisted till his cheeks became the colour of the blossom of pomegranates, and his tearful eyes sparkled with indignation. He cast a significant glance at Nouronihar, which the Caliph noticing, asked, "Is that, then, your Gulchenrouz?" – "Sovereign of the world!" answered she, "spare my cousin, whose innocence and gentleness deserve not your anger!" – "Take comfort," said Vathek, with a smile: "he is in good hands. Bababalouk is fond of children: and never goes without sweetmeats and comfits." The daughter of Fakreddin was abashed, and suffered Gulchenrouz to be borne away without adding a word. The tumult of her bosom betrayed her confusion, and Vathek becoming still more impassioned, gave loose to his frenzy; which had only not subdued the last faint strugglings of reluctance, when the emir suddenly bursting in, threw his face upon the ground, at the feet of the Caliph, and said: "Commander of the faithful! abase not yourself to the meanness of your slave." – "No, emir," replied Vathek, "I raise her to an equality with myself: I declare her my wife; and the glory of your race shall extend from one generation to another." – "Alas! my lord," said Fakreddin, as he plucked off a few grey hairs of his beard; "cut short the days of your faithful servant, rather than force him to depart from his word. Nouronihar is solemnly promised to Gulchenrouz, the son of my brother Ali Hassan: they are united, also, in heart; their faith is mutually plighted; and affiances, so sacred, cannot be broken." – "What then!" replied the Caliph, bluntly, "would you surrender this divine beauty to a husband more womanish than herself; and can you imagine, that I will suffer her charms to decay in hands so inefficient and nerveless? No! she is destined to live out her life within my embraces: such is my will: retire; and disturb not the night I devote to the worship of her charms."

The irritated emir drew forth his sabre, presented it to Vathek, and, stretching out his neck, said, in a firm tone of voice: "Strike your unhappy host, my lord! he has lived long enough, since he hath seen the prophet's vicegerent violate the rights of hospitality." At his uttering these words, Nouronihar, unable to support any longer the conflict of her passions, sunk down in a swoon. Vathek, both terrified for her life, and furious at an opposition to his will, bade Fakreddin assist his daughter, and withdrew; darting his terrible look at the unfortunate emir, who suddenly fell backward, bathed in a sweat as cold as the damp of death.

Gulchenrouz, who had escaped from the hands of Bababalouk and was, that instant, returned, called out for help, as loudly as he could, not having strength to afford it himself. Pale and panting, the poor child attempted to revive Nouronihar by caresses; and it happened, that the thrilling warmth of his lips restored her to life. Fakreddin beginning also to recover from the look of the Caliph, with difficulty tottered to a seat; and, after warily casting round his eye, to see if this dangerous Prince were gone, sent for Shaban and Sutlememe; and said to them apart: "My friends! violent evils require violent remedies; the Caliph has brought desolation and horror into my family; and, how shall we resist his power? Another of his looks will send me to the grave. Fetch, then, that narcotick powder which a dervish brought me from Aracan.[1] A dose of it, the effect of which will continue three days, must be administered to each

---

1   Aracan: the most westerly part of Lower Burma. [*Islam2* I, 606]

of these children. The Caliph will believe them to be dead; for, they will have all the appearance of death. We shall go, as if to inter them in the cave of Meimouné,[1] at the entrance of the great desert of sand and near the bower of my dwarfs. When all the spectators shall be withdrawn, you, Shaban, and four select eunuchs, shall convey them to the lake; where provision shall be ready to support them a month: for, one day allotted to the surprise this event will occasion; five, to the tears; a fortnight to reflection; and the rest, to prepare for the renewing of his progress; will, according to my calculation, fill up the whole time that Vathek will tarry; and I shall, then, be freed from his intrusion."

"Your plan is good," said Sutlememe, "if it can but be effected. I have remarked, that Nouronihar is well able to support the glances of the Caliph: and, that he is far from being sparing of them to her: be assured, therefore, that notwithstanding her fondness for Gulchenrouz, she will never remain quiet, while she knows him to be here. Let us persuade her, that both herself and Gulchenrouz are really dead; and, that they were conveyed to those rocks, for a limited season, to expiate the little faults, of which their love was the cause. We will add, that we killed ourselves in despair; and that your dwarfs, whom they never yet saw, will preach to them delectable sermons. I will engage that every thing shall succeed to the bent of your wishes." – "Be it so!" said Fakreddin, "I approve of your proposal: let us lose not a moment to give it effect."

They hastened to seek for the powder which, being mixed in a sherbet, was immediately administered to Gulchenrouz and Nouronihar. Within the space of an hour, both were seized with violent palpitations; and a general numbness gradually ensued. They arose from the floor where they had remained ever since the Caliph's departure; and, ascending to the sofa, reclined themselves upon it, clasped in each other's embraces. "Cherish me, my dear Nouronihar!" said Gulchenrouz: "put thy hand upon my heart; it feels as if it were frozen. Alas! thou art as cold as myself! hath the Caliph murdered us both, with

---

1 Meimouné: perhaps named after Maymūna Bint al-Harith, Mohammed's last wife.

his terrible look?" – "I am dying!" cried she, in a faultering voice: "Press me closer; I am ready to expire!" – "Let us die then, together," answered the little Gulchenrouz; whilst his breast laboured with a convulsive sigh: "let me, at least, breathe forth my soul on thy lips!" They spoke no more, and became as dead.

Immediately, the most piercing cries were heard through the harem; whilst Shaban and Sutlememe personated with great adroitness, the parts of persons in despair. The emir, who was sufficiently mortified, to be forced into such untoward expedients; and had now, for the first time, made a trial of his powder, was under no necessity of counterfeiting grief. The slaves, who had flocked together from all quarters, stood motionless, at the spectacle before them. All lights were extinguished, save two lamps; which shed a wan glimmering over the faces of these lovely flowers that seemed to be faded in the spring-time of life. Funeral vestments were prepared; their bodies were washed with rose-water; their beautiful tresses were braided and incensed; and they were wrapped in simars[1] whiter than alabaster.

At the moment, that their attendants were placing two wreaths of their favourite jasmines, on their brows, the Caliph, who had just heard the tragical catastrophe, arrived. He looked not less pale and haggard than the goules that wander, at night, among the graves. Forgetful of himself and every one else, he broke through the midst of the slaves; fell prostrate at the foot of the sofa; beat his bosom; called himself "atrocious murderer!" and invoked upon his head, a thousand imprecations. With a trembling hand he raised the veil that covered the countenance of Nouronihar, and uttering a loud shriek, fell lifeless on the floor. The chief of the eunuchs dragged him off, with horrible grimaces, and repeated as he went, "Aye, I foresaw she would play you some ungracious turn!"

No sooner was the Caliph gone, than the emir commanded biers to be brought, and forbade that any one should enter the harem. Every window was fastened; all instruments of music

1   simars, symars: light, flowing robes.

were broken; and the Imans[1] began to recite their prayers. Towards the close of this melancholy day, Vathek sobbed in silence; for they had been forced to compose, with anodynes, his convulsions of rage and desperation.

At the dawn of the succeeding morning, the wide folding doors of the palace were set open, and the funeral procession moved forward for the mountain. The wailful cries of "La Ilah illa Alla!"[2] reached the Caliph, who was eager to cicatrize himself, and attend the ceremonial: nor could he have been dissuaded, had not his excessive weakness disabled him from walking. At the few first steps he fell on the ground, and his people were obliged to lay him on a bed, where he remained many days in such a state of insensibility as excited compassion in the emir himself.

When the procession was arrived at the grot of Meimouné, Shaban and Sutlememe dismissed the whole of the train, excepting the four confidential eunuchs who were appointed to remain. After resting some moments near the biers, which had been left in the open air; they caused them to be carried to the brink of a small lake, whose banks were overgrown with a hoary moss. This was the great resort of herons and storks which preyed continually on little blue fishes. The dwarfs, instructed by the emir, soon repaired thither; and, with the help of the eunuchs, began to construct cabins of rushes and reeds, a work in which they had admirable skill. A magazine also was contrived for provisions, with a small oratory for themselves, and a pyramid of wood, neatly piled to furnish the necessary fuel: for the air was bleak in the hollows of the mountains.

At evening two fires were kindled on the brink of the lake, and the two lovely bodies, taken from their biers, were carefully deposited upon a bed of dried leaves, within the same cabin. The dwarfs began to recite the Koran, with their clear, shrill voices; and Shaban and Sutlememe stood at some distance, anxiously waiting the effects of the powder. At length Nouronihar

---

1 Iman, *Imam*: originally the spiritual leader of Islam. The Imam and the Caliph were the same. In modern times, the office is held by prominent theologians in Islamic communities. [*Islam2* III, 1163]
2 La Ilah illa Alla!: "There is no God but God!"

and Gulchenrouz faintly stretched out their arms; and, gradually opening their eyes, began to survey, with looks of increasing amazement, every object around them. They even attempted to rise; but, for want of strength, fell back again. Sutlememe, on this, administered a cordial, which the emir had taken care to provide.

Gulchenrouz, thoroughly aroused, sneezed out loud: and, raising himself with an effort that expressed his surprise, left the cabin and inhaled the fresh air, with the greatest avidity. "Yes," said he, "I breath again! again do I exist! I hear sounds! I behold a firmament, spangled over with stars!" – Nouronihar, catching these beloved accents, extricated herself from the leaves and ran to clasp Gulchenrouz to her bosom. The first objects she remarked, were their long simars, their garlands of flowers, and their naked feet: she hid her face in her hands to reflect. The vision of the enchanted bath, the despair of her father, and, more vividly than both, the majestic figure of Vathek, recurred to her memory. She recollected also, that herself and Gulchenrouz had been sick and dying; but all these images bewildered her mind. Not knowing where she was, she turned her eyes on all sides, as if to recognize the surrounding scene. This singular lake, those flames reflected from its glassy surface, the pale hues of its banks, the romantic cabins, the bullrushes, that sadly waved their drooping heads; the storks, whose melancholy cries blended with the shrill voices of the dwarfs, every thing conspired to persuade her, that the angel of death[1] had opened the portal of some other world.

Gulchenrouz, on his part, lost in wonder, clung to the neck of his cousin. He believed himself in the region of phantoms; and was terrified at the silence she preserved. At length addressing her; "Speak," said he, "where are we? do you not see those spectres that are stirring the burning coals? Are they Monker and Nekir[2] who are come to throw us into them?

---

1 angel of death, Asrael, *Izra'il*: a being pitiless and strong, which drags the souls of unbelievers from their bodies. [*Sale* 7; *Islam2* IV, 292]

2 Monker and Nekir, *Munkar* and *Nakir*. These angels ask preliminary questions of the dead person on matters of faith; ignorance of the teachings of Islam sends him to hell. [*Islam2* VI, 217; *Sale* 101; *D'Herbelot* 58]

Does the fatal bridge[1] cross this lake, whose solemn stillness, perhaps, conceals from us an abyss, in which, for whole ages, we shall be doomed incessantly to sink."

"No, my children," said Sutlememe, going towards them, "take comfort! the exterminating angel, who conducted our souls hither after yours, hath assured us, that the chastisement of your indolent and voluptuous life, shall be restricted to a certain number of years, which you must pass in this dreary abode; where the sun is scarcely visible, and where the soil yields neither fruits nor flowers. These," continued she, pointing to the dwarfs, "will provide for our wants; for souls, so mundane as ours, retain too strong a tincture of their earthly extraction. Instead of meats, your food will be nothing but rice; and your bread shall be moistened in the fogs that brood over the surface of the lake."

At this desolating prospect, the poor children burst into tears, and prostrated themselves before the dwarfs; who perfectly supported their characters, and delivered an excellent discourse, of a customary length, upon the sacred camel; which, after a thousand years, was to convey them to the paradise of the faithful.

The sermon being ended, and ablutions performed, they praised Alla and the Prophet; supped very indifferently; and retired to their withered leaves. Nouronihar and her little cousin, consoled themselves on finding that the dead might lay in one cabin. Having slept well before, the remainder of the night was spent in conversation on what had befallen them; and both, from a dread of apparitions, betook themselves for protection to one another's arms.

In the morning, which was lowering and rainy, the dwarfs mounted high poles, like minarets, and called them to prayers. The whole congregation, which consisted of Sutlememe, Shaban, the four eunuchs, and a few storks that were tired of fishing, was already assembled. The two children came forth from their cabin with a slow and dejected pace. As their minds were in a tender and melancholy mood, their devotions were per-

---

1   the fatal bridge: The Islamic idea of the soul crossing a bridge after death is drawn from the religion of Zoroaster.

formed with fervour. No sooner were they finished than Gulchenrouz demanded of Sutlememe, and the rest, "how they happened to die so opportunely for his cousin and himself?" – "We killed ourselves," returned Sutlememe, "in despair at your death." On this, Nouronihar who, notwithstanding what had past, had not yet forgotten her vision said – "And the Caliph! is he also dead of his grief? and will he likewise come hither?" The dwarfs, who were prepared with an answer, most demurely replied: "Vathek is damned beyond all redemption!" – "I readily believe so," said Gulchenrouz; "and am glad, from my heart, to hear it; for I am convinced it was his horrible look that sent us hither, to listen to sermons, and mess upon rice." One week passed away, on the side of the lake, unmarked by any variety: Nouronihar ruminating on the grandeur of which death had deprived her; and Gulchenrouz applying to prayers and basket-making with the dwarfs, who infinitely pleased him.

Whilst this scene of innocence was exhibiting in the mountains, the Caliph presented himself to the emir in a new light. The instant he recovered the use of his senses, with a voice that made Bababalouk quake, he thundered out: "Perfidious Giaour! I renounce thee for ever! it is thou who hast slain my beloved Nouronihar! and I supplicate the pardon of Mahomet; who would have preserved her to me, had I been more wise. Let water be brought, to perform my ablutions, and let the pious Fakreddin be called to offer up his prayers with mine, and reconcile me to him. Afterwards, we will go together and visit the sepulchre of the unfortunate Nouronihar. I am resolved to become a hermit, and consume the residue of my days on this mountain, in hope of expiating my crimes." – "And what do you intend to live upon there?" inquired Bababalouk: "I hardly know," replied Vathek, "but I will tell you when I feel hungry – which, I believe, will not soon be the case."

The arrival of Fakreddin put a stop to this conversation. As soon as Vathek saw him, he threw his arms around his neck, bedewed his face with a torrent of tears, and uttered things so affecting, so pious, that the emir, crying for joy, congratulated himself, in his heart upon having performed so admirable and unexpected a conversion. As for the pilgrimage to the mountain, Fakreddin had his reasons not to oppose it; therefore, each ascending his own litter, they started.

Notwithstanding the vigilance with which his attendants watched the Caliph, they could not prevent his harrowing his cheeks with a few scratches, when on the place where he was told Nouronihar had been buried; they were even obliged to drag him away, by force of hands, from the melancholy spot. However he swore, with a solemn oath, that he would return thither every day. This resolution did not exactly please the emir — yet he flattered himself that the Caliph might not proceed farther, and would merely perform his devotions in the cavern of Meimouné. Besides, the lake was so completely concealed within the solitary bosom of those tremendous rocks, that he thought it utterly impossible any one could ever find it. This security of Fakreddin was also considerably strengthened by the conduct of Vathek, who performed his vow most scrupulously, and returned daily from the hill so devout, and so contrite, that all the grey-beards were in a state of ecstasy on account of it.

Nouronihar was not altogether so content; for though she felt a fondness for Gulchenrouz, who, to augment the attachment, had been left at full liberty with her, yet she still regarded him as but a bauble that bore no competition with the carbuncle of Giamschid. At times, she indulged doubts on the mode of her being; and scarcely could believe that the dead had all the wants and whims of the living. To gain satisfaction, however, on so perplexing a topic; one morning, whilst all were asleep, she arose with a breathless caution from the side of Gulchenrouz: and, after having given him a soft kiss, began to follow the windings of the lake, till it terminated with a rock, the top of which was accessible, though lofty. This she climbed with considerable toil; and, having reached the summit, set forward in a run, like a doe before the hunter. Though she skipped with the alertness of an antelope, yet, at intervals, she was forced to desist, and rest beneath the tamarisks to recover her breath. Whilst she, thus reclined, was occupied with her little reflections on the apprehension that she had some knowledge of this place; Vathek, who, finding himself that morning but ill at ease, had gone forth before the dawn, presented himself, on a sudden, to her view. Motionless with surprise, he durst not approach the figure before him trembling and pale, but yet lovely to behold. At length, Nouronihar, with a mixture of pleasure and affliction, raising her fine eyes to him, said: "My lord! are you then come hither to eat rice and hear sermons with me?" – "Beloved phantom!" cried Vathek, "thou dost speak; thou hast the same graceful form; the same radiant features: art thou palpable likewise?" and, eagerly embracing her, added: "Here are limbs and a bosom, animated with a gentle warmth! – What can such a prodigy mean?"

Nouronihar, with indifference answered: "You know, my lord, that I died on the very night you honoured me with your visit. My cousin maintains it was from one of your glances; but I cannot believe him: for, to me, they seem not so dreadful. Gulchenrouz died with me, and we were both brought into a region of desolation, where we are fed with a wretched diet. If you be dead also, and are come hither to join us, I pity your lot: for, you will be stunned with the clang of the dwarfs and the storks. Besides, it is mortifying in the extreme, that you, as well as myself, should have lost the treasures of the subterranean palace."

At the mention of the subterranean palace, the Caliph suspended his caresses, (which indeed had proceeded pretty far) to seek from Nouronihar an explanation of her meaning. She then recapitulated her vision; what immediately followed; and the history of her pretended death; adding, also, a description of the place of expiation, from whence she had fled; and all, in a manner, that would have extorted laughter, had not the thoughts of Vathek been too deeply engaged. No sooner, however, had she ended, than he again clasped her to his bosom and said: "Light of my eyes! the mystery is unravelled; we both are alive! Your father is a cheat, who, for the sake of dividing us, hath deluded us both: and the Giaour, whose design, as far as I can discover, is, that we shall proceed together, seems scarce a whit better. It shall be some time, at least, before he finds us in his palace of fire. Your lovely little person, in my estimation, is far more precious than all the treasures of the pre-adamite sultans; and I wish to possess it at pleasure, and, in open day, for many a moon, before I go to burrow under ground, like a mole. Forget this little trifler, Gulchenrouz; and" – "Ah! my lord!" interposed Nouronihar, "let me intreat that you do him no evil."– "No, no!" replied Vathek, "I have already bid you forbear to alarm yourself for him. He has been brought up too much on milk and sugar to stimulate my jealousy. We will leave him with the dwarfs; who, by the bye, are my old acquaintances: their company will suit him far better than yours. As to other matters; I will return no more to your father's. I want not to have my ears dinned by him and his dotards with the violation of the rights of hospitality: as if it were less an honour for you to espouse the sovereign of the world, than a girl dressed up like a boy!"

Nouronihar could find nothing to oppose, in a discourse so eloquent. She only wished the amorous monarch had discovered more ardour for the carbuncle of Giamschid: but flattered herself it would gradually increase; and, therefore, yielded to his will, with the most bewitching submission.

When the Caliph judged it proper, he called for Bababalouk, who was asleep in the cave of Meimouné, and dreaming that the phantom of Nouronihar, having mounted him once more on her swing, had just given him such a jerk, that he, one moment, soared above the mountains, and the next, sunk into the abyss. Starting from his sleep at the sound of his master, he ran, gasping for breath, and had nearly fallen backward at the sight, as he believed, of the spectre, by whom he had, so lately, been haunted in his dream. "Ah, my lord!" cried he, recoiling ten steps, and covering his eyes with both hands, "do you then perform the office of a goul! have you dug up the dead? yet hope not to make her your prey: for, after all she hath caused me to suffer, she is wicked enough to prey even upon you."

"Cease to play fool," said Vathek, "and thou shalt soon be convinced that it is Nouronihar herself, alive and well, whom I clasp to my breast. Go and pitch my tents in the neighbouring valley. There will I fix my abode, with this beautiful tulip, whose colours I soon shall restore. There exert thy best endeavours to procure whatever can augment the enjoyments of life, till I shall disclose to thee more of my will."

The news of so unlucky an event soon reached the ears of the emir, who abandoned himself to grief and despair, and began, as did his old grey-beards, to begrime his visage with ashes. A total supineness ensued; travellers were no longer entertained; no more plasters were spread; and, instead of the charitable activity that had distinguished this asylum, the whole of its inhabitants exhibited only faces of half a cubit long, and uttered groans that accorded with their forlorn situation.

Though Fakreddin bewailed his daughter, as lost to him for ever, yet Gulchenrouz was not forgotten. He dispatched imme-diate instruction to Sutlememe, Shaban, and the dwarfs, enjoin-ing them not to undeceive the child, in respect of his state; but, under some pretense, to convey him far from the lofty rock, at the extremity of the lake, to a place which he would appoint, as safer from danger, for he suspected that Vathek intended him evil.

Gulchenrouz, in the meanwhile, was filled with amazement, at not finding his cousin; nor were the dwarfs less surprised; but Sutlememe, who had more penetration, immediately guessed what had happened. Gulchenrouz was amused with the delu-sive hope of once more embracing Nouronihar, in the interior recesses of the mountains, where the ground, strewed over with orange blossoms and jasmines, offered beds much more inviting than the withered leaves in their cabin; where they might accompany with their voices, the sounds of their lutes, and chase butterflies. Sutlememe was far gone in this sort of description, when one of the four eunuchs beckoned her aside, to apprize her of the arrival of a messenger from their fraterni-ty, who had explained the secret of the flight of Nouronihar, and brought the commands of the emir. A council with Sha-ban and the dwarfs was immediately held. Their baggage being stowed in consequence of it, they embarked in a shallop,[1] and quietly sailed with the little one, who acquiesced in all their proposals. Their voyage proceeded in the same manner, till they came to the place where the lake sinks beneath the hollow

---

1 shallop: a light open boat.

of a rock: but, as soon as the bark had entered it and Gulchen-rouz found himself surrounded with darkness, he was seized with a dreadful consternation, and incessantly uttered the most piercing outcries; for he now was persuaded he should actually be damned for having taken too many little freedoms, in his life-time, with his cousin.

But let us return to the Caliph, and her who ruled over his heart. Bababalouk had pitched the tents, and closed up the extremities of the valley, with magnificent screens of India cloth, which were guarded by Ethiopian slaves with their drawn sabres. To preserve the verdure of this beautiful inclosure in its natural freshness, white eunuchs went continually round it with gilt water vessels. The waving of fans was heard near the imperial pavilion; where, by the voluptuous light that glowed through the muslins, the Caliph enjoyed, at full view, all the attractions of Nouronihar. Inebriated with delights, he was all ear to her charming voice, which accompanied the lute: while she was not less captivated with his descriptions of Samarah, and the tower full of wonders; but especially with his relation of the adventure of the ball, and the chasm of the Giaour, with its ebony portal.

In this manner they conversed the whole day, and at night they bathed together, in a basin of black marble, which admirably set off the fairness of Nouronihar. Bababalouk, whose good graces this beauty had regained, spared no atten-tion, that their repasts might be served up with the minutest exactness: some exquisite rarity was ever placed before them; and he sent even to Shiraz, for that fragrant and delicious wine which had been hoarded up in bottles, prior to the birth of Mahomet. He had excavated little ovens in the rock, to bake the nice manchets which were prepared by the hands of Nouronihar, from whence they had derived a flavour so grate-ful to Vathek, that he regarded the ragouts[1] of his other wives as entirely maukish:[2] whilst they would have died of chagrin at the emir's, at finding themselves so neglected, if Fakreddin, notwithstanding his resentment, had not taken pity upon them.

---

1   ragouts: A stewed dish of small pieces of meat and vegetables; highly seasoned.
2   maukish; mawkish: having a faint, sickly flavour.

The sultana Dilara, who, till then, had been the favourite, took this dereliction of the Caliph to heart, with a vehemence natural to her character: for, during her continuance in favour, she had imbibed from Vathek many of his extravagant fancies, and was fired with impatience to behold the superb tombs of Istakhar, and the palace of the forty columns; besides, having been brought up amongst the magi,[1] she had fondly cherished the idea of the Caliph's devoting himself to the worship of fire: thus, his voluptuous and desultory life with her rival, was to her a double source of affliction. The transient piety of Vathek had occasioned her some serious alarms; but the present was an evil of far greater magnitude. She resolved, therefore, without hesitation, to write to Carathis, and acquaint her that all things went ill; that they had eaten, slept, and revelled at an old emir's, whose sanctity was very formidable; and that, after all, the prospect of possessing the treasures of the pre-adamite sultans, was no less remote than before. This letter was entrusted to the care of two woodmen, who were at work in one of the great forests of the mountains; and who, being acquainted with the shortest cuts, arrived in ten days at Samarah.

The Princess Carathis was engaged at chess with Morakan-abad, when the arrival of these wood-fellers was announced. She, after some weeks of Vathek's absence, had forsaken the upper regions of her tower, because every thing appeared in confusion among the stars, which she consulted relative to the fate of her son. In vain did she renew her fumigations, and extend herself on the roof, to obtain mystic visions; nothing more could she see in her dreams, than pieces of brocade, nosegays of flowers, and other unmeaning gew-gaws. These disappointments had thrown her into a state of dejection, which no drug in her power was sufficient to remove. Her only resource was in Morakanabad, who was a good man, and

---

1   magi: This is the first reference to the religion of Zoroaster, the dominant religion in Persia before the arrival of Islam. Beckford makes religious tension between Islam and Zoroaster an important source of conflict in *The Episodes*. Richardson's *Dissertation* is likely Beckford's main source, but his Zoroastrianism is highly embellished by his own imagination.

endowed with a decent share of confidence; yet, whilst in her company, he never thought himself on roses.

No person knew aught of Vathek, and, of course, a thousand ridiculous stories were propagated at his expense. The eagerness of Carathis may be easily guessed at receiving the letter, as well as her rage at reading the dissolute conduct of her son. "Is it so!" said she: "either I will perish, or Vathek shall enter the palace of fire. Let me expire in flames, provided he may reign on the throne of Soliman!" Having said this, and whirled herself around in a magical manner, which struck Morakanabad with such terror as caused him to recoil, she ordered her great camel Alboufaki to be brought, and the hideous Nerkes, with the unrelenting Cafour, to attend. "I require no other retinue," said she to Morakanabad: "I am going on affairs of emergency; a truce, therefore, to parade![1] Take you care of the people; fleece them well in my absence, for we shall expend large sums, and one knows not what may betide."

The night was uncommonly dark, and a pestilential blast blew from the plain of Catoul, that would have deterred any other traveller however urgent the call: but Carathis enjoyed most whatever filled others with dread. Nerkes concurred in opinion with her; and Cafour had a particular predilection for a pestilence. In the morning this accomplished caravan, with the wood-fellers, who directed their route, halted on the edge of an extensive marsh, from whence so noxious a vapour arose, as would have destroyed any animal but Alboufaki, who naturally inhaled these malignant fogs with delight. The peasants entreated their convoy not to sleep in this place. "To sleep," cried Carathis, "what an excellent thought! I never sleep, but for visions; and, as to my attendants, their occupations are too many to close the only eye they have." The poor peasants,[2] who were not overpleased with their party, remained open-mouthed with surprise.

Carathis alighted, as well as her negresses; and, severally stripping off their outer garments, they all ran to cull from those spots where the sun shone fiercest, the venomous plants that

---

1 a truce ... to parade: forego ... ceremonials.
2 peasants: Beckford is referring here to the wood-fellers.

grew on the marsh. This provision was made for the family of the emir; and whoever might retard the expedition to Istakhar. The woodmen were overcome by fear, when they beheld these three horrible phantoms run; and, not much relishing the company of Alboufaki, stood aghast at the command of Carathis to set forward; notwithstanding it was noon, and the heat fierce enough to calcine even rocks. In spite however, of every remonstrance, they were forced implicitly to submit.

Alboufaki, who delighted in solitude, constantly snorted whenever he perceived himself near a habitation; and Carathis, who was apt to spoil him with indulgence, as constantly turned him aside: so that the peasants were precluded from procuring subsistence; for, the milch goats and ewes, which Providence had sent towards the district they traversed to refresh travellers with their milk, all fled at the sight of the hideous animal and his strange riders. As to Carathis, she needed no common aliment:[1] for, her invention had previously furnished her with an opiate, to stay her stomach; some of which she imparted to her mutes.

At dusk, Alboufaki making a sudden stop, stampt with his foot; which, to Carathis, who knew his ways, was a certain indication that she was near the confines of some cemetery. The moon shed a bright light on the spot, which served to discover a long wall with a large door in it, standing a-jar; and so high that Alboufaki might easily enter. The miserable guides, who perceived their end approaching, humbly implored Carathis, as she had now so good an opportunity, to inter them; and immediately gave up the ghost. Nerkes and Cafour, whose wit was of a style peculiar to themselves, were by no means parsimonious of it on the folly of these poor people; nor could any thing have been found more suited to their taste, than the site of the burying ground, and the sepulchres which its precincts contained. There were, at least, two thousand of them on the declivity of a hill. Carathis was too eager to execute her plan, to stop at the view, charming as it appeared in her eyes. Pondering the advantages that might accrue from her present situation, she

---

1 aliment: that which is necessary for the proper functioning of the mind and body, used most often in reference to food.

said to herself, "So beautiful a cemetery must be haunted by
gouls! they never want for intelligence: having heedlessly
suffered my stupid guides to expire, I will apply for directions
to them; and, as an inducement, will invite them to regale on
these fresh corpses." After this wise soliloquy, she beckoned to
Nerkes and Cafour, and made signs with her fingers, as much as
to say: "Go; knock against the sides of the tombs and strike up
your delightful warblings."

The negresses, full of joy at the behests of their mistress; and
promising themselves much pleasure from the society of the
gouls, went, with an air of conquest, and began their knockings
at the tombs. As their strokes were repeated, a hollow noise was
heard in the earth; the surface hove up into heaps; and the
gouls, on all sides, protruded their noses to inhale the effluvia,[1]
which the carcases of the woodmen began to emit. They
assembled before a sarcophagus of white marble, where
Carathis was seated between the bodies of her miserable guides.
The Princess received her visitants with distinguished polite-
ness; and, supper being ended, they talked of business. Carathis
soon learnt from them every thing she wanted to discover; and,
without loss of time, prepared to set forward on her journey.
Her negresses, who were forming tender connexions with the
gouls, importuned her, with all their fingers, to wait at least till
the dawn. But Carathis, being chastity in the abstract, and an
implacable enemy to love intrigues and sloth, at once rejected
their prayer; mounted Alboufaki, and commanded them to take
their seats instantly. Four days and four nights, she continued
her route without interruption. On the fifth, she traversed
craggy mountains, and half-burnt forests; and arrived on the
sixth, before the beautiful screens which concealed from all
eyes the voluptuous wanderings of her son.

It was day-break, and the guards were snoring on their posts
in careless security, when the rough trot of Alboufaki awoke
them in consternation. Imagining that a group of spectres,
ascended from the abyss, was approaching, they all, without ceremony, took to their heels. Vathek was, at that instant, with

---

1   effluvia: a noxious or disagreeable exhalation as from a putrefying substance.

Nouronihar in the bath; hearing tales, and laughing at Baba-balouk, who related them: but, no sooner did the outcry of his guards reach him, than he flounced from the water like a carp; and as soon threw himself back at the sight of Carathis; who, advancing with her negresses, upon Alboufaki, broke through the muslin awnings and veils of the pavilion. At this sudden apparition, Nouronihar (for she was not, at all times, free from remorse) fancied, that the moment of celestial vengeance was come; and clung about the Caliph, in amorous despondence.

Carathis, still seated on her camel, foamed with indignation, at the spectacle which obtruded itself on her chaste view. She thundered forth without check or mercy: "Thou double-head-ed and four-legged monster! What means all this winding and writhing? Art thou not ashamed to be seen grasping this limber sapling in preference to the sceptre of the pre-adamite sultans? Is it then, for this paltry doxy,[1] that thou hast violated the con-ditions in the parchment of our Giaour! Is it on her, thou hast lavished thy precious moments! Is this the fruit of the knowl-edge I have taught thee! Is this the end of thy journey? Tear thyself from the arms of this little simpleton; drown her, in the water before me; and, instantly follow my guidance."

In the first ebullition of his fury, Vathek had resolved to rip open the body of Alboufaki and to stuff it with those of the negresses and of Carathis herself, but the remembrance of the Giaour, the palace of Istakhar, the sabres, and the talismans, flashing before his imagination, with the simultaneousness of lightning, he became more moderate, and said to his mother, in a civil, but decisive tone; "Dread lady! you shall be obeyed; but I will not drown Nouronihar. She is sweeter to me than a Myrabolan[2] comfit; and is enamoured of carbuncles; especially that, of Giamschid; which hath also been promised to be con-ferred upon her: she, therefore, shall go along with us; for, I intend to repose with her upon the sofas of Soliman: I can sleep no more without her." – "Be it so!" replied Carathis, alighting; and, at the same time, committing Alboufaki to the charge of her black women.

---

1   doxy: a loose woman.
2   Myrabolan comfit: a plum preserved in sugar.

Nouronihar, who had not yet quitted her hold, began to take courage; and said, with an accent of fondness, to the Caliph: "Dear sovereign of my soul! I will follow thee, if it be thy will, beyond the Kaf, in the land of the afrits. I will not hesitate to climb, for thee, the nest of the Simurgh; who, this lady excepted, is the most awful of created beings." – "We have here then," subjoined Carathis, "a girl, both of courage and science!" Nouronihar had certainly both; but, notwithstanding all her firmness, she could not help casting back a thought of regret upon the graces of her little Gulchenrouz; and the days of tender endearments she had participated with him. She, even, dropped a few tears; which, the Caliph observed; and inadvertently breathed out with a sigh: "Alas! my gentle cousin! what will become of thee!" – Vathek, at this apostrophe, knitted up his brows; and Carathis inquired what it could mean? "She is preposterously sighing after a stripling with languishing eyes and soft hair, who loves her," said the Caliph. "Where is he?" asked Carathis. "I must be acquainted with this pretty child: for," added she, lowering her voice, "I design, before I depart, to regain the favour of the Giaour. There is nothing so delicious, in his estimation, as the heart of a delicate boy palpitating with the first tumults of love."

Vathek, as he came from the bath, commanded Bababalouk to collect the women, and other moveables of his harem; embody his troops; and hold himself in readiness to march within three days: whilst Carathis, retired alone to a tent, where the Giaour solaced her with encouraging visions: but, at length, waking, she found at her feet, Nerkes and Cafour, who informed her, by their signs, that having led Alboufaki to the borders of a lake; to browse on some grey moss, that looked tolerably venomous; they had discovered certain blue fishes, of the same kind with those in the reservoir on the top of the tower. "Ah! ha!" said she, "I will go thither to them. These fish are past doubt of a species that, by a small operation, I can render oracular. They may tell me, where this little Gulchenrouz is; whom I am bent upon sacrificing." Having thus spoken, she immediately set out, with her swarthy retinue.

It being but seldom that time is lost, in the accomplishment of a wicked enterprize, Carathis and her negresses soon arrived at the lake; where, after burning the magical drugs, with which they were always provided; they stripped themselves naked, and waded to their chins; Nerkes and Cafour waving torches around them, and Carathis pronouncing her barbarous incantations. The fishes, with one accord, thrust forth their heads from the water; which was violently rippled by the flutter of their fins: and, at length, finding themselves constrained, by the potency of the charm, they opened their piteous mouths, and said: "From gills to tail, we are yours; what seek ye to know?" – "Fishes," answered she, "I conjure you, by your glittering scales; tell me where now is Gulchenrouz?" – "Beyond the rock," replied the shoal, in full chorus: "will this content you? for we do not delight in expanding our mouths." – "It will," returned the Princess: "I am not to learn, that you are not used to long conversations: I will leave you therefore to repose, though I had other questions to propound." The instant she had spoken, the water became smooth; and the fishes, at once, disappeared. Carathis, inflated with the venom of her projects, strode hastily over the rock; and found the amiable Gulchenrouz, asleep, in an arbour; whilst the two dwarfs were watching at his side, and ruminating their accustomed prayers. These diminutive personages possessed the gift of divining, whenever an enemy to good Mussulmans approached: thus, they anticipated the arrival of Carathis; who, stopping short, said to herself: "How placidly doth he recline his lovely little head! how pale, and languishing, are his looks! it is just the very child of my wishes!" The dwarfs interrupted this delectable soliloquy, by leaping, instantly, upon her; and scratching her face, with their utmost zeal. But Nerkes and Cafour, betaking themselves to the succour of their mistress, pinched the dwarfs so severely, in return, that they both gave up the ghost; imploring Mahomet to inflict his sorest vengeance upon this wicked woman, and all her household.

At the noise which this strange conflict occasioned in the valley, Gulchenrouz awoke; and, bewildered with terror, sprung impetuously and climbed an old fig-tree that rose against the acclivity of the rocks; from thence he gained their summits, and ran for two hours without once looking back. At last, exhausted with fatigue, he fell senseless into the arms of a good old genius, whose fondness for the company of children, had made it his sole occupation to protect them. Whilst performing his wonted rounds through the air, he had pounced on the cruel Giaour, at the instant of his growling in the horrible chasm, and had rescued the fifty little victims which the impiety of Vathek had devoted to his voracity. These the genius brought up in nests still higher than the clouds, and himself fixed his abode, in a nest more capacious than the rest, from whence he had expelled the Rocs[1] that had built it.

These inviolable asylums were defended against the dives and the afrits, by waving streamers; on which were inscribed in characters of gold, that flashed like lightning, the names of Alla and the Prophet. It was there that Gulchenrouz, who, as yet remained undeceived with respect to his pretended death, thought himself in the mansions of eternal peace. He admitted without fear the congratulations of his little friends, who were all assembled in the nest of the venerable genius, and vied with each other in kissing his serene forehead and beautiful eye-lids. – Remote from the inquietudes of the world; the impertinence of harems, the brutality of eunuchs, and the inconstancy of women; there he found a place truly congenial to the delights of his soul. In this peaceable society his days, months, and years glided on; nor was he less happy than the rest of his companions: for the genius, instead of burthening his pupils with perishable riches and vain sciences, conferred upon them the boon of perpetual childhood.

Carathis, unaccustomed to the loss of her prey, vented a thousand execrations on her negresses, for not seizing the child, instead of amusing themselves with pinching to death two insignificant dwarfs from which they gain no advantage. She returned into the valley murmuring; and, finding that her son was not risen from the arms of Nouronihar, discharged her ill-humour upon both. The idea, however, of departing next day for Istakhar, and of cultivating, through the good offices of the

---

1 Roc, *Rukhkh*: in Arabian fable, a bird capable of carrying an elephant, often, by assimilation, confused with Simurgh. [*Islam2* VIII, 595]

Giaour, an intimacy with Eblis[1] himself, at length consoled her chagrin. But fate had ordained it otherwise.

In the evening as Carathis was conversing with Dilara, who, through her contrivance had become of the party, and whose taste resembled her own, Bababalouk came to acquaint her that the sky towards Samarah looked of a fiery red, and seemed to portend some alarming disaster. Immediately recurring to her astrolabes[2] and instruments of magic, she took the altitude of the planets, and discovered, by her calculations, to her great mortification, that a formidable revolt had taken place at Samarah, that Motavakel,[3] availing himself of the disgust, which was inveterate against his brother, had incited commotions amongst the populace, made himself master of the palace, and actually invested the great tower, to which Morakanabad had retired, with a handful of the few that still remained faithful to Vathek.

"What!" exclaimed she; "must I lose, then, my tower! my mutes! my negresses! my mummies! and, worse than all, the laboratory, the favourite resort of my nightly lucubrations, without knowing, at least, if my hair-brained son will complete his adventure? No! I will not be dupe! immediately will I speed to support Morakanabad. By my formidable art, the clouds shall pour grape-shot in the faces of the assailants and shafts of red-hot iron on their heads. I will let loose my stores of hungry

---

1   Eblis, *Iblis*: an angel, sent from heaven to chastise Gian Ben Gian, the last pre-adamite sultan. After defeating Gian Ben Gian, he began to govern in his place. When Adam was created and all the earth ordered to obey him, Eblis, composed of the element of fire, scorned submission to a creature formed of clay. He rebelled against the Divine will and was joined in his revolt by the Dives. [*Richardson* 141-43] D'Herbelot's account of Eblis presents him as the anti-Christ and emphasizes his loss of hope for God's mercy. He quotes Persian poet Esfahani: "The fire that is the origin of his nature and pride will be endlessly the instrument of his punishment." Pride and disobedience are his two primary sins. [*Islam2* III, 669]

2   astrolabe, *asturlab*: an astronomical instrument for measuring altitudes of heavenly bodies, determining the hours of the day or night, and casting horoscopes. It is mentioned in Arab treatises starting in AD 815 and remained a popular subject in Islamic astronomy. The first European astrolabes followed Islamic models. [*Islam2* I, 722]

3   Motavakel, *al-Mutawakkil*: Vathek's brother and successor. Beckford's account bears no resemblance to history. [*Islam2* VII, 777]

serpents and torpedos,[1] from beneath them; and we shall soon see the stand they will make against such an explosion!"

Having thus spoken, Carathis hasted to her son who was tranquilly banqueting with Nouronihar, in his superb carnation-coloured tent. "Glutton, that thou art!" cried she, "were it not for me, thou wouldst soon find thyself the mere commander of savoury pies. Thy faithful subjects have abjured the faith they swore to thee. Motavakel, thy brother, now reigns on the hill of Pied Horses: and, had I not some slight resources in the tower, would not be easily persuaded to abdicate. But, that time may not be lost, I shall only add a few words: – Strike tent to-night; set forward; and beware how thou loiterest again by the way. Though, thou hast forfeited the conditions of the parchment, I am not yet without hope: for, it cannot be denied, that thou hast violated, to admiration, the laws of hospitality by seducing the daughter of the emir, after having partaken of his bread and his salt. Such a conduct cannot but be delightful to the Giaour; and if, on thy march, thou canst signalize thyself, by an additional crime; all will still go well, and thou shalt enter the palace of Soliman, in triumph. Adieu! Alboufaki and my negresses are waiting at the door."

The Caliph had nothing to offer in reply: he wished his mother a prosperous journey, and ate on till he had finished his supper. At midnight, the camp broke up, amidst the flourishing of trumpets and other martial instruments; but loud indeed must have been the sound of the tymbals, to overpower the blubbering of the emir, and his grey-beards; who, by an excessive profusion of tears, had so far exhausted the radical moisture, that their eyes shrivelled up in their sockets, and their hairs dropped off by the roots. Nouronihar, to whom such a symphony was painful, did not grieve to get out of hearing. She accompanied the Caliph in the imperial litter; where they amused themselves, with imagining the splendour which was soon to surround them. The other women, overcome with dejection were dolefully rocked in their cages: whilst Dilara

---

1   torpedos: a weapon, intended to be buried, which explodes when trodden upon; a mine.

consoled herself, with anticipating the joy of celebrating the rites of fire, on the stately terraces of Istakhar.

In four days, they reached the spacious valley of Rocnabad. The season of spring was in all its vigour, and the grotesque branches of the almond trees, in full blossom, fantastically chequered with hyacinths and jonquils, breathed forth a delightful fragrance. Myriads of bees, and scarce fewer of santons, had there taken up their abode. On the banks of the stream, hives and oratories were alternately ranged; and their neatness and whiteness were set off, by the deep green of the cypresses, that spired up amongst them. These pious personages amused themselves, with cultivating little gardens, that abounded with flowers and fruits; especially, musk-melons, of the best flavour that Persia could boast. Sometimes dispersed over the meadow, they entertained themselves with feeding peacocks, whiter than snow; and turtles, more blue than the sapphire. In this manner were they occupied, when the harbingers of the imperial procession began to proclaim: "Inhabitants of Rocnabad! prostrate yourselves on the brink of your pure waters; and tender your thanksgivings to heaven, that vouchsafeth to shew you a ray of its glory: for, lo! the commander of the faithful draws near."

The poor santons, filled with holy energy, having bustled to light up wax torches in their oratories, and expand the Koran on their ebony desks, went forth to meet the Caliph with baskets of honeycomb, dates, and melons. But, whilst they were advancing in solemn procession and with measured steps, the horses, camels, and guards, wantoned over their tulips and other flowers, and made a terrible havoc amongst them. The santons could not help casting from one eye a look of pity on the ravages committing around them; whilst the other was fixed upon the Caliph and heaven. Nouronihar, enraptured with the scenery of a place which brought back to her remembrance the pleasing solitudes where her infancy had passed, intreated Vathek to stop: but he, suspecting that these oratories might be deemed, by the Giaour, an habitation, commanded his pioneers to level them all. The santons stood motionless with horror, at the barbarous mandate; and, at last, broke out into lamentations;

but these were uttered with so ill a grace, that Vathek bade his eunuchs to kick them from his presence. He then descended from the litter, with Nouronihar. They sauntered together in the meadow; and amused themselves with culling flowers, and passing a thousand pleasantries on each other. But the bees, who were staunch Mussulmans, thinking it their duty to revenge the insult offered to their dear masters, the santons, assembled so zealously to do it with good effect, that the Caliph and Nouronihar were glad to find their tents prepared to receive them.

Bababalouk, who, in capacity of purveyor, had acquitted himself, with applause, as to peacocks and turtles; lost no time in consigning some dozens to the spit; and as many more to be fricasseed. Whilst they were feasting, laughing, carousing, and blaspheming at pleasure, on the banquet so liberally furnished; the moullahs, the sheiks,[1] the cadis,[2] and imans of Shiraz (who seemed not to have met the santons) arrived; leading by bridles of riband,[3] inscribed from the Koran, a train of asses which were loaded with the choicest fruits the country could boast. Having presented their offerings to the Caliph; they petitioned him, to honour their city and mosques, with his presence. "Fancy not," said Vathek, "that you can detain me. Your presents I condescend to accept; but beg you will let me be quiet; for, I am not over-fond of resisting temptation. Retire then: – Yet, as it is not decent, for personages so reverend, to return on foot; and, as you have not the appearance of expert riders, my eunuchs shall tie you on your asses with the precaution that your backs be not turned towards me: for, they understand etiquette." – In this deputation, were some high-stomached sheiks who, taking Vathek for a fool, scrupled not to speak their opinion. These Bababalouk girded with double cords; and having well disciplined their asses with nettles behind, they all started, with a preternatural alertness; plunging, kicking, and running foul of one another, in the most ludicrous manner imaginable.

Nouronihar and the Caliph mutually contended who should

---

1   Shiek, *shaikh*: the patriarch of a tribe or family. [*Islam1 VII, 275*]
2   cadi, *Kadi*: a magistrate who decides on points of law and religion. [*Islam2 IV, 373*]
3   riband: ribbon.

most enjoy so degrading a sight. They burst out in peals of laughter, to see the old men and their asses fall into the stream. The leg of one was fractured; the shoulder of another, dislocated; the teeth of a third, dashed out; and the rest suffered still worse.

Two days more, undisturbed by fresh embassies, having been devoted to the pleasures of Rocnabad, the expedition proceeded; leaving Shiraz on the right, and verging towards a large plain; from whence were discernable, on the edge of the horizon, the dark summits of the mountains of Istakhar.

At this prospect, the Caliph and Nouronihar were unable to repress their transports. They bounded from their litter to the ground; and broke forth into such wild exclamations, as amazed all within hearing. Interrogating each other, they shouted, "Are we not approaching the radiant palace of light? or gardens, more delightful than those of Sheddad?"[1] – Infatuated mortals! they thus indulged delusive conjecture, unable to fathom the decrees of the Most High!

The good Genii, who had not totally relinquished the superintendence of Vathek; repairing to Mahomet, in the seventh heaven; said: "Merciful Prophet! stretch forth thy propitious arms, towards thy vicegerent; who is ready to fall, irretrievably, into the snare, which his enemies, the dives, have prepared to destroy him. The Giaour is awaiting his arrival, in the abominable palace of fire; where, if he once set his foot, his perdition will be inevitable. "Mahomet answered, with an air of indignation:"He hath too well deserved to be resigned to himself; but I permit you to try if one effort more will be effectual to divert him from pursuing his ruin."

One of these beneficent Genii, assuming, without delay, the exterior of a shepherd, more renowned for his piety than all the derviches and santons of the region, took his station near a flock of white sheep, on the slope of a hill; and began to pour forth, from his flute, such airs of pathetic melody, as subdued

---

1   Sheddad, *Schedad*: legendary King of Persia who built a sumptuous palace and delightful gardens. He may have been punished for pride and presumption. He and his court were destroyed by a terrible noise from heaven. [Sale, *Koran*, 490n, *D'Herbelot* 780]

Persepolis
From Cornelis de Bruin, *Voyage par la Muscovie en Perse* (1718)
Courtesy Cambridge University Library.

the very soul; and, wakening remorse, drove, far from it, every frivolous fancy. At these energetic sounds, the sun hid himself beneath a gloomy cloud; and the waters of two little lakes, that were naturally clearer than crystal, became of a colour like blood. The whole of this superb assembly was involuntarily drawn towards the declivity of the hill. With downcast eyes, they all stood abashed; each upbraiding himself with the evil he had done. The heart of Dilara palpitated; and the chief of the eunuchs, with a sigh of contrition, implored pardon of the women, whom, for his own satisfaction, he had so often tormented.

Vathek and Nouronihar turned pale in their litter; and, regarding each other with haggard looks, reproached themselves – the one with a thousand of the blackest crimes; a thousand projects of impious ambition; – the other, with the desolation of her family; and the perdition of the amiable Gulchenrouz. Nouronihar persuaded herself that she heard, in the fatal music, the groans of her dying father; and Vathek, the sobs of the fifty children he had sacrificed to the Giaour. Amidst these complicated pangs of anguish, they perceived themselves impelled towards the shepherd, whose countenance was so commanding that Vathek, for the first time, felt overawed; whilst Nouronihar concealed her face with her hands. The music paused; and the Genius, addressing the Caliph, said: "Deluded prince! to whom Providence hath confided the care of innumerable subjects; is it thus that thou fulfillest thy mission? Thy crimes are already completed; and, art thou now hastening towards thy punishment? Thou knowest that, beyond these mountains, Eblis and his accursed dives hold their infernal empire; and seduced by a malignant phantom, thou art proceeding to surrender thyself to them! This moment is the last of grace allowed thee: abandon thy atrocious purpose: return: give back Nouronihar to her father, who still retains a few sparks of life: destroy thy tower with all its abominations: drive Carathis from thy councils: be just to thy subjects: respect the ministers of the Prophet: compensate for thy impieties, by an exemplary life: and, instead of squandering thy days in voluptuous indulgence, lament thy crimes on the sepulchres of thy ancestors. Thou beholdest the clouds that obscure the sun: at the instant he recovers his splendour, if thy heart be not changed, the time of mercy assigned thee will be past for ever."

Vathek, depressed with fear, was on the point of prostrating himself at the feet of the shepherd; whom he perceived to be of a nature superior to man: but, his pride prevailing, he audaciously lifted his head, and, glancing at him one of his terrible looks, said: "Whoever thou art, withhold thy useless admonitions: thou wouldst either delude me, or art thyself deceived. If what I have done be so criminal, as thou pretendest, there remains not for me a moment of grace. I have traversed a sea of blood, to acquire a power, which will make thy equals tremble: deem not that I shall retire when in view of the port; or, that I will relinquish her, who is dearer to me than either my life, or thy mercy. Let the sun appear! let him illume my career! it matters not where it may end." On uttering these words, which made even the Genius shudder, Vathek threw himself into the arms of Nouronihar; and commanded that his horses should be forced back to the road.

There was no difficulty in obeying these orders: for, the attraction had ceased: the sun shone forth in all his glory, and the shepherd vanished with a lamentable scream.

The fatal impression of the music of the Genius, remained, notwithstanding, in the heart of Vathek's attendants. They viewed each other with looks of consternation. At the approach of night, almost all of them escaped; and, of this numerous assemblage, there remained the chief of the eunuchs, some idolatrous slaves, Dilara, and a few other women; who, like herself, were votaries of the religion of the Magi.

The Caliph, fired with the ambition of prescribing laws to the powers of darkness, was but little embarrassed at this dereliction. The impetuosity of his blood prevented him from sleeping; nor did he encamp any more, as before. Nouronihar, whose impatience, if possible exceeded his own, importuned him to hasten his march, and lavished on him a thousand caresses, to beguile all reflection. She fancied herself already more potent than Balkis,[1] and pictured to her imagination the Genii falling prostrate at the foot of her throne. In this manner they advanced by moon-light, till they came within view of the two towering rocks that form a kind of portal to the valley, at the extremity of which, rose the vast ruins of Istakhar.[2] Aloft, on the mountain, glimmered the fronts of various royal mausoleums, the horror of which was deepened by the shadows of night. They passed through two villages, almost deserted; the only inhabitants remaining being a few feeble old men: who, at

---

1 Balkis, *Bilkis*: Queen of Sheba. Islamic legends and commentaries abound with stories of Solomon and Sheba. In some they marry and become Muslim. [*Islam2* I, 1219]

2 Istakhar: Beckford's description follows closely the accounts of Chardin and Le Brun of Persepolis. Le Brun, in particular, mentions the vastness of the platform and a stairway to subterranean passages where no one dares enter. [*Chardin*, III, 100-139; *Le Brun* II, 261, 267]

the sight of horses and litters, fell upon their knees, and cried out: "O Heaven! is it then by these phantoms that we have been, for six months tormented! Alas! it was from the terror of these spectres and the noise beneath the mountains, that our people have fled, and left us at the mercy of the malificent spirits!" The Caliph, to whom these complaints were but unpromising auguries, drove over the bodies of these wretched old men; and, at length, arrived at the foot of the terrace of black marble. There he descended from his litter, handing down Nouronihar; both with beating hearts, stared wildly around them, and expected, with an apprehensive shudder, the approach of the Giaour. But nothing as yet announced his appearance.

A death-like stillness reigned over the mountain and through the air. The moon dilated on a vast platform the shades of the lofty columns which reached from the terrace almost to the clouds. The gloomy watch-towers, whose number could not be counted, were covered by no roof; and their capitals, of an architecture unknown in the records of the earth, served as an asylum for the birds of the night, which, alarmed at the approach of such visitants, fled away croaking.

The chief of the eunuchs, trembling with fear, besought Vathek that a fire might be kindled. "No!" replied he, "there is no time left to think of such trifles; abide where thou art, and expect my commands." Having thus spoken, he presented his hand to Nouronihar; and, ascending the steps of a vast staircase, reached the terrace, which was flagged with squares of marble, and resembled a smooth expanse of water, upon whose surface not a blade of grass ever dared to vegetate. On the right rose the watch-towers, ranged before the ruins of an immense palace, whose walls were embossed with various figures. In front stood forth the colossal forms of four creatures, composed of the leopard and the griffin, and though but of stone, inspired emotions of terror. Near these were distinguished by the splendour of the moon, which streamed full on the place, characters like those on the sabres of the Giaour, and which possessed the same virtue of changing every moment. These, after vacillating for some time, fixed at last in Arabic letters, and prescribed to the Caliph the following words: – "Vathek! Thou hast violated the conditions of my parchment, and deserveth to be sent back, but in favour to thy companion, and, as the meed for what thou hast done to obtain it; Eblis permitteth that the portal of his palace shall be opened; and the subterranean fire will receive thee into the number of its adorers."

He scarcely had read these words, before the mountain, against which the terrace was reared, trembled; and the watch-towers were ready to topple headlong upon them. The rock yawned, and disclosed within it a staircase of polished marble, that seemed to approach the abyss. Upon each stair were plant-ed two large torches, like those Nouronihar had seen in her vision; the camphorated vapour of which ascended and gath-ered itself into a cloud under the hollow of the vault.

This appearance, instead of terrifying, gave new courage to the daughter of Fakreddin. Scarcely deigning to bid adieu to the moon, and the firmament; she abandoned, without hesita-tion, the pure atmosphere, to plunge into these infernal exhala-tions. The gait of those impious personages was haughty, and determined. As they descended, by the effulgence of the torch-es, they gazed on each other with mutual admiration; and both appeared so resplendent, that they already esteemed themselves spiritual intelligences. The only circumstance that perplexed them, was their not arriving at the bottom of the stairs. On hastening their descent, with an ardent impetuosity, they felt their steps accelerated to such a degree, that they seemed not walking but falling from a precipice. Their progress, however, was at length impeded, by a vast portal of ebony which the Caliph, without difficulty, recognized. Here, the Giaour awaited them, with the key in his hand. "Ye are welcome!" said he to them, with a ghastly smile, "in spite of Mahomet, and all his dependents. I will now usher you into that palace, where you have so highly merited a place." Whilst he was uttering these words, he touched the enameled lock with his key; and the doors, at once, flew open with a noise still louder than the thunder of the dog days,[1] and as suddenly recoiled, the moment they entered.

---

1   dog days: the sultry period between July and September.

The Caliph and Nouronihar beheld each other with amazement, at finding themselves in a place, which, though roofed with a vaulted ceiling, was so spacious and lofty, that, at first, they took it for an immeasurable plain. But their eyes, at length, growing familiar to the grandeur of the surrounding objects, they extended their view to those at a distance; and discovered rows of columns and arcades, which gradually diminished, till they terminated in a point radiant as the sun, when he darts his last beams athwart the ocean. The pavement, strewed over with gold dust and saffron, exhaled so subtile an odour, as almost overpowered them. They, however, went on; and observed an infinity of censers, in which, ambergrise[1] and the wood of aloes, were continually burning. Between the several columns, were placed tables; each, spread with a profusion of viands; and wines, of every species, sparkling in vases of crystal. A throng of Genii, and other fantastic spirits, of either sex, danced lasciviously, at the sound of the music, which issued from beneath.

In the midst of this immense hall, a vast multitude was incessantly passing; who severally kept their right hands on their hearts; without once regarding any thing around them. They had all, the livid paleness of death. Their eyes, deep sunk in their sockets, resembled those phosphoric meteors, that glimmer by night, in places of interment. Some stalked slowly on; absorbed in profound reverie: some shrieking with agony, ran furiously about like tigers, wounded with poisoned arrows; whilst others, grinding their teeth in rage, foamed along more frantic than the wildest maniac. They all avoided each other; and, though surrounded by a multitude that no one could number, each wandered at random, unheedful of the rest, as if alone on a desert where no foot had trodden.

Vathek and Nouronihar, frozen with terror, at a sight so baleful, demanded of the Giaour what these appearances might mean; and, why these ambulating spectres never withdrew their hands from their hearts? "Perplex not yourselves, with so much at once," replied he bluntly; "you will soon be acquainted with

---

1 ambergrise: Grey amber or ambergris is also called *musk*, a sweet-smelling secretion of the sperm whale, valued as perfume and medicine.

all: let us haste, and present you to Eblis." They continued their way, through the multitude; but, notwithstanding their confidence at first, they were not sufficiently composed to examine, with attention, the various perspective of halls and of galleries, that opened on the right hand and left; which were all illuminated by torches and braziers, whose flames rose in pyramids to the centre of the vault. At length they came to a place, where long curtains, brocaded with crimson and gold, fell from all parts in solemn confusion. Here, the choirs and dances were heard no longer. The light which glimmered, came from afar.

After some time, Vathek and Nouronihar perceived a gleam brightening through the drapery, and entered a vast tabernacle hung round with the skins of leopards. An infinity of elders with streaming beards, and afrits in complete armour, had prostrated themselves before the ascent of a lofty eminence; on the top of which, upon a globe of fire, sat the formidable Eblis. His person was that of a young man, whose noble and regular features seemed to have been tarnished by malignant vapours. In his large eyes appeared both pride and despair: his flowing hair retained some semblance to that of an angel of light. In his hand, which thunder had blasted, he swayed the iron sceptre, that causes the monster Ouranbad,[1] the afrits, and all the powers of the abyss to tremble. At his presence, the heart of the Caliph sunk within him; and he fell prostrate on his face. Nouronihar, however, though greatly dismayed, could not help admiring the person of Eblis: for, she expected to have seen some stupendous giant. Eblis, with a voice more mild than might be imagined, but such as penetrated the soul and filled it with the deepest melancholy, said: "Creatures of clay, I receive you into mine empire: ye are numbered amongst my adorers: enjoy whatever this palace affords: the treasures of the pre-adamite sultans;[2] their fulminating sabres; and those talismans,

---

1 Ouranbad, *Urranbad*: a fierce flying monster, probably the Arabian version of the simurgh. [*Richardson*, 148]

2 pre-adamite sultans: the universal monarchs of the world (*sultan* means *power, authority*) before the creation of Adam. D'Herbelot lists the most renowned as Soliman Hiat, Soliman Raad, Soliman Daki, Soliman Imlak, Soliman Schadi, Soliman Virani, Soliman Bouaki, Soliman Tchaghi, and finally the Soliman called Gian Ben Gian, who ruled the world immediately before the creation of Adam. [*D'Herbelot* 820]

that compel the dives to open the subterranean expanses of the mountain of Kaf, which communicate with these. There, insatiable as your curiosity may be, shall you find sufficient objects to gratify it. You shall possess the exclusive privilege of entering the fortresses of Aherman,[1] and the halls of Argenk,[2] where are portrayed all creatures endowed with intelligence; and the various animals that inhabited the earth prior to the creation of that contemptible being whom ye denominate the father of mankind."

Vathek and Nouronihar feeling themselves revived and encouraged by this harangue, eagerly said to the Giaour; "Bring us instantly to the place which contains these precious talismans." – "Come," answered this wicked dive, with his malignant grin, "come and possess all that my sovereign hath promised; and more." He then conducted them into a long aisle adjoining the tabernacle; preceding them with hasty steps, and followed by his disciples with the utmost alacrity. They reached, at length, a hall of great extent, and covered with a lofty dome; around which appeared fifty portals of bronze, secured with as many fastenings of iron. A funereal gloom prevailed over the whole scene. Here, upon two beds of incorruptible cedar, lay recumbent the fleshless forms of the preadamite kings, who had been monarchs of the whole earth. They still possessed enough of life to be conscious of their deplorable condition. Their eyes retained a melancholy motion: they regarded one another with looks of the deepest dejection; each holding his right hand motionless, on his heart. At their feet were inscribed the events of their several reigns, their power, their pride, and their crimes; Soliman Daki; and Soliman, called Gian Ben Gian, who, after having chained up the dives in the dark caverns of Kaf, became so presumptuous as to doubt of the Supreme Power. All these maintained great state; though not to be compared with the eminence of Soli-

---

1 Aherman, *Ahriman*: ancient Persian principle of evil, opposed to the principle of good, Ormozd. Greeks and Latins call them Arimanius and Oromazdes when explaining the doctrine of Zoroaster touching the two principles. [*D'Herbelot*]
2 Argenk, *Arzang*: a dive who reigned in the mountains of Kaf. His gallery contains the statues of 72 pre-adamite Solimans. [*D'Herbelot*]

man Ben Daoud.[1] This king, so renowned for his wisdom, was on the loftiest elevation; and placed immediately under the dome. He appeared to possess more animation than the rest. Though, from time to time, he laboured with profound sighs; and, like his companions, kept his right hand on his heart; yet his countenance was more composed, and he seemed to be listening to the sullen roar of a cataract visible in part through one of the grated portals. This was the only sound that intruded on the silence of these doleful mansions. A range of brazen vases surrounded the elevation. "Remove the covers from these cabalistic depositaries," said the Giaour to Vathek; "and avail thyself of the talismans which will break asunder all these gates of bronze; and not only render thee master of the treasures contained within them, but also of the spirits by which they are guarded."

The Caliph, whom this ominous preliminary had entirely disconcerted, approached the vases with faltering footsteps; and was ready to sink with terror when he heard the groans of Soliman. As he proceeded, a voice from the livid lips of the prophet articulated these words: "In my life-time, I filled a magnificent throne; having, on my right hand, twelve thousand seats of gold, where the patriarchs and the prophets heard my doctrines; on my left, the sages and doctors, upon as many thrones of silver, were present at all my decisions. Whilst I thus administered justice to innumerable multitudes, the birds of the air, hovering over me, served as a canopy against the rays of the sun. My people flourished; and my palace rose to the clouds. I erected a temple to the Most High, which was the wonder of the universe: but, I basely suffered myself to be seduced by the love of women, and a curiosity that could not be restrained by sublunary things. I listened to the counsels of Aherman, and the daughter of Pharaoh; and adored fire, and the hosts of heaven. I forsook the holy city, and commanded the Genii to rear the stupendous palace of Istakhar, and the terrace of the watch towers; each of which was consecrated to a star. There, for a while, I enjoyed myself in the zenith of glory and pleasure. Not

---

1 Soliman Ben Daoud: Based on the biblical Solomon, son of David, Beckford creates a fictional adaptation of this character and makes him a convert to Zoroaster.

only men, but supernatural beings were subject also to my will. I began to think, as these unhappy monarchs around had already thought, that the vengeance of Heaven was asleep; when, at once, the thunder burst my structures asunder, and precipitated me hither: where, however, I do not remain, like the other inhabitants, totally destitute of hope; for, an angel of light hath revealed that in consideration of the piety of my early youth, my woes shall come to an end, when this cataract shall forever cease to flow. Till then I am in torments, ineffable torments! an unrelenting fire preys at my heart."

Having uttered this exclamation, Soliman raised his hands towards heaven, in token of supplication; and the Caliph discerned through his bosom, which was transparent as crystal, his heart enveloped in flames. At a sight so full of horror, Nouronihar fell back, like one petrified, into the arms of Vathek, who cried out with a convulsive sob; "O Giaour! whither hast thou brought us! Allow us to depart, and I will relinquish all thou hast promised. O Mahomet! remains there no more mercy!" – "None! none!" replied the malicious dive. "Know, miserable prince! thou art now in the abode of vengeance and despair. Thy heart, also, will be kindled like those of the other votaries of Eblis. A few days are allotted thee previous to this fatal period: employ them as thou wilt; recline on these heaps of gold; command the infernal potentates; range, at thy pleasure, through these immense subterranean domains: no barrier shall be shut against thee. As for me, I have fulfilled my mission: I now leave thee to thyself." At these words he vanished.

The Caliph and Nouronihar remained in the most abject affliction. Their tears were unable to flow, and scarcely could they support themselves. At length, taking each other, despondingly, by the hand they went faltering from this fatal hall; indifferent which way they turned their steps. Every portal opened at their approach. The dives fell prostrate before them. Every reservoir of riches was disclosed to their view: but they no longer felt the incentives of curiosity, of pride, or avarice. With like apathy they heard the chorus of Genii, and saw the stately banquets prepared to regale them. They went wandering on, from chamber to chamber; hall to hall; and gallery to gallery; all without bounds or limit; all distinguishable by the same louring gloom; all adorned with the same awful grandeur; all traversed by persons in search of repose and consolation; but, who sought them in vain; for every one carried within him a heart tormented in flames. Shunned by these various sufferers, who seemed by their looks to be upbraiding the partners of their guilt, they withdrew from them to wait, in direful suspense, the moment which should render them to each other the like objects of terror.

"What!" exclaimed Nouronihar; "will the time come when I shall snatch my hand from thine!" – "Ah!" said Vathek, "and shall my eyes ever cease to drink from thine long draughts of enjoyment! Shall the moments of our reciprocal ecstasies be reflected on with horror! It was not thou that broughtest me hither; the principles by which Carathis perverted my youth, have been the sole cause of my perdition! it is but right she should have her share of it." Having given vent to these painful expressions, he called to an afrit, who was stirring up one of the braziers, and bade him fetch the Princess Carathis from the palace of Samarah.

After issuing these orders, the Caliph and Nouronihar continued walking amidst the silent crowd, till they heard voices at the end of the gallery. Presuming them to proceed from some unhappy beings, who, like themselves, were awaiting their final doom; they followed the sound, and found it to come from a small square chamber, where they discovered, sitting on sofas, four young men, of goodly figure, and a lovely female, who were holding a melancholy conversation by the glimmering of a lonely lamp. Each had a gloomy and forlorn air; and two of them were embracing each other with great tenderness. On seeing the Caliph and the daughter of Fakreddin enter, they arose, saluted, and made room for them. Then he who appeared the most considerable[1] of the group, addressed himself thus to Vathek: – "Strangers! who doubtless are in the same state of suspense with ourselves, as you do not yet bear your

---

1   most considerable: Alasi, King of Kharezme, is the highest ranking of the narrators of *The Episodes*. His narrative is the first episode.

hand on your heart, if you are come hither to pass the interval allotted, previous to the infliction of our common punishment, condescend to relate the adventures that have brought you to this fatal place; and we, in return, will acquaint you with ours, which deserve but too well to be heard. To trace back our crimes to their source, though we are not permitted to repent, is the only employment suited to wretches like us!"

The Caliph and Nouronihar assented to the proposal; and Vathek began, not without tears and lamentations, a sincere recital of every circumstance that had passed. When the afflicting narrative was closed, the young man, who first addressed him, began in the following manner:[1] – "The history of the princes and friends, Alasi and Firouz, confined in the palace of subterraneous fire." The next was: – "The history of Prince Barkiarokh, confined in the palace of subterraneous fire." Then: "The history of Prince Kalilah and Princess Zulkais, confined in the palace of subterraneous fire." The third prince had reached the midst of his adventures, when a sudden noise interrupted him, which caused the vault to tremble and to open.

Immediately a cloud descended, which gradually dissipating, discovered Carathis on the back of an afrit, who grievously complained of his burden. She, instantly springing to the ground, advanced towards her son, and said, "What dost thou here, in this little square chamber? As the dives are become subject to thy beck, I expected to have found thee on the throne of the pre-adamite kings."

"Execrable woman!" answered the Caliph; "cursed be the day thou gavest me birth! Go, follow this afrit; let him conduct thee to the hall of the Prophet Soliman: there thou wilt learn to what these palaces are destined, and how much I ought to abhor the impious knowledge thou hast taught me."

"Has the height of power, to which thou art arrived, turned thy brain?" answered Carathis: "but I ask no more than permission to shew my respect for Soliman the prophet. It is, how-

---

1 Apparently Beckford intended *The Episodes* to be inserted at this point. It does no damage to continuity, however, to bring *Vathek* uninterrupted to its sublime ending and then to supply *The Episodes*.

ever, proper thou shouldest know that (as the afrit has informed me neither of us shall return to Samarah) I requested his permission to arrange my affairs; and he politely consented. Availing myself, therefore, of the few moments allowed me, I set fire to the tower, and consumed in it the mutes, negresses, and serpents, which have rendered me so much good service: nor should I have been less kind to Morakanabad, had he not prevented me, by deserting at last to thy brother. As for Bababalouk, who had the folly to return to Samarah, to provide husbands for thy wives, I undoubtedly would have put him to the torture; but being in a hurry, I only hung him, after having decoyed him in a snare, with thy wives: whom I buried alive by the help of my negresses; who thus spent their last moments greatly to their satisfaction. With respect to Dilara, who ever stood high in my favour, she hath evinced the greatness of her mind, by fixing herself near, in the service of one of the magi; and, I think, will soon be one of our society."

Vathek, too much cast down to express the indignation excited by such a discourse, ordered the afrit to remove Carathis from his presence, and continued immersed in thoughts which his companions durst not disturb.

Carathis, however, eagerly entered the dome of Soliman, and without regarding in the least the groans of the prophet, undauntedly removed the covers of the vases, and violently seized on the talismans. Then, with a voice more loud than had hitherto been heard within these mansions, she compelled the dives to disclose to her the most secret treasures, the most profound stores, which the afrit himself had not seen. She passed, by rapid descents, known only to Eblis and his most favoured potentates; and thus penetrated the very entrails of the earth, where breathes the sansar, or the icy wind of death. Nothing appalled her dauntless soul. She perceived, however, in all the inmates who bore their hands on their heart, a little singularity, not much to her taste.

As she was emerging from one of the abysses, Eblis stood forth to her view; but notwithstanding he displayed the full effulgence of his infernal majesty, she preserved her countenance unaltered; and even paid her compliments with considerable firmness.

This superb monarch thus answered: "Princess, whose knowledge, and whose crimes, have merited a conspicuous rank in my empire; thou dost well to avail thyself of the leisure that remains: for, the flames and torments, which are ready to seize on thy heart, will not fail to provide thee soon with full employment." He said, and was lost in the curtains of his tabernacle.

Carathis paused for a moment with surprise; but resolved to follow the advice of Eblis, she assembled all the choirs of genii, and all the dives, to pay her homage. Thus marched she, in triumph, through a vapour of perfumes, amidst the acclamations of all the malignant spirits; with most of whom she had formed a previous acquaintance. She even attempted to dethrone one of the Solimans, for the purpose of usurping his place; when a voice, proceeding from the abyss of death, proclaimed: "All is accomplished!" Instantaneously, the haughty forehead of the intrepid princess became corrugated with agony: she uttered a tremendous yell; and fixed, no more to be withdrawn, her right hand upon her heart, which was become a receptacle of eternal fire.

In this delirium, forgetting all ambitious projects, and her thirst for that knowledge which should ever be hidden from mortals, she overturned the offerings of the genii; and, having execrated the hour she was begotten and the womb that had borne her, glanced off in a rapid whirl that rendered her invisible, and continued to revolve without intermission.

Almost at the same instant, the same voice announced to the Caliph, Nouronihar, the four princes, and the princess, the awful, and irrevocable decree. Their hearts immediately took fire, and they, at once, lost the most precious gift of heaven: – HOPE. These unhappy beings recoiled, with looks of the most furious distraction. Vathek beheld in the eyes of Nouronihar nothing but rage and vengeance; nor could she discern aught in his, but aversion and despair. The two princes who were friends, and, till that moment, had preserved their attachment, shrunk back, gnashing their teeth with mutual and unchange-able hatred. Kalilah and his sister made reciprocal gestures of imprecation; all testified their horror for each other by the most ghastly convulsions, and screams that could not be smothered. All severally plunged themselves into the accursed multitude, there to wander in an eternity of unabating anguish.

Such was, and such should be, the punishment of unre-strained passions and atrocious deeds! Such shall be, the chas-tisement of that blind curiosity, which would transgress those bounds the wisdom of the Creator has prescribed to human knowledge; and such the dreadful disappointment of that rest-less ambition, which, aiming at discoveries reserved for beings of a supernatural order, perceives not, through its infatuated pride, that the condition of man upon earth is to be – humble and ignorant.

Thus the Caliph Vathek, who, for the sake of empty pomp and forbidden power, had sullied himself with a thousand crimes, became a prey to grief without end, and remorse with-out mitigation: whilst the humble, the despised Gulchenrouz passed whole ages in undisturbed tranquillity, and in the pure happiness of childhood.

THE EPISODES OF VATHEK

THE HISTORY OF THE TWO PRINCES
AND FRIENDS, ALASI AND FIROUZ

translated by Kenneth W. Graham

I REIGNED in Kharezme[1] and would not have exchanged my kingdom, circumscribed as it was, for the huge empire of Caliph Vathek. No, it was not ambition that brought me into this dismal place. My crimes had a more comely cause. Alas, this heart, which will soon burn in the fires of divine vengeance, throbbed with tenderness and breathed only for sensual delights. The sweet sentiments of friendship glided eas-ily into a soul like mine. They invaded it entirely and made it like the soul of my friend, whose passions were violent, impetuous, and strange. It is then to this friend, whom you see here with me, that I owe the fate for which I tremble in advance; and I tremble, not so much because the fate is ghastly but because I fear that I will have to reproach him for that fate, him in whose presence I find happiness even in this terrible abode.

I was only eighteen when I ascended the throne. Several hours before his death, the King, my father, bade me approach his bedside.

"My son," he said, "I have arranged for you to receive excellent instruction from skilled masters. They tell me that you have profited from your lessons and I am happy to believe them. I know, myself, that you excel in music and dance with much grace and lightness. These talents are much admired by my subjects but I doubt that they are sufficient to make you a good ruler. You lack neither wit nor judgment; use them to suppress your desires when they draw you too much toward frivolous designs that are not without danger. The duties of a sovereign take the greater part of his time. Alas, I have never had enough to fulfill them in their entirety."

---

1   Kharezme, *Kharazm*: A province of the Khalifate on the Oxus River and extending to the Aral Sea; present-day Turkmenistan makes up much of the province. [*Islam2* IV, 1060]

The Queen, my mother, was there when these words were spoken. She saw that they disconcerted me and that I hung my head without answering. To rescue me from my predicament, she said to the King, "Let your Majesty be reassured about Alasi. His innate kindness will be preserved by the very arts whose effects you fear. By bringing sweetness to his soul, they will protect him against youthful impulsiveness and make him beloved of his subjects and the source of their happiness."

"May Heaven make it so," replied my father, who was in no condition to argue, "but I never believed that music and dance could close the heart to passion except that the one excites the soul and the other the body, something which is not at all desirable. As a precaution, send for, without delay, Roudabah, Princess of Ghilan,[1] who has been promised to me for Alasi; let him marry her as soon as she arrives. These are my last wishes. Without believing that you are mistaken in your hopes, I have good reason to wish my son attached to a woman who combines wisdom and courage of spirit with beauty."

In fact, my mother was not at all mistaken. When poetry and music plunged me in tender melancholy, I treated my people with increased attentiveness and affability. My taste was fastidious, exquisite, my pleasures refined; but through a goodness of soul rare in a sovereign, I did not want to please myself at the expense of my subjects. I hoped that they would be as happy as I. I encouraged extravagance in the rich to make the poor more comfortable and to that end I put on elaborate festivities which usually tired me to death and frustrated my penchant for solitude.

After such disturbances, I did not fail to seek relaxation and peace in a palace situated in the midst of a forest inhabited by wild but harmless animals, whose lot I often envied. In this place I was protected less by the few slaves who served me than by the love of my subjects. Here had been assembled all that a voluptuous heart could cherish, and I savoured everything with exquisite pleasure. I had some trees felled to form a little clear-

---

1 Ghilan, *Gilan*: A province of the Khalifate extending along the south-west shore of the Caspian Sea. It had only two considerable cities: Rasht or Rachut, on the sea, and Lakshan, also known as Ghilan, situated inland. [*D'Herbelot, Islam2* II, 1111]

ing and round it flowed a stream with waters as clear as those of Rocnabad.[1]

In the midst of this clearing I arranged the construction of four pavilions which, by their differing aspects, formed in turn a refuge against the discomforts of each successive season. The rest of the site was a parterre[2] interspersed with flowers, varied by bowers of scented shrubs, and watered by a hundred fountains of jasper.[3]

From this place, which resembled the full moon shining in the dark blue of the sky, I was often drawn into the gloomy depths of the surrounding woods to admire and to dream.

One day, stretched out on the moss caressing a young deer that with me was tame, I heard, not far away, the sound of a horse's gallop, and soon after appeared a rider unknown to me. His dress was outlandish, his countenance fierce, his eye haggard. But he did not hold my attention for long. A young boy, more beautiful than the morning star, drew my gaze entirely. The stranger held the lad clasped against his chest and seemed anxious to prevent him from calling out. Enraged at what I took to be an act of violence, I leapt up and barred the stranger's way, my glistening sabre flashing toward his eyes.

"Stop, wretch," I cried, "do you dare commit such a crime in the sight of the King of Kharezme?"

Hardly had I spoken these words when the stranger sprang to the ground, without relinquishing his precious charge, and saluting me with every mark of respect, said, "Prince Alasi, it is you that I seek. I wish to entrust to you a priceless treasure. Filanshaw,[4] King of Shirvan,[5] the intimate friend of the King your father, is reduced to dire extremity. His rebellious subjects hold him besieged in his palace at Samakhié.[6] The troops of

---

1   Rocnabad: a brook that flows close to the city of Schiraz in the province of Fars.
2   parterre: a level space usually occupied by patterned arrangements of flower-beds.
3   jasper: a kind of stone speckled with colours and precious in ancient times; in the most valued kinds, green predominates.
4   Filanshaw, *Filanshow*: Ruler of Shirwan during the reign of Vathek.
5   Shirvan, *Shirwan*: A province in Persia extending to the western shore of the Caspian Sea, to the north and west of Ghilan. It includes, roughly, present day Azerbaijan. Vathek added the province to his empire. [D'Herbelot, *Islam2* VII, 382]
6   Samakhié: *Schamakie* was the capital of *Shirwan*; it is present day Shemakha in Daghestan.

the Caliph Vathek support them in their revolt. They have sworn to kill their sovereign. Filanshaw accepts undaunted the decrees of fate so far as he himself is concerned, but anxious, if that be yet possible, to save alive his only son, the lovely child whom you see here, he has commanded me to place him in your hands. Hide this pearl of incomparable price in your bosom; suffer its origin, the shell in which it was formed, to remain unknown, until such time as the years bring security. And so farewell. I fear pursuit. Prince Firouz[1] will himself tell you all else that you may wish to know."

I had, while he was speaking, opened my arms to Firouz, and Firouz had sprung into them. We held one another, embracing with a tenderness that seemed to fill the stranger with joy. He mounted his horse and was gone in a moment.

"Take me away from here, my dear prince," said Firouz then in a voice softer than the sound of a celestial lute, "now indeed do I fear to fall into the hands of my persecutors. Ah! would they tear me from the side of the friend Heaven has given me – the friend toward whom my whole heart gives one bound?"

"No, masterpiece of nature," I cried, "nothing shall tear you from my side. My lands, my subjects, my very life will be used for your protection. But why hide your birth in a place where nothing can harm you?"

"It must be so, most generous defender," replied Firouz, "my father's foes have sworn to extirpate his race. They would brave death itself in obedience to their oath; they would stab me in your very presence if I were recognized. The Magus,[2] who brought me here and has guarded me through my infancy, will do all he can to persuade them I am no longer alive. Find someone to father me – it matters not whom – I shall have no other pride save that of loving you, and deserving that you should love me in return."

---

1 Firouz, *Firuz*: Persian word for the third day of the five added at the end of the solar year. It signifies *victorious* and *triumphant*. [*D'Herbelot*]

2 magus, magi: Priests of the Zoroastrian faith. The religion of Zoroaster associates light with the good principle and involves worship in temples of fire. This ancient Persian religion was fiercely suppressed with the rise of Islam. Some of the magi driven out of Persia went to India where they are called Parsi. Beckford gives Zoroastrianism a demonic bent that is not historical.

Thus speaking, we came to my summer pavilion; it was hung with grey silk on which branches of flowering thorn were lightly patterned in silver matte. Firouz appeared enchanted with the place.

"That colour is so cleverly contrived to moderate the sun's rays! The vases of agate and of topaz match it perfectly! How our tastes agree! But," he continued, clasping me tightly, "please show me the other three pavilions; give me, if it pleases you, a thousand tokens of the sweet sympathy that links us."

I was so delighted with the enthusiasm of this loving child, who would taste of no refreshments until I had satisfied his admiring curiosity, that I led him immediately to my other pavilions. The rose coverings that I had conceived for the autumn pavilion, the green for the spring, the orange for the winter pavilion, all seemed to him well contrived, their several decors well matched. Everything had his approval; his accurate comments and modest conclusions expressed a tenderness for me.

I was overcome with pleasure and amazement. "Is this not," I said to myself, "a conjuring trick that some genie,[1] enemy of my repose, has contrived? Perhaps this charming phantom is going to disappear before my eyes and abandon this heart, which as yet has loved no one, to the bitterness of a pointless emotion."

It seemed that Firouz read my thoughts: at least, he spared no effort to dispel my fears and to make me taste the true sweetness of a reciprocal friendship. Although he was hardly thirteen, his judgment was as developed as mine. What am I saying, companions in misfortune! Is this fearful setting a place for flattery? No. My friend will pardon me if I say that at his tender age, he had already acquired all the perversity of heart and soul that a vicious education can provide. And yet, because an apparent simplicity and an appealing manner concealed these vices, the first steps that I took toward an attachment that nothing has ever altered, followed a path strewn only with flowers without thorns.

---

1   genie, genii, *jinn*: demons or giants, possessing magical powers, created by God before Adam.

I had already prolonged several times the customary interval I devoted to my seclusion. Its duration, so short to myself, seemed long to my people. A return to Zerbend became imperative. Some days before our departure, I caused a shepherd living in the neighbourhood of my retreat to be brought before me, and commanded him, on pain of death if he divulged our secret, to acknowledge Firouz as his son. The precaution seemed to reassure my little friend. His vivacity and natural gaiety intensified.

The day before our departure, we went for a walk in the forest. My beloved deer, that Firouz had petted hundreds of times, bounded in front of us.

"What a pretty animal!" I said. "How I love it."

"You love it!" cried Firouz. "A deer shares your heart with me! It will die."

Saying these words he drove his dagger into the heart of the poor deer which fell at my feet with a reproachful look for not having come to its defense.

Firouz had committed this cruel act so suddenly that I had not time to stop him. He appeared to enjoy my surprise, my anguish, and my indignation. For several moments his manner was scornful and irritated. Then, taking an aggrieved tone, he said to me, "King of Kharezme, do not weep useless tears. Avenge your beloved. Here is the blade stained with her blood! Here is my breast that I bare for you. Pierce it! Dispel from my heart your own image, or out of pure shame of cherishing it still, I will make myself the quarry."

These words, the sight of his heaving chest as white as alabaster, drove me to distraction. My heart was overwhelmed. I took my friend in my arms. I dried his tears, which began to flow abundantly, all falling on my chest. I begged pardon for having distressed him. In a word, he had all the triumph that he could wish. Such was the first test of my blind attachment. I admit that it cost me more than all the others. It heralded an alarming future. But how to prevent it? Against whom should I guard myself? Against a child whom I had vowed to protect, whom I loved more than my life, who had, if possible, more grace than art, and who, by his seductive caresses allowed not one of my reflections the time to mature?

We left for Zerbend where Firouz won the admiration of all eyes and the interest of all hearts. My courtiers, reassured by the low birth that I encouraged them to suppose, did not see him as a dangerous favourite, and the Queen, my mother, charmed by the attentions he paid her, praised him unceasingly.

What happy days I spent with my friend! How they flew! No, happiness is a bird of passage. It has but a single season: it never returns twice, at least not in all its freshness. Firouz's conduct was such that people saw in him only what was amiable. In my heart's intoxication, I reproached myself for the alarm the adventure with the deer had given me. Now I saw no more than a jealousy, flattering to me, which had caused in his sensitive heart a ferocious reaction that would not be repeated.

Given this disposition, I was not a little surprised to see him coming to me, one day, wild and furious. "Prince," said he, "why have you deceived me? If you were not prepared to love me, and me alone, you ought not to have accepted me as your friend. Send me back to the Magus. I do not want to witness your transports over the Princess Roudabah, whom we are awaiting."

This new outburst surprised me, but I did not have the strength to be angry. To calm my friend down, I excused myself when I should have rebuked him vigorously. I explained that the orders of my father made it impossible to send Roudabah back. I entreated him not to leave me and assured him that he would always be for me the object of my most cherished affections.

"If only," he cried, drying several tears that he tried to hold back, "I were sharing your affections with a friend worthy of you! But with a woman! Oh! It is a hundred times worse than the deer. This sex is lower than a beast for malice: without faith, without virtue, dissembling, unfaithful, made for man's misfortune. The Magus told me. You will be tormented, and I will die of sorrow to see you suffer."

Such sentiments could make no great impression on me:

they were too commonplace. But the tears of my beloved were irresistible. In truth, I did not promise him never to wed Roudabah, but I consoled him with the assurance that she would not be coming soon, and when she arrived we would test her character before proceeding with the engagement that he feared for my sake.

Firouz hardly ever left me, neither days nor nights. He had, nevertheless, one of the most pleasant apartments in my palace, his own servants, and all the power of limitless favour. I had provided him with instructors – whom he exasperated; with superb horses – which he rode to death; and with slaves – whom he ill-treated without mercy. But all this was hidden from me, and had I become aware, it would have made no difference.

A moullah,[1] esteemed for his age and piety, was commissioned to explain to him the wholesome moral teachings of the Koran[2] and caused him to read and learn by heart its sacred verses; of all tasks, this was the most irksome to the son of Filanshaw. But I attributed his distaste to any cause but the true one. He had not dared to teach me the sentiments that the Magus had inspired in him.

One day, when I had spent more than two long hours without seeing Firouz, I went to look for him, and found him in a large hall, dancing around an ass whom he made to caper with him. "Ah, my dear prince," cried he, running up to me open-armed; "you have before you the very strangest spectacle in the world. My moullah is transformed into an ass – the king of asses, since he talks even as he talked before!"

"What do you mean?" cried I; "what game are you playing now?"

"It's not a game," replied the moullah, contained in the form of this low animal. "I am as I appear, and I entreat your Majesty to find no evil in what I am doing."

At these words I stood confounded. I doubted that it was truly the voice of the moullah, and almost believed that it was a

---

1   moullah, *molla*: A general term of respect, normally applied to clergy and learned men. [*Islam2* VII, 221]
2   Koran, *Qu'ran*: The holy book of Islam.

real donkey which, by some miracle, had been endowed with the gift of speech. Vainly did I ask Firouz for an explanation. He only laughed immoderately and replied, "Ask the donkey."

Finally, my patience quite exhausted, I was about to order that the ass be gutted or the voice machine demolished, when Firouz assumed his most serious air, and said: "Sire, you will, I hope, forgive the innocent artifice by which I have endeavoured to demonstrate how much you, and other princes, are deceived as to the character of the people about them. This moullah has, doubtless, been presented to you as a man of very superior merit; and, as such, you have appointed him to act as teacher to your friend and ward. Well! be it known to you that, in order to obtain one of my most hideous Negro women, with whom he is madly in love, he has consented to remain three days thus ridiculously accoutred, and so to be a universal laughing-stock. And, indeed, you must agree that he presents the form and figure of an ass in a highly satisfactory manner, and that his speech does no discredit to the performance."

I asked the moullah if what Firouz said was true.

"Not quite," he replied, "the girl he is to give me, though black as night, is beautiful as day; the oil that gives lustre to her charms is scented with orange-flowers; her voice has the bitter-sweet of the pomegranate; when she toys with my beard, her fingers, prickly like thistles, titillate my very heart! Ah! so that she may be mine, suffer me, suffer me to remain for three days in the form and figure of an ass!"

"Die in that form, wretch," I cried with an indignation I could not contain, "and let me never hear speak of thee again."

I retired as I spoke those words, casting at Firouz looks of a kind to which he was in no way accustomed.

The rest of the day I spent in reflecting on Firouz's ill-nature, and the infamous conduct of the moullah; but, when evening came, I thought only of again seeing my friend. I had him summoned. He came at once, timid and affectionate. "Dear prince," said he, "you don't know what grief I have felt all day at the thought that you seemed angry with me. In order to obtain forgiveness, I have lost not a moment in executing your commands. The ass is dead and buried. You will never hear speak of him again."

"This is another of your ill-timed jests," I exclaimed. "Do you ask me to believe that the moullah, who spoke with such vigour this morning, is dead to-night?"

"He is, and by your command," replied Firouz. "One of my Negro slaves, whose mistress he wished to appropriate, despatched him, and he was buried without ceremony, like the donkey he was."

"This is really too much!" cried I. "What! Do you think you can, with impunity, assassinate a man whose head you yourself had turned?"

"I executed your orders," he rejoined. "I executed them to the letter. Surely the loss of so vile a creature is not to be regretted. Farewell, I go to weep over my own imprudence, and the fragility of your affections – which the least little event can shatter."

He was about to retire. I stopped him; I took him in my arms; I overwhelmed him with caresses. We had dinner; we continued our debauch well into the night, and I was again weak enough to laugh at all his jokes and jibes about his donkey.

The public did not take the death of the moullah so lightly. It was said that Firouz, in derision of the faith of the true believers, had administered some philtre[1] to the holy man, causing him to go mad. They detested his cruelty; they accused me of inexcusable weakness for a child whose low birth had given him low inclinations. The Queen, my mother, felt herself bound to bring these mutterings of discontent to my attention. She spoke of them openly, in front of Firouz so as to moderate his arrogance, if that were possible, and made to us both sensible and affectionate reprimands, but for which my friend never forgave her.

He was specially outraged by the contempt heaped upon him because of the humble birth we had imagined for him, and told me it was absolutely necessary his true parentage should be disclosed. I represented the dangers involved, dangers he had himself set before me in such strong terms, and entreated him

---

1 philtre: a love potion.

to wait at least for the return of the envoys I had sent to Shirvan. But he was too impatient to wait, and, in order to overcome my objections, bethought himself of a device which I could certainly never have foreseen.

One morning, when we were about to go hunting, he pretended sickness. I wished to remain by him; but he urged me not to stay, assuring me that, with a little rest, I should find him, on my return, in a fit condition to share with me in such amusements as would be a pleasant relaxation after the fatigues of the day – amusements that he would himself devise.

Accordingly, I did find on my return a superb collation, prepared and served in a little grove of trees and decked and illumined after a fashion all the prince's own – in other words, with the utmost taste and refinement. We sat under a canopy formed of the intertwining branches of orange trees and honeysuckle. The petals of a thousand flowers, strewn at our feet, formed a rich carpet. Crystal vases in all colours were arranged around us, reflecting the light of small aromatic lamps which had been hung with great artistry from the trees, and choirs of musicians were so placed as to charm our ears without interrupting our discourse.

Never was evening more delicious; never had Firouz shown himself more gay, more amiable. He had dismissed my attendants. He wanted, he said, to serve me himself. He carried out the duties attentively and I responded with enchantment. He played only too well the role of cupbearer, but his pleasant mirth enlivened me more than the wine. When he perceived that my head was in a whirl of pleasant bewilderment, he knelt before me on one knee, and, taking both my hands in his, said: "Dear Alasi, I had forgotten to ask you to forgive a wretch who has deserved death."

"Speak, beloved," I replied, clasping him to my breast; "you know that from me you have but to ask in order to obtain; and, besides, I should be pleased indeed to find your heart sensible to compassion."

"The matter stands thus," rejoined Firouz. "I was to-day in my apartment, surrounded by your flatterers, who at once hate me and seek to win my favour, when the shepherd, my supposed father, came in, open-armed, to embrace me. At that moment the blood of Filanshaw surged rebellion in my heart. 'Hence, churl,' said I to the shepherd, 'go and stifle thy misbegotten brats with thy clumsy caresses! Wouldst thou have the unblushing effrontery to maintain that I am thy son?' 'That I am bound to do so, you very well know,' he replied firmly. 'I will maintain it with my life.' This reply of his was, no doubt, in strict accordance with his duty; but, curious to see how far we can really depend on those to whom we entrust our secrets, I ordered the man, who seemed so resolute, to receive the bastinado.[1] He endured it but a short time – he revealed all. After your express orders, and the punishment with which you threatened him, he is no doubt worthy of death; but I pray you forgive him."

"The test was a little severe," I stammered. "You are always cruel, but always far too kind."

"It is true," he replied, putting his arms around me, "I do not endure mankind as patiently as you do. I find them false to their protestations, flighty in their feelings and so fragile in their vows that I can hardly bear them. Why are we two not alone in the world? We suffice, one for the other, and the earth, swarming with the vile and wretched, might boast itself inhabited by two close friends, faithful and fortunate."

It was thus that Firouz brought me to tolerate this new proof of the essential badness of his heart. The rest of the night passed as if we were really alone in the world. I learned on the morrow that the son of Filanshaw had not told me the whole story. It was by his own orders, and at his suggestion, indirectly conveyed, that the shepherd had come into his presence, and accosted him as he had done; I learned that the poor bumpkin had the fortitude to endure his punishment almost unto death before infringing my commands. I sent the unhappy creature a sum of money, but I made no reproach to Firouz. It was impossible for me to adopt for a moment a severe tone with him, and I lacked the strength to resist the torrent which pulled me along.

---

1 bastinado: To beat the soles of the feet with a stick.

As this scene had filled all my court with indignation, and seemed to reflect more blame on Firouz than he actually deserved, I publicly, and with some pomp, declared his real birth, and the reasons why it had been hidden. I also thenceforward surrounded him with guards and was not a little surprised to see that those who had hitherto been most bitter against him were now all eagerness to do him service. This made me mistrust somewhat their real intentions, but Firouz reassured me: "Don't take unnecessary alarm, my dear friend," said he, laughing; "you can entrust the care of my person to these people just as safely as to their fellows; their affection changed as my birth changed. I am now no longer the sly and cruel little shepherd lad; I am a great prince, good and humane of disposition. I could have the heads of five or six of them cut off daily to play bowls, and the rest would continue to sing my praises while trusting to be more fortunate than their companions."

Such speeches – and I knew only too well how true they were! – served insensibly to harden my heart. It is a great evil to look upon mankind with a too clear vision. You seem to be living among wild beasts, and you become a wild beast yourself. I had feared that, in his new rank, Firouz would yield more freely than before to his evil bent; but in this I was mistaken. He showed himself noble in manner and sensible in conduct, and his bearing toward great and small was affable and obliging. In short, he completely obliterated the bad impression produced by his former practices.

These days of quiet and pleasure lasted till the arrival of Roudabah. I was with Firouz when the news was brought and I tremble even yet to remember his reactions. A deathly pallor overspread his countenance, his movements became convulsive, and at last he fell in my arms, senseless. I carried him myself to the sofa. I wept immoderately; my burning tears, better than any other comfort, returned him to his senses. He tried to push me away and said to me in a weak and trembling voice: "Ah, cruel friend; let me die."

Then, entirely beside myself, I swore to him, making the most horrible threats against myself in case I violated my vow, not to marry Roudabah unless he consented and to treat her, after having married her, only as he would instruct me himself. He listened to me avidly and the life returned to his beautiful eyes.

During these moments, so bitter, yet altogether so delicious, and these outpourings of an affection so perfectly mutual, the Princess of Ghilan, who had in vain slowed her progress to give me time to go to meet her, had finally been forced to arrive. She was at the palace of the Queen, my mother. Firouz wanted to follow me there. I tried to explain that Roudabah would find it strange that I would bring someone with me. He said that he would die of anxiety if I went without him, and that was enough to convince me. On our way, I hoped to be able to reassure Firouz that the Princess of Ghilan was not beautiful.

Nevertheless, she was beautiful, but of a beauty that inspired awe rather than desire; very tall, of majestic bearing, her whole aspect proud and austere. Her long hair, black as ebony, enhanced the whiteness of her complexion, and from her eyes, of the same hue, darted glances more imposing than seductive. Her mouth, though graceful in its lines, had no inviting smile, and when her coral lips opened, the words were words of sense indeed, but very rarely moving and persuasive.

Stung, as it seemed, by my want of a lover's ardour, and offended because, contrary to all use and custom, I had come accompanied by my friend, Roudabah no sooner perceived us advancing than she turned to my mother and said; "Which of these two princes is the one to whom I am destined?"

"To both, if you please," replied Firouz unhesitatingly and mockingly, so that I almost burst out laughing. I restrained myself, however, with an effort, and was preparing to find some excuse for my friend's ill manners, when the Princess of Ghilan, after looking me over attentively from head to foot, and casting a disdainful look at Firouz, remarked – always addressing herself to the Queen: "Those who allow an insult to pass unnoticed deserve to be insulted. And you Kali," continued she, turning to the chief of her eunuchs, "make all the necessary preparations for my return to Ghilan this very night."

Saying these words she retired, and my mother was not slow to follow her, only stopping to threaten us with all the calamities we would face once plunged in a war that we had just brought upon ourselves by offending Roudabah. But we were at that moment in no humour for alarm.

As soon as we found ourselves alone we laughed as if to outdo each other at the scene that had just taken place. "Is that a woman?" asked Firouz. "No, it is the ghost of Roostum,[1] or of Zalzar[2] – the soul of these famous warriors, Roudabah's ancestors, has seized possession of that long figure that we are asked to look upon as hers. Oh, my dear Alasi, prepare yourself for a far different combat than what one expects on a normal wedding-day. Polish your sabre; you will need it to defend your life if you do not in all things exactly conform to all the formalities which your Amazon believes her due and which will be dictated to you in silver tones by the all-powerful Kali."

"Do you not fear for the loss of my heart?" I asked Firouz.

"Oh! I fear nothing at all," he replied; "you cannot love Roudabah for you have loved me. We are so different, she and I. I have the manner of a lamb, though I am not precisely that. She is a lioness in every sense. Besides, if she wishes to devour us, she will begin with me and I will have no regrets at all to bestow on you."

We chatted in this tone until the Queen's return interrupted us. She had nearly appeased Roudabah and wished me to complete her task. Her representations, dictated by a mother's love, were strong and urgent, and I yielded to them, but before following her, I said to my dear friend in a low voice that nothing would make me forget my pledge.

The jests that we had directed at Roudabah returned to my mind when I approached her, but I found them insipid as soon as she spoke. Reason has a power over the human spirit which the passions can never entirely remove. I found in the Princess

---

1   Roostum, *Rustam*: A great Persian hero and general, celebrated as a model of strength and courage. He killed the dive Argenk, or *Arzang*. [*Richardson* 132, 146]

2   Zāl, Zāl-zar: According to the *Shah-nama*, he was the son of Persian king-hero, Sām. He was brought up by Simorgh and, at maturity, returned to his father and became his heir. He married Princess Rudāba, daughter of Mehrāb, King of Kābol: "all radiance, harmony and delectability." After a difficult pregnancy and assisted by Simorgh, Rudāba gave birth to Roostam. Given her name, Firouz naturally connects Roudabah with these legendary heroes.

of Ghilan all the qualities that my father had mentioned and, moreover, a gentleness that the love she had developed for me doubtless inspired in her. The more I examined her, the more I felt that the affront I would have to give her, covered me with shame.

These thoughts gave me a wistful and dejected air which Firouz detected from the moment he saw me. Immediately, taking an affectionate inflection and embracing me with redoubled tenderness, he said to me, "Don't torment yourself, my dear prince, by useless battles between honour and friendship. I surrender my over-delicate sensitivity to your peace and glory. Heaven preserve me from being a cause that dishonours my friend in the eyes of the world and loses him the trust of his subjects. Marry the Princess of Ghilan; I resolve to share your heart with her. If she takes it from me entirely, I will have but a short time to regret the loss."

I believed at first that Firouz wanted to beguile me. But eventually he persuaded me that he spoke sincerely and wanted himself to organize the celebrations that were to mark the occasion of my marriage.

These preparations took time. I saw Roudabah every day and I never left her without a greater degree in estimation for her. At his entreaty, Firouz accompanied me to several of these visits. She appeared never to recall the insult that he had inflicted on her. She spoke with interest of his plight and offered to see to it that Ghilan's armies would join with mine to help him to secure his hereditary throne, for Filanshaw was dead and the rebels who supported Caliph Vathek asked no more than to throw off his yoke. Firouz for his part displayed ample sensitivity to the kindness of Roudabah. He pointed out her good qualities to me, but I saw how much he was pleased to hear me say: " Well, my reason renders her justice but my heart is not touched. I am able to love only you."

On the day preceding that fixed for the marriage ceremonies, I rose earlier than usual. I was anxious, agitated, for I clearly saw that a sadness which he tried in vain to hide from me, consumed my darling Firouz. I went down alone into the gardens deploring the fate of kings who are obliged ceaselessly to sacrifice themselves to responsibilities that no one would demand of common people. I wandered through the darkest alleys and entered at last into a grotto where the day's light hardly pierced. I chose the blackest shade, so as to dream undisturbed. I had been there but a quarter hour when Amnì, the son of my vizir,[1] came and seated himself at the other end of the grotto. He was on the side where a little light penetrated so he could not see me. I spoke not a word. A moment later I saw the eunuch Kali enter with an air of mystery. He went up to Amnì, "Handsome Amnì," he said to him, "rejoice. You shall have what your heart desires. My mistress, who, as you know, can deceive the most perceptive eyes, will come to this place this night. The first of her love-pledges will be yours; the King of Kharezme will have her second vows tomorrow, which she will violate every time he amuses himself with his insolent favourite."

Amnì kissed the ground in token of submission, clapped his hands three times to express his joy, and gave some money to the eunuch. They left together.

I was about to follow, and wash out the affront in blood; but a moment's reflection arrested this first impulse. I had no love for Roudabah. I was marrying her, with a sense of loathing, only to avoid public censure and out of pity for her. No longer would I make myself unhappy on such grounds. I had only to bring her criminal perfidy into full light, and I should be quit of her, and recover my own freedom with all honour.

These thoughts passed swiftly through my brain. I thanked whatever lucky star had led me just in time to this important discovery, and ran to impart it to Firouz. What was my dismay when, on entering his apartment, I found him lying on the floor, his clothes torn, his beautiful tresses cut, his eyes pouring out torrents of tears. I lacked the strength to utter a word. I fell down next to him and sobbed in turn. My speechless anguish, my agitation, forced him finally to break the silence.

"Calm yourself, generous Alasi! It is my condition that troubles you? Surely it should cause you no surprise; but forget that

---

1   vizir, *wazir.* Director of the central bureaucracy.

you have seen me thus. Notwithstanding these tears, this hair that I have given to the flames because you would not gaze upon it any more, I wish you every happiness with Roudabah – yes, though it should cost me my life!"

"Ah," cried I, "perish a thousand Roudabahs to spare one of those musk-coloured[1] curls which adorned your head, even if they had been as faithful as our Roudabah is perfidious.

"What!" cried Firouz in turn, "Have I heard aright? Are you speaking of the Princess of Ghilan? For pity's sake explain yourself?"

I then told him all that had happened in the grotto, and my determination to blaze abroad to all men the shame of Roudabah. He fully approved my design, and made no effort to hide his joy at the course things were taking. Now he embraced me with rapture; now he regretted the loss of his hair because it pleased me; and yet again he assured me that happiness would make his hair soon grow back. Finally, he spoke and contrived so many extravagances, that if I had suffered real sadness, he would have eliminated it entirely.

We resolved not to reveal our secret to the Queen, my mother, until the time came for taking her with us to surprise Roudabah. Firouz mistrusted women's discretion, and I did not lack reasons for believing his every word on all the defects that he attributed to them. We passed the day together. I sent my excuses to Roudabah that business prevented me from seeing her: I thought she was not worth the trouble that moment of dissimulation had cost me.

"She will count every moment that you squander with me," said Firouz, "and will compensate herself with her handsome Amnì."

"I don't believe it," I said, "although I am resolved to spare Roudabah's life and to content myself with driving her away in disgrace. But Amnì will pay with his blood for his inordinate insolence."

The Queen seemed more astonished than grieved when we went to her apartment and told her what had brought us thith-

---

1   Dark brown or auburn.

er so late. Friendship among women is rarely sincere and never lasting. My mother's had cooled toward Roudabah as mine had appeared to increase. Nevertheless, she had not been able to help respecting her, and never ceased, while following us, to exclaim over this adventure. Firouz, on his part, laughed, and for more reasons than one.

We went down into the garden. A faithful slave, whom I had set to watch the place, came and told us that the two culprits had been in the grotto for some minutes. Immediately we entered, with torches, and in such numbers that those whom we thus surprised must, as one would have thought, fall dead for very shame. They seemed, however, in no wise disconcerted. They held each other in a close embrace and seemed more distressed at being interrupted than embarrassed at being discovered. Their impudence left me speechless. My mother was averting her gaze when Roudabah addressed her.

"What are you doing here, Queen of Kharezme? Your sex must constrain you from rejoicing in my misfortune and you cannot judge the fault that I appear to have committed. You had a husband who loved you alone; the one destined to be mine loves only his Firouz. As Firouz is to Alasi, so my lover is to me. I am Alasi's equal. I may be permitted as well to have a favourite. If all women thought like me, either men would have to change the unjust laws that they have passed, or we would stop nourishing with our milk the tyrants who subjugate us."

Roudabah's brazen discourse made me forget that I had resolved to spare her life. I drew my sword in a fury and thought, with one blow, to send their two wretched heads rolling on to the ground; but my sword clove the empty air alone: they vanished from my sight!

Instantly a cry arose: "The Princess of Ghilan has forced the guard at the entrance to the grotto!" And she appeared before us. "King of Kharezme," she said in clear tones, modest but unabashed, "I am advised that a plot is being hatched in this place against my honour; and I am come to confound my enemies. What is going on here?"

"Fly, wretched creature," said the Queen, "or my son will

repeat the blow you have just evaded by your magic arts."

"I do not fear death," replied Roudabah, not at all disconcerted. "Alasi has made no attempt on my life. If you have been misled by some seeming prodigy, I ask you to tell me what was its nature. I rely on the help that Heaven gives to innocence and dare to flatter myself that I can undeceive you."

Roudabah's proud and noble bearing, her gaze that commanded respect, all served to confound me. I almost doubted the evidence of my eyes and ears, when Firouz exclaimed: "Oh! we must indeed confess that the Princess of Ghilan's memory is of the shortest! We find her in the arms of her beloved Amnì. She holds a conversation with us full of effrontery and disappears with her darling. When, an instant later, it pleases her to return to the scene, she has forgotten entirely all that has taken place."

At these words Roudabah changed colour. The flush died on her cheeks, and left them deadly pale. She turned upon me eyes that were full of tears. "Oh, most unhappy prince!" she said, "I now see the full depth of the abyss yawning at thy feet. The monster dragging thee thitherward will not fail of his prey! The spirits of darkness are at his beck and call. I cannot save thee, and yet I shudder at abandoning thee to thy fate. Thou hast covered me with infamy, but it is thy ruin only that pierces my heart!"

Having thus spoken, Roudabah retired with majestic steps, none daring to stay her.

We stood as if turned to stone, and looked fixedly at one another, unable to speak. "Surely we must all have lost our wits," cried the Queen at last. "What! the cool effrontery of an unworthy sorceress would make us disbelieve the evidence of our eyes and ears! Let her go, and deliver us forever from her hateful presence! It is the best thing that could happen."

I acknowledged the truth of her words; and Firouz, who appeared confused and alarmed, made sincere undertakings never to see her again.

We each took ourselves back to our apartments. My thoughts were so confused and troubled that I did not consider telling Firouz to accompany me to mine, though he did so without my noticing him. I could not suppress a shudder of horror when I found we were alone together. Presentiments sent to us from heaven, you have no effect on corrupted hearts. Firouz threw himself impetuously into my arms. He was seized by a shivering which alarmed me. He sobbed; he cried out. I became frantic. I drew him to me; I sought to reassure and calm him. Finally, when he had captured my complete attention and all my thoughts, he spoke to me.

"Oh, why did you give me shelter? Why did you not leave me to die with my father? I was then but a child; no one could have accused me of being a magician. Is it at this court of yours, and here by your side, that I have learned the art of conjuring up the dives?[1] And yet Roudabah, the wicked Roudabah, has almost persuaded you. Will she not also say I have gained your friendship by some evil charm? You know well enough that the only charm I have used is to cherish you a hundred times more than my own life!"

But why dwell upon the scene; all of you can foresee its inevitable outcome. Like the Caliph Vathek, I had heard the voice of a beneficent spirit, and, like he, I hardened my heart against its saving influence.[2] Roudabah's words were forgotten, the doubts, faint and confused, that I felt for my friend, were replaced by a limitless confidence. That moment was the turning-point that determined my fate.

We heard on the following morning that Roudabah had departed during the night, with all her retinue. I ordered public rejoicings.

A few days afterwards Firouz said to me, before my mother: "You must see, my dear Alasi, that we are going to have a war with the King of Ghilan. He will wish to avenge his daughter who will have ample cunning to persuade him that she is innocent. Forestall him; raise an army; invade Ghilan, and ravage the country: you are the aggrieved party!"

---

1   dives, *diw*. Persian name for spirits of evil and darkness, creatures of Ahriman, the personification of sin. [*Islam2* II, 322]

2   Near Istakhar, a genie offered Vathek one last chance to repent of his crimes; he refused.

My mother agreed with Firouz, and even if she had not, I was left with no resolve other than that of my friend.

We had never been able to find Amnì; I had ordered him sought everywhere, but in vain. His father, who had taken him with him to the court of Ghilan when he proposed to Roudabah on my behalf, had fled, fearing without doubt, that I suspected he had encouraged the criminal amour of his son. The position of vizir was vacant. On the recommendation of Firouz, I gave it to Montaleb, a man proud and enterprising, but inexperienced in state business and incapable of governing well.

All was soon ready for our expedition and we began our march at the head of a numerous host. The fires of courage sparkled in the eyes of Firouz as they did when the famous Asfendiar,[1] glowing with youth and beauty, rode out of his tower for the first time and flew to the aid of his father when a powerful enemy had attacked.

The frontiers of Ghilan were undefended; we ravaged them without difficulty. The ardour with which Firouz caused damage on all sides inflamed his blood. He fell dangerously ill. I camped with my troops and by so doing gave my enemy time to arm themselves. I was absorbed only with my friend: I spent days and nights beside his bed, counting the feverish beats of his heart, observing the alterations of his face. Finally he began to recover but was too feeble for us to resume our march. It was necessary for him to reaccustom himself to exercise, little by little. So we rode our horses each day, without venturing too far from our camp.

One day, when we had extended our ride a little further than usual, we found ourselves in a valley clothed in moss so fresh, watered by a stream so lovely, and surrounded by hills so green, that Firouz insisted on dismounting and resting there. As

---

1 Beckford's allusion to the *Shah-nama*, the great epic of the Persian kings by Ferdowsi, is doubly relevant. Isfendiar was both a great champion and a promoter of fire worship. Defending his father, the King of Persia, against the victorious armies of the King of China, Isfendiar rode out boldly on a powerful horse and in single combat killed a demon [dive or *diw*], the champion of the invading forces. Isfendiar went on to conquer many countries for his father and convert them to the new religion of fire worship.

the valley was long and narrow and as we had a large enough company with us, I could not see any danger in satisfying my friend's wishes. I had them serve us refreshments on the grass, and we ate while conversing on the beauty of the scene.

Firouz ordered our followers to take themselves behind one of the hills. We were alone; it seemed that this charming place revived all his gaiety. He was telling me a thousand uproarious stories when we saw, tripping by not far from us, a doe whiter than snow. Firouz, who did not like animals, let fly an arrow. It hit its target and she fell. We ran to the spot.

A peasant, perceiving us, cried: "What have you done? You have killed the holy woman's doe!"

This exclamation seemed to amuse Firouz. But his mirth was of short duration. An enormous dog, the doe's companion, leapt upon him, dragged him to the ground, held him pinned down with heavy paws, and seemed to be only waiting some master's orders before putting its fangs through his throat. It was a dreadful moment! I dared neither to speak nor attack the dog, for fear of enraging it the more; nor could I attempt to shear off its head: the dog was pressed too closely to my friend for me to risk it.

At last, when I own I was almost terrified to death, I saw approaching a woman, veiled, who forced the dog to relinquish its hold, and then, turning to me, said: "I did not think, King of Kharezme, to find you here, in a place where I had come to bury myself alive. I have just, according to the divine precept, returned good for evil, in saving the life of Firouz. Do not you, on your part, return evil for good by destroying this people, who, far from seeking to avenge my wrongs, are quite ignorant of my misfortune."

As she finished speaking these words she lifted her veil, and disclosed the majestic countenance of Roudabah. Then she turned on her heel, and retired with quick steps, leaving us in a state of inexpressible surprise.

Firouz was the first to recover. "Well," said he, "do you still doubt that Roudabah is not a fearsome magician? What shall we do to protect ourselves against her arts? I know but one remedy: let us surprise her this very night; let us take a band of our trusted followers, and burn her alive in her retreat – which we can discover by skilful inquiry; or else we may resign ourselves to being torn to pieces by the Afrites,[1] who serve her in the shape of savage beasts."

"Shame!" cried I. "Would you thus repay the service she has just done us? Whatever she may be, she has this moment saved you from a cruel death."

"Too credulous prince," rejoined Firouz, "do you not see that the infamous sorceress defers her vengeance. She was only fearful of gaining, with her haste, the unrelenting resentment of our army. She will employ all her art to kill us little by little. She has already begun with me. My illness resulted from her spells. She let me recover a little to assault me with her dog instead of the fever. Each day will bring some new evil. But since you wish to expose me here, I consent. I dare hope that after my death she will spare your life and be satisfied with making you her slave!"

This speech, not less than convincing, produced its desired effect. I was not master of my own judgement when Firouz made me glimpse the least danger to himself. I became as eager as even he could wish, in the execution of his black design. The flames that consumed Roudabah's rustic dwelling were kindled by my hands as well as his; and, notwithstanding the cries of the peasantry – whom we slaughtered as a reward for their generous efforts on her behalf – we did not leave the spot till we had left Roudabah buried as we believed, beneath a heap of smoking ashes.

We returned to our camp. Firouz could not contain his joy, whereas I hardly concealed the remorse that always followed my crimes, a remorse that never spared me from a single one of them.

A few days afterwards I had my army advance into the interior of the country; but soon found my way blocked by the enemy's forces, under the personal command of the King of Ghilan and his son. It became necessary to offer battle. Firouz

---

1   afrit, *ifrit*: to the Arabs, the most terrible, cruel, and cunning monster of the race of Genii, or djinn [*Islam2* III, 1050]; the Persian equivalent is dive or *diw*.

insisted on fighting by my side. He parried the blows aimed at me. I threw myself in front of him to block the thrusts aimed at my friend. Neither suffered his sight to be diverted from the other. No one could doubt that each, in defending the other's life, was defending a life dearer than his own.

The Prince of Ghilan had sought me out everywhere. We met at last, and, swooping on me with uplifted sword, he cried: "King of Kharezme, thy life shall pay forfeit for the atrocious wrongs done to my sister; had I known of them before, I should have sought thee out in thy very palace and defied all the spirits of darkness that dwell there!"

Scarcely had he spoken these words than the hand that held the avenging sword fell to the ground, struck off at the wrist by a back-handed blow from the blade of Firouz. The King of Ghilan rushed up, foaming with rage, and aimed at us two crashing blows. I avoided the one; and the other went home on Firouz's shoulder. I saw him reel in the saddle. To send the old King's head flying in the air, to take Firouz on to my own horse, to spur out of the battle – all this was but the work of a moment.

Firouz had lost consciousness. I was scarcely in a better plight. Instead of returning to my camp, I plunged into a deep forest. There I lay Firouz on the ground. I tore off my turban to bind his wound. My sobs attracted a woodman who was working nearby.

"This young man is in very poor condition," he said. "This is your brother, no doubt. If you wish, we can carry him to my father's cabin. With God's help, he will make him better, for he is as skilled as he is charitable."

Straight away, we cut off tree branches to fashion a stretcher, and we carried Firouz to the cabin. The old man looked at Firouz, ran to fetch an elixir, and made him drink of it. Then he said to me, "But a moment more, and this young man would have been dead. He has lost nearly all his blood. The first thing to be done was to repair that loss. I see," he continued, examining the wound, "that there is no longer any danger. He will regain consciousness and in a few days will be healed."

This hope was substantiated in an instant. Firouz opened his eyes and cried, "Ah, my dear friend, where are we? Was the battle lost?"

"No, no," I interrupted, putting my hand on his mouth. "We have won since your precious life has been saved. But keep calm. You do not know how much harm might result if you speak too much."

Firouz understood the full meaning of my words; he kept silent. Then, turning to the woodman's son, I handed him a purse full of gold and pressed him to obtain for my friend some necessary comforts of which this place had none.

"Oh, nothing could be easier," he responded; "with money we have everything. We are near a large town, and luckily five leagues from the spot where the armies slaughter themselves."

I could not understand how in so little time, it seemed to me, I had gone such a way. I saw clearly that when one fears for a loved one, one can be too distracted to be able to calculate distances.

Meanwhile, a gentle sleep had imperceptibly taken possession of Firouz. The old man observed him with a contented eye while my respirations harmonized with the rise and fall of my friend's chest. He slept thus for several hours and only awoke when the peasant returned. He brought nothing I had asked for. I was about to manifest my amazement to him when Firouz, who had regained most of his vivacity, said to him: "You must have some news to recount."

"Yes, yes," said he, "and the very best of news. The army of the Kharezmians has been cut to pieces, and their camp pillaged. The victory would be complete if they could only catch those wicked princes, Alasi and Firouz, who have escaped, after killing our King and his son. But the princess Roudabah, who has ascended the throne, is having them sought everywhere. She offers such great rewards for finding them that they must soon be in her power."

"I am delighted at what you tell me," cried Firouz, without suffering any change to appear in his countenance. We had been assured that Roudabah was burned to death in her woodland dwelling; and I had been most grieved to hear it, as I knew she is a most excellent princess."

"She is even better than you think," replied the peasant with a cunning look; "and that is why Heaven has kept her from harm. The prince, her brother, chanced upon her retreat, and took her away some hours before the attempted assassination you mention, which, please God, will not long remain unpunished."

While saying this in a tone which showed how much he knew who we really were, he made a sign to his father to follow him.

They went out of the room together. Afar we heard the trampling of many horses. Firouz immediately rose to a sitting posture, and, presenting me with a razor, which he took from under his clothes, said in a low voice: "You see, dear friend, the danger we are in. Hurry, cut off my hair and throw it into these flames. Do not speak a word. If you lose a moment it is all up with us!"

I could but comply with such a pressing command; and I did so. A few seconds later, the cabin shook. A dive in the form of an Ethiopian appeared and asked Firouz what he wanted with him. "I desire thee," he replied, "to carry me this instant, with my friend, to the cavern of the Magus, thy master, and as thou passest, to crush the worthless wretches who are bargaining for our lives!"

The dive needed no second orders. He took us both in his arms, sprang from the hut – causing it, with one kick, to fall on our hosts, and then shot through the air so rapidly that I lost consciousness.

When I came to myself, I was in the arms of Firouz, and at first saw only his charming face, lovingly pressed against mine. I softly closed my eyelids again, as one does when wishing to prolong a pleasant dream, but reopened them when Firouz's voice invited me to look around. I opened my eyes and thought myself transported beneath a new firmament, encrusted with stars a thousand times more brilliant and nearer to us than the stars in the natural world. I looked round on every side, and it seemed to me I was in a vast plain, and that round it were transparent clouds. I breathe, and it is the comely aroma of the most enlivening perfumes. I listen, and a heavenly symphony ravishes my heart. My rapture lasts several moments. Finally I cry, "Here we are, then, carried into Cheheristan.[1] We are together in the eternal abode of joy."

"It is only the cave of the Magus," Firouz replied. "It is true that we find here quite a number of spirits superior to our race. Indeed, these lamps are attached invisibly to the azure vault; these crystals are set artistically into the rock and, reflecting one another, multiply to infinity the shrubs, the flowers, the decorative shell-work in varieties of colours. All this is not the work of human hands. But such is this place, and whosoever it may be that lives here, your slightest desires are anticipated. Is that not so, father?" he continued, raising his voice.

"Yes," responded the Magus, advancing toward me with a gesture of respect. "Prince Alasi will be treated here as he treated my dear son, and to begin with what is at this moment the most necessary, you are being served all the dishes that delight your taste-buds."

He had no sooner spoken when a table covered just as he had instructed, and a sideboard well stocked with wines, sparkling in their vessels, appeared in front of us. Young boys, as fair and graceful as the jasmine sprays engarlanding their heads, presented themselves to serve us, sliding forward three magnificent sofas for the Magus and for us.

I had no need to ask Firouz if he were better. He ate with an appetite that encouraged my own and which delighted the Magus, all the while indulging in a thousand good-natured pranks with our pretty cup-bearers.

We drank, we laughed, we frolicked. The Magus indulged us with the best grace in the world. After which, having commanded that we be left on our own, he said to me, "King of Kharezme. I do not wish your curiosity to keep you awake tonight and I am going to reply in advance to all that you could wish to know. You are doubtless surprised that, with the power

---

1 Cheheristan, perhaps *Shehrizur*. A fertile plain in Kurdistan; its southern boundary is the River Sirwan.

I possess, I should have taken the trouble to seek and obtain your protection for Firouz. Here were some of my reasons. I had flattered myself that the people of Shirvan would repent of their revolt and that they would remember that Firouz is descended from a race of heroes. But if he had to reign, he must not be raised here where miracles and pleasures might increase his distaste for the restrictions of royalty. It was preferable that he improve his knowledge of men. The ideas that I had given him of them sufficed for him to appreciate their just value. You know that my views have prevailed. The hope of recovering his kingdom is at an end. His faithless subjects groan in the Caliph's chains and do not know how to break them. They are not worthy of my employing supernatural powers. For that matter, what more can Firouz desire? He possesses the universe in possessing the heart of his friend."

"Oh, I am certain at present that his heart is mine," said Firouz, "but I have been in great danger of losing part of it, and if my beautiful tresses had not helped me to exclude Roudabah by having a dive, acting in an unofficial capacity, represent her, I do not know what might have happened. What do you have to say about this, my dear Alasi?"

"Only that yet again I pardon this injustice, although it was a little extreme," I replied.

"The word *injustice* excites your suspicions, Prince Firouz," replied the Magus, but the King of Kharezme cannot ignore that every being has the right, by all possible means, to remove harmful objects from its path; and that the moments of anger or fear which impel us are born of the living force of nature. But that is enough for tonight; it is late and you have need of rest."

Straight away we stood up; the young boys reappeared. They led us to a dimly-lit bedroom where, arranged beneath an embroidered canopy, two beds invited us to lie down. Then they took off our clothes, and having wished us goodnight with the best grace in the world, left the room.

Firouz had not the least desire to let me sleep. He was so overcome by joy to find himself in the place where he had spent his first years that he behaved extravagantly and impulsively. He related to me how, in a moment, the Magus cured his wound. He praised the Magus's powers and advised me to ask to see his chamber of fire. He confessed that he had been raised in the religion of Zoroaster and that he thought it the most natural and rational of all religions. "Consider," he added, "could I ever have been pleased by the absurdities of the Koran? Would that all your Mussulman[1] doctors had shared the fate of the moullah whose discourses wearied me to death! That moment when I changed him into an ass was delicious for me. I should have taken a like pleasure in plucking out all the feathers from the wings of the Angel Gabriel, and thus punishing him for having furnished a pen to the man who wrote therewith so much nonsense."[2]

There was a time when such words would have seemed to me unspeakable impiety; indeed, I did not much like them then. But any remaining scruples could not hold against the caresses with which Firouz accompanied each word.

A voluptuous sleep took possession of us at last; and we did not wake till the lively song of birds proclaimed broad day. Surprised by a music which I had no reason to expect in this place, I ran to the entrance of a kind of grotto where we found ourselves and I saw that it opened on a garden where were gathered all the delights that nature has to offer. The sea, which bordered it, enhanced the riches that the land presented to our eyes.

"Is this still part of the Magus's cavern?" I cried.

"It's one of its exits," Firouz replied, "but it would take you more than one day to explore all the beauties of the place. The Magus says that everything has been made for man's use, and that man must possess himself of everything he wants whenever the opportunity offers. He has spent part of his life in acquiring his power, and is spending the remainder in enjoying it."

As soon as our kind pages heard that we were up, they came in zealously and presented us with our clothes – most singular

---

1   Mussulman, Muslim: A follower of the religion of Islam. *Mussulman* was current in
    western Europe in Beckford's time.
2   Muslim tradition identifies the Angel Gabriel as inspiring Muhammad to write the
    Koran.

in their convenience and cleanliness. We descended into the garden where, under a trellis from which hung most appetizing grapes, we found the Magus who, just as we, did justice to the excellent breakfast served to us. I did not fail to express to the Magus a very strong desire to see his Temple of Fire.[1] "It will please you," said he, with a satisfied air; "but I cannot conduct you thither until you have visited my baths, and been invested with robes suitable to the majesty of the place."

I have never been impressed by ceremonies: I had too often experienced their dulness. Those of the Magus, instead of exciting my curiosity, awoke instead my aversion through the importance that he imposed on everything. I did not hurry to leave the bath where our little friends amused us with pretty stories. I endured all the paraphernalia of a rich and bizarre costume I was given, only because it pleased Firouz.

But what were my feelings on entering the Temple of Fire? Never has spectacle, except the sight that met my eyes on entering this dire palace, so filled me with surprise and terror. The fire that the Magus worshipped seemed to issue from the bowels of the earth and to soar up to the clouds. The flames sometimes shone with an unendurable brightness; sometimes they shed a blue and lurid light, that helped make all surrounding objects appear even more hideous, if that is possible, than they actually were. The rails of glowing brass that separated us from this dread deity did no more than partially reassure me. From time to time we were enveloped in a whirlwind of sparks, which made the Magus feel deeply honoured – an honour with which I would very gladly have dispensed. In the part of the temple where we stood, the walls were hung with human hair of every colour; and, from space to space, human hair also hung in festoons from pyramids of skulls set in gold and ebony. Besides all this, the place was filled with the fumes of sulphur and bitumen,[2] oppressing the brain and taking away the breath.

I trembled; my legs seemed to give way; Firouz supported me. "What are you afraid of, dear prince. Would I take you

---

1 Zoroastrianism erected temples of fire as places of worship.
2 bitumen: inflammable mineral pitch; asphalt.

into a place of danger? There is the god of nature in all his terror. Let us now see him in his glory."

Speaking thus, he led me into another place that I do not know how to describe to you since I was hardly able to glance at it. I was dazzled by an infinity of beams shining from a vault, brighter than the sun, whose light it reproduced, reverberating from numberless gems that surrounded us. I closed my eyes and whispered to Firouz, "I am no better here than in the other place. Take me away from the presence of your god. Nothing save your own nearness has enabled me to bear for a moment *his* nearness."

I was in need of recuperation and of the exquisite dinner placed before us. I was again in a condition to listen to the Magus with renewed patience after the table had been cleared. All that he told us about his religion was not new, and I paid little heed to this part of his discourse. But his moral teachings were much more useful. He extolled his temple of fire: we learned that the dives had built it, but that he, himself, had chosen its decorations in the course of his life. I asked him for no explanations on this point; I feared, in fact, that he might provide some. Those skulls and the human hair that he called decorations I disliked to a sovereign degree, and if I had not been sure of the heart of Firouz, I would have been very ill at ease with the Magus. Fortunately, I was not called upon to listen to our formidable host more than once a day. The rest of our time was spent in amusements and pleasures of every kind. The young boys would artfully vary the tableaux they presented and in which they played parts, but Firouz, who was acquainted with my tastes, always made his own contribution. These enveloping attentions spread such a voluptuousness over all my moments that I was hardly in a state to keep any account of time. The present had so far obliterated the past that I never once thought of my kingdom. But the Magus put an end, all too soon, alas, to this period of delirium.

One day, he said to us, "We are about to separate, my dear children; the hour of bliss, for which I have sighed for such long years, is approaching; I am expected in the Palace of Subterranean Fire[1] where I shall bathe in joys and possess treasures passing human imagination. But there I will not forget you. If only I could flatter myself that I will see you two there. It is there that true friends can frolic together in perfect rapture, for neither death nor the vicissitudes of things can ever separate them.. They live there in mutual tenderness for a happy eternity."

"Ah, where is that divine abode?" I cried. "Let us follow you there."

"You must, before all things, adore my god," replied the Magus. "Do homage to the powers that serve him and win his favour by the sacrifices that he ordains."

"I will worship any god you like," said I, "if he will suffer me to live for ever with Firouz, and free from the horrible fear of seeing pale sickness or bloody steel attack his beautiful days. What must I do besides?"

"You must, " replied the Magus, "cause the religion of Zoroaster to be received in your dominions, by choice or by force. You must raze the mosques to the ground and erect temples of fire in their stead. Finally, you must sacrifice without pity all whom you cannot convince and who refuse to embrace the true faith. This is what I have myself done, though not so openly as you can do it; and, as a sign of what I have been able to accomplish, see all these locks of hair that ornament my Hall of Fire – dear testimonies that will open the gates of the only abode where happiness reigns."[2]

"Quick, quick! let us go and cause heads to be cut off," said Firouz, "and so amass a treasure of human hair. The sacrifice of crazy wretches who will not accept our beliefs is as nothing if we can obtain thereby the supreme felicity of loving each other for all time!"

This loving enthusiasm of Firouz obtained my complete

---

1 Palace of Subterranean Fire: The Hall of Eblis, introduced in *Vathek*.
2 Malignant Zoroastrians appear in the pro-Islamic *Arabian Nights*. "The Adventures of Hasan of Basrah" on the 582nd night introduces a magician named Bahram: "I worship the Flame and the Spark, I worship the Sun and the Light of the Sun. I have already raped nine hundred and ninety-nine Mussulmans into my power ..." Beckford's Magus derives from sources like this.

assent, and the Magus, having reached the height of his wishes, resumed: "I esteem myself happy, King of Kharezme, in seeing you, at last, convinced of the truth of my faith. Several times have I despaired, and I should certainly not have taken so much trouble about you if you had not been the friend of the son of Filanshaw. Ah! What honour will be mine when your conversion is known in the Palace of Subterranean Fire! Hence, therefore! Depart at once. A ship, ready equipped, awaits you upon the shore. Your subjects will receive you with acclamation. Do all the good you can. Remember that to destroy those who are obstinate in error is accounted a great merit by the stern god you have promised to serve. When you deem that your reward is fully earned, go to Istakhar,[1] and there, on the Terrace of the Beacon Lights, make a conflagration of the hair of those whom you have immolated in so good a cause. The nostrils of the dives will be gratified by that sweet-smelling sacrifice. They will discover to you the steep stairway, and open the ebony portal: I shall receive you in my arms, and you will receive the honours due to two such perfect friends."

Thus did I yield to the last seductions of the Magus. I had heaped scorn on his exhortations, but my heart was too interested in his promises to be able to resist. For a moment indeed I thought they might be false; but soon I decided that, in view of the reward, every hazard must be risked. No doubt the Magus, urged on by ambition and covetousness, had made a similar calculation – to find himself ultimately deceived, as are all the miserable wretches who find their way to this place!

The Magus wished to see us embark. He embraced us affectionately on the shore and advised that we should keep in our service, as followers on whom we could always rely, the twenty Negroes appointed to navigate our ship. Scarcely had we set sail when we heard a terrible sound – a sound like thunder makes as it goes crashing among the mountains and heaping up the valleys with ruin. We saw the rock we had just left crumble into the sea. We heard the cries of joy with which the exultant

---

1 Istakhar: The location (in Persia) of the ruin that, according to *Vathek*, leads to the Palace of Subterranean Fire.

dives then filled the air; and we judged that the Magus was already on his way to Istakhar.

Our twenty Negroes were such good sailors, so adroit and alert, that we should have taken them to form part of the Magus's supernatural following, if they had not assured us that they were simple fire-worshippers, and no more. As their chief, Zouloulou by name, seemed very well acquainted with all the mysteries of the cavern, I asked him what had become of the little boys for whom we had conceived a liking. He replied that the Intelligences,[1] who first gave them to the Magus, had disposed of them, doubtless for the best, and that we could not do better than to leave them in their hands.

I cannot express the joy with which my subjects celebrated my return. I was moved and quite blushed at the designs I entertained against them. Firouz saw this and immediately distracted my attention with several of his charming witticisms.

We discovered that my visir, Motaleb, was now in the good graces of the Queen, my mother, but that he had thrown into disorder all the business with which he was entrusted. Irritated on both counts, Firouz wanted to cut off his head. He whispered in my ear, "He has such a good head of hair." But I was satisfied with deposing him from his office. I appointed in his stead a feeble old man who said yes to everything, and who quickly demolished the Great Mosque at Zerbend as soon as I relayed the order.

My mother came in haste to ask what I meant by an act so impious. "We mean," answered Firouz arrogantly, "never again to hear mention of Mahomet and his dreams, and to establish in Kharezme the religion of Zoroaster, as being the only religion worthy of credence."

Outraged at this reply and also piqued on the subject of Motaleb, the Queen could not contain her anger and responded with abuse. She heaped upon us imprecations – which have been only too terribly effectual. I listened to her without resentment; but Firouz prevailed on me to commit her to a

---

1 Intelligences: Spiritual beings; the term, in this instance, seems to refer to djinn.

tower, where, not long afterwards, she ended her life in bitterness of spirit, and cursed the hour when she had brought me into the world.

These iniquities did not trouble me much. I was resolved to stop at nothing to allay the fears that are inseparable from true love. At first I met with so little resistance to my wishes that Firouz, who saw how easily the courtiers and the army yielded, would say: "Where can we get hair? How many locks I see that would be of admirable use to us if only the heads that bear them were a little more obdurate! We must hope that they will change their minds, or we stand in danger of never getting to Istakhar."

At last there came a change indeed! Most of those who frequented the Temples of Fire I had erected were only waiting for a favourable moment to rise in rebellion. Several plots were discovered, and then our sacrifices began. Firouz wished to proceed with order. As he was fully acquainted with the talents of Zouloulou, he established him as head preacher. He caused him to get up, every day, on to a tall stage, erected in the midst of the city square, to which the people most resorted. There the brazen Negro, vested in a robe of vermilion, his countenance assured, his voice piercing, would pour forth his sermons, while his nineteen compeers stood ready, with drawn swords, at the bottom of the steps leading to the stage, and cut off the heads of all who would not believe what others wanted them to believe; and neither, of course, did they forget to secure the hair of their victims.

Mine was still the stronger side. I was beloved by the soldiery, who generally care very little what god they serve so long as they are flattered by their king.

Persecution produced its ordinary effect. The people courted martyrdom. They came from all parts to deride Zouloulou – whom nothing disconcerted – and to get their heads cut off.

The carnage became at last so great that the army itself was scandalised. Motaleb incited them to rebellion. He sent secretly, in the name of the nobles, to offer the crown of Kharezme to Roudabah – inviting her to come and avenge the death of her father, and of her brother, and her own wrongs.

We were not without information regarding these secret machinations – for parasites seldom altogether abandon a monarch so long as the crown still glitters on his head; but we felt no serious alarm till we perceived that we were becoming the weaker party. My guards had already, on more than one occasion, suffered the Negroes to be beaten – at a cost, to Zouloulou, of his two ears. He was the first to advise us not to lose the fruit of our labours.

By the care and vigilance of this zealous follower, everything was soon made ready for our departure. In the middle of the night I left my kingdom, which was by this time in almost full rebellion against my rule – left it with a heart as triumphant as if I had been a conqueror. We mounted, Firouz and I, two superb Arab horses; the twenty Negroes each led a camel, ten of which were laden with human hair.

Though anxious to reach our journey's end, we did not hurry overmuch. Firouz stopped everywhere to make mischief, ably seconded by Zouloulou who was equally spirited and equally mischievous. I was rarely along on these expeditions but Firouz recounted them to me with a gaiety and grace that always enchanted me.

One night when I had awaited him in my tent longer than usual, he arrived out of breath and announced to me, "To horse, my friend, we have to reach the great desert, only a few parasangs[1] from here. Zouloulou knows all the byways and will lead us to some spot where we may find shelter from the danger that threatens us. Do not ask me to say any more. You shall know all when we are safe."

I understood easily that by one of his usual tricks, Firouz had brought pursuit on us, but I made no reproach. I gave orders to strike the tents and left.

At daybreak we found ourselves in the middle of a large thicket of trees so bushy that it was necessary to enter in order to persuade ourselves that the paths were negotiable. We dismounted in a grove where interlaced branches formed a

---

1 parasang, *farsakh*: Measurement of distance based on how far troops can march in an hour. To D'Herbelot, it equals two French leagues, or 8 km, or 5 miles. The modern equivalent of one parasang is 6 km. [*Islam2* II, 812]

canopy that the sun could hardly penetrate. Straight away the Negroes served refreshments; then Firouz, filling his goblet with Shiraz[1] wine, remarked to me, "Prince, let us drink the health of that awesome queen that the Kharezmians are going to place on the charming Alasi's throne."

"If the venture that made us hasten on our march has a bearing on your banter, relate it to me now so that we can both laugh," I returned.

"Oh my friend," he asserted, "such pleasure have I never had. I could purchase it for a hundred times the fatigue that we have suffered. Know that when last night Zouloulou kept me behind, it was to tell me that Roudabah was only about a hundred paces from us, that she had wandered some little distance from the army she was leading into Kharezme, and that she was at that moment resting in her pavilion, with no other following than a few of her guards, all of whom were sleeping soundly. At these words my heart was seized with fear and fury. I felt the keen edge of my sword and cried, 'Then let us be away, Zouloulou, let us sacrifice this hateful princess who means to usurp my friend's throne. She believes in the Koran, and her long black hair will make a good prize.'

'Moderate this enthusiasm,' the African replied, 'and learn that you can accomplish nothing against the life of Roudabah. The Magus ordered me to tell you so, if occasion required, and to tell you further that you would yourself perish in the attempt. A power against whom nothing can prevail protects the Princess of Ghilan. But if you will be calm, and listen to my advice, we can do much worse to her than cut off her head.'

'Speak quickly then,' I replied. 'It is only by bringing my rage to the test that you can appease it.'

'Follow me then, and no noise,' he directed. 'I will cause Roudabah's guards to inhale certain fumes, and sleep for a long time without waking. We shall easily make our way, undetected, as far as her pavilion, and can then, as our fancy dictates,

---

1   *Shiraz*, in Persia, is, in Beckford's work, the site of civilized luxuries, like wine. Wine was and is forbidden to devout Muslims, so Firouz and Alasi are demonstrating their opposition.

bedaub the face of your enemy with this unguent, which possesses the power of making the most beautiful countenance ugly and repulsive.'

So said, so done. We deepened the sleep of Roudabah's women, but her we left natural and undrugged. I rubbed so hard that she awoke with a start, almost unnerving me. Her colour was already a livid bluish-gray, her mouth spread as far as her ears, and her eyes were blood-red. At her cry when she recognized me I was afraid that she would swoon, and in losing consciousness, would steal from me a part of the pleasure that I hoped to gain. But happily her courage, so praised, sustained her, and I had time to detach a mirror that hung from the sash of one of her women and to present it to her, saying, 'Acknowledge, majestic princess, that the little monster of a Firouz is a model of courtesy; he flatters himself that this beautifying make-up, which he has just applied to your countenance, will cause you to remember him – always!'

I was unable to say any more. As soon as she had glanced at her budding charms, she fainted away, and we withdrew. As we were not able to prevent her from returning to consciousness and from setting her army on our tails, I urged you to get away. That is my story. I am now finished with Roudabah. I have taken her lover and her beauty away from her. What more can one do to a woman?"

The gaiety with which Firouz told his little story did not deflect my attention this time from the atrocity of the crime which he had just committed. I was surprised that, with a heart so tender and full of feeling where I was concerned, he was so spiteful; but more than that, I was struck by what had prevented the murder attempt from going any further. "The power that protects Roudabah," said I to myself, "must love the good, for that princess is good. It is not then the same power that is about to receive cruel beings such as us. But if it reigns supreme over all other powers, what is to become of us? Oh Mahomet! Thou art beloved of this supreme power, but I have renounced thee. Thou hast certainly forsaken me utterly! What refuge have I, save with thine enemies?"

With this despairing thought came the last feelings of

remorse I was destined to experience. Such feelings I always owed to the Princess of Ghilan; but, alas! they always came in vain!

I willingly helped Firouz to lure me from such melancholy reflections. I could not revoke the past; probably I would not have wished it if I could. I had no other course but to throw myself, eyes firmly closed, into the abyss of futurity.

Instead of taking the planned route across the desert of Nouderbigian,[1] we skirted it for several days on the advice of Zouloulou, who still feared the army of Ghilan. Everyone knows that the borders of the desert offer the pleasantest scenes of nature and are peopled by guileless and happy inhabitants. Such places precisely suited Firouz: he mixed with the good people, singing, dancing with them, making himself warmly loved, but never leaving them without making them repent having known him.

Since, to please him, I often extended our halts at the same place, we were persuaded to attend a wedding in a pleasant valley where we pitched our tents. Firouz accepted the invitation with pleasure, resolved to bring trouble to some others. He kept such a close watch on the two lovers that he was able to surprise them, alone and tête-à-tête, in a little grove of palms where a waterfall had formed a deep basin. First, he heard their reciprocal protestations of tenderness, then, accompanied by Zouloulou, who followed him everywhere, he approached them, sabre in hand, and announced in a menacing voice, "Know, wretches, that I have promised the afrite Gulfakair to sacrifice to him two hearts truly smitten with love. I have just been listening to you. You are the ones I am looking for, so prepare to die this instant."

"Oh, I am not the one you should take as your victim," immediately replied the young woman. "I do not love Assán at all; my mother wants me to marry him and I really had to say sweet things to him."

"Then, it is Assán whom I will sacrifice for the present, while I wait for someone else," replied Firouz.

---

1   Perhaps the Great Salt Desert between Ghilan and Isfahan.

"You will choose badly," said Assán; it is Kérima who sought after me. She is the one with the heart that you want. Me, I love other things as much as her."

"Are you rich?" asked Firouz.

"We each have a herd and a cottage," they replied.

"Since it is not for gain that you are marrying," replied Firouz, "you must be doing it for love, but so as to be sure of my facts, the one who loves the least has only to throw the other into that pool to save his life."

Speaking thus, he brandished his sabre around their heads. Kérima moved first. She started to push Assán toward the water; he, in turn, seized her around the middle with the same design. Kérima did not lack strength. They began, thus, to wrestle, ever nearer the brink, until they fell into the deep waters, to the great amusement of Firouz, who, as he helped them to drown, laughed heartily.

My friend recounted the story in the pleasantest manner and finished it saying, "Believe me, dear Alasi. If all who pretend to love were put to the same proof, none would stand up to it except you and I. As for women, there isn't one of them who would not hurry to drown her lover, or her husband, to save her own life, and I hope that the men would respond in kind."

As the villagers were ignorant of the accident that had just happened, they gathered the next day for the wedding; but when no one could find the bride and groom, the rejoicing changed to lamentation. Firouz appeared as afflicted as the rest, but sought only to redouble their sorrow.

The cruelties that I had brought to bear on my subjects had hardened my heart. All these scenes entertained me and I helped out several times in order to please Firouz.

The last of these bizarre and atrocious whims happened as we were coming out of the desert. For several days we had been hearing of the unusual piety of a santon[1] who lived in a chapel at the foot of a small hill.

"I must visit this extraordinary man," Firouz said to me. "I am curious to know if he deserves his reputation."

---

1 Santon: A European designation for a Muslim monk or hermit.

So, one evening, he took Zouloulou with him, and having arranged together what they were going to do, he approached alone the door of the chapel. He knocked and in soft and plaintive tones, began to speak.

"Heavenly sir, have pity on a young boy who risks his life if you do not offer him charitable refuge."

At these words, an elderly gentleman with a long white beard, grey robe, enormous turban, and a lantern in hand, opened the door, but taking three steps back upon spying Firouz, cried, "Beauteous angel, who does me honour with your presence, what would you have of me."

"Father," replied Firouz, with an air of modesty and embarrassment, "angels know nothing of the needs of human nature, and I am dying of starvation. Deign to give me something to eat, and then I will tell you who I am."

"You are welcome here, my son," exclaimed the santon with joy, giving him a little stroke on the cheek. "Enter without further ceremony, sit yourself down, and I will find some rice, dates, and water to appease your appetite."

"Alas, I must seek shelter elsewhere," replied Firouz in a mournful tone; "I am not used to such dishes. I had counted on making good cheer with you and spending a merry night here."

"Oh, stay," replied the old man, "and since you have such good intentions, I will find the means to wine and dine you according to your desires."

Speaking thus, he took from a sideboard a cut of roast venison, some cakes and confections, and a bottle of Shiraz wine. He put it all on a little table of cedarwood and sat himself on a rattan sofa beside Firouz, who started to eat as if he had an importunate hunger.

The convivial goblet was not forgotten, nor the tender words of gratitude from Firouz, whose words sent the old man into raptures of delight. Suddenly they heard a rude pounding on the door. Firouz pretended terror and begged the santon on no condition to open it; then the blows doubled in strength, the door burst open, and Zouloulou appeared wrathfully before them.

"Is it thus," he said to the old gentleman, "that you harbour in your own house a young vagabond who left the tent of his elder brother, the prince, to avoid being punished for his faults?"

"Don't be so harsh, my dear Zouloulou," cried Firouz. "For two days now my brother has starved me because I said that I admired the keen countenance and beautiful white beard of this amiable man before us. Is it strange that I escaped to come to see him? Consider, instead of getting angry, partake with us of this little supper, seasoned with the captivating conversation of our host."

Zouloulou appeared appeased by these words and, urged by the santon, he took his place at the table, saying, "It must be admitted that my master is indeed violent and thoroughly stubborn, but his brother is answerable to him and nothing can be done about that."

Firouz did not fail to cause several glasses to be drunk by the Negro; then, having looked at him affectionately, he said, "You know, honest Zouloulou, that my brother, despite his bad temper, often lets you manage things. Do me a service with him that I will never forget. He wanted to give me a tutor; have him accept our host in this capacity. I will owe you my life's happiness."

"Do you think," Zouloulou replied brusquely, "I can induce the prince to put close to you a zealous Muslim, he who detests the religion of Mahomet and is an adorer of fire?"

"Alas, I did not think of that," said Firouz with consternation. "Let us not speak of it again. I have lost all hope."

"Why, my son," cried the santon, who had listened to them without saying a word and without ceasing to gaze at Firouz, "why discourage yourself so soon. Could we not persuade your brother that I have changed my faith and that I think like him?"

"He will not believe that easily," replied the Negro. "He will want proofs of it."

"As for that, we will see," replied Firouz; "and if my dearly-beloved father would accompany us from this time on, we will soon know where we stand."

Zouloulou was of a mind to complete his supper and to empty another two bottles, after which he told them that he was going ahead of them, and if they followed closely, they would find the prince predisposed in favour of their joint enterprise.

He came, in fact, to tell me everything. I saw that the adventure was dear to Firouz's heart, and I promised to play my role appropriately. First I made difficulties. Then I insisted that when the country people came the next morning to ask, according to their custom, for the blessing of the santon, he should preach to them the adoration of fire, and damn Mahomet as energetically as he could.

The poor wretch, his head turned by the attractions of Firouz, consented to all, on the promise that we protect him from the anger of the peasants and that we take him immediately along with us.

For safety, Firouz wanted to keep him the night in our tent and let him go only when we saw the rustic devotees make their way toward the chapel. Then we, and our escort of blacks, gathered with them as if we enjoyed the same pious sentiments.

The santon kept his word, but we did not keep ours. We were the first to cry out against the impieties that he spouted. The names, *blasphemer*, *villain*, were not spared him. Finally, so effectively did we stir up the anger of these good people that they launched themselves all at once at the chapel, demolished it, set fire to the ruins, and burnt the preacher with his chapel. He had the ill-fortune to see Firouz laugh full-throatedly at his fate.

With the santon dispatched, the peasants turned to go each to his own work, but that did not suit us. We barred their way, reproaching them for the death of the santon and our Africans began to cut off heads, right and left.

At their cries and at all the tumult, several pious hermits came running who, profoundly alarmed, asked to know what was the matter. "It is a matter of having your venerable beards to compensate us for the one we regretfully saw burnt," Firouz shouted to them..

As he spoke, he knocked off with a single blow the most

frizzy head that I had ever seen. A few others, quite well adorned, I made fly in the air. The Negroes managed the rest with dispatch. Several of these unfortunates, in the hope of saving their lives, tore out themselves their long beards and threw them in our faces. That reconciled us not at all, for the wind carried away half. Finally, masters of the battle-field, we gathered up the precious plunder which we so greatly prized and, persuaded that we had ample to please the dives of the subterranean palace, we resumed our route with a cheerful eagerness that did not relax until our arrival at Istakhar.

It was already night when we came to the Terrace of the Beacon Lights; we travelled the length of it with a kind of horror, notwithstanding all we could say to one another of endearment and encouragement. There was no moon in the firmament to shed upon us its soft rays. The stars alone were shining there; but their trembling light only seemed to intensify the sombre grandeur of all that met our gaze. We regretted, indeed, none of the beauties, none of the riches of the world we were about to leave. Nor did we dream of the pleasures to come. We thought only of the bliss of being together forever; and yet invisible ties seemed still to draw us back toward the world.

We could not repress a shudder when we saw that the Negroes had done piling up our enormous heap of human locks. With trembling hands we approached our torches to set it on fire; and we thought we would die of fright when the earth opened before our feet, rock shattering into millions of frightening fragments. At the sight of the stairway that seemed so easy of descent, and the torches illuminating it, we were somewhat reassured. Overcome with joy, we embraced, and, each taking the other's hand, began cautiously to descend – when the twenty Negroes, who were far from our thoughts, hurled themselves upon us so impetuously that we fell, headlong, against the ebony portal at the bottom.

I will not describe the dread, impressed upon us by the prospect of the place in which we were – all who are here have had that fearful experience – but one object of terror peculiar to ourselves was the sight of the Magus. He was pacing to and fro amid the restless, miserable crowd, with his right hand on his breast. He saw us. The flames devouring his heart leapt out through his eyes. He darted upon us a fearful glance, and hurried away. A moment after, we encountered a malevolent dive, who, to insult Firouz, advised him that Roudabah had recovered all her beauty, and reigns peacefully in Kharezme. He assured him that she would never come here.

At last Eblis declared all the horror of our fates. What a god have we served! What fearful doom has he pronounced upon us! What! Must we hate one another, we who have loved so much? We who came here to enjoy an eternity of love, shall we hate one another eternally? Oh, dire, accursed thought – let our beings be obliterated this instant!

Sobbing, sobbing these last words, the two princes threw themselves into each other's arms and for a long space a mournful silence reigned in that unhappy company. But at last this silence was broken by Vathek, who asked the third prince to relate his story. His curiosity was still intact. It was reserved for the final victim to extinguish in these criminal souls every feeling save hatred and despair.

THE HISTORY
OF PRINCE BARKIAROKH[1]

translated by Sir Frank T. Marzials

MY crimes are even blacker than those of the Caliph Vathek. No rash and impetuous counsels hastened my ruin, as they have hastened his. If I am here, in this abode of horror, it is because I spurned the salutary advice, oft repeated, of the most real and loving friend.

I was born on the borders of the Caspian Sea, in Daghestan,[2] not far from the city of Berdouka. My father was a fisherman, a worthy man, who lived quietly and in comfort by his toil; and I was his third son. We lost our mother while still too young to feel her loss; but we saw our father weeping, and we wept too. We were, my brothers and I, very industrious, very obedient, and not altogether ignorant. A dervish,[3] my father's friend, had taught us how to read, and how to form various characters. He often came to spend the evening in our dwelling; and, while we were making wicker baskets, would pass the time in discourses of a pious nature, and explain to us the Koran. Alsalami, for such was the dervish's name, was really a man of peace, as his name suggested: he settled our little differences, or else prevented them, with a mildness and affection that endeared him to us all. When his maxims and apophthegms seemed over-serious and to incline to dullness, he would enliven them with stories, and thus the principles he wished to inculcate became the more acceptable.

A fairly large garden, which we had planted under the dervish's direction, supplied him with a new field for our occu-

---

1 Barkiarokh, *Barkyaruk* (d. AD 1105): Son of Malikshah, and briefly sultan of the Arabian provinces. Except for its authenticity, it is not clear why Beckford used the name. He probably found it in *Anecdotes Arabes*. [*Anecdotes Arabes*, 592–93; *Islam2* I, 1051]

2 Daghestan, *Daghistan*: A mountainous region on the Caspian Sea, divided into two parts by the pass of Derbend. It was also divided in religion, a Christian part ruled by a prince with the title, Filanshah or Kilanshah. It was not converted to Islam until the eighteenth century. [*Islam2* II, 87]

3 dervish: a Muslim friar who has vowed to live in poverty and austerity.

pation and amusement. He taught us the art of cultivating plants, and their virtues. We went with him to gather such flowers as are health-giving or agreeable, for distillation, and were transported with pleasure as we watched them undergoing transformation in our alembics.[1] I was active and eager to learn, so that Alsalami treated me with a flattering distinction. His favour made me vain, but I affected great modesty while in his presence, only to indemnify myself by a greater arrogance when he was away; and, in the quarrels which ensued between my brothers and myself, I always had the art of putting them in the wrong. By the profits derived from our distilled waters, our wicker baskets, and our fishing we lived in relative affluence. Two black slaves kept our sylvan dwelling in a state of cleanliness that added much to its charm; the food they prepared for us was, if simple, always wholesome and pleasant to the taste; and finally, baths, conveniently disposed, helped to afford a degree of comfort which few persons, in our condition of life, were able to enjoy.

Surrounded by so much that was agreeable and calculated to make life pleasant, my evil nature yet asserted itself more strongly day by day. There was, in the wall of one of the upper chambers of the house, a cupboard which my father never opened before us, often declaring that he would bestow the key upon the one of his three sons who showed himself most worthy of that distinction. This promise was so frequently repeated, and the dervish let fall so many vague hints implying that we were by birth superior to our present obscure position, that we imagined the cupboard contained some great treasure. My brothers coveted its possession, no doubt, but did not on that account refrain from indulging, among our friends and neighbours, in the amusements natural to their age. As for me, I languished, I withered, at home, and could think of nothing but the gold and precious stones which, I supposed, were hidden in that fatal receptacle, and my one desire was to get them into my own hands. My seeming steadiness, my assiduity in all home

---

1 alembic: a still.

duties, were greatly approved; my father and his friend never tired of praising my industry and wisdom: but, ah! how far were they from reading my heart!

One morning my father said to all three of us, in presence of the dervish: "You have now, my children, reached the age at which a man should select a companion to help him in bearing the ills and sorrows of life. But I in no wise wish to influence your choice. I was allowed to make mine in full freedom, and I was very happy with your mother. I think I may fairly hope that each of you will find a good wife. Go and look for her. I give you a month in which to prosecute your search, and here is money sufficient for your needs during that time. If, however, you should return this very day, you would give me a very agreeable surprise, for I am old, and desire very passionately to see my family increased before my decease."

My brothers bent their heads in token of submission. They went out with an alacrity from which I augured that they would not have the slightest trouble in satisfying my father's wishes.

I was outraged at thinking of the advantage they would thus obtain. I had nothing better to do, however, than to go out as they did. They went off to their friends in the neighbourhood, and I, who had made no friends, addressed my steps to the adjacent city. As I went through the streets I asked myself: "Where am I going? How can I find a wife? I know of none. Shall I accost the first woman I meet? She will laugh at me, and look upon me as a fool. No doubt that, in strict terms, I have a month before me; but my brothers seem quite ready to satisfy our father's wishes this very day. He will bestow his key upon the one or the other of them, and that dear, that sweet, that lovely treasure, the treasure that has cost me so many sighs, will be lost to me for ever. Wretch that I am! Better never to see the place again than not return home before nightfall! Shall I go and see the dervish? – this is the hour when he is usually in his oratory. He has always preferred me to my brothers, and will take pity on my trouble. Pity!" I repeated, "oh yes; the pity of contempt! 'This boy,' he will say – 'I thought him a lad of spirit, and here, at twenty years of age, he is incapable of finding a wife! He is nothing but a goose, and does not deserve the key of the cupboard."'

A prey to these bitter reflections, I traced and retraced my steps over the same ground; I wandered hither and thither, restlessly, aimlessly; the mere sight of a woman made my heart beat. I went two steps towards her and made four steps backwards. Every one laughed at me; the passers-by thought me crazy. "Is that the son of Ormossouf, the fisherman?" said some, "How wild he looks! has anyone molested him?" "What a pity," said others, "that he has gone out of his mind; fortunately he seems quite harmless."

Outraged by these insults, worn out by fatigue, and seeing that night was coming on, I took my way at last towards a caravanserai,[1] determined to leave Daghestan on the morrow, and so never suffer the mortification of seeing my brothers in the enjoyment of the treasure I had myself so greatly coveted.

It was already rather dark, and I was walking slowly, with my arms crossed over my breast and despair written large upon my countenance, when, at the corner of the street, I saw, coming from some distance towards me, a little woman, veiled, who appeared to be in great haste. She stopped suddenly, however, as we passed, and, after bestowing on me a gracious salutation, inquired: "What ails you, young man? At your age, and with a face so pleasing, grief ought to be a thing unknown, and yet you seem altogether borne down with trouble."

I took heart on hearing these words. I seized the woman by her hand – which she left in mine – and replied: "Auspicious star, that hidest thyself behind this thin cloud of lawn,[2] is it not possible that Heaven intends thee to be my guiding star indeed? I am looking for a woman ready to espouse me this very night, and to accompany me instantly to the house of my father; and such a woman I have been unable to find."

"She is now found, if so be that you are yourself willing," she replied, in gentle and timid accents. "Take me. I am neither young nor old, neither beautiful nor ugly, but I am chaste,

---

1 caravanserai: inns built on trade routes with storage space for merchandise, stables for animals, and rooms for travellers.
2 lawn: Finely woven linen.

industrious, and prudent; and my name is Homaïouna,[1] which is a name of happy augury."

"Oh, I take you right willingly!" cried I; "for even if you are not all that you say, yet there can be no question of your goodness, since you are thus ready to follow one who is quite unknown to you; and goodness was the one indispensable quality required by my father. Quick, quick; let us hasten to anticipate, or at least not to be behind, my two brothers."

Immediately we began to walk – or rather to run – as fast as we could towards our house. Poor Homaïouna was very soon out of breath, and I perceived that she limped slightly. I was myself very strong, and I took her on my shoulders, not putting her on the ground till we reached the door. My brothers, and their two intended brides, had arrived long before me; but the dervish, who was ever my friend, had insisted on waiting till nightfall, so that the three marriages might, if possible, take place simultaneously. My future sisters-in-law were still veiled, but when I contrasted their entrancing figures with that of Homaïouna my face grew red with shame. And I felt even more perturbed when, after our vows had been reciprocally exchanged, the time came for raising my wife's veil: my hand trembled; I was tempted to turn my eyes away; I fully expected to disclose the features of a monster. But what a pleasant surprise awaited me! Homaïouna was not indeed of extraordinary beauty, like the wives of my two brothers, but her features were regular, her face expressive and intelligent, and she was attracted by an air of indescribable candour. Alsalami, who perceived the ironical smiles of my brothers, whispered in my ear that he was quite sure I had made the best choice of the three, and would see reason to congratulate myself over the wife who had fallen to my lot.

The fatal cupboard was in our sleeping apartment; and, though I was not insensible to my wife's charms, I could not help sighing, as I always did, when looking at that mysterious article of furniture. "Have I the misfortune of not pleasing you?" said Homaïouna tenderly.

---

1 Homaïouna: Perhaps Beckford drew the word from *humayun*, a Persian epithet meaning *fortunate, glorious, royal*. [*Islam2* III, 574]

"By no means," said I, kissing her. "But, in order quite to reassure you, let me explain that this cupboard contains a treasure of which my father has promised the key to the one of his three sons who proves most worthy. He is not in as great a hurry to make his choice as we are to obtain possession of the treasure!"

"Your father is wise," rejoined my wife; "he is afraid of choosing rashly. It remains for you, by your conduct, to solve his doubts. Nevertheless, bear in mind that I am called Homaïouna, and should bring you luck."

The gracious and affectionate air with which she pronounced these words made me entirely forget, for that night at least, the riches that filled my imagination; and, if I had not been the most foolish of men, I should have forgotten them altogether, since I already possessed the greatest, the most inestimable of treasures – a real friend. And indeed I soon perceived that chance had done more for me than foresight had done for my brothers. Their wives were idle, full of vanity, and constantly quarrelling with each other; and though they did not love Homaïouna, whose modesty and housewifely virtues constantly brought them to blush, yet they always referred to her in their differences because they could not help regarding her with respect. My father saw all this well enough, though he said not a word; but I read his thoughts in the looks he cast at the dervish, who, without making any bones about it, praised my wife highly.

One day, having drawn me apart, he said: "Barkiarokh, I have a question to ask, and you must answer it truthfully, for I ask it in your own interest: How did you come to know Homaïouna?"

I hesitated a moment; but, finally, the wish to know the reason of his curiosity prevailed, and I replied fully and without disguise.

"That is a very strange adventure," cried he, "and your story confirms me in an opinion I had already formed. Have you observed, my son, that when your wife is coming and going in the garden, the flowers, as she passes, assume livelier colours and a more delicious fragrance; that the plants and the shrubs, as she touches them, grow visibly; and that the water shed from the watering-pot by her hands rivals in its effects the bright and fertilising dews of the later spring! I have seen your wicker baskets take on an unwonted lustre and fineness as she arranged them for market upon the camel's back. Twice has she got ready your nets, and on both occasions the draught of fishes was miraculous in abundance. Oh, she is assuredly protected by some powerful jinn! Cherish her. Therefore, honour her as the destined source of all your happiness."

I assured Alsalami that I should have no difficulty in following his advice, seeing how well I knew my wife's inestimable qualities. And immediately I retired, being anxious to think over what I had just heard. "If it be true – and all appearances point that way" – said I to myself, "that Homaïouna enjoys the favour of some supernatural power, why does she not open the cupboard, or, at least, determine my father to give her the key? Probably she has never turned her thoughts that way. Shall I suggest it to her? Ah! but dare I? Her wise conversation, her heavenly looks, hold me in awe. Let me rather studiously hide my excessive covetousness in my own bosom. If she knew me as I really am she would despise me, and certainly not aid or abet my evil designs. To veil their vices from the sight of the good is the only resource of those who are not blind and know themselves to be vicious." Thus was I confirmed in habits of hypocrisy; and these, for a time, worked only too effectually to my advantage.

So all went well, and peaceably enough, in our little family; till one night, when we came home, my brothers and I, from selling our fish, we found our father suffering from a most acute attack of gout – a malady to which he had for some time been subject, though he had never before experienced an attack of such violence. Immediately we assumed an air of great consternation, and squatting down on our knees, at a little distance from him, remained in mournful silence. The dervish and the two black slaves held him up, while my wife busied herself about such alleviations to his sufferings as were possible.

As to my sisters-in-law, they had retired to their own rooms, under pretext that they were not strong enough to witness so harrowing a spectacle.

The acute paroxysms of Ormossouf's malady at last left him. Then, turning his eyes upon us, he said: "My dear sons, I know, and very well perceive, how much you love me; and I make no doubt that, however weary, you will hasten to satisfy a whim that has just entered into my head. I have eaten nothing all day, and I should greatly like to have for supper fishes of a rare kind, and pleasant to the taste. Take your nets, therefore, and see what you can do for me. But let each keep apart whatever he chances to catch, so that his wife may cook and prepare it separately. Nevertheless, do not cast your nets into the sea more than once: I give you this direction because it is late, and some accident might befall you. I am not in a condition to bear the anxiety that would ensue if your return were long delayed."

We rose immediately, and, taking our boat, which was moored to the shore close by, went some little way, to what we knew to be a likely spot. There we threw in our nets, each, as we did so, making vows for his own success and the failure of his two brothers. The night was dark. It would have been impossible to examine then and there what we had taken. We returned home, therefore, in ignorance; but, during our short walk from the boat, my brothers suffered all the pangs of envy, for they saw that I was nearly borne down by the weight of my nets, while they carried theirs without the slightest difficulty. Their anxiety however, proved to be only transient. How did they triumph when it turned out that each had taken an enormous fish of a rare kind, and covered with magnificent scales, while mine was so small, and of a colour so brown and uniform, that it looked rather like a reptile than a denizen of the sea! It needed not the shouts of laughter of my sisters-in-law and their husbands to add to my confusion and mortification. I threw my seemingly worthless fish on to the ground, and was about to trample it underfoot, when my wife, having picked it up, said in my ear: "Take courage, my dear Barkiarokh; I am going to cook this little fish, which troubles you so much, and you shall see that it is the best of the three." I had such confidence in her that these words caused hope to revive in my breast, and I quite came to myself.

Ormossouf could not help smiling when he saw that atomy of a fish, which had been placed between the other two on the platter, and presented a most pitiful appearance. "Whose fish is this?" said he.

"It is my husband's," answered Homaïouna; "and a most exquisite delicacy, though it will make but two mouthfuls. Deign, therefore, to eat it entirely yourself, and pray eat it at once. May it do you as much good as I desire. May every best wish we could form for your health and welfare be accomplished as you partake of it!"

"Any article of food coming from thy hand must needs be delicious, seeing how graciously it is offered," replied the good old man; "therefore I will satisfy thee, my dear daughter." Saying these words, he put a piece of the fish into his mouth.

Then me elder brother, jealous of this small act of favour, cried: "Ah! if good wishes only are wanted to win favour here, then who can go further than I, who would willingly exchange my age for that of my father, and give him my strength to take upon myself his weakness!"

"I say the same," interrupted my second brother, "and with all my heart!"

"Oh, I do not yield to either of you in filial tenderness!" cried I, in turn. "I would willingly take to myself the gout that torments my most cherished father, and so deliver him from it for ever, and that is much worse than merely assuming to oneself the wrinkles of his age."

Though I pronounced these words with every show of enthusiasm, yet I held my eyes down, and fixed on the table, for fear that Homaïouna should see how far they were from expressing my real thoughts. But suddenly, at the sound of the piercing cries uttered by my sisters-in-law, I lifted up my head. Oh, marvel unspeakable! oh, miracle! – which still causes my heart to cease beating when I think of it! I saw my brothers bent half double, wrinkled, and showing all the signs of age, and my father irradiated with youth!

Terror took hold upon me. I had, as they had, uttered a rash wish! "Heavens!" I cried, "must I ..." I was able to say no more. Sharp pains shot through me, taking away all powers of speech. My limbs stiffened. My heart failed me. I fell to the ground in a sort of trance – from which, however, I was soon recalled by the noise and tumult in the room. My sisters-in-law were heaping a thousand reproaches on their unhappy husbands, and upbraiding them for the wishes they had uttered. They, on the other hand, were crying out that they had not meant what they said, and that what they had really said could not properly be described as wishes. On this Homaïouna, having told them that Heaven, to unmask knaves, often takes them at their word, they all fell on her, calling her a witch and a wicked Dive, and began to beat her. Ormossouf and the dervish, who undertook to defend my wife, were not spared; but they returned the blows they received a hundredfold, the one having regained his old vigour and strength, and the other having never lost them: thus they necessarily had the advantage of men broken and trembling with age, and of two women rendered incapable by a blind fury. At last my father, weary of such a disgraceful scene, and outraged by his wicked children's want of filial piety, took a scourge armed with a hundred knots, and drove them out of the house with the curses they deserved.

During this scene, in which I would otherwise willingly have taken the part of my brothers, I did, notwithstanding my sufferings, remember the key of the cupboard, and prudently judged that, in order to gain possession of it, I must put a curb on the rage by which I was possessed. To this end I stifled my involuntary cries by putting the end of my robe into my mouth, and remained as if senseless, stretched upon the floor.

So soon as my brothers and their wives were out of the house, the dervish, Homaïouna, and my father ran to me, and tried to lift me up. Their care, and the pity I read in their looks, touched me but little. I was especially furious against my wife, whom I regarded as the cause of all that had taken place. In order to contain myself I had need of the self-control acquired during a long course of habitual hypocrisy. "Deign," said I, in a voice interrupted by many groans, "deign to have me carried to my bed, where I may, perhaps, obtain some relief to my most excruciating pains; but, whatever happens, I shall never repent having delivered my dear father from such an insupportable malady."

"Oh! it is thou, and thou alone, who by the filial piety hast deserved to possess the key of the fatal cupboard," cried Ormossouf. "Here it is," continued he, presenting it to me. "In thee will be accomplished the promises made to my race. Ah! what joy will be mine when I see thee glorious and happy!"

"To contribute to thy happiness will ever be my only joy," said I, with a grateful look; "but I am in great suffering, and at the present moment nothing but sleep can afford me any pleasure."

Immediately I was carried into my room – the room that contained the cupboard – and where I was burning to find myself; and left alone with my wife.

"Here," she said, "it is a healing balm which I will apply to the soles of your feet. It will ease your pain."

"Oh, I have not the slightest doubt that you know what you are about," said I, looking at her gloomily enough; "there does not seem much that you do not know."

Homaïouna made as though she did not notice my ill-humour. She applied the balm, and my sufferings ceased. This good office reconciled me to her somewhat. I kissed her as I passed, and ran to the cupboard. Then I turned the key, trembling with curiosity. I expected to be dazzled by the brightness of the gold and precious stones I should find there, but, in lieu of any such treasure, I found only a very small iron box, containing a leaden ring, and a piece of parchment well folded and sealed. At the sight of this I was utterly confounded. The idea of all it had cost me to obtain possession of what I regarded as pure rubbish stopped the beating of my heart and took away my breath.

"Do not be too soon discouraged," said my wife, "and especially do not begin to regret your act of filial piety; read."

I did as Homaïouna advised, but not without blushing because she had divined my thoughts, and I read these words, written in fine characters upon the parchment: "Take this ring.

When placed on the little finger of thy left hand, it will make thee invisible. By this means thou shalt be enabled to regain the kingdom of thy ancestors, and to reign as either the best, or the vilest, of kings."

At these last words Homaïouna cried out, in a voice so loud and piercing that the very chamber shook withal; "O Allah, Allah! Leave not the choice of this alternative to the husband thou hast given me! Compel him to be good and let me remain for ever a simple mortal. I consent never to revisit my own happy home, and to pass all my days in this my present exile, provided only that my dear Barkiarokh becomes the good king mentioned in this parchment!"

At these words, and on seeing the rays of light that seemed to issue from Homaïouna's eyes, and her form as if transfigured, I fell at her feet with my face to the ground, and, after a few minutes' silence, cried in turn: "O you, whom I scarcely dare to look upon, deign to lead my steps in the way that is set before them, and may your generous wish on my behalf be accomplished!"

"The decrees of Heaven are supreme, and they only are sure of accomplishment," said she, raising me up softly and tenderly; "nevertheless, listen with all your ears, and may my words be engraved upon the tablets of your heart. I will hide nothing that relates to myself, and nothing that relates to your own future duties and responsibilities; and then I shall submit to my fate, whatever it may be." She spoke, sighed deeply, and then began her story in the following words: –

The Story of the Peri Homaïouna

"I know, O son of Ormossouf, that you and Alsalami, the dervish, have come to the conclusion that I am protected by some celestial Intelligence; but how far, even so, were you from guessing to what a glorious race I belong! I am a true daughter of the great Asfendarmod, the most renowned, the most puissant, and, alas! the most severe of all the Peris![1] It was in the

---

1 peri: a species of jinn, renowned for grace, beauty, and goodness.

superb city of Gianhar, the capital of the delightful country of Shaduka,[1] that I came into the world, together with a sister, who was called Ganigul. We were brought up together, and loved one another tenderly, notwithstanding the differences in our dispositions. My sister was mild, languid, quiet – she only cultivated a poetic restfulness – while I was alert, active, always busy about something, and especially desirous of doing good whenever I could find an opportunity.

"My father, into whose presence we never came without trembling, and who had never seemed to trouble his head much about us, caused us one day to be summoned to the foot of his resplendent throne. 'Homaïouna, and you, Ganigul,' said he, 'I have had you both under my observation. I have seen that the beauty, which is the common inheritance of all the Peris, shows equally in the face and form of both of you – but I have also seen that your dispositions are different. Such diversities of character exist, and must exist: they contribute to the general good. You have come to an age when it is fitting that each should consult her own heart, and choose in what manner she prefers to pass her life. Speak! what can I do for you? I am the sovereign of one of the most marvellous countries in Ginnistan – a country in which, as its name implies, desire and its fulfilment, so often separated, go nearly always hand in hand – and you have but to ask in order to obtain. Speak first, Homaïouna.'

"'My father,' I replied, 'I am fond of action. I like to succour the afflicted, and make people happy. Command that there be built for me a tower, from whose top I can see the whole earth, and thus discover the places where my help would be of most avail.'

"'To do good, without ceasing, to mankind, a race at once flighty and ungrateful, is a more painful task than you imagine,' said Asfendarmod. 'And you, Ganigul,' continued he, addressing my sister, 'what do you desire?'

"'Nothing but sweet repose,' replied she. 'If I am placed in possession of a retreat where Nature unveils her most seductive charms – a retreat from which envy and all turbulent passions

---

1 Shaduka: Beckford also spells it Shadukan in this story and Shadukian in *Vathek*. It is the city of "pleasure and desire" in Ginnistan, the land of the peris.

are banished, and where soft pleasure, and a delightful indolence for ever dwell – then I shall be content and happy, and shall, with every returning day, bless a father's indulgence.'

"'Your wishes are granted,' said Asfendarmod. 'You can, at this moment, betake yourselves to your respective habitations. At a glance from me the Intelligences, who do my bidding, have already made every preparation for your reception. Go! we shall meet again. You can sometimes come hither, if such is your wish, or visit one another. Nevertheless, bear in mind that a decision once taken in Shaduka is taken for ever. The celestial race, to which we belong, must never know the unstable desires, still less the feelings of envy, that afflict the feeble race of man.'

"After saying these words, my father motioned to us to retire; and immediately I found myself in a tower, built on the summit of mount Kaf – a tower whose outer walls were lined with numberless mirrors that reflected, though hazily and as in a kind of dream, a thousand varied scenes then being enacted on the earth. Asfendarmod's power had indeed annihilated space, and brought me not only within sight of all the beings thus reflected in the mirrors, but also within sound of their voices and of the words they uttered.

"The first scene that chanced to attract my attention was such as to fill me with righteous anger. An impious mother-in-law was endeavouring, by feigned caresses and artful words, to induce her weak husband to give his daughter in marriage to a negro, hideously deformed, who, as she declared, had seduced the girl's innocence. The young virgin, like a lily already half severed from its stem, bent her lovely head, and awaited, pale and trembling, a fate she deserved so little; while the monster to whom she was destined asked pardon, with the eyes of a basilisk,[1] and the sighs of a crocodile, for an offence he had not committed, and was careful to hide in his heart, which was as black as his countenance, the crimes he *had* committed with the mother-in-law. In the twinkling of an eye, I saw all this in their faces, and flew, quick as lightning to the spot. With my

---

1 basilisk: a mythical reptile whose breath and gaze are fatal.

invisible wand – in which lies concentrated a celestial power distinctive of the higher order of Peris – I touched the wicked woman and her vile paramour. Instantly they altered their tone, looked upon one another with fury, recriminated the one upon the other, and said so much that the husband, transported with rage, cut off both their heads. He then caused his trembling daughter to approach, wept over her tenderly, and afterwards, having sent for a youth as beautiful as herself, had them married on the spot.

"I retired to my tower, well satisfied with having performed an act of justice and equity, and made two amiable creatures happy. And thereupon I passed a delightful night.

"At the point of day I ran to my mirrors: the one before which I stopped reflected the harem of an Indian sultan. I saw there a superb garden, and in it a woman of great beauty, of majestic figure, and of proud and haughty bearing, who seemed to be in a state of great agitation. She was walking on a terrace, with large strides, and looking in every direction most anxiously; nor was her anxiety allayed till she saw a black eunuch coming towards her. He approached with every mark of assiduity and respect, and said, bowing almost to the ground: 'Queen of the world! Your commands are obeyed. The imprudent Nourjehan is confined in the black grotto. The sultan will certainly not look for her there; and to-night the slave dealer, with whom I have conferred, will take her hence for ever.'

"'You have only done your duty,' said the lady; 'but I shall not fail to reward you liberally. Tell me, however, how you succeeded in overmastering my odious rival without disturbance, or clamour on her part?'

"'I accosted her as she came out of the apartment of our lord and master, whom she had left asleep,' replied the eunuch. 'She was about to retire to her own apartment, when, quicker than lightning, I seized hold of her, and wrapped her up in a rug, with which I had provided myself; I then carried her, running as fast as I could, to the black grotto. Then, in order somewhat to allay her fears, I told her she should depart this night with a slave merchant, who might, perhaps, sell her to another king; nor could she hope for a better lot. Calm yourself, therefore, I conjure you, my dear mistress. As soon as the sultan awakes, he will wish to see you, for, notwithstanding his fits of inconstancy, you, and you alone, reign supreme in his heart.'

"'I would not share his love with the unworthy Nourjehan,' cried the lady; 'nevertheless, since I am avenged, I will smother my just anger.'

"I misliked this plot, and its instruments, the lady more especially, and resolved to protect the unfortunate object of her jealousy. So I flew to the black grotto, unclosed the secret door, and, having plunged Nourjehan into a deep slumber, enveloped her with a cloud that rendered her invisible, and in this state bore her to the side of the sultan, who was still asleep. Then I took my flight towards the immense city adjoining the imperial palace.

"I passed the rest of the day in floating over streets and houses, and observed several matters that seemed somewhat out of order, which I proposed to redress. Nevertheless, I felt a certain curiosity to see what was happening in the harem, and returned thither at nightfall. What was my surprise when, in an immense hall, illumined by a thousand lamps, I saw the dead body of the haughty lady whom I had left alive in the morning: it lay in a coffin of aloes wood, and was all covered with livid spots. The sultan, at one time plunged in speechless sorrow, shed torrents of tears, at another time foamed with rage, and swore he would discover the atrocious hand that had cut short the days of his favourite sultana. All the women, ranged in circles round the bier, sobbed in a heartrending manner, and, amid groans and sighs, uttered the most touching eulogies upon the departed. None manifested more sorrow than Nourjehan, nor was more prodigal of her praises. I looked at her fixedly. I read her heart. I enmeshed her in my occult influence. Immediately rolling on the floor like one possessed, she accused herself of having slipped poison into a bowl of sherbet that was being prepared for her rival – and added that she had been led to commit an act of such atrocity by a dream; she had dreamt that the favourite had caused her to be confined in the black grotto, and meant to have her handed over to a slave merchant. The sultan, in a fit of fury, ordered the culprit to be taken from his presence, and immediately strangled. I let things take their course, and returned, pensive, and in confusion, to my tower.

"'Ah!' said I to myself, 'Asfendarmod spoke only too truly when he warned me that the task of benefiting mankind is hard and ungrateful; but ought he not rather to have said that we cannot tell, when we think to do good, whether we may not be really doing harm! I prevented certain designs inspired by jealousy and revenge, but not involving the death of the victim, and have, on the other hand, been the cause of a horrible crime, committed by a furious woman acting under the influence of what she took to be a dream. How perverse are these creatures of clay[1] to whom I have devoted my care! Would it not be better to let them prey upon one another, and to live as my sister does, in the enjoyment of the happiness inherent to natures as perfect as ours? But what am I saying? Am I still in a position to choose? Did not my father tell me that my choice once made was irrevocable? What shall I do? I shall not always be able to read people's hearts from the expression of their countenances. Their stronger emotions I may be able to follow from outward, involuntary signs; but premeditated malice will ever hide behind a mask. It is true that my mysterious influence excites remorse, and leads to the criminal's confession of his crime; but by that time the harm is done, the crime is committed. I cannot anticipate the intention of the wicked; and my intervention, however well meant, may be the cause of a thousand evils.

"These thoughts tormented me night and day. I remained inactive in my tower. In vain did the objects that presented themselves to my gaze excite my compassion, and seem to call for intervention. I refrained from yielding to such impulses. If I saw a grand vizier trying to ruin a rival by vile intrigue, and all the arts of flattery and calumny, I would be on tiptoe to contravene his designs – and then I would stop suddenly, at the thought that that rival might perchance be even more wicked than himself, and a worse oppressor of the people, and that I should thus possibly hear, at the great day of judgement, thou-

---

1 creatures of clay: human beings, formed by God out of earth, and thus elementally different from peris, who are formed from fire.

sands of voices crying out against me. 'Allah, avenge us!' Events, as they passed before me in their daily pageant, almost always justified these previsions.

"One day, having cast my eyes on the flourishing city of Shiraz, I saw, in a very decent dwelling, a woman whose modest beauty and grace charmed me. She had but just entered a very pretty chamber in which there was a little oratory, when she first attracted my attention. Kneeling there, she began to pray with edifying fervour; but, as she was so occupied, her husband burst in the door, which she had closed from the inside, seized her by the hair, took a whip of knotted cords from underneath his tunic, and beat her unmercifully. At the sight of this piece of savagery, I could not contain myself, and hastened to the poor creature's help, arriving, however, just in time to hear the sound of a most sonorous sneeze that came from a cabinet hidden behind some Indian matting. The husband ran to the place from which the sound proceeded, and dragged, out of an obscure recess, a fakir[1] hideous to behold. His hair was matted, frizzled and filthy, his beard red and disgusting, his complexion olive and oily, his body almost naked and covered with old scars. The exasperated Persian was no less confounded than I at the sight of such an object. He looked at it for some moments speechless, and then at last broke out: 'This, then, you infamous creature, is the fine lover you prefer to myself! I knew well enough that a man was shut up with you here, but I never expected to find a monster such as this! And you, continued he, addressing the fakir, 'how did you have the impudence to come here?'

"'I came,' replied the hypocrite, quite unabashed, 'to do what you yourself can evidently do far better than I. Flagellation is meritorious. It mortifies the body, and uplifts the soul. I came to apply the whip to your wife, who is in the habit of confiding to me her little spiritual troubles. For the purpose I had brought with me the penitential instrument which you see here, but you have forestalled me. Sufficient for the day – she has had enough, and so I withdraw.' Saying these words, he took

---

1   fakir: a religious beggar; fakirs normally lived religious lives of great austerity.

from a kind of belt, which composed his only habiliment, a large scourge, thickly knotted, and stepped towards the door.

"The husband stopped him, half mechanically, for he remained quite confused and uncertain. His wife, seeing this, at once threw herself down at his feet. 'Ah, my beloved spouse,' cried she, 'finish your work, make me die beneath your blows, but do not imperil your soul by falling foul of this worthy man. He is the friend of our holy Prophet;[1] beware, yes, beware of the curse that will surely light upon your own head if you molest him and do him wrong.'

"'What does all this mean?' said the unhappy Persian, utterly bewildered and almost convinced of the innocence of his wife. 'I am not so easily frightened. Be more coherent, and explain how this pretended saint came to be here, and how long have you known him. I should be glad enough to believe that you are less guilty than you at first appeared, but I must have a full and reasonable account of what has taken place, and, above all, I must have the truth.'

"He had it only too completely, for at that moment I touched his perfidious spouse with my wand, and she rose from the ground like a wild thing, and cried in a loud voice, 'Yes, I love this vile seducer to distraction, and more than I ever loved thee, thou tyrant of my life! A hundred times have I kissed his bleared eyes, and his livid, discoloured mouth; in a word, I have made him master not only of thy means, but of my person. On his side he has taught me to laugh at Allah[2] and his Prophet, to utter the most infamous blasphemies, and to deride the most sacred things. I knew that thou wert spying on me, and had knelt down in prayer, so as to deceive thee – not anticipating the trivial accident that revealed my paramour's presence. Such are my crimes. I hold them in abhorrence. Something, I know not what, compels me to disclose them. Let my accomplice refuse to reveal *his* if he dares.'

"The fakir, though utterly confounded, opened his lips to reply. I don't know what he might have said for himself – I had not taken the trouble to subject him to my influence – but the

---

1 Muhammed: the inspired founder of Islam.
2 Allah: God.

enraged Persian did not give him time to utter one syllable. He took him by the middle, and hurled him from the top of the balcony, and then sent the wife the same way. They fell from a very great height, into a courtyard paved with sharp stones, and were dashed to pieces.

"I was returning, very pensively, to my tower, when lamentable shrieks, coming from a thick wood, assailed my ears. I ran forward, and saw a young man, more beautiful than the angels in the seventh heaven, defending himself against three negroes, whose shining scimitars[1] had already wounded him in several places, and who cried to him without ceasing: 'Where is your brother! What have you done with your brother?'

"'Barbarous wretches,' he replied, 'he is, alas! where you wish to send me. You have murdered him, and it is now my turn.'

"These words touched me. The air of the youth, scared as he was, seemed so interesting, that I thought I might venture to intervene. I was about to snatch him out of the hands of his enemies, by whom he had at last been disarmed, when another youth, covered with blood, appeared behind the scene, painfully dragging his wounded body from behind some bushes. 'My friends,' said he, in a feeble voice, to the negroes, who ran forward to meet him, 'carry me instantly to the palace of my beloved Adna. Let my last looks be fixed on her, and may Heaven grant me enough life to give her my troth. You could find no better means of avenging me of my brother, who has only murdered me in order to prevent our union, and to possess my goods. I see that you became aware, but too late, of his atrocious designs, and have begun to punish him. Go no further. Let us leave him to bleed in this remote spot. That will be punishment enough. We are not bound to help him further.'

"The negroes obeyed. They bore away their master. The criminal remained, stretched upon the ground, pale and haggard as a spectre come from hell; nor was I in any wise tempted to give him any help of mine.

"These two adventures convinced me, finally, that acts of

---

1   scimitar: a curved sword.

benevolence, on my part, might often be much misplaced. I resolved to make appeal to the justice of Asfendarmod with regard to the change which such events had naturally operated in my sentiments.

"Nevertheless, as I well knew how stern and strict he was, I thought it would be to my advantage to obtain my sister's countenance and help. So I left my tower, and took flight for her habitation.

"The habitation Ganigul had obtained from my father was in every respect conformable to her tastes and wishes. It was situated on a little island, which a river, translucent and bordered with flowering thorns, encircled seven times. In the interspaces between these circles the grass was so moist and fresh that the fishes would often leave the silvery waters of the river and disport themselves there. Various kind of grass-eating animals browsed in these moist meads, which were starred with flowers; and all enjoyed such happiness in the regions assigned to them that they never thought to stray. The island itself was at once a flower garden and an orchard. It seemed as if the sweet-smelling shrubs had joined in friendship with the fruit-trees, so closely were their branches interlaced. The daintier flowers grew on the more immediate border of the stream, and the shores of the stream itself were of the finest gold sand. A bower of orange-trees and myrtle, surrounded by a palisade of gigantic roses, formed my sister's palace, and was the spot to which she retired at night, together with six Peris who had attached themselves to her company. This delightful retreat was situated in the centre of the island; a brook ran through it, formed by a thousand rivulets of water, that joined on entering its confines, and separated again at their exit. As these running streamlets ran over a stony, uneven bed, they made a constant melodious murmur, that harmonised perfectly with the voice of the nightingales. On both sides of the brook were ranged beds, made of the shed petals of flowers, and of feathers of divers colours which the night birds had shaken from their tiny wings; – and on these beds one slept voluptuously. Thither Ganigul often retired in the daytime to read in quiet the marvellous annals of the Jinns, the chronicles of ancient worlds, and the prophecies relating to the worlds that are yet to be born.[1]

"After the days of agitation I had spent in my tower, I seemed to pass into a new life on entering into this abode of peace. My sister received me with a thousand caresses, and her friends were no less eager to provide for my entertainment. Sometimes they challenged the creatures of lightest foot to run races with them; sometimes they joined their heavenly voices to the voices of the birds; or they sported with the goats, which, like the ewes and cows, would gladly present to them udders full of milk; or else they matched themselves in feats of agility against the sprightly gazelles. Amid all the creatures thus daily ministering to their pleasure, the dog, faithful and caressing, the lithe and supple cat, were not forgotten. But none were more amiable and delightful than a little Leiki which never quitted the happy Ganigul. The divine warbling of this lovely bird, the brilliant colours of its plumage, were even less to be admired than the extreme sensibility of its heart, and the supernatural instinct with which it had been endowed by some superior power. Whether at rest in the bosom of its mistress, or whether, fluttering among the shadeful myrtles, it gave voice to a song of an endless variety, it never ceased to be attentive to all her movements; and it seemed ever on the watch to forestall and obey her every wish. By the beating of its wings it expressed its joy when anything was found for it to do: it would dart like lightning to fetch the flowers, the fruits, that Ganigul desired; it would bring them in its vermeil beak, which it would lovingly insinuate between her lips as asking to be rewarded for its service. I occasionally had a share in its caresses, and returned them willingly; but as I did so I sighed to think I had no such companion in my solitude.

---

1   worlds that are yet to be born: "The fabulous Asiatic ages stretch far beyond the creation of man. They suppose the world to have been repeatedly peopled by creatures of different formation, who were successively annihilated or banished for disobedience to the Supreme being. An Eastern Romance introduces the hero Caherman in conversation with the monstrous bird or Griffon *Simurgh*; who tells him, that she had already lived to see the earth seven times filled with creatures, and seven times a perfect void: that the age of Adam would be seven thousand years; when the race of man would be extinguished, and their place supplied by beings of another form and more perfect nature ..." [*Richardson*, 141-42].

"My sister had wisely reminded me that this was the time of the great assemblage of the Peris, over which Asfendarmod presided in person, and that it would be better, therefore, to defer our proposed visit to a more convenient season. 'My dear Homaïouna,' said she to me one day, 'you know how tenderly I love you, and you know also that I desire nothing better than to have your company. Would to Heaven that you had, like myself, made choice of the peace and tranquillity of this abode! May my father allow you to share in its delights! Nevertheless, I advise you to make further trial, for a little while, of the kind of life you yourself selected. Either you will find therein unexpected satisfaction, or you will have new reasons to allege in urging the stern Asfendarmod to relieve you from further trials. As to the time of your departure, let us postpone it as much as possible. Rejoice here in my friendship, and in all the delights by which I am surrounded. Art is excluded from my domain; but Nature is here prodigal of her gifts. I possess everything I had desired, and even more; for I had no conception of such a gift as a happy chance has bestowed upon me.'

"'You mean, doubtless, your beloved bird,' said I, much moved. 'How did you obtain possession of it?'

"'Oh, I am quite ready to tell you the story,' answered she. 'I always think of it with renewed pleasure. I was seated in the shade of that great lilac-tree, whose flowers diffuse such a pleasant odour, when, suddenly, the sky put on the liveliest colours, rosier than the most brilliant sunrise. A light, intense beyond description, spread over all, diffusing everywhere a feeling of unspeakable joy and content. It was a light that seemed to pour down direct from some sanctuary, or, if I may dare to say so, from the very throne of the Supreme Power. At the same time strains of a divine harmony floated in the air – strains ravishing, indefinite, that appeared to lose themselves in the vague infinity of space. A cloud of almost indistinguishable birds went sailing across the firmament. The murmur of their innumerable wings, mingling with the far flutings of their song, threw me into an ecstasy. While I was lost in the enjoyment of these marvels, one bird detached itself from the rest, and fell, as if exhausted, at my feet. I lifted it up tenderly. I warmed it in my breast. I encouraged it to resume its flight; but it refused to leave me. It came back and back, and seemed desirous of becoming altogether mine. Its shape, as you see, is that of a Leiki, but its gifts of mind and soul equal those of the most favoured creatures. A heavenly inspiration seems to breathe through its songs; its language is that of the empyrean;[1] and the sublime poems it recites are like those which the ever-happy Intelligences declaim in the abodes of glory and immortality. Supremely marvellous, even in a country where everything is a marvel, it follows me, it serves me like the most willing of slaves, I am the object of its tenderest gratitude – it is the object of my admiration, and of my care. Ah! how rightly it is called the Bird of Love!'

"These last words troubled me so that I had some difficulty in hiding my perturbation. Envy took possession of my soul: no doubt I had contracted that degrading passion in my inter-course with mankind, for, so far, it had not been known among us. Everything about me turned to gall and wormwood. I longed to be alone, and, when alone, could not bear my own company. I issued at night from my sister's bower of perennial blossoms, to stray, as chance dictated, through the surrounding wilderness of leaves, and, when there, the brilliant light shed by thousands of glow-worms only served to exasperate me. I would fain have trampled on these little creatures, whose amaz-ing numbers and marvellous brilliance had before excited my admiration. Darkness was what I sought as a fit cloak for my shameful thoughts. 'Oh, Ganigul!' I said, 'how happy are you, and how wretched am I! What comparison is there between your isle of peace and my tower of discordant sighs, between your delightful leisure and my continual agitation, between the smiling natural beauties, the innocent and faithful creatures that surround you, and the rude world, the wicked and ungrateful race of man, that I have ever before my eyes? Ah! your sweet bird is more necessary to me than to you! You have friends ever assiduous to please you, an infinite number of creatures at beck and call for your amusement – why, why should I not have at

---

1   the empyrean: the highest reaches of heaven.

least this one thing which would stand to me in lieu of all the rest? Yes, I will have it. I will take it from you, for you would doubtless refuse to give it me. I will take it away with me, and you will certainly not remain uncomforted for its loss in this delightful sojourn.'

"Though at first I put away with horror the thought of such a crime, yet, insensibly, I grew accustomed to it, and all too soon there occurred a sad opportunity for the perpetration of the theft. One day I was alone in a little grove of jasmine and pomegranates, when the Leiki came thither seeking for flowers. I called him. He flew to me. Immediately, binding his feet and wings with a slight piece of fibre, I hid him in my bosom. As I was about to fly with the stolen bird, I heard my sister's voice calling me. I trembled in all my limbs. I was unable to move a step. 'What do you want with me?' cried I, in a peevish tone?

"'Ah! why,' asked Ganigul tenderly, as she hastened up, 'why do you thus seek to be alone? In the name of all our love for one another, let me at least have a share in your troubles.'

"'No,' cried I, in great agitation, and pressing to my heart the bird, which was trembling pitifully, and which I wished to keep from uttering any sound. 'No, I will no longer burden you with my presence. Adieu, I am going hence.'

"Scarcely had I pronounced these words, when a thick, black cloud cast its veil over the firmament, and dimmed the brilliancy about us; and the hiss of rain and growling of a storm filled the air. At last my father appeared, borne on a meteor whose terrible effulgence flashed fire upon the world. 'Stay, wretched creature,' said he, 'and behold the innocent victim that hath fallen a sacrifice to thy barbarous envy!'

"I looked, and, oh, horror! I had smothered the marvellous, the greatly loved bird!

"At this moment all grew dark before my eyes. I tottered, I fell to the ground lifeless.

"When the great voice of Asfendarmod brought me back to my senses, I saw neither my sister, nor her friends, nor her fatal Leiki. I was alone with my inexorable judge.

"'Daughter of crime,' said he, 'go and crawl upon that earth where Allah alone is the dispenser of events, and whence thou hast carried away nothing save its vices. Study mankind at leisure before pretending to afford them help and protection. Thou shalt still retain some of the privileges inherent in thy nature, but thou shalt at the same time be liable to some of the most cruel sufferings to which men are liable. And you, O winds, mysterious invisible powers, who do my bidding, bear her to the obscure sojourn of men! May she there, by patience and wisdom, regain her title to come back once more to our regions of light!'

"On hearing this fulminating sentence, I threw myself, utterly distracted on my knees, and, unable to speak, lifted up to my father's suppliant hands. Then, all of a sudden, a whirlwind, palpable, overmastering, surrounded me, and having lifted me from the place where I knelt bore me downward, circling ever, during seven days and seven nights. At the end of that time, I was deposited on the dome of a palace overlooking an immense city, and I knew that I had reached my destination. I acquiesced very humbly in the fate I had so well deserved.

"When I began to examine my surroundings, I was at once struck by the signs of utter gloom that reigned throughout the city. Men, women, children, all had put ashes on their heads, and were running hither and thither in great perturbation. Little by little they trooped together in a large place before the palace, and seemed to be in expectation of some extraordinary event. As I was not sure of having retained the power of moving at will from place to place, I formed a wish, trembling as I did so, to mingle with the crowd: and, at the same moment, found myself side by side with a great black eunuch, who was trying to keep order with his cane, striking out to right and left. Notwithstanding his truculent air, I thought he looked really good-natured, and tried to attract his notice. At last he turned his eyes upon me.

"'What are you doing here, girl?' said he, in tones half of reproof, and half friendly. 'Here, and without your veil, like a wanton! Yet you seem to be a modest girl too, unless your looks belie you. Follow me into the palace. You would certainly be insulted in this crowd; and, besides, I like to hear tell of adventures, and you can tell me yours.'

"I bent my head in submission, and taking hold of the eunuch by his robe, made it my business to follow him. He forced a way through the press with his cane. By his orders the guard at the palace gate allowed me to pass, and he led me into his apartment, which was cleanliness itself. 'Sit down,' said he, 'you must be tired. I have no time at the present moment, to listen to a long story. Tell me only, and in a few words, who you are, and how you came to be outside, in the midst of the populace, half dressed, and, as it seemed to me, quite alone?'

"'I am,' I replied, 'the unfortunate daughter of a mighty prince, who dwells very far from hence. I have been carried away from the palace – by whom I know not. My captors compelled me for several days to travel so rapidly that I was quite unable to distinguish the road by which I was being taken. At last I was left by them in the place where you found me, and in the same apparel, the apparel I wore when they tore me from my home; and,' I added, 'I shall be less unhappy than I thought myself if I succeed in obtaining your distinguished protection.'

"'Yes,' said Gehanguz, for that was the eunuch's name, 'such apparel as you have on you is fine; and, moreover, there is an air of distinction about you conforming fairly well with what you tell me concerning your birth. But be quite frank with me, and tell me truly whether your captors committed any outrage against your person during the journey?'

"'O, by no means,' I replied. 'Revenge was their motive, and revenge closes the heart against the ingress of all other passions.'

"'Enough for the present,' said Gehanguz, 'you do not seem wanting in intelligence, and may be as useful to me as I to you. Rest here a while, and take some refreshment; dress yourself as befits. I will see you again in a few hours.'

"Having spoken these words, he clapped his hands, gave various orders to several young girls who instantly appeared, and departed.

"The young girls drew near to me with great respect, put

me in a bath, rubbed me all over with precious essences, clothed me in a very beautiful dress, and served me with an excellent collation. Nevertheless, being plunged in the deepest sadness, I maintained the while an absolute silence. 'What shall I do?' said I to myself. 'Shall I stay here under the charge of Gehanguz? He seems to be kindly and humane, but I have learnt to distrust appearances. I feel that it is within my power to take flight to any habitable corner of the earth; but wherever I go, I shall find men and wherever there are men I shall have to face the same troubles and anxieties. Will it not be better, seeing I deserve my punishment, to undergo that punishment in its entirety, and submit altogether to my fate, only using my supernatural powers in circumstances of absolute necessity? Besides, the dread executors of Asfendarmod's decree brought me hither. That is a further reason for remaining where I am, and striving, by an unbounded submission, to re-enter those happy regions from which I am not to be for ever excluded.'

"Sleep at last closed my eyelids. A happy dream took me back to Shaduka: I stood beside Ganigul in the bower of orange-trees and myrtle. She looked at me with sad eyes full of pity. Her Leiki flew about her uttering plaintive cries. As she strove to quiet it, I threw myself at her feet. Then she took me in her arms and held me tenderly to her bosom.

"But at this point, while still in this ecstasy of happiness, I was awakened by the voice of the eunuch. 'Come,' said he in his harsh voice, harsh yet not altogether unsympathetic, 'come, let us for a while discuss your affairs; and begin by telling me your name.'

"'I am called Homaïouna,' said I, uttering a deep sigh. 'It was without a doubt, a mistake to bestow that name upon me.'

"'Not at all!' cried Gehanguz; 'there is no life, however fortunate, in which at least one reverse does not occur. That reverse you have just experienced. Henceforward we shall have nothing but uninterrupted prosperity. Now, listen, and I will explain matters. You are now in the famous city of Choucan, the capital of the greatest and richest country in the Indian peninsula. The king who reigned here a few days ago, had twenty other kings as vassals, elephants without number, treasures that could not be counted, and an untold host of subjects both industrious and obedient; but, with all this, he has had to fall asleep, like any ordinary man. He was placed this morning on the bed of everlasting rest; and that is why you saw all the people in mourning.'

'"That means," I interrupted, 'that this great king is dead, and that he has just been buried.'

'"Fie! fie!' cried the eunuch, with a sour look. 'How dare you utter words so offensive to self-respecting ears. Such expressions are banished from Choucan. Keep a strict watch over your tongue, or you would at once give the lie to all I mean to say concerning your birth, and the superior education it should imply.'

'"Fear nothing,' I rejoined, with a smile. 'I shall know how to conform to so delicate a custom.'

'"Very well,' he pursued in a milder tone, 'you must know then that our good king never had any children save two daughters, twins, and equally beautiful and amiable. Whether he found it difficult to make a choice between the two, or whether he had some reason or other for leaving the question open, I know not; but he never, during his lifetime, gave people to understand which of the two was to inherit his crown. Nevertheless, a little time before he entered into his last sleep he summoned four old men, whose profound wisdom had never once been found wanting during the fifty years they had served him as viziers – and to those old men he entrusted the sacred parchment containing his last instructions, and signed with the twenty-one seals of the Empire. This parchment was opened a few moments ago, and it decides nothing.'

'"How,' said I, 'he has not named a successor?'

'"No,' replied Gehanguz; 'all he has left to his daughters is a problem for their solution – a problem which, as I am assured, is full of difficulty, – with the order that the one who best solves it, according to his own views, as communicated to the four viziers, shall be proclaimed Queen absolute of Choucan and its dependencies. I had received some inkling of his intentions from one of the favourite sultanas, who has extended me her protection, even more because of my zeal in my office than because I am chief of the eunuchs. But, as she did not herself know the question to be propounded, she was unable to impart it to me. If one may judge by the countenances of the princesses to whom alone it has been communicated by the four viziers, it must indeed be thorny. They seemed to be plunged in deep thought on leaving the divan. They were even overheard whispering to each other that they would require every one of the forty allotted days in order to ponder out a solution. This is the present state of things,' continued Gehanguz, 'and here is my project: I will assign you as companion to the two princesses, who live together, to all appearances, in perfect harmony. They will receive you gladly, for they like novelty, and are tired of all their girl slaves. You will insinuate yourself into their good graces, and so divide your attention as to retain the confidence of the one who ultimately becomes Queen. You will speak to them often about me, and dissipate, as far as may be, the effect of anything that the little crazy-pated slave girls may have said to my disadvantage. If you see that one of the two is better disposed in my favour than the other, you will help her with your advice, and with mine, in case she confides to you the question of questions. In any case you will do your best to keep me in favour with both. The few words I have heard you speak, show that you possess intelligence; your eyes give promise of even more. You will have no difficulty, therefore, in obtaining over the princesses that ascendancy which people of intelligence naturally acquire over those who are not so gifted. Moreover, in acting as I propose, you will cause me to retain my office, and be yourself the favourite of a great Queen – a position not to be despised. And I may say that it is not ambition, and still less self-interest that prompts me in this. It is the desire to see the harem maintained in the admirable order I have established here. I should be in absolute despair if any wrong-headed person were to come and destroy the work I have accomplished with such unimaginable pains. You will see for yourself the results of my efforts, and, I make no doubt, will from a feeling of justice consent to serve me. But that will in no way dispense me from acknowledging my indebtedness.'

"I had listened to what Gehanguz was saying. I had carefully watched his eyes to see if I could detect in them a little cloud of embarrassment almost certain to appear when a speaker is animated by some sinister design; but I had been able to discover nothing save zeal, kindliness and sincerity. Nevertheless, I determined to be circumspect and careful in the observations which, by his means, I should be in a position to pursue, and only to serve his interests in so far as he might be worthy of assistance.

"On the same day he presented me to the Princesses Gulzara and Rezie, indulging in such eulogies and encomiums on my merits as would not have been excessive even if he had known my real condition. At everything he invented concerning my ability and accomplishments, I could not help smiling, and looking at him in a way that disconcerted him somewhat. But I took pity on him, and reassured his mind by another look, intended to signify that I should perform every thing he promised.

"There was I, then, late a sovereign in Shaduka, now a slave in Choucan – my heavenly beauty a thing of the past, my face and form quite ordinary, my youth gone too, and an indeterminate and unattractive age assigned to me instead; and condemned to remain under this altered shape, an exile for a limitless period, and to be subject to evils both unknown and unforeseeable. My fall was indeed terrible; but I had brought it on myself, and I did not repine.

"Both my new mistresses conceived for me, from the first, a lively affection. I told them interesting and amusing stories. They were transported with pleasure when I sang, accompanying my voice, which was melodious, upon the lute. If I devised for them some new adornment, it seemed to add to their beauty; the refreshments poured by my hands were always agreeable to the taste, and diversified in flavour. At all my successes poor Gehanguz opened great eyes, and went into ecstasies of surprise and pleasure.

"Gulzara I liked much better than her sister. But I had the best of reasons for mistrusting first impressions – those instinctive attractions that are, for the most part, deceptive. I was not sorry, therefore, when the two princesses took to quarrelling as to which should have most of my company in private. This would give me an opportunity of better studying their characters. I took advantage of it, and soon became convinced that, in this particular instance, my first inclination had not played me false. Rezie, under the outward seeming of a seductive affability, hid an evil heart; she might have imposed, if her violent passions had not sometimes caused her to reveal her real self. When her vanity had made her believe that I preferred her to Gulzara, she opened her mind to me freely, and acquainted me, not only with the question propounded by the King her father, but also with her proposed reply. I saw with pleasure that she had no chance of becoming queen; she deserved to be queen so little! All her intentions were unjust as concerned the people, and malicious as concerned her sister. Gulzara, more reserved, did not give me her confidence so easily. I had to merit it by devotion, and kindly care, which, indeed, cost me nothing, because I really loved her, and wished to do her service. At last she confessed, in tones that were persuasive, because simple and unaffected, that she had no ambition, and only wished to be queen for the sake of the good she might do; but that in this respect she was fully prepared to trust her sister, and had not even troubled her head to think about her father's question. All she said made me deem her so worthy to rule that I thought it only right to tell her it was her duty, in conformity with the King's last wishes to aspire to the throne. She hesitated, however; but was at last persuaded – especially after I had thrown light on the perplexing problem propounded by the late King, and had furnished a reply with which she appeared to be more than satisfied.

"On the day when this great matter was to be settled, the city resounded with the noisy instruments of music in use in that country. The people again trooped together with the murmur and rustle of swarms of angry bees. And Gehanguz, drawing me aside, asked if I had any idea of what was likely to be the issue.

"'Set your mind at rest,' said I. 'All will be well. You will be retained in your office, because I am convinced that you only desire to remain chief eunuch from good motives.'

"At these words he began to caper like a roebuck, and ran to open the door of the divan for the princesses, whom I was following.

"The assembly was already complete, and the spectacle most striking. At the end of an immense mysterious hall stood a throne of blue enamel, all dotted over with unnumbered phosphorescent lights like stars, brilliant and terrible. This symbolic throne was raised on four columns – two of jasper, blood-red, and two of the purest alabaster – and I knew at once that the Jinns had fashioned it. I understood that the red columns stood for justice, and the white for mercy, and that the stars symbolized the rays that emanate from a good king, and serve as light to lighten his people. The four old viziers entrusted with the commands of the late monarch, now asleep, stood within a latticed grating of steel, surmounted with spikes, that surrounded the throne. A few paces from it carpets were set, similar to those used for prayer in the Mosques, and on those carpets knelt the ambassadors of twenty kings, vassals of the King of Choucan. The grandees of the State knelt at a greater distance, all profoundly inclined, and holding a finger to their lips.

"The princesses advanced up to the steel grating, with their eyes lowered and hands crossed over their breasts. Then one of the viziers, having shown to the assembly the seal of the King, inscribed in large characters on the parchment, read these words, in a loud voice: 'Rezie and you, Gulzara, I have not thought it well to decide which of you two shall pass beyond the sharp spikes of steel that guard the royal seat. I make you the arbiters of your own fate. Reply: which is the more worthy of reigning – a virgin princess who marries, loves her husband, and provides heirs to the throne, or a virgin princess who, not marrying, has yet a whole multitude of sons and daughters whom she cherishes like the apple of her eye?'

"'Wise and reverend sires,' said Rezie, 'it must be clear to you that the King, when he propounded this strange question, wished to pass a jest upon us; and that it is only a woman chaste, and solely attached to her husband, who can be worthy to fill his throne. My sister doubtless thinks as I do, and we will reign together, if such be your good pleasure.'

"The viziers answered not a word. They turned towards Gulzara, who, with modest mien, spoke thus: 'I think the King, our father, wished to intimate that a princess whose whole desire is to be the mother of her subjects, who thinks rather of making them happy during her lifetime than of providing them with masters after her death, and who has no other care save the public good, that such a princess is most worthy of being a queen. I promise never to marry, and to have no children save my people.'

"Scarcely had she uttered these words than the four viziers, having impetuously opened the door of the steel grating, threw themselves at her feet, crying with all the strength of their lungs: 'Honour and glory to Gulzara, Queen of Choucan! Happy for ever be Gulzara our Queen!'

"The ambassadors and grandees repeated these acclamations in even louder tones, so that their shouts reached the people assembled before the palace. These latter made the air resound with their cries, at the same time beating one another without mercy. Blows, cuffs, even dagger thrusts, passed freely on all sides. The hubbub was so terrible that I should have been frightened if I had been susceptible to fear. 'What does this mean?' said I, in a low voice, to Gehanguz. 'Have all these people gone mad?'

"'No, no,' he replied; 'they are only doing what they aught to do. Here it is customary, when any great and happy event takes place, to grave it on the popular memory after this manner. Recollection is thereby greatly quickened. Fortunate are those who, on such occasions, have lost an eye or a limb! Their family is then regarded as really zealous for the public good; and children, seeing upon their fathers such honourable scars, glory in them from generation to generation. Indeed, the custom is sound and salutary, for the people are ever fickle and forgetful, and would keep nothing in mind unless some special means were taken to jog their memory.'

"Meanwhile the four viziers had displayed to the whole divan the writing of the King, showing that Gulzara had answered according to his intentions, and ought to be made queen. She was accordingly installed formally upon the throne, at the foot of which Rezie came to do homage, with a smile that seemed to the assembly generally a smile of congratulation, but that to my eyes showed only as a mask for spite and disappointment. The new Queen assured her sister of her love – then raising her own right hand three times above her head to command attention, she said: 'Venerable councillors of my father, I shall never undertake anything of importance without your advice; but who will serve as an intermediary in our communications, and inform you of my decisions? Who will enter with me into such details as are necessary for the good of the state? I am a virgin, and I have promised to remain so, always. Daily intercourse with a man would in no way be convenient. I declare, therefore, that Homaïouna, whose ability and competence are well known to me, shall be my grand vizier; and I ordain that she shall be invested with all the powers appertaining to that office.'

"The four old councillors, the twenty ambassadors, and the grandees of the kingdom, all acquiesced unanimously. Gehanguz came, trembling with joy, and led me to the first step of the royal dais. All spoke my praises in a loud voice – not one of them having the least knowledge of me. Then Rezie, no longer able to contain herself, asked permission to retire, and whispered in my ear as she passed: 'This is another new trick of yours, vile slave; you shall pay dearly for your presumption and insolence!' I pretended not to hear the threat or the insult, deciding to hide them from Gulzara, whom they would only have grieved and alarmed. Indeed, I was filled with admiration for that amiable princess, having received no previous intimation of the generous engagement into which she had entered for the good of her people.

"'Why, my Queen,' said I, when we were alone, 'why have you promised not to marry? It would surely have sufficed if you had merely replied according to the views of the King, your father.'

"'The sacrifice was not so great as you imagine, my dear Homaïouna. But more I cannot tell you. To go into details would but envenom the wound still bleeding in my heart; and we must devote our attention to other matters. I feel that in you there is something above nature; and it is on you that all the weight of kingship must devolve. Rule in my empire; and, if I am at all dear to you, so rule that my reign shall be famous to all time for justice and good government. The hope of living with glory in the memory of men will comfort me for having lived my life among them unhappily.'

"I respected Gulzara's secret, and succeeded, even beyond her hopes, in fulfilling the wishes she had formed for her people's good. All India resounded with her name. The prosperity of her Empire was the admiration and envy of all kings. The twenty princes, her vassals, insisted on paying a double tribute, and mostly brought their tribute to the capital in person. Bands of musicians were constantly posted on the beautiful terraced roofs of the palaces of the great in Choucan, and there they sang the praises of the Queen, or played loud and lively music, to which the people danced. All this contributed to Gulzara's gaiety. As to Gehanguz, he could not contain himself for joy, and blessed the day when he had come across me.

"For five years my efforts had been thus successful, and I was congratulating myself on having, at last, made so many people happy, when one day, the zealous eunuch entered my apartment looking utterly terrified and bewildered. 'Homaïouna,' said he, 'come quickly to the Queen. She has quite lost her wits. She laughs and cries at the same time, passes from a transport of joy to the extremity of despair, and shows every symptom of complete mental derangement. Ah! we are lost! Rezie will wish to govern. The great fabric of happiness which you have erected in Choucan, and my own little masterpiece of good government in the harem, will alike fall to pieces. O, unhappy day! Oh, day for ever marked with a black sign! Why did I not die before seeing its baleful light?'

"I did not trouble to answer Gehanguz; I made haste to follow him. Gulzara ran to meet me with wild eyes. Seizing my hand, she cried: 'He is come! He is not dead! His lovely eyebrows alone were burned, and his hair singed! But eyebrows and hair have grown again, magnificent as ever, and he asks to see me! What unforseen unhappiness! Ah, no! what an overwhelming misfortune,' continued she, throwing herself on a sofa and shedding a torrent of tears. 'I have renounced him for ever! Alas, I did not do so for want of love, but because I loved him too well! What is to become of me? Advise me, Homaïouna! Mayhap I shall follow your advice – mayhap you will lose my favour by giving it me!'

"'Calm yourself, my Queen,' said I, 'and explain. I don't understand what you mean, nor do I know of whom you are speaking.'

"'True,' she rejoined, 'I have never told you about Prince Tograi,[1] my mother's nephew – Prince Tograi whom I have cherished from my earliest infancy; who responded to my love with all his heart; who was said to have perished in a great fire; and who now returns, now when, faithful to his memory, I have promised never to marry. What will he say?'

"'He will,' I replied, 'be overwhelmed doubtless with grateful feelings when he knows that the sacrifice – vaunted everywhere as an act of unspeakable generosity – was really made for his sake; and, if worthy of you, he will applaud you greatly.'

"'You speak coldly and calmly, wise Homaïouna,' rejoined the Queen. 'You are as unendurable snow to the fire burning in my heart! Retire, and do you, Gehanguz, at once introduce the Prince Tograi.'

"I obeyed, condemning myself even more than Gulzara did, for having tried to make head against the assault of a passion so violent and overwhelming, instead of allowing somewhat for its first fury.

"During three hours – the saddest hours passed since my exile from Shadukan – I did nothing but sorrow over my amiable princess, and deplore the instability of the happiness I had thought to build on secure foundations. It was she herself who broke in upon my sad forebodings. She came to me open-

---

1 Tograi; al-Tughra'i, Mu'ayyid al-Din: Arab poet from Isfahan (ca. 1061-1121). While of no significance to Beckford's character, the name is indicative of Beckford's concern with authenticity.

armed, and began by flooding me with tears. At last, growing somewhat calmer, she said: 'I have come back to my senses, dear Homaïouna, but my deep grief will not pass away as easily as my fit of unreason. Listen, tremble, and pity me! The Prince Tograi appeared before my eyes looking as though he had just bathed in the Prophet Kedder's Spring of Immortality.[1] He was radiant with beauty, youth and, as it seemed to me, with love. He threw himself on his knees to kiss the hem of my garment. I held out my hand, and would, I think, have kissed him, if the presence of Gehanguz, whom I had ordered to stand near by, had not restrained me. He read in my eyes the feelings of my heart; but instead of showing the loving gratitude of which you spoke a while ago, he began to upbraid me angrily. I forgave his first outburst. I tried to pacify him. I went so far as to offer to resign the crown of Choucan so that we might be united. I told him I must certainly renounce the throne if I infringed the solemn engagement into which I entered when I accepted it, but I protested truly that, with him, I should never regret my abdication. 'And indeed,' I added, 'how could I cherish my people like a tender and loving mother, when my husband was the sole object of my affection, and occupied all my thoughts? The fame I earned,' I told him, 'was but a small alleviation to the grief caused by your loss. Now that I possess you once more, I can well do without it.'

"'I feel,' continued the Queen, addressing me, 'all the shame attaching to such a confession. But will you believe it, Homaïouna, the ungrateful Tograi dared to take advantage of my weakness. He was not afraid to unveil to my eyes a heart as black as the face of an Ethiopian. 'What talk is this about abdicating the throne of the Empire of Choucan?' cried the arrogant prince. 'Is it Gulzara, the Queen, who holds such language – nay, who utters a rhapsody worthy of the hermits of the desert of Hejaz?[2] Let us put all this rubbish aside, and talk seri-

---

1   the Prophet Kedder's Spring of Immortality: Al-Khadir, a mysterious, fabled wise man, lived by the Spring of Immortality. A story concerning him is told in the Koran. [Islam2 IV, 903]
2   Hejaz: Islam's holy land; a province in Arabia where Mecca and Medina are situated. [D'Herbelot, Islam2 III, 362]

ously. If you have really sighed over my exile, if you love me as you say you do – place me at once on the blue throne with the phosphorescent stars. All your father's nonsense can in no way affect your right to the throne – the more so that you are in assured possession. That right I will maintain, and that possession I will confirm by my valour. Rivers of blood shall be made to flow before a word of reproach reaches your ears. All those who come near you will respect you, as they respect me. Whosoever occupies a throne is bound by no promises. Meanwhile, begin by getting rid of a wretched creature whom you have ridiculously appointed to be your Grand Vizier. She is suspected of being a witch, and is, perhaps, only artful and malicious – but that is quite reason enough for putting her in a sack and throwing her into the river. Go, my well-beloved, and settle this at once; don't look so startled. Have you not waited all too long for the happiness you are to enjoy in my arms?'

"'Tograi was quite right in saying I was startled and troubled. I felt as if I should die. But my horror at such impiety and insolence reanimated me. Instead of replying, I clapped my hands; Gehanguz whistled; and immediately fifty eunuchs appeared with their swords drawn. Yet, such is the marvellous power of a passion which shame itself cannot utterly destroy, that I took pity upon him, and said, rather firmly than angrily: 'My mother's nephew, I give thee life in consideration of the ties of blood by which we are united. Go from my presence, and let me never see thee more, unless thou art prepared to undergo the punishment thou hast justly deserved, and be cut into a thousand pieces by these glittering swords.' Having uttered these words, I made signs to the eunuchs to remove the unhappy prince. But they had to carry him out; so terrified was he that he could scarcely stand. For a whole hour I remained as if turned to stone on my divan. Then a crowd of quick and agonising thoughts coursed through my brain, and threw me into a kind of delirium. I thought I saw before me Tograi, amiable and compliant, as, when banished by my father, he came to say good-bye to me, seven years ago – and then that old Tograi vanished, and, behold, the new Tograi, overbearing and perfidious, took his place, and gave me advice, or rather commands, unrighteous and dishonourable. Never, never, Homaïouna, will these two images cease to haunt me. Death alone can deliver me from them; but I shall die worthy of your regrets. Nevertheless, listen, and observe these my orders: come every day, after the hour when the Divan has been held, and be a witness to my tears, and, if you will, mingle with those tears your own. See that Gehanguz makes the interior of my palace as sad and sombre as is my heart. I direct that my musicians sing and play doleful and dirge-like airs, and such airs only. I shall not cause all public rejoicings to cease; but whoever appears before me with a smile upon his lips will add to my pain.'

"I assured Gulzara that it would be to me a solace to mingle my tears with hers, and that she would be strictly obeyed; for I had resolved rather to cheat than openly combat her sorrow. The duties of her position furnished opportunities and means of distraction, which I did not neglect to utilise, and, without a fatal occurrence I should perhaps have succeeded in restoring peace to that generous spirit.

"Rezie had retired to a palace she possessed on the top of a neighbouring mountain. She appeared rarely in the presence of her sister, and then only to play such parts of feigned affection as she had studied in solitude; while Gulzara, who had not yet unmasked her real character, repaid her false attachment with genuine affection. It was long since the perfidious princess had made her appearance in Choucan, when, one day, her chief eunuch came, on her part, to ask for an audience. I wished to retire, but the Queen kept me back. The messenger was introduced, and spoke thus: 'The Princess Rezie, whose seal of credence I here present, prostrates herself at your august feet, and recognises that your Highness has, by her superior lights, justly earned the throne to which she had herself aspired. Nevertheless, she ventures to ask, as some compensation, that you will suffer her to espouse the Prince Tograi, who now basks only in her presence, and who, moreover, stands in need of some consolation for the misfortune into which he has fallen – the misfortune namely of losing the good graces of his glorious sovereign. The uncertainty in which my princess stands with regard to the nature of your reply keeps her in a state of cruel anxiety, and the prince himself does not dare to appear in your presence. Without these obstacles, they would both have come to ask you, on their knees, to graciously accomplish the common desire of their hearts.'

"On seeing the pallor that had overspread the countenance of Gulzara, and the heaving of her breast, I saw she was about to faint. I told the fatal eunuch to leave us, and wait in the neighbouring gallery for a reply to his message. Gehanguz, who, like myself, had taken immediate alarm, at once put him out, and was just in time to help me in holding up the Queen, as she fell into my arms. We had no wish to cause her enemies to triumph, and so did what was necessary without calling for help. She remained senseless for some time. At last she opened her eyes, turned them sadly on me, and said, after some moments of silence, and with a fairly tranquil air: 'What shall I do, Homaïouna?'

"'What the generosity of your heart dictates,' I replied.

"'But my sister,' she rejoined, 'could not be happy with a man so depraved, and my people would most certainly, at a day which cannot be far distant, be most miserable. Should I not save them all, while I am yet able, by causing Tograi's head to be immediately cut off? I tremble at being reduced to such an extremity; but here, as it seems to me, cruelty is a necessary evil. What do you say, Homaïouna?'

"'It belongs to Allah alone,' I answered, 'to rule the present in view of the future, for he only sees the future unclouded.'

"'You would have me then give my consent to this odious union?' said she, in a voice choked by emotion. 'Very well, let me do this further violence to my heart. But the blow will be mortal. Go, Gehanguz, go, and carry a favourable reply to my sister's request, and to her ...' She did not conclude, but uttered a sad and piercing cry, and fell back senseless on her divan.

"We were now no longer able to hide her condition. The twelve leeches[1] in attendance were summoned. They all felt the pulse of the unconscious Gulzara at the places where the pulse is most marked. I was plunged in the most agonised

---

1   leeches: physicians.

uncertainty, till these birds of evil omen croaked the cruel words: 'She sleeps, she sleeps for ever!' They spoke but too truly, Gulzara had just expired.

"It is impossible to depict the sorrow I felt at this terrible catastrophe; and my grief was all the greater in that I thought I had myself to blame for the premature demise of the amiable Gulzara. 'Fool that I was,' said I to myself, 'I spurred this too generous princess to an effort beyond her powers, and thereby hastened to its end her useful life. I do not yet understand the violence of human passion, or the infirmity of human reason; and yet I wish to govern men! O bitter experience, which has cost me a friend almost as dear as Ganigul herself and her fatal bird! But should I have allowed her to soil her conscience with the blood of a prince whose only fault was ambition, and whose designs Allah could have made to be dust as blown before the wind? Should I have suffered her so to act that her sister could accuse her of mean jealousy, and that she herself would be humiliated in the eyes of her subjects? O fair and radiant soul, now receiving the reward of virtue in the company of heavenly Intelligences, forgive the excess of my zeal! Thou shalt live, as thou didst desire to live, in the memories of men, and never to the end of time shall thy sweet and lovely image fade from my heart.'

"Absorbed in these thoughts, I was kneeling beside the royal bed, which I was watering with my tears, when Rezie's eunuch, having rudely struck me on the shoulder, said: 'What are you doing here, too brazen Homaïouna? Why have you not, like your companions, retired to your own apartment? It is the rule here that the slaves of the sleeping Queen should be confined to their rooms till she is borne to the place of her long rest. Come, follow me; you have ceased to be Grand Vizier. You are no more than a vile and dangerous slave.'

"I rose at once, and followed the eunuch without answering a word. He caused food for three days to be brought to me, said a few more rude things, and took great care to see that my door was secured. I could easily have braved him, and escaped out of his hands, but I was curious to see what Rezie would do with me. I wished also to take public part in the funeral of Gulzara.

Moreover, the sounds of lamentation, which I heard on all sides, were as balm to my own grief.

"She is sleeping, our good Queen is sleeping,' cried unnumbered voices, 'and she will never wake again. She who was our mother is asleep, and perhaps Homaïouna, who did us so much good, will slumber likewise!' These sad words, ceaselessly repeated round and about the palace, echoed in my ears during three days. On the morning of the fourth day, the same eunuch who had shut me up in my apartment same, bringing with him a long robe of red silk, striped with black, and a thick veil of the same colours, and, having himself dressed me in them, said: 'This is the mourning worn by the personal slaves of Gulzara. You will lead the women – that is the place of honour assigned to you. Similarly Gehanguz will lead the eunuchs. The two bands will be placed, one to the right, and the other on the left of the equipage which is to convey the sleeping Queen to the plain of tranquility. Follow me!'

"We proceeded to the great court of the palace, in the centre of which stood a litter of sandalwood, drawn by four black unicorns. Amid the strident strains of a thousand lugubrious instruments of music, and the cries, even yet more piercing, of the inhabitants of Choucan, the body of Gulzara was placed on this litter, and over her was spread a pall of cloth of silver, while the gracious countenance of the lovely princess – who indeed appeared to be only sleeping – was left uncovered.

"Several persons on horseback, singularly accoutred, and bearing in their hands what looked like sceptres of white agate, ordered the procession. At once we began to move forward; but the flowers strewn upon our way in ever-increasing quantities – for the people never ceased to throw them in large basketfuls – made our progress extremely slow. At last we reached a silent and solitary plain, where, by order of succession, were ranged the tombs of the kings and queens of Choucan since unnumbered ages. The aspect of the place was strange and striking. Only the domes of the tombs were visible, and these domes were of black marble, highly polished, and from each protruded a large number of golden pipes. All save the domes was underground, and we descended by an easy declivity to a vault of seemingly limitless extent. As an infinite number of perfumed wax tapers made this gloomy place as light as day, I looked on all sides for the doors of the tombs whose domes I had admired outside. But I could see none. I perceived at last that each tomb was walled in, and marked with a great slab of gold, on which these words were graven: 'Here lies such and such a king. He reigned so many years. Let no one dare to touch this wall, or trouble his repose. His memory alone is at the mercy of the people.'

"We had to go a very long way before reaching the tomb assigned to Gulzara; and we entered it, without disturbing the order of our procession, through a very large door, which had just been removed. The internal walls were covered with the same black marble that we had seen outside; but a quantity of little golden lamps, suspended from the dome, shed a pure bright light, and diffused a delightful perfume.

"The litter was placed in the midst of this vast sepulchre. The viziers, the twenty ambassadors, and the grandees of the State came, one after the other, and prostrated themselves before the sleeping Queen, wishing her a pleasant repose. Tograi himself, the iniquitous Tograi, dared to fulfil this pious duty, but he presented himself at last, and stammered his complimentary words with a haggard and troubled look. I shuddered as I looked upon him, and felt greatly tempted to punish his temerity, when an old man, pale, fleshless, and sinister of aspect, cried out with a shrill, harsh voice: 'Homaïouna, and you, Gehanguz, be it known to you that the wise viziers who govern Choucan during this short interregnum have decreed that, as you were the two favourite slaves of Gulzara, you must keep her company. Be duly grateful for the honour shown to you, and fail not in respect for your Queen.'

"Having said these words, and produced some most lamentable sounds out a brazen trumpet, he resumed, in tones even more dismal and lugubrious: 'The Queen Gulzara is in the bosom of eternal rest. Suffer her to sleep, and let all due honour be paid to her.'

"I scarcely heard these last words, so utterly confounded was I by the dread sentence that had preceded them! All the assistants had retired, and the door had almost been bricked up, and still I had not cast one glance at poor Gehanguz, whereas his faithful and loving heart was only afflicted on my behalf. He was the first to break the silence, crying: 'Oh, Gulzara! oh, my beloved mistress, here is your dearly loved Homaïouna, the divine damsel who has made your subjects so happy – here is she immured for ever! You wished to save her: I was to have taken her out of your kingdom. Alas! you never anticipated falling so suddenly asleep!'

"'Is it then,' said I very quietly to Gehanguz, 'an established custom in Choucan to bury people alive?'

"'Yes, yes,' he replied. 'It is one of those absurd and cruel customs which the people of Choucan have taken it into their heads for ages to call sacred and venerable: it is a compliment they pay to the most faithful servants of their kings and queens, a distinction, be it said, with which those upon whom the so-called honour happens to fall would very willingly dispense. I have always thought the custom barbarous, and unworthy of an intelligent people; but the lamps of love and gratitude, to which we owe the lovely light now shining here – that at least is a fine conception?'

"'Explain yourself,' cried I.

"'You have seen,' said he, 'all the golden pipes that bristle on the dome of each tomb. Well, they answer to the lamps suspended within, and, by a curious contrivance, are used to feed those lamps with oil, and supply them with wicks. The cost of these is not defrayed by the State. It is defrayed by the people in their gratitude. When they have lost a good king or a good queen, men and women, old and young, are eager to maintain in his or her tomb such an illumination as you see here. Their zeal, in this respect, is more or less lively according to the benefits received, and is maintained from father to son. There is, you must know, an aperture at the top of each dome, and in that aperture a mirror of polished metal. Looking into this one may see, in some of the tombs, the lamps still burning, though the king has been asleep for several centuries, while in the greater number of tombs the lamps have long gone out. There are even some unjust sovereigns who have found themselves in total darkness at the end of two or three days, for their favourites, as wicked as themselves, were necessarily ungrateful, and never thought of supplying the wicks and oil they might owe to their benefactors. It is with reason, therefore, that these lamps are called the lamps of Love and Gratitude, and the brilliant mirror of polished metal, the Eye of Justice. Oh! we are never likely to find ourselves in darkness here. The tomb of Gulzara, thanks to all your cares, will shine resplendent till the day of judgement!'

"I was so touched with the sentiments of Gehanguz, and with the holy calm that reigned over his countenance in a moment so terrible, and when all human help seemed altogether hopeless, that, wrapping myself up in pious thoughts, I addressed this prayer to Asfendarmod from the very bottom of my heart: 'Sovereign of Shadukan the blessed, you who, as a reward for your zeal in the cause of the holy Prophet, are able to hear the voice of your subjects in whatsoever part of the world they may happen to be, vouchsafe to grant to your unhappy daughter the power of saving this honest and generous creature. I know by experience that I have lost the faculty of affording any active help to others save the help of counsel and care, but oh! grant me your aid, at this time, so that Gehanguz may not die in this place a lingering and cruel death.'

"Suddenly, in a moment, I was filled with that feeling of confidence which, in beings of our nature, is always a presage of success. I went up to the eunuch, and said, taking him by the hand: 'Your pious resignation and serenity are about to be rewarded. Take firm hold of me, and have no fear.'

"Scarcely had I said these words, when, the dome opening above our heads, I sprang upward, and, in accordance with my wish, found myself, together with the eunuch, at the gates of Ormuz.[1] 'Here you are in safety,' said I to him. 'Remember the Peri Homaïouna, and ever continue to be beneficent and just.'

"The surprise and astonishment of Gehanguz prevented him from replying, and I must have been far away indeed before he

---

1   Ormuz; *Hormuz*: trading center in the east side of the entrance to the Persian Gulf.

would sufficiently recover to open his lips. As for me, I took flight back to Choucan. I wished to know what had become of Rezie and Tograi. I wished – but the night is already far spent," said my wife, interrupting herself. "I will finish my story at greater leisure. We will now discuss your own affairs, and then take some rest. Suffice it to say that Rezie and Tograi were never united: on the contrary, they came to hate one another cordially, and were mutually destructive. I had left them a long time, and wandered through various countries, and been the witness of a thousand calamities – in which, however, I took no part – when, after visiting the mountains of Daghestan, I met you in the streets of Berdouka. You pleased me, notwithstanding the wildness of your looks: a feeling to which I had so far been a stranger took possession of my heart. You know the rest, and whether I have kept the promises I have made. I had often, while in Shadukan, read the annals of the Jinns, and as soon as you spoke of the fatal cupboard, I knew what it contained. But I could think of no just means of inclining your father to give his decision in your favour till the little fish, which you caught, provided an expedient. A Jinn was hidden in that vile shape, a Jinn who, for his crimes, had been thus transformed by Asfendarmod. His restoration to his own form offered great difficulties. It was first necessary that the fish should be caught, and this was not easy, owing to the smallness of its size, and its great weight, so that it always either slipped through the meshes of the net, or else broke them. It was then necessary that the indwelling spirit should be squeezed out of the fish, while still alive, and without injury. Being aware of all this I effectually liberated the Jinn; and, as he had sworn to fulfil any wish uttered in favour of whomsoever should eat the little fish from whose body he had been happily delivered, I urged Ormossouf to eat the fish, and afterwards induced you all three to make vows in Ormossouf's favour – vows which you alone did not afterwards seek to revoke. Thus you have deserved to ascend the throne which one of your ancestors lost through not following the advice of a Peri who protected him, and who, as some consolation, gave him the wonderful ring contained in the leaden box – at the same time telling him that one of his descendants would open the box and regain possession of the throne of Daghestan. The tradition of this promise passed from father to son for several generations, but every effort to open the box had proved ineffectual. At last your father, who had vainly made the attempt himself, resolved, on the advice of Alsalami, to give it to the one of his sons who should display the most filial piety.

"Those are the facts, with which it is right you should be made acquainted; and now this is what you ought to do. So soon as Ormossouf and the dervish are up, you will apprise them of your intentions, and ask them to give you their blessings, and then make your way to Berdouka, with the ring on your left finger. You will thus enter, without being seen of any, into the King's garden. At the bottom of the garden, you will find the trunk of a large tree, which no one has ever been able to destroy. Touch the tree with your ring. It will at once fly open, and you will find therein a bag made of serpent's skin – of which you will take possession. The bag contains an assortment of gems more brilliant than any in Shadukan; bring these gems to me, and I will go and sell them wheresoever I am most likely to find the best market.

"With the money so obtained, we shall have no difficulty in enlisting the services of the hillmen in Daghestan, who indeed are attached to your family, and hate the usurper. Thus you will be able, as becomes a prince, to take possession of your kingdom at the head of an army."

End of the Story of the Peri Homaïouna

Here Homaïouna ceased speaking; and I, utterly confounded, and indeed terrified, by the marvels she had related, knelt down again at her feet, assuring her of my unbounded respect and limitless obedience. This seemed not to please her at all. She asked, with tears in her eyes, whether what I now knew about her had in any way altered my affection. Then I kissed her. We retired to bed; and I made believe to sleep, so that I might, without interruption, consider my position; a position, no doubt, infinitely superior to any for which I could have dared to hope; and yet I was in despair. "What," I said to myself, "shall I gain by being king? It is this most redoubtable Peri, and not I, who will really bear rule in my kingdom. She will want to treat me as she treated the Queen of Choucan, and insist on my doing all her behests, even though I should die for it! What do I care about the public good, regarding which she prates so much? My own private good is the one thing I have at heart, and *that* I shall never secure with her. Well enough even if she confined herself to advice and reproaches – mere words I could treat with contempt – but, though she speaks modestly enough of what remains of her former supernatural powers, she may be deceiving me, even as I am deceiving her. She may still have in reserve her terrible wand. She made no mention of it in her story about Gulzara, but then that story is not yet finished. I must hear her tale to the end, so as to lay this most cruel doubt. Ah! better a hundred times to remain a poor fisherman than to be a slave upon a throne!"

The storm had not ceased raging in my evil heart, when the day appeared. I was about to curse its light and might indeed have done so with very good reason, for it was by that day's light that I took the first step leading to the abyss in which we now are.

I used all my powers of hypocrisy so as to hide my perturbation of spirit from my wife, my father, and the dervish, and left them offering up, on my behalf, prayers, which I have always taken good care to render vain.

On my way to Berdouka, I met several persons whom I knew very well, and as not one of them seemed to see me I began to feel in my ring a confidence which had so far been wanting. I entered with some assurance into the King's garden, and ran to the tree Homaïouna had described. I touched it. It opened, and I took out the bag of serpent-skin. I was so impatient to behold the incomparable Shadukan gems that I could not wait till I was out of the garden. I took them from the bag one after the other, and, though half blinded by their brilliancy, examined them again and again. They were sixteen in number:

four diamonds, four carbuncles,[1] four emeralds and four rubies, each of the size of a Khoten[2] orange.

To contemplate them at greater leisure, I placed them on the grass in an unfrequented alley to which I had retired, and was in an ecstasy of joy and admiration when a dwarf, who was perched in a tree, and whom I had not observed, leapt toward me. I had only just time to return my treasures to the bag, and hurry away, the dwarf, meanwhile, in great agitation, peering about under the grass, and scratching the earth with his nails. He cried at last: "Alas! The resplendent vision has disappeared! But it may return. I will go and fetch my beautiful princess – if some Jinn be about, playing his pranks, he will not refuse to gratify her with such a lovely sight." Speaking thus he sped towards the palace, so light of foot that the grass and flowers scarce bent beneath his tread.

Clearly I had rendered the gems visible by suffering them to leave my hand, and I was frightened at the possible consequences of this act of imprudence. I thought the best thing I could do was to get out of the garden as soon as possible; but, as I was a long way from the gate by which I had entered, I had time to think – though I sped along quickly enough: "Where am I going? Shall I venture to place these inestimable gems in a woman's hand? Even supposing that my wife is above her sex's passion for jewellery, supposing she faithfully brings back to me the price she obtains for them, what good shall I derive from the purchase of a throne on which I shall sit loaded with her chains? No! Far better sell them myself and indulge freely in all pleasures and delights – better far to live forgotten but happy, in some obscure corner of the earth! It is to be hoped that Homaïouna may not discover my place of retreat. She knows not everything; still less does she know all she would like to know. I will go down to the port. I will enter, invisible, into the first ship that sails hence. I can have my being quite happily without bidding good-bye to the Peri, Ormossouf, and Alsalami. Enough that the one should have inflicted upon me her

---

1   carbuncle: a fiery red precious stone, a ruby or sapphire.
2   Khoten: a province of China bordering on Persia's north-east. In the *Shah-nama*, Rustem conquers Khoten on behalf of his king, Kai-khosráu.

exhortations, and the other his gout – while as to the third, he is of no account. I shall not regret one of them."

While indulging in these reflections, I perceived that I had lost my way among the garden walks, which formed a kind of labyrinth. What was my surprise at finding myself once more close to the place where I had discovered the precious gems; and I now heard the accursed dwarf screaming to a whole crowd of eunuchs who were following him: "Yes – this is the spot where I saw those marvels, I saw them with my two eyes, I swear it by my own tiny soul, and by the great heart of the Princess Gazahidé, my dear mistress."

On this I was going to fly, when a young beauty, more dazzling than my diamonds, my rubies, my emeralds, and my carbuncles, pressed forward through the throng, and with an air of wilfulness that became her well, and was not without dignity, cried: "Silence, all! and listen to the commands of the daughter of your King, the princess Gazahidé! Be it known to you that I firmly believe all that the little Calili has just told us: cease, therefore, to treat him as a mere visionary. I insist on seeing the precious stones which the Jinn has spread out upon the grass, and I shall compel the Jinn to show them me by all such persistent means as my curiosity may dictate. Come, erect a pavilion for me on this very spot – I shall not leave it till I have obtained sight of the gems. If any of you says a single word of objection, I will give him cause for repentance. If the objection comes from my father, I will take vengeance upon him by refusing to wear in my hair the aigrette[1] of blue flowers he likes so well!"

While Gazahidé spoke, my eyes were fixed on hers, my soul seemed ready to take to itself wings to fly to her. Nor did I regain my presence of mind – so was I intoxicated with love – till I saw that her attendants were preparing to satisfy her caprice. Then did all the tremors of an anticipated delight go coursing through my frame. I leant against a tree at a little distance, fully determined, at all hazards, to personate the imaginary Jinn.

Standing thus, I grew impatient at the dilatoriness with

---

1   aigrette: normally a tuft of feathers to ornament the hair; in this case a tuft of flowers.

which the eunuchs prepared the pavilion, and would, most willingly, have torn in pieces all the ornaments with which they slowly decorated it. She had said she wished to be left alone, and by the orders of the King, who had done nothing but laugh at her whims, every wish of hers was to be satisfied. It was about the middle of a fine summer day; but the heat was tempered by the thick umbrage of the trees, and by gauze curtains that interrupted such of the sun's rays as would have done more than diffuse a soft and voluptuous light.

I had again to keep my soul in patience while jars of excellent sherbet, and basins of comfits and ginger, were presented to Gazahidé, with a lengthy ceremonial. She partook of these dainties very quickly, so as the sooner to be quit of her eunuchs and slave girls. They retired at last; and to such a distance that they could only have come to the help of their young mistress if summoned in very loud tones.

I went forward on tiptoe, I warily raised the curtains and entered into this paradise of delights. Gazahidé lay at full length on the too happy divan, and my greedy eyes feasted their full on her fair proportions and delicate limbs. My emotion was such that I could scarcely stand. I had thrown myself on the ground not far from the princess, when, raising herself suddenly, she put her little white hands together, and cried: "Oh, Jinn, mighty Jinn, who hast shown thy precious gems to my dwarf, refuse not, I pray, to grant the same favour unto me."

Scarcely had she uttered these words, when I placed on the ground a carbuncle whose rays would have put to shame the rays of the sun. Gazahidé's surprise was so great that, fearing lest she should cry aloud, I whispered: "Admire in silence what is less beautiful than yourself."

She smiled, and, emboldened by my flattering words, advanced, precipitately, to take hold of the carbuncle, which I, as rapidly, withdrew.

"Oh, heavens!" cried she, "I did not mean to steal it; I only wanted to hold it in my hands for an instant. You speak passionate words to me, but ah! you are cruel!"

"No, Queen of Beauty," I replied, "I am far from desiring to give you pain; but you can only touch these precious stones on one condition – and that I will tell you after I have placed them all, and all together, before your eyes. Lie down again, therefore, on your divan, and have patience for a few moments."

Gazahidé obeyed me with an air of respect, and even of fear. Then I arranged the jewels in a square, placing them in such juxtaposition that each should add to each a new lustre; and this I did, hiding them the while with the skirt of my robe, so that all might be uncovered at once.

I had every reason to repent of the effect of the spectacle thus presented to the amiable Gazahidé. She was so dazzled and bewildered that she fell backward on her divan, and looked as if life itself had flown. Frightened in turn, I ran towards her, first taking the precaution to replace my treasures in the serpent-skin bag, which I attached to my belt. I found her pale, with her eyes closed, and deprived of all power of motion. But how lovely she was in that state! I opened her dress to give her air.... I was quite beside myself, when reviving from her trance, she cried: "Who has dared to touch me?"

"It is the Jinn Farukrouz, who has come to your help," I replied.

"Ah!" she rejoined, in softer accents, "your name is not so fair as your jewels! But where are they? Tell me what I must do to obtain leave to hold them in my hands, one after the other: and, above all, do not show them to me all at once, for fear of accidents."

"For each one you must give me a kiss," I replied, in a voice trembling with fear and hope.

"What! no more than that!" she said. "Oh! most willingly. The kiss of a spirit will be as the breath of the wind blown from the evening star; it will cool my lips and rejoice my heart."

I did not ask her to repeat a permission so delicious. My kiss was a long one. She accepted it with a kind of agreeable impatience, and was about to complain of an ardour she had so little expected, when I placed in her hand a ruby, whose brilliant hue harmonised with the charming blush my kiss had raised upon her cheeks. She turned the stone over and over, with an abstracted air, and then, giving it back to me, said: "Let me now have an emerald of the same value."

As I gave her the second kiss, I pressed her in my arms so closely that she gave a start, and said, with some emotion in her voice: "Farukrouz, as you are palpable, you can doubtless make yourself visible. Ah! I would rather see you yourself than your precious stones!"

I had too high an opinion of my own face and figure to be bashful about showing them, and, moreover, I had that day donned my best attire. I therefore removed the ring from the little finger of my left hand; and, as I saw that the first glance Gazahidé cast upon me was favourable, I immediately took her back into my arms. At first she returned my caresses with a very good grace, when, suddenly, she violently shook herself free, and cried out in great wrath: "Go! you are a rough and wicked Jinn; go away! I won't listen to another word about your precious stones; if you are so bold as to come near me again, I shall call out with all my might."

This threat made me tremble. My invisibility was not like that of the Peri, whose body became not only invisible but impalpable, so that no obstacle could arrest its movements. I could be imprisoned, and in various way made to perish. During a few moments I remained thoughtful and silent; but the danger in which I stood and the love still burning within me, sharpened my wits, and I cried: "O daughter of the King, fairest of earthly women! I see it is now time to reveal the glory and happiness to which you are destined. Be assured, and listen to me. You will then do me justice, and become more kindly and sweet than the Leiki, whose grace and sensibility you possess."

"Speak," said she eagerly; "I will give you all my attention. But seat yourself at the other end of the divan, and, above all, don't touch me."

Then, with Homaïouna's marvellous story still fresh in my memory, I began the following recital of my own imaginary adventures:–

"You have doubtless heard tell of the great Asfendarmod, monarch of Shadukan, and sovereign over all the Peris, Jinns and Dives who have existed either before, or after, the Preadamite kings. Well, I am his son, his favourite son, in whom he has placed his full confidence. He gave into my charge two of my sisters who are as flighty as the bulbul,[1] and unruly as the zebra, and directed me never to lose sight of them. In order to facilitate my task, he had removed their wings, and shut them in a tower – of which I safely held the key. A friendly Jinn took it into his head to deliver them, and set to work for that purpose with considerable cunning. We had been, he and I, on terms of great friendship for a long time, and were accustomed to spend whole days together. For half-a-moon he kept away from me, and when I reproached him, on the occasion of our first meeting, he only answered my reproaches with a deep sigh. My friendship took alarm; I pressed him to open his heart.

'"Ah!' cried he, at last, 'only a Peri, nay, only the son of Asfendarmod himself is worthy of her. I am mad to have lost so much time in contemplating her charms! Yes, dear Farukrouz,' continued he, 'the Princess Gazahidé, only daughter to the King of Daghestan, ought to belong to you and to none other. I saw her emerging from her bath like the sun rising from the bosom of the sea; a portion of her hair, pure gold and like to rays of blinding light, still floated in the transparent waters, while the remaining locks enriched her ivory forehead; her eyes a tint more lively and brilliant than the azure of the firmament, were agreeably shaded by the tiny threads of black silk that went to form her delicate eyebrows and long eyelashes; her nose suited well the little portals of supple coral that neighboured it – little portals that enclosed the loveliest pearls of the Sea of Golconda.[2] As to the remainder of her charms, do not expect me to describe them: I saw naught because I saw too much. I only know that that perfect shape seemed to have come straight from the studio of the celebrated Mani,[3] who

---

1 bulbul: the nightingale.
2 Golconda: a hill fort west of Hyderabad in southern India; an important trade center for diamonds.
3 Mani: famous painter and sculptor from China.

had not forgotten to add the lovely hues of life to a form whiter than snow.'

"This portrait, which, as I have since discovered, was in no wise flattering, inflamed me to such a point that I cried: 'Ah! cease to torment me, my cruel friend! You know that I cannot abandon care of my sisters, who at every moment ask me for some new thing. Wherefore, then, inflame me thus? Yes, I burn to see Gazahidé, but alas! how can I?'

"'Go, my dear Farukrouz,' said the Jinn, in tones of affection; 'go and satisfy a desire that is so natural. *I* will remain in the tower, and do the behests of the daughters of Asfendarmod, who will never know that you have left them under my care. Give me the keys, and go.'

"Madcap that I was, I accepted the offer of the false and malicious Jinn. I took my flight hither. What he had told me of your charms was so true that I never entertained a suspicion of his treachery, and thus he had full leisure to escape with my sisters before I thought of returning to Shadukan. I was looking at you; I was following your steps; I was altogether forgetting my own existence; when, suddenly, the whirlwinds that execute my father's commands seized upon me, bore me hence, and placed me at the foot of his throne. Asfendarmod heaped upon me the reproaches I deserved, and, in the first fury of his indignation, condemned me to remain a hundred years among men in the shape you now behold – but without depriving me of my invisibility. More afflicted because I had offended him than because of the punishment to which I was condemned, I embraced his knees, and watered them with my tears. He read my heart, and was touched by my filial affection: 'Unhappy Farukrouz,' he said, 'I cannot revoke my sentence, but I will make thy lot more endurable. As Gazahidé is the cause of thy disgrace, so shall it be its consolation. Go, go to her once more; gain her in love; marry her; and tell her that, for a wedding gift, I allow her to retain, unimpaired, her beauty and her youth, during the hundred years she will live with thee!'

"After speaking these words, he gave me the jewels you have seen, promised me his help on due occasion, and caused me to be borne hither. The fear of alarming you by a too sudden apparition suggested the thought of first awaking your dwarf's curiosity, and so exciting your own. I succeeded, and should now be altogether satisfied, if only you had loved me enough to take me as your husband before learning my history."

Gazahidé had listened to this rhapsody of mine with such marks of credulity and admiration as afforded me the liveliest pleasure. She came nearer when I finished speaking, and, taking my two hands in hers, said: "My dear Lord, do not doubt my love. The first look you cast upon me gave you the possession of my heart; but I have a good father, to whom respect is due, and in that respect I must not be found wanting. He alone can dispose of me. Let me direct Calili to go for him at once. He will be transported with joy when he hears of the honour you propose to do me. All will be settled according to your wishes, and in a manner conformable to the position of the son of Asfendarmod."

I had come too far to turn back. Besides, I imagined that the King of Daghestan, like most of his fellows, would not be over-gifted with sense, and I hoped to impose upon him as easily as I has imposed on his daughter. She, therefore, with my consent, left the tent, and called loudly for Calili.

The dwarf ran up out of breath. "Well, my Princess," said he, "what have you seen? The jewels, doubtless?"

"Go," she replied. "I have seen something much better than jewels; run and tell my father that happiness and wonders transcending all he can imagine await him here."

"What?" cried the dwarf, "have you seen anything more beautiful than what I saw myself? Oh! tell me what it is, dear mistress; tell me what it is, I conjure you. I cannot walk a step unless you satisfy my curiosity."

As he was repeating these words with a quite childish importunity, Gazahidé boxed his ears twice soundly, which caused him to run off so quickly that she could not help laughing with all her heart. She then called me – for I had made myself invisible before Calili – and, having asked me to entrust her with one of the carbuncles, told me to listen to the conversation she was about to hold with her father, and only show myself at the right moment.

At the sight of the King, and at the first words he uttered, I perceived that he could be easily gulled. He listened to my story, and considered my carbuncle with large astonished eyes and a mouth widely opened. Then he cried: "Oh, son of Asdendarmod! generous Farukrouz, appear! appear! Suffer me to pay you such honours and give you such thanks as are justly due. This very day you shall be the husband of Gazahidé, and to-morrow I will abdicate in your favour. I ask for no greater boon than to see my daughter always fair, young and happy – unless, indeed, you should be willing to add to your favours by prolonging my days so that I may behold the lovely children to be born of your union."

The sight of me did not in any way diminish the good monarch's predilection in my favour. My attire was not indeed magnificent, but the precious gems made up for any deficiency in that respect. I offered them as a wedding gift for his daughter; but he refused, saying that the carbuncle – which he would keep for the love of me – was of greater value than all the women in the world – a statement that caused Gazahidé to pout her lips very prettily.

We all returned to the palace. The eunuchs, on seeing me issue from the tent, were filled with fear and grimaced hideously; the slave girls, too, were somewhat scared, but soon reassured. As to Calili, whether from aversion, or some presentiment of evil, he always looked at me askance.

After having been bathed, perfumed, and clad in garments of great magnificence, I was married to Gazahidé, putting the while a veil upon the extravagance of my joy so as to maintain an air of dignity conformable to the splendour of my supposed origin. The remainder of the day was spent in regales, dances, and concerts, which amused me not at all, and in which my princess seemed to take but little pleasure. It was otherwise with the King. His satisfaction was huge. He played like a child with the pages and slave girls, and made the vaults of the chamber re-echo to the shouts of his laughter.

When he bade us good-night, he again told me that, on the morrow, he would resign to me his crown; but I asked him to defer the honour, and to suffer that I should spend three days in the harem, altogether devoted to me dear Gazahidé, and enjoying the pleasures of his royal company; and this he conceded, very graciously, and even with thanks. I had my reason for proffering the request. I was madly in love, and wished to enjoy my happiness, without interruption, during the three days in question, not doubting that Homaïouna would come and disturb it so soon as she knew of my adventures – adventures so contrary to what she had herself intended. But who can be quite happy while haunted with the fear of what he has only too richly deserved? I was seized with terrors in the very midst of my delights. At the slightest noise I was on the point of snatching myself from the arms of Gazahidé – fearing to be surprised by the incensed Peri. In fine, those three days – which are yet the only days in my whole life that remain dear to my memory – passed in alternate transports of love and paroxysms of terror.

The fourth morning had scarce begun to show on the horizon when whole files of eunuchs came to conduct me to the divan. My heart beat. I was filled with the most dire presentiment, but could find no plausible excuse for further delay. Nor would the King have brooked it. He had, with infinite trouble, composed and learned by heart a harangue in which my story was set out, and greatly amplified, and would have been afraid to trust his memory further. He delivered his address accordingly, to the amazement of his hearers, who never ceased looking at me all the time he was speaking. He was at last about to affix the royal plume to my turban, when an aged emir, whom I knew very well, approached and spoke some words in his ear. The good monarch changed colour, said that he did not feel well, and broke up the assembly; and I was escorted back to the harem.

A few minutes afterwards Gazahidé was summoned to her father's apartment. She came back all in tears. "Ah! my beloved husband," said she, "a strange accusation is being made against you! The Emir Mohabed says that you are the son of the fisherman Ormossouf, that you used to come and sell your fish at his house, and that he has spoken to you a hundred times as you passed along the streets. He declares that your story is but a fable, and that your precious stones are all false, and only seem to be genuine by magic art – and, in a word, that you are an imposter, and upheld by some wicked Dive. My father is not altogether convinced, but he doubts; and he trembles, more-over, at the mere mention of Ormossouf, whom he knows to have a better right than himself to the throne of Daghestan – and whom, for that reason, he holds in execration. He was about to send to the good fisherman and have him arrested, together with all his family, and to subject them to a most rig-orous examination, but I besought him to delay this order until to-morrow, I represented that, if you really were Farukrouz, you would never forgive such an outrage, that he would draw upon himself the vengeance of Asfendarmod, and make me miserable for the remainder of my days. I ended by assuring him that you loved me well enough to give me your entire confidence, and that whatever confession you might make to me would be fully imparted to him. Tell me, then, the whole truth, without hesi-tation, and place entire reliance both on my heart and my troth. If you really are Barkiarokh, the son of Ormossouf, I love you none the less, and I do not despair of so arranging matters that we may yet be happy."

I was myself too false to have faith in anyone; and I was very far from wishing to place myself at the mercy of my second wife – the power which my first wife exercised over me was too terrible for *that*. I was for the moment embarrassed, and Gazahidé renewed her entreaties in the tenderest manner – when, suddenly, an atrocious thought occurred to me, and seemed, in my utter perversion, to afford a means of escape. I affected confidence and security, and said to the princess, smil-ing: "I admire your prudence; you know that pleasures in the hand are worth more than pleasures in anticipation, and have been unwilling to resign those of to-day. I am far, indeed, from being of a contrary opinion, and it will not be my fault if we do not pass this day as pleasantly as the three which preceded it. Besides, if all the circumstances I related to you – circumstances which you can, in turn, relate to your father to-morrow – fail to content him, he may, if he likes, consult every fisherman in

Berdouka. In the end he will beg my pardon, and I shall forgive him for the love of you."

Like a rose well-nigh faded in the noon-day heat, and into which a light cloud distills new freshness, so did Gazahidé breathe life from my words. Her cheeks resumed the sweet rose tints of their full beauty; her eyes sparkled with love and joy; I became more inflamed with love for her than ever. I returned, transported, all the caresses she lavished upon me, striving thus to make her forget the indignity to which, as she thought, I had been subjected; and every moment confirmed me in the resolution of doing my utmost not to lose the happiness I was then enjoying. The hours passed only too quickly. Towards evening the King, who, doubtless, did not dare to appear before me, sent the chief of his eunuchs to inquire how his daughter fared. She caused him to be informed, in reply, that she had never been better in her life, and that he might sleep in peace.

I had not forgotten my promise to give the princess a more circumstantial account of my history, but had deferred doing so till a time when I could frame it in such a manner as to further my designs. Shortly after we were in bed I began my story, but made it so absurd, so long, and so tiresome, that, as my intention was, I sent her to sleep, and should have gone to sleep myself – but dark plots are ever wakeful.

The night was far advanced when, after placing the ring on my left hand, I took my way to the King's apartment, which I knew, as he had before conducted me thither. Calili, the dwarf, and Gazahidé's other eunuchs, slept in her antechamber. Those who guarded the King himself watched in rows on either side of the entrance to his sleeping-room, which was closed by a curtain only. I passed noiselessly between the eunuchs, and found the venerable monarch plunged in the deepest slumber. By the light of the tapers illuminating the room, I applied a cushion to his countenance, and stifled him so adroitly that he never even exhaled a single sigh. I then arranged the body with the head drooping over the side of the bed, in such a way that any clots of blood found upon him might seem due to some natural accident, and retraced my steps, trembling. I was so distracted that, losing my way, I traversed two or three unknown corridors. At last, however, I succeeded in discovering where I was, and had come to Gazahidé's door, when, making a false step, I fell at full length upon the floor. Aghast at my fall, to which I attributed a supernatural cause, I whispered in low and fearful tones, "Oh! cruel Homaïouna, do not so soon subject me to your too terrible influence; let me at least, for a little while, enjoy the fruits of my crime!" I suffered, however, on that occasion, from nothing worse than fright. I picked myself up quickly, and went to lie down again by the princess, only keeping as far from her as possible, for fear lest she should wake, and perceive that I myself was not asleep.

I had some fear that I might be troubled by remorse; but such was so far from being the case that I began to find excuses for my horrible deed – was it not right to defend my own life? And then I congratulated myself on possessing the love of the heiress to the throne, and so being sure of the throne itself.

Amid these reflections, I saw the day dawn without anxiety, and was in no wise alarmed by the cries that soon resounded through the harem. Gazahidé woke with a start, half rose, and then fell back upon the bed, senseless, on hearing of the sudden death of the King her father. Her slave girls, her eunuchs, utterly distraught, ran hither and thither in the palace. Calili alone remained near her, and helped me to try to bring her back to consciousness. For a long time our efforts proved vain; at last she opened upon me her beautiful eyes, as if to ask for my pity! I stretched out to her my perfidious arms; but, before I could clasp her to my breast, I received on my left side, which was uncovered, a terrible blow from the fatal wand. It struck me prostrate, and, rolling on the ground, I cried like a mad creature: "Cursed be thy existence, O infamous Barkiarokh! Cursed be thy perversity, thy hypocrisy, thy ingratitude to Homaïouna, and thy wicked perfidy towards the innocent Gazahidé! Cursed above all be thy ring, which, by making thee invisible, has favoured the perpetration of this thy last crime! May the earth open to swallow up the murderer of his sleeping sovereign, of the venerable old man who had adopted thee as his son! Ah! let me, at least, with my teeth, tear in pieces these horrible hands by which he was done to death, and thus avenge outraged nature!"

Shrieking out these furious imprecations, I bit my arms, I beat my head upon the floor, and my blood flowed freely, while Gazahidé, as if turned to stone, looked upon me, not hindering. After about half an hour thus spent in agony, the terrible overmastering influence ceased to operate, and my evil nature reasserted itself. I saw I was lost unless I had recourse to some new stratagem, and with a deep-drawn sigh I said: "Heaven be thanked! this fit of madness is over; be assured, my dear wife, it will not recur for a long while. This is only the second fit I have had in my life."

Saying these words, I tried to drag myself towards her bed, when the dwarf, his eyes ablaze with anger, threw himself between us, crying: "Don't come near my princess, detestable monster! Vainly wouldst thou attribute to a momentary aberration the confession of the monstrous act of which thou art really guilty. I heard thee myself, this very night, return from the King's apartment. Thou didst fall down at four paces' distance from thy couch, and didst there entreat that very Homaïouna, whom thou hast just named once more, to suffer thee to enjoy the fruits of thy crime. I thought I had only dreamt some evil dream, but I had heard the truth only too well! If thou darest to come forward one single step I will, with these nails of mine, tear off the remains of flesh which this supernatural fit of remorse has left upon thy bones!"

Though my recent attack had left me in a state of extreme weakness, rage at being thus convicted of what I sought to deny, supplied me with sufficient strength to rise, to seize Calili, and to hurl him into the sea, which, on that side, bathed the walls of the palace. Unfortunately for me, instead of drowning, he swam off with a surprising agility.

I then stood confounded, and Gazahidé fell back into a swoon, when, suddenly, an infinite number of voices rang through the palace: "Vengeance! Vengeance! Let all doors be closed, let every sword be drawn! Barkiarokh has killed our King, let us not suffer the wretch to escape!"

At this fearful tumult, I trembled for my life, like a coward; I abandoned the princess, and, having rendered myself invisible, I made all haste to get out of the palace. But every avenue was closed; swords swept glittering in all directions. In this extreme peril I seized hold of a sycamore, some fifty cubits[1] high, that grew in the middle of the great court, climbed up quickly, and perched myself as well as I was able, on the top. Thence I looked down, with unspeakable terror, upon the multitude of people who swarmed below seeking my life. They increased in number with every moment, while the furious dwarf never wearied in urging them on. This scene, of which I was at once the wretched spectator, and the horrible cause, lasted without intermission during the whole day and the following night; and, to add to my miseries, the uncomfortable posture I had to adopt, and my agitation, brought on an attack of the accursed gout from which I had relieved my father. I could have screamed so as to make the welkin[2] ring, but fear restrained me. And, as I felt that I was growing weaker from hour to hour, I unwound my turban, and bound myself firmly to the tree so as not to fall on the pikes and spears of my enemies.

In this condition, with unuttered curses on my lips, and despair in my heart, I spent yet another day in contemplating the frightful confusion that reigned below. At last I began to see things dimly, as through a cloud, and to hear nothing distinctly, and almost to lose consciousness of my own existence, when a great noise of axes, applied from the outside to the gates of the palace, caused me to start and tremble and lose all consciousness.

What was my surprise, on coming to my senses, to find myself softly lying on silk mattresses bedewed with the most delightful odours! I opened my eyes, and perceived, by the light of a great crystal lamp, that I was in a long chamber, at the other end of which was an oratory. In this oratory a dervish was muttering prayers with great fervour, and repeating my name over and over again in his orisons.[3] I knew not what to make of such a vision. I looked on in silence for a long time, and at last

---

1   cubit: the distance from the elbow to the tip of the middle finger, about 20 inches.
2   welkin: the vault of heaven.
3   orisons: prayers.

thought I must be in the regions of the dead. Much surprised at my favourable treatment there, I could not help exclaiming: "Ah! little have I deserved to receive such mercies!" These words caused the dervish to turn round. He made haste to come to me, and I recognized Alsalami. "My son," said he, "I like to hear these first ejaculations of a contrite heart. Heaven be praised! You will not die in a state of impenitence!"

"Am I still in the land of the living?" I inquired.

"Yes," he replied; "thanks to the benevolence of Homaïouna."

"If my life had depended on that cruel Peri," I rejoined, "I should long since have ceased to breath – she has done everything for my destruction!"

"No, no!" returned Alsalami; "she has only done what she ought to have done. It would not have become a pure intelligence, such as she is, to suffer you to touch Gazahidé with hands still reeking of the breath of which you just deprived her father. She made you feel her formidable power, not in order to divulge your crime, but so that you might not add to that crime an element of such atrocity. Nevertheless, when she saw you suspended to the sycamore – for you could not make yourself invisible to her eyes – she took pity upon you. 'He must be saved,' said she, 'and have time given him for repentance.' Immediately she took flight, sought out the brave men who live among the mountains, and induced them to take arms for your release. Under her leadership, they vanquished your enemies, broke open the gates of the palace, and, after she had made you visible by removing the fatal ring to another finger, took you down from the tree. Then she gave you such care as your condition demanded; and now, leaving me here to watch the effect of her restoratives, is gone to complete the work of assuring the throne to your family. You might easily have ascended that throne without a crime, O Barkiarokh! But now the steps thereto must be fashioned out of your repentance. Daoud was a murderer even like yourself, but he became the best of kings."[1]

---

1 Daoud; David: The reference is probably to King David's plot to have Uriah the Hittite killed in battle so that he might marry Uriah's wife, Bathsheba. [II Samuel 11]

This consolatory and pious discourse, which I deemed to be in the last degree dull and commonplace, made me feel that if ever hypocrisy could be of use to me, it was now. I began, therefore, to beat my breast, with no great violence indeed, but with an air of well-feigned compunction. I accused myself, I condemned what I had done in no measured terms, and besought the dervish to intercede for me. At last, after seeing the holy man bathed in tears, I said: "Alas! what has become of the innocent princess whom I have caused to be an orphan?"

"She is in this palace," he replied, "and very ill, in the bed where you left her. But Homaïouna is taking care of her, and will, I have no doubt, restore her to life and health. The Peri has also appeased the friends of the dead King. Though she has been strictly careful to tell no lies they are beginning to doubt whether you are really guilty of the crime Calili alone imputes to you; for Gazahidé herself has never opened her lips on the subject; she has never even uttered your name."

"What have they done with that accursed dwarf?" cried I passionately.

"Peace, peace, my son," said the dervish. "You must yourself forgive, if you wish Allah to forgive you. The dwarf has fled, and has not been pursued."

"May heaven be his guide!" said I, with an air of compunction. "Who indeed can be as wicked as I? But may I see my father, and testify my gratitude to Homaïouna?"

"Ormossouf," he replied, "governs the kingdom, though he has not yet assumed the title of king. He is too busy, at the present moment, to see you, and, to tell you the truth, he does not seem to have any great wish to do so. As to the Peri, you will no doubt see her, as such is your desire. But now keep quiet. Too much excitement might be hurtful." Saying these words, he returned to the oratory.

I asked for nothing better than to be left to my own reflections. I had to think out some plan for obtaining possession of the crown, which I should mainly value as a means of pacifying Gazahidé, or at least subduing her to my ends: for that too charming princess was ever present in my thoughts. But my fate for the present depended on Homaïouna, and it was not so easy to cajole her as the dervish. Exaggerated protestations, all untoward grimacing and show, would have been lost upon her. I indulged in neither. I left it to my looks and actions to convince her, not only of my repentance, but also of a return of tenderness towards herself. Notwithstanding her previous experiences, Homaïouna was not suspicious; and she loved me. Alsalami spoke strongly in my favour, and Ormossouf himself wanted to return to obscurity and quiet. So they decided among them that I should be proclaimed King of Daghestan. Nor did I think it wise to feign reluctance. I merely said to the Peri: "I can only repeat the words which the Queen of Choucan spoke to you on a similar occasion. 'All the burden of kingship will fall on you, my dear Homaïouna.'"

This utterance afforded great satisfaction to my active spouse; and in my own interests, I thoroughly acted up to it during the first days of my reign. I allowed her to make all the arrangements she liked; and even to appoint Alsalami as my Grand Vizier, though, to myself, in truth, such a choice seemed somewhat ridiculous. What I wanted was to gain the love and respect of my people, and I neglected no steps to that end. I was constant in my attendance at the mosques,[1] where I distributed great alms to the poor, and gave excessive gifts to the imans.[2] I administered justice almost every day in person, and only allowed Alsalami to take my place occasionally, and to gratify Homaïouna.

One day, when they were both particularly well pleased with me, and I stood high in their good graces, I caused the conversation to turn on the subject of destiny, and allowed them to embark, according to their custom, in a long disquisition upon that subject. After listening to them for some time, with apparent interest, I said: "Alas! who more than myself can believe that we are the slaves of fate! My love for Gazahidé caused me to commit a crime which I shall never cease to deplore, and yet, notwithstanding, I burn to see once again that unfortunate princess; the thought of her follows me everywhere; it troubles me in my devotions; and if I do not satisfy this unconquerable

---

1 mosques: houses of worship.
2 imans; *imams*: scholars of Islamic law.

desire, I shall never be myself again. Do not be angry at my saying this, dear Homaïouna," I continued, "my tenderness towards
you is founded on admiration and gratitude, and will be eternal. My blind passion for your rival can only last so long as it is
thwarted."

"I am not jealous," replied the Peri, with an air of majesty,
calm and unruffled, "but I fear the violence of your character,
and foresee, with great pain, the evils you are drawing down
upon yourself. Gazahidé holds you in such abhorrence that she
would rather see the Deggial[1] than yourself. Your presence
might kill her."

"Oh! people do not die so easily," said I. "I shall succeed in
pacifying her if you do not set yourself to counteract my
efforts; and, as to that, your energies might be more profitably
employed in other directions."

"As you please," said she. "I must submit. But I have the
most dread presentiments."

I pretended not to hear these last words, and still less the
deep sighs with which Alsalami accompanied them; and
instantly made my way towards Gazahidé's apartment.

The eunuchs and the princess's slave girls were transfixed
with terror at my approach, and at the intimation of my desire
to see their mistress; but I ordered them on pain of death to
keep silence, and forbade them to follow me. I entered noiselessly, but, for fear of alarming Gazahidé, without making
myself invisible, and looked at her for some time unperceived.
Seated on a pile of cushions, her back was nearly turned to the
door. Her flowing hair looked like golden embroidery on the
simar[2] in which she was clothed. With her head bent over her
knees, she bedewed with tears the carbuncle which I had presented to her father – and which he had given her to keep. I
went round behind her on tiptoe, and, throwing myself at her
feet, clasped my arms round her, and held her tight, for fear she
should endeavour to escape.

As, notwithstanding all my hardihood, I could not, without
strong emotion, see and touch a woman for whom I enter-

---

1 Deggial is the Muslim Antichrist. [*D'Herbelot; Sale* 80]
2 simars: light, flowing robes.

tained such a violent passion, and whom I had so deeply wronged, I was scarcely able to stammer a few words of excuse; but she at once interrupted them by a heartrending cry, and fell back in a fainting fit that seemed to be accompanied by every symptom of death.

So dire an accident ought to have been as a curb to my passion; on the contrary, it acted as a spur.... Ashamed and despairing, I issued from the apartment, hiding my head with the skirt of my robe, and ordering the eunuchs and the slave girls to go to the help of their mistress.

I stood at that moment in no need of strokes from the fatal wand; my heart was already sufficiently tortured, but rather with despite and rage than remorse. This first visit was followed by several others of a similar kind. The woman I sought to embrace was always inert and seemingly dead, and I always quitted her with horror. Often, after issuing from Gazahidé's apartment, I rushed away to the Mosque, and there beat my breast with such violence that the spectators were lost in admiration at seeing a king as zealous, as much a martyr in the cause of penitence, as the most enthusiastic of fakirs.

All this time Homaïouna, who could not have been ignorant of my fatal visits to Gazahidé, never spoke of them to me; and she acted wisely, for I regarded her as the first cause of this unspeakable misfortune that had befallen me, and should have lost all patience with her. Alsalami did indeed venture to utter a halting word of remonstrance, but I reduced him to silence in tones that froze the very blood in his veins. He took to his bed and remained there till he died. It was the Peri who came to tell me of his death, and to propose another vizier in his stead. I was too embittered against her to comply. I reproached her with having utterly overburdened a poor recluse who, from his youth up, had been accustomed to live a quiet life, and had naturally succumbed beneath the weight of the duties she had absurdly imposed upon him; and I gave her to thoroughly understand that henceforward I should choose my own Grand Vizier.

"I understand," cried she, and her air was rather sad and pitiful than angry; "you will only give your confidence to one who flatters the inordinate and unruly passion by which you are now tormented – a passion that makes you the byword of your harem. Ah! unless Heaven intervenes, you are about to become the wicked king with whose advent the fatal parchment threatens mankind."

She retired after saying these words, and I was tempted to make her repent having uttered them, by beating her to the ground; for I knew by what she had told me of her history that, though it was not possible to kill her, it was possible to inflict upon her the most cruel and excruciating torments. Only fear lest she should find means of depriving me altogether of my princess restrained me; but alas! I soon lost this reason for remaining with her on decent terms.

I was scarcely awake the following morning, when I heard terrible sounds of lamentation coming from Gazahidé's apartments. I got up in alarm. I ran thither; her eunuchs, her slave girls, prostrated themselves to the ground before me, vociferating hideously. Altogether beside myself, I stepped over them, I entered into the princess's chamber. There on her divan, I found my carbuncle, and a paper containing these terrible words: "Take back thy accursed carbuncle, detestable Barkiarokh! The sea is about to receive this miserable body of mine, and will never give it up again into thine arms. Would to heaven that the waters had engulfed it ere that first fatal hour when it was profaned by thee!"

Like a sick man, who, though consumed by present evils, thinks of a long life, and feels the sudden dart of the Angel of Death, so was I smitten to the heart by the loss of her who was my daily torment. I threw myself down on the divan, and remained there, heedless of outward things, for half the day. At last I regained the power of consecutive thought, and my first use of it was to accuse the Peri. "She it is," said I to myself, "who, with that wretched little fish of hers, caused me to acquire the fatal ring, and with it to take upon myself my father's gout. She is who, in her spite and jealousy, compelled me to confess my crime before Gazahidé. and placed me in extreme peril. She it is, doubtless, who threw the princess into these deathlike swoons which prevented her from listening to me; for, had the princess been in a condition to hear my excuses, she was far too gentle, and loved me far too much, not to have forgiven me; nor certainly was it of her own motion that she preferred death to myself. But is she really dead? Has she thrown herself into the sea? Should I attach implicit faith to a piece of writing placed here perhaps only to deceive? It is true that Gazahidé could not otherwise escape, save by supernatural means. The height of these walls, and the incorruptibility of her guards, make this certain. But can I be equally certain that the Peri has not spirited her away, and removed her to other lands? Did she not obtain that power and make use of it, when she succoured the eunuch Gehanguz? Did she not, in some sort, warn me yesterday that she might exercise it again? Ah! I would rather Gazahidé were really drowned than in another man's arms! In any case I must be revenged on Homaïouna, and to be revenged I must dissemble."

After these reflections I concocted a plot quite worthy of my own turpitude, and left that fatal chamber, with a countenance sad indeed but composed, and retired to my own apartments. Far from refusing to admit Homaïouna, who came to me almost at once, I received her with a grateful air. "You had told me," said I, "that Heaven would put an end to my criminal excesses; you are a true prophet. Unfortunately, I always believe your warnings after the event and too late. I am now myself again, and though I cannot help deploring the loss I have experienced, I shall bear it with resignation. Help me with your counsels; continue to rule over my kingdom; while I devote myself to those pious exercises so necessary to my soul's welfare."

"Now, Allah and his Prophet be praised for this return of your better self!" cried the Peri. "But, alas! was it necessary, in order to bring you to your right mind, that that poor princess should be sacrificed and forfeit her life? I loved her, and would at least have wished to pay due honour to her mortal remains. Vain hope! Nothing of her has been recovered save this veil found floating on the surface of the waters. She must have sought to rest for ever buried beneath the waves."

"You think, then," said I, looking fixedly at Homaïouna, "that the amiable Gazahidé has perished irretrievably?"

"Do I believe it?" replied she. "I believe it only too assuredly. And you yourself, can you still have doubts? Ah! dear Barkiarokh, cease to entertain visionary hopes that would neutralise your good intentions. Seek a refuge from your sorrow rather in such pleasures as are lawful. If you are happy without shame, and without crime, my utmost desires will be accomplished!"

This affectionate speech, instead of touching me, only served to further exasperate me against the Peri. I knew her to be incapable of falsehood; and was assured, therefore, that she had not actually removed Gazahidé; but still I regarded her as the prime cause of Gazahidé's loss. I became more than ever determined to execute my cruel designs for her punishment, and carried out those designs to the full, after giving her, for three days, so as to allay her suspicions, every mark of affection and confidence.

The wicked easily recognise wickedness in others. I had discovered that Ologou, chief of my eunuchs, was a thorough scoundrel, and just such an instrument as I required. I ordered him to find among his fellows two or three cut-throats fit for any act of violence. He brought me two, and said he could answer for them. "My friends," said I, "by a fatal mischance I am married to a magician, who first presented herself to me as a simple and innocent creature. Shortly after our wedding, she did indeed perform, at my expense, two or three of the tricks of her trade; but, as these were of no great malignity, I passed them over in silence. Afterwards she passed to deeds of atrocity. In order that I might reign, or rather in short order that she might herself exercise sovereign power, she stifled the late King, and, in her jealousy, has just thrown the princess into the sea. I am bound to punish crimes so execrable; the trouble is to find the means. She can disappear at pleasure, and at pleasure move about from place to place. It would be useless, therefore, to give her up to public justice. Only by surprising her asleep can she be punished as she deserves."

"Sire," interrupted Ologou, "I have long been aware of the wickedness and hypocrisy of Homaïouna; if you so order, we will, this very night, enter, fully armed, into her chamber, and run her through and through before she can wake to consciousness."

"I am perfectly agreeable," I replied; "the act will be an act of justice, and not go unrewarded."

This new crime of mine was executed to my entire satisfaction. The Peri would have died a thousand deaths if she could have died at all. Her body was one great wound, when, by the exercise of her supernatural powers, it disappeared from before the eyes of her cruel assailants, who, by my orders, published the crimes of which I accused her, and the magician's trick by which she had eluded the full punishment I meditated.

The veneration in which I was held, and the number of my witnesses, caused these lies to be generally believed. Men pitied me. The partisans of the murdered King, and of the drowned princess thanked me for the justice I had wished to execute, and suggested that I should forbid any of my subjects, on pain of death, to afford help, or shelter, to Homaïouna. Ormossouf alone could have thrown light on this mystery of iniquity; but he was naturally indolent, and no longer supported by his friend the dervish, so that he caused but little anxiety; as a matter of fact, he gave me no trouble whatever.

Nothing could equal my joy at the thought that the Peri would now be fully occupied in getting healed of her wounds, and must perforce leave me alone for some time. I resolved to take advantage of these moments of respite, and to drown in debauchery my too poignant memories of Gazahidé. The tranquil pleasures of the harem were too insipid for such a purpose. My ring could procure me delights of a more pungent nature, and without loss of my reputation for sanctity. I imparted my design to Ologou, and he brought me a list of the most beautiful women of Berdouka. Among these was the favourite of Mohabed, the Emir who had so unseasonably recognised me as Barkiarokh at the very moment when I was about to be made King under the name of Farukrouz.

It was with genuine delight that I began my adventures with this lady. In order to effect my purpose, I sent Ologou, at the point of day, to the Emir, summoning him at once to attend the divan. I entered her apartment invisibly, at the same time as my messenger, and squatted own in a corner. There I listened to the good old man's comic complaints. "Must I leave thee, Light of my Eyes?" he said to his wife. "That fool of a Barkiarokh, who is much more fit to be a fisherman than a king, wants to make men move about by starlight as he used to propel his boat hither and thither in the old days. Moreover, he has lost two wives, and does not want to take to himself any more, and is restless at nights. He does not bear in mind that husbands more fortunate than himself do not like to rise so early in the morning."

"Ah! speak no evil of that pious monarch," cried a soft and silvery voice, "he is so good and so beneficent that all the world should love him. Go – don't keep him waiting, I shall remain patiently in bed till you return."

The Emir murmured a few words more – made his adieux, and departed.

His back was no sooner turned than the lady cried out in indignant tones: "Go, odious old bag of bones! and may you never come back! Alas! why do I not belong to that amiable Barkiarokh, who is more beautiful than the sun at noonday!"

With a woman already so favourably disposed, any great precautions on my part were unnecessary. At first she was somewhat alarmed by my sudden appearance, but not long: I soon reassured her, and we spent together the whole time that the Grand Vizier – who for that day presided over the Divan in my stead – occupied in idle discussion – and in the art of idle speech he was a past master.

I several times renewed my visits to this lady, and witnessed various scenes, to which she gave occasion for my amusement, between herself and her husband. Then I became inconstant, and the wife of the Iman of the Great Mosque took my fancy. Her husband had in no way offended me. On the contrary, we were the best of friends. But what did that matter? I had the same success here as in my first adventure, and indeed never failed in any of the similar adventures in which I subsequently embarked. Ologou, who frequented all the harems where he thought I might find advantage, would adroitly prepossess the ladies in my favour, and they, in their own interests, kept my doings secret.

But oh! my unhappy companions, how ill do these frivolities consort with our horrible situation here! I shall dwell on them no more, but pass at once to events more fitted for recital in this our present abode.

Though I regarded my adulteries as little more than a multiplicity of jokes, yet I could not but be surprised that the Peri paid so little attention to them. She must, by this time, have been long healed of her wounds, and nevertheless I received no strokes from her fatal wand. At last I came to the conclusion that the daggers of my eunuchs had brought her to a more reasonable frame of mind, and that she had elected some other field for her energies.

Pleasures so facile at last brought satiety. After some years my fits of gout became more frequent, and the hypocrisy, which I continued to practice, became insupportable. Ologou, who had made himself master of all my secrets, often journeyed to divers parts of the world to find for me young beauties, whom he had afterwards the mortification of seeing me despise. I did nothing but talk to him about Gazahidé, whose charms, now that I was more than satiated with chance amours, assumed in my memory even brighter hues than before. At last the wretched slave was at his wits' end, and knew not what to do, when an accident occurred, very unexpectedly, that woke me from my lethargy.

One day, when I was giving audience to the people, two women, veiled, presented themselves at the foot of the throne, and, with timid and suppliant voices, besought me to hear them in private. Without knowing why, I felt moved by their accents, and had them conducted into my harem, whither I shortly followed. What was my surprise on seeing my two sisters-in-law, as pretty and as fresh as in the days when they had first excited my admiration. "Wives of my brothers," I said, "be assured of my good-will, but let us postpone to some future time whatever communication you may desire to make to me. In my harem pleasure is the first business of all, and to that business every other is postponed."

I devoted, therefore, some days assiduously to their entertainment. Afterwards I reminded them that they had something to say to me.

"Oh! we had forgotten our old husbands," cried the younger, "and no wonder, seeing what wretched creatures they are, and how utterly incapable of work, or doing anything for us! We have wandered from city to city, living by the alms of the faithful, ever since the day when Ormossouf drove us from his door. The faithful gave us bread, but no comfort. The Afrite of the Miry Desert alone seemed to enter into our troubles; but your brothers were afraid to avail themselves of the remedy he proposed."

My sister-in-law blushed as she uttered these words, and was silent.

"Conclude," said I sharply. "You have excited my curiosity. I desire to know the whole of this adventure."

Story of Barkiarokh's Younger Sister-in-Law

"Well, you shall know it," she rejoined; "but you will be even more frightened than your brothers. This it is: a good woman, to whom we had told the story of the little fish, and of the misfortunes it had brought upon us, came one day, in great haste, to the hovel into which we retired at night-time. 'My children,' she said, 'I have just been told something that may be of use to you, and I have lost no time in coming to impart it. It is confidently asserted that at thirty mountains' distance from here is to be found the Miry Desert, inhabited by an Afrite, who is very obliging, and never refuses advice, or help, provided only that the applicant does not go counter to any of his singular fancies; and as you are good folk, easy and obliging because you are poor, you will doubtless be welcome. True, the distance is somewhat great, but, as you are always on the move, begging hither and thither, distance in your case must be a slight matter. I think it will be to your advantage to undertake the journey; and if you gain nothing, why, you will lose nothing, seeing that you have nothing to lose.' This conclusion was unassailable. We thanked the good old woman, and instantly set out.

"We travelled no great distance day by day, our husbands being feeble and unable to walk long at a time. As to my sister and myself, we were buoyed up by the hope that the poor old things might recover their youth and strength, and were as light of foot as two does pursued by a hunter. Nor should we fail to acknowledge what we owe to the good Mussulmans who inhabit that great stretch of country, and allowed us to want for nothing. True, we never told them the end and object of our pilgrimage, for fear of scandalising them – the Afrites being no friends to the Holy Prophet in whose name the alms were bestowed upon us.

"At last we reached the Miry Desert. But there our hearts failed us, so evil and horrible was the place. Picture to yourself an immense tract of land covered with thick black mud – neither pathways, nor trees, nor any beasts save certain swine that wallowed in the filth, and added to its horror. We perceived, afar off, the caverned rock, the dwelling of the Afrite; but we were fearful of being swallowed up in the slime, or torn to pieces by the porkers, before we could reach it. As to the odious brutes, we had no means of attacking or repelling them, and from their numbers it was evident their master greatly liked their company.

"'Let us retrace our steps,' cried your two brothers. 'Nothing can be more unendurable than this!' At these words my sister and I lost all patience. We upbraided them so hotly both for their wretchedness and our own, that, after much weeping, they suffered us to drag them into the slough. Here we upheld them as best we could, notwithstanding the difficulty we experienced in extricating ourselves. The sun darted upon us its fiercest rays, and this seemed greatly to enliven the pigs, which, without appearing to notice us, indulged at our sides in a thousand gambols, and tumblings, splashing us in such a manner as to make us frightful and filthy to behold. Nevertheless, what with swimming, and wading, and falling, and getting up again, we at last succeeded in reaching the foot of the rock, which was situated in the midst of the Miry Desert, and surrounded by dry moss – the latter very comforting.

"We found the Afrite seated at the entrance of a spacious cavern, and enveloped in a robe of tiger skins, so long and so ample that it stretched round him for several cubits. His head was out of proportion with his gigantic stature, for it was of ordinary size, and his face was strange to a degree. His complexion was of fine yellow; his hair, his eyebrows, his eyelids and his beard, purple; his eyes black as night; his lips pale red; his teeth narrow, white and sharp like fish bones, and the general effect rather extraordinary than pleasing. He received us graciously. 'Poor people,' said he; 'I'm so filled with pity for all you have suffered in coming here, that you may be sure I shall do my utmost to help you. Speak boldly therefore; in what can I serve you?'

"Encouraged by these words we related to him our woes in greatest detail, and then asked if he knew of any remedy.

"'Yes, yes,' he replied; 'I know of a remedy sure enough, and a very easy one; but we will speak of it by-and-by; go now to the bottom of my cave, and you will find there a spring of pure water; cleanse yourselves thoroughly; then, turning to the right, you will see clothing of all sorts; take the garments you most fancy and, after donning them, come back and rejoin me here.'

"The offer came opportunely and we accepted it with joy and gratitude. We bathed deliciously, and were no less glad to change our old rags. We afterwards found the Afrite at the same place where we had left him, and arranging fruit of all kinds in baskets. 'Sit here near me,' said he, 'and eat, for you must be hungry.'

"And so indeed we were. The Afrite laughed with all his heart when he saw how we devoured our food. At last he observed: 'You don't at all look like over-scrupulous Mussulmans, and, I take it, would drink wine with pleasure if it were offered. Come,' he continued, seeing from our looks that we wished for nothing better, 'you shall have it in abundance.'

"Saying these words he stretched out his hand over the dirty waters surrounding us, and these changed immediately into a stream flowing with red wine, whose smell was a delight, and along the stream grew fruit trees. The swine had disappeared. In their stead an immense number of gracious and graceful children played about the stream, and presented to us great vases of crystal full of the sparkling wine, which we relished with transports of delight. For a whole hour we had only opened our lips to drink, when our elder brother, quite hilarious, cried: 'Ah! how happy you are, my Lord Afrite, and how happy should we be in turn if you would consent to keep us with you here!'

"'Poor fool,' replied the Afrite; 'poor fool who, like the rest of mankind, dost judge of happiness by outward appearances! See if I am happy.' Speaking thus he lifted up his robe, and we saw that his two legs were fixed into the ground as far as the knees. At this strange spectacle, terror and compassion were depicted upon our countenances. He saw it, and resumed, with a more tranquil air: 'Do not be too sorry for me, my friends. Though the power who holds me half buried here, may cheat the eyes of those who come to visit me, by making that appear a filthy slough which is indeed a delightful watercourse, yet he cannot prevent my ultimate deliverance – which is perhaps not far distant. However that may be, I cannot retain you here. Go, leave me with these fair children whom you mistook for swine, and of whom, very happily, I have not been deprived; but before we separate, let me tell you this: the imprudent wish by which you brought upon yourselves age and its infirmities can only cease to have effect with the death of your father. It is for you to consider how far you are prepared to wait for that event – which, in the ordinary course of nature, may still be far distant – or to hasten its approach. As for me, I know very well that if I had a hundred fathers, I should not spare a single one of them in order to put an end to misery such as yours and that of your amiable consorts.'

"By our consideration, by our silence, the Afrite perceived that his suggestion failed to meet with our approval. This appeared to disconcert him; and suddenly changing his manner he said rudely: 'Go, and pursue your reflections elsewhere. I am mistaken in you. I thought we might meet again to our common advantage; but you are no better than cowards. Go this minute. I dispense with all ceremony and farewells.'

"We were too frightened to wait for a repetition of this command. We rose without saying a word; but, O heavens! the beautiful stream, which it would have been a joy to traverse, had become once again a slough, foul and infamous. And now our husbands, who were even more indignant against the Afrite than ourselves, showed us the way. They threw themselves, without hesitation, into the muck heaps, and we followed dolefully. The horrible passage proved far more difficult than before. We were up to our necks in filth, and the swine molested us in a thousand ways. Vainly did we say one to another that we were wading in clear wine, and surrounded by pretty children. The lie was too palpable.

"Weary to death, we emerged at last from the Miry Desert, and reached dry land. Immediately your elder brother cried: 'Cursed ever be that child of Eblis who dared advise us to commit parricide.'

"'Cursed,' said your second brother, 'be the infamous breath that uttered the impious words; cursed, I say, be he who spoke them, cursed from his purple locks to the soles of his feet – if, indeed, he has any feet, as he pretended.'

"'Cursed,' added my sister, 'be everything that belongs or has belonged, to that monster, save only his clear wine, and the good clothes we are carrying away with us.'

"After these just imprecations, we sat down under a big tree to rest for the night, which was approaching with great strides. Our feeble husbands, thoroughly worn out, slept profoundly, while my sister and I kept awake consulting as to what was to be done. In the morning I made the two old men acquainted with the conclusions at which we had arrived. 'Believe me,' said I, 'banish all false shame, and the fears that have hitherto prevented you from appealing to the King, your brother. Barkiarokh is too good, too full of piety, to blush at your poverty, or to bear in mind our ancient quarrels. Let us go and throw ourselves at his feet, and tell him all that has befallen us. He will help us if only to spite the Afrite, for he has sufficiently proved, by the banishment of Homaïouna, that he has no love for such malign spirits.' We set forth once more, and, after a long and tiring journey, at last reached Berdouka – where our husbands are awaiting your reply."

End of the Story of Barkiarokh's Younger Sister-in-Law

I had trembled with joy on learning, in the course of this narrative, that I might hope one day to be delivered from my fatal gout. The means by which the happy hour could be hastened had at first somewhat startled me, but my heart, in its utter depravity, soon grew reconciled to the horrible thought.

The only question was how to commit such an odious crime without exciting suspicion; and to this point I had addressed my thoughts during the latter portion of my sister-in-law's story.

She had told it in such a way as to make me understand, even if I had not known it already, what kind of woman I was dealing with. So, when she had done speaking, I said to her, in a tone of contempt: "Hence, leave my palace, you women who have neither spirit, sense nor courage! You are unworthy of what I intended to do for you. What! you did not persuade your husbands to recover their youth and vigour by taking the life of a monster, devoid of right feelings, who showed indeed that he was no father of theirs, by hounding them out of his house in their infirm condition – a condition they had assumed out of love for himself – and who afterwards had such fearful inhumanity as to see them perishing with want! Had you not sufficient influence over your husbands to compel them, if need were, to enter secretly, by night, into a house of which every nook and corner was well known to them, and to cut off the wretch's head? Conduct so just and energetic, far from exciting my anger, would have deserved my praise. Hence, hence, I say! and let me never hear speak of you again!"

More was not wanted. My sisters-in-law were altogether beside themselves. They had been hoping to see their husbands no more, and to go on living with me. So they threw themselves distracted at my feet, and began to embrace my knees, crying out, both together: "Forgive us, dear lord, forgive us; it is not our fault, if your brothers are irresolute and spiritless. We were not as base as they. But what could we say or do? They would have killed *us* if we had insisted on their following the counsels of the Afrite. Now, however, since you tell us Ormossouf is not really their father, we know perfectly well what to say to them. Promise to take us back into your good graces – which we value far more than the restoration of our husbands to youth and vigour – and we will show that we have more spirit and sense than you think."

And here, O my companions! I must draw a veil over an act too abominable to be spoken of without horror, even in these subterranean halls of Eblis. My sisters-in-law succeeded only too well; and, in concert with them, I caused their wretched husbands to be surprised at the very moment when they had consummated their abhorred murder. Ologou, to whom I had given orders to that effect, had their heads cut off on the spot, and brought their wives to my harem. I was alone with the two wretches, and coldly listening to the recital of their accursed crime, when the Peri's wand struck me with such force that I fell down as if killed. A moment after I rose from the ground in an inconceivable fury, and having seized my two accomplices, I pierced them through and through again and again with my dagger, and cast their bodies into the sea. To this involuntary act of justice succeeded new transports of despair. I yelled imprecations against myself, till my voice failed and I fell into a swoon.

Ologou had seen all through the door curtains, but had taken good care not to come near during my frenzy. He entered when he saw the paroxysm was over, and, taking me in his arms, without calling for assistance, dressed the wounds I had inflicted on myself, and brought me back to my senses. I asked him, with a feeble voice, if there had been any dangerous witnesses to the scene just enacted. He reassured me on this point, but was as terrified as myself by this evidence that the Peri had not forgotten me. We grew calmer by degrees, and determined, by a conduct above reproach, to keep clear of the fatal wand for the future.

A fish might more easily live on the apex of a rock than a man accustomed to crime live a life of virtue. Vainly did the eunuch invent day by day new and innocent amusements – I was dying of rage and ennui. "Ah! I would brave Homaïouna," I used to say, "if only I were sure she would not punish me in public. The convulsions of remorse that she persists in inflicting upon me would only take the place of the attacks of gout, from which I am now delivered – but I risk all if ever she exposes me publicly in the eyes of my subjects."

The strictness I was compelled to impose upon my own conduct, made me so hard and harsh in my dealings with others that I was on the point of being hated by my people as much as I had formerly been beloved, when one day Ologou came to tell me, with an air of triumph, that he had found a sovereign remedy for my woes. "You have doubtless heard," he continued, "of Babek Horremi,[1] surnamed the Impious, because he believed in no religion at all, and preached a universal subservience to enjoyment, and to every conceivable kind of pleasure. You know also with what ease he perverted all Persia and the adjacent provinces, and how, being followed by a prodigious number of his adherents, he made head against the troops sent for his destruction by the Caliphs Mamoun[2] and Motassem; and how, finally, he was captured by the latter through the treachery of a dog, the son of a dog. Well, this great man has not altogether perished. Naoud, his confidant and minister survives him. He has escaped from the prisons of Samarah,[3] and, after wandering from land to land for several years, has, at last, come hither. I met him this morning in the neighbourhood of Berdouka, and greeted him as he deserves. He had been my master in old days, so I knew him well, and ventured to acquaint him with your sorrows. He pitied you, and offers you his services. Take him as your Grand Vizier; he is the man you want. The present holder of the office is but a fool, who carries out to the letter such orders as you may deign to give him. The ingenious Naoud will do much more – he will know how to preserve you from Homaïouna's wand, which he in no wise fears so far as he himself is concerned. Meanwhile, and little by little, he will establish the Horremitic sect in Daghestan, so that if you should throw off the mask of piety, which you have so far assumed, your subjects will be rather rejoiced than scandalized."

I eagerly seized upon this hope. I saw Naoud, and made no

---

1 Babek Horremi, *Babak Alkorremi*: Head of Khurrami sect located in parts of Persia and holding hedonistic and libertine views that everything agreeable to the senses is permitted, including wine and promiscuity. The movement, anti-Arab and anti-Muslim, drew ideas and supporters from Zoroastrianism. They fomented revolts against the Arab Caliphate in the eighth and ninth centuries AD. [*Islam2* I, 844]
   Babak revolted against Vathek's father, who sent an army against him and with great difficulty defeated, captured, and executed him. [*D'Herbelot* 159]
2 Mamoun; *al-Ma'mun*: Abbasid caliph who reigned 813-833. Succeeded by *al-Mu'tassim* (Motassem) in 833 and *al-Wathiq* (Vathek) in 842.
3 Samarah: Islamic capital city, founded by Motassem.

doubt that, with his gifts of seduction, he would soon relieve me of all anxiety. We conferred together several times. At last we settled the day on which I should, in full divan, declare him my Grand Vizier. I was thus hurrying to my ruin, without a thought that to establish impiety in my states would be the most unpardonable of my crimes. In a very few moments I was to perceive my error, but too late. Naoud, clothed in magnificent attire, was at my right; I pointed him out with my hand to the emirs, and grandees of the kingdom, who waited respectfully to hear my commands. "Here," said I, "is the man of whom I make choice to help me in governing you, and making you happy...." I was about to enlarge on the scoundrel's imaginary good qualities, when the fatal wand, without striking me to the earth, or troubling me in its accustomed manner, compelled me to change my tone: "He is," I continued, "with the exception of myself, the most infamous of men; he is the impious friend and disciple of the impure Babek Horremi; he has undertaken to corrupt you all, to make you abandon the religion of Mahomet, and to adopt instead the worship of unbridled enjoyment and illicit pleasure; he is well worthy to be the vizier of a monster, who has murdered your King, so outraged your princess that she was forced to throw herself into the deep, caused the Peri who protected him to be pierced with a thousand wounds, taken advantage of all your wives, and finally impelled his brothers to assassinate his and their father. Here is the ring that has favoured my crimes. It is the ring that made me invisible when you, the Iman of the Great Mosque, said doatingly to your wife that she was a little mouse whom the Angel Gabriel had let fall into the room of a prophet; it is this ring that enabled me to listen while you, Mohabed, on being summoned to the Divan, said I was more fit to be a fisherman than a king; but I forgave you, because I instantly took your place in your harem. A power, supernatural, irresistible, which often before has made me utterly beside myself, is this day constraining me after a different fashion. It leaves me just enough of reason to convince you, circumstantially, that I am the most atrocious, the most detestable monster that the earth ever bore upon its surface. Glut your vengeance. Tear in pieces Ologou, my accomplice, and the perfidious Naoud; but beware lest you come near me. I feel that I am reserved for a yet more terrible fate."

After speaking thus, I was silent, looking around me with haggard eyes and a ferocious mein. I seemed to defy the general fury, which, as I looked, took the place of what had at first been consternation. But, when every sword was uplifted against me, I quickly put the ring on the little finger of my left hand, and, crawling like a reptile, escaped through the furious crowd. As I passed the court of the palace I heard the cries of Ologou, and of Naoud; but these were less fearful to me than the sight of the sycamore from which, in fancy, I saw myself a second time suspended – and the terror of it still held me long after I had left Berdouka.

During all the remainder of the day, I walked, or rather ran, mechanically, and not knowing whither I went. But at nightfall I stopped short, gazing fearfully at a forest that stretched out before me. The feeble and confused glow of twilight made everything loom large, and the dark green of the trees was so gloomy and lugubrious that I hesitated before penetrating into that black abode of solitude. At last, impelled by an evil fate, I entered the woods, groping. Scarce had I taken a couple of steps, when I was thrown down amid the thorns and briars by the great branches, that seemed to my fancy, so strong and irresistible were they, like great arms intent on repelling and keeping me out.

"Wretch that thou art," cried I, "even inanimate things have thee in horror! For thee there is no mercy in the heavens, or on the earth. Remain where thou art, a prey for the evil beasts of the forest, if even *they* do not disdain to devour thee! Oh, Homaïouna, well art thou avenged; triumph in my miseries; I am not worthy to excite thy pity!"

I had just done uttering these words when thousands of ravens and crows began croaking from the tops of the trees, and what they croaked was: "Repent, repent."

"Ah!" cried I, "is there still room for repentance? Yea, I may dare to hope so, and will do penance resignedly. I shall wait for the return of daylight in the place where I now am, and then, setting forth once more, I will make haste to leave Daghestan. Fortunately the precious stones are still in my possession. I will sell them, and distribute the money as alms among the poor. Then I will retire into some desert, and browse on the grass of the field, and drink the water of heaven. I have been the abominable king foretold in the parchment, but I may yet become a holy hermit."

Amid these good resolutions, which somewhat quieted my spirit – and being, moreover, overwhelmed with fatigue – I fell asleep on my couch of briars and thorns, and slept as profoundly as if I had lain on a divan with velvet cushions. The sun was already up when lamentations, proceeding from no great distance, awoke me with a start. A soft and childish voice was crying: "Oh, Leilah, unhappy Leilah, shalt thou leave thy mother's body to the vultures, or shalt thou still continue to drive them away, notwithstanding the hunger pinching thee so sore? Alas! my death is sure if I remain here. These ravenous birds will devour us all, and my mother will never be buried, according to her passionate wish, in the same earth as her father, who was murdered so inhumanely. Oh! why is Calili dead also? He would have helped me to honour the last wishes of his dear princess. Barkiarokh, cruel Barkiarokh! I will not curse thee, for thou art my father, and Gazahidé forbade it, but I curse the day that I owe to thee."

Surprised and utterly bewildered by such an amazing adventure, I was on the point of uttering a piercing cry in answer to my daughter's complaints; but I refrained, so as not to frighten her, perhaps to death; and, remembering that I was invisible, I advanced, without noise, to the place where she still sobbed out her heart. A palisade, bristling with spikes as sharp as javelins, barred my way. I looked through, and saw the innocent Leilah lying on the grass before a little house made of palm branches intertwined in reeds. Her lovely eyes were turned towards the gate of the palisade; though those eyes were tear-bedimmed, they seemed to shoot at me their full rays, and those rays pierced my heart – a heart which they reached indeed through accustomed ways, for their light was the same as Gazahidé's eyes had so often darted upon me. I was carried back to the fatal moment when my princess caused her tent to be set up over the spot where the dwarf first saw my precious stones. Leilah was about the same age as her mother at that time – her features, her hair, her figure, her entrancing beauty, all were alike. Startled, beside myself, I did not know what to do. Clearly it was imperative that I should hide my name; but supposing anyone had given my daughter a faithful description of my person, how would it then be possible to escape recognition? Still something had to be done. I could not leave the lovely child without help. I removed the ring, therefore, from my little finger, and knocking at the gate of the palisade said, with a lamentable voice: "Whosoever you may be that inhabit this dwelling of canes and palm leaves, I pray you to afford your hospitality to a poor wretch whom the impious Barkiarokh has reduced to utter misery."

"Now Allah and his Prophet be praised for the help they have sent me," cried Leilah, rising hastily, and leaping at one bound to the gate of the palisade, which she opened. "Come," continued she, "dear stranger, whom Barkiarokh persecutes; you will here behold other victims of his cruelty, and help me to bury my mother and her dwarf, so that the vultures may not devour them."

As she said these words she invited me to enter.

Considering how contrite I had been only a few hours before, who would not have thought that the sight of Gazahidé's body, even more effective than the Peri's wand, would overwhelm me with remorse? But, ah! the horrible effect of habitual indulgence in crime! I experienced, at that terrible moment, nothing but wild, ungovernable passion, and vowed that my daughter, my own daughter, should ere long become my prey! I called on Eblis to give me success in this my sinister design; and immediately set to work to carry out Leilah's filial wish with regard to the interment of her mother's body, so as thus to gain her confidence, and ultimately bring her into my arms!

I dug a large pit in which we deposited the corpse of Gazahidé and that of the dwarf – on whom, in my inmost heart, I showered a thousand curses. Then, taking Leilah by the hand, I said: "Dry your tears. Let me lead you to some place where we can obtain the assistance of which you stand so greatly in need. Barkiarokh's wickedness has driven me out into this forest. I fancied I saw, a long way off, some peasants' cottages; let us go in that direction. You have done your duty to your mother. It is now time to think of yourself."

"I will follow you anywhere," she replied; "for surely Heaven has sent you to be my protector. Be a father to me, since my own father is a monster, whom both you and I have every reason to detest."

Leilah had more courage than strength. She could scarcely stand. I took her in my arms, and bore the lovely burden through the forest – not without trembling lest I should meet some one who knew me, for I dared not use my ring except in case of absolute necessity, since its history must be well known to my daughter, and its use, therefore, would have involved instant recognition. I pressed the innocent creature to my bosom; and the impure fire within me was increasing in violence, when a sudden thought put an end to my infamous transports. "Fool that I am," said I to myself, "of what am I thinking? Homaïouna is hovering about me. It is she who, yesterday, caused the ravens and crows of the forest to utter their warnings. As she has no supernatural means of reading men's hearts, she may believe it is only paternal love that makes me take care of Leilah; but if I yielded to my present mad desires, she would not spare me the worst effects of her fatal power. Then, by confessing my crimes, I should make myself known to my daughter, and the horrible scenes that I had erewhile with Gazahidé would be renewed. Oh! is there no spot in all this wide world to which the terrible Peri cannot follow me? And if there is, cannot the Afrite of the Miry Desert point it out? His advice to my brothers shows well enough that all things are known to him; and that he hesitates at nothing. I will go and consult him; till then, I will hold myself well in hand with Leilah, and not even kiss her as a friend."

The honest peasants to whom we addressed ourselves, not only supplied our immediate and urgent needs, but also sold us a good horse. So I took Leilah up behind me, and made haste to leave Daghestan.

When I had nothing more to fear, I stopped in a large city; and there, having disposed of one of my emeralds to the best advantage, I caused fine clothes to be made for Leilah, and gave her two woman slaves. She did not know how to thank me enough. The name of "father" which she bestowed upon me, her real affection, her innocent caresses, all excited me beyond measure; but I still had perforce to hold myself firmly, if reluctantly, in hand.

The necessary preparations for our journey to the Miry Desert required time. I had no desire to remain whole months on the way, like my brothers and my sisters-in-law. One quiet evening, after a very stormy day, I asked Leilah to tell me her mother's story; which she immediately did, with ready submission. That story I already knew only too well up to the time when I thought Gazahidé had thrown herself into the sea, and I paid little heed to what Leilah was saying, till she reached this point:

The Story of Leilah, Barkiarokh's Daughter

"My mother only recovered from the swoons of which the unworthy Barkiarokh took such infamous advantage, to abandon herself to the most terrible despair. Neither her slaves, nor even the good Homaïouna, could comfort her. She pined away visibly, and must, ere long, have died; but, one night, when she had risen from her couch, and was, as usual, weeping over the accursed carbuncle, she heard, through the window, the voice of Calili saying: 'Open to me, dear mistress, open to me! I have risked all to save you.'

"And indeed the faithful dwarf had, at the peril of his life, climbed a gigantic fig-tree, which, rising from the border of the sea, covered with its branches the walls of Gazahidé's chamber. By the help of a silken ladder, which he attached to this tree, my mother escaped, with great courage, after leaving on the dais a writing intended to throw Barkiarokh off the scent. The dwarf, after detaching the ladder, slid down, and made the princess enter into a little boat – by which he himself had come to the place – and then, for he rowed quite as well as he swam, he hugged the shore, and ultimately reached the forest, and the dwelling in which you found me. That dwelling belonged to a holy woman called Kaioun, who had retired thither to pray and meditate. She had given shelter to Calili, and, hearing from him of Barkiarokh's crimes, and the sorrows of Gazahidé, had not hesitated to second that zealous servant in his enterprise. The poor princess was received with much respect and kindness by this pious recluse, so that she never ceased to thank Heaven for the refuge she had found; and when Calili wished afterwards to persuade her to quit Daghestan, she refused to listen to his advice, protesting that she would end her days with Kaioun, and be buried in the earth of the same land that held the bones of her father. As Barkiarokh made no attempt to find the fugitive, the dwarf became more easy in his mind; and my mother was beginning to find comfort and peace, when a new misfortune befell her: she found that she was with child. 'Oh, heavens!' said she, 'must I bear a child to that detestable monster! Ah! may it not be like him.'

"It was then with tears, and anguish, in the most mortal anxiety, that, at last, she brought me into the world. I did not want either for care, or good instruction, during my infancy – my mother, Kaioun, Calili, all had no thought but for me. I was grateful and submissive, and, I may say, happier than I shall ever be again. I sometimes went to the neighbouring town with the charitable Kaioun. She had bought a supply of sandal-wood, with which we made little boxes, very neat, that we sold at considerable profit. It was not necessary to enjoin silence upon me with regard to the place of our retreat; for my mother had told me her story, and I feared even more than she did to fall into the hands of Barkiarokh, whom I hated with all my soul.

"So the years passed pleasantly and peacefully. We regarded the savage spot in which Heaven had placed us, as a real paradise; when, suddenly, the hand of providence, that so far had been our stay, ceased to give us its support. My mother fell sick of a slow fever, and we were greatly alarmed. Calili and I never left her for a single moment. Kaioun alone went to the town to purchase such necessities as we required. She always remained away as short a time as possible, but at last a day came when she went and never returned. We passed the next two days in an indescribable torment of anxiety. At last Calili, seeing that his dear mistress was getting worse for want of the necessary food and comforts, resolved to brave all chance of discovery. He repeated without ceasing: 'I am the cause of all that has happened, it is all due to my idiotic admiration for the accursed jewels of the thrice-accursed Barkiarokh; it is for me to do whatever can be done to remedy the irremediable.'

"My mother suffered him to depart out of pity for me. But, seeing that he did not return, any more than Kaioun, and fearing that he had been recognised and delivered over to Barkiarokh, she lost all hope, and had not the courage to suggest any remedy to our desperate circumstances. Indeed we had nothing left for our support save the water of the cistern, and she herself was far too weak to go outside our retreat, even had I dared to let her do so. I already felt the pangs of hunger most poignantly, and though I took great pains to hide this from Gazahidé, she perceived my agonies all too soon, and they added terribly to her own distress. She was dying like a lamp in which the oil is exhausted. I saw it. I mourned by her side in silence. She lost consciousness, to my inexpressible anguish, and then, coming to herself again, took me in her arms, and said: 'Daughter, most beloved, and most unfortunate, I recommend thy innocence to the protection of Allah. May he keep thee from falling into the hands of Barkiarokh, nay, take thy life with mine, if such be his will. Never curse thy father; but flee from him as thou wouldst flee from the fiery mouth of a dragon! If thou dost survive me, if Calili does not return, depart hence; seek out some charitable person who will help thee in thy distress, and see to my burial. I refused to leave Daghestan so that my bones might rest in the same mould as the bones of my father, and I should not like the vultures to carry them to some other land. O Allah! O Prophet! forgive me for having been the cause of the death of so good a father, and take pity upon my daughter.'

"She never spoke again, and I lay upon her breast almost as lifeless as she. I know not how long I so remained. I only came to myself when I felt, trickling down my throat, some liquor, which Calili was pouring out with a trembling hand. I opened my eyes. Oh, horror! It was blood, his own blood, he was making me swallow!

"'Unhappy Leilah,' said he, 'this beverage, odious as it is, will sustain you somewhat. I have been pursued by a tiger. I was quick enough to prevent him from seizing me altogether, but once, once he managed, to catch hold of me, and tore my side with his claws. My blood has nearly all run out through this great wound. I am about to follow my dear mistress. I go to Allah's judgement seat, there to ask for justice on Barkiarokh, and help for yourself.'

"Having said these words, the good, the generous Calili, laid himself down at my mother's feet, and expired.

"I had slightly recovered my strength, but would only, in my despair, have used it to put an end to my own life, if it had not been for the fear lest vultures should eat the body of Gazahidé, and her last wishes thus remain unfulfilled. The same fear prevented me from leaving the spot. I contented myself, therefore, with uttering loud complaints outside the house, so that any chance passers-by might hear them. Full oft, however, did I go in again to shed hot tears over my mother's body. And I did the same over that of Calili! Alas! it was to his blood that I owed my small remnant of life. At last you came to save me. You helped me to bury my dear mother and her faithful dwarf. What a debt of gratitude is mine! But gratitude is not the only feeling I entertain for you. You inspire in me an affection akin to that I felt for Gazahidé. I should be happy with you anywhere, provided you were safe from the pursuit of Barkiarokh, who, as you tell me, is ever on the watch to take your life. Let us make haste, therefore, to go to the friend of whom you have spoken, and who, as you hope, will be able to show us the way to some place of retreat where the name of that cruel prince is detested. No fatigues daunt me, I am far more afraid for you than for myself. And be assured that I shall be guilty of no indiscretion. I was not myself when, in the forest, I uttered those complaints which might have caused me to fall into the hands of Barkiarokh. Fortunately they were poured into the ears of his enemy – his enemy who is for ever to be the friend of unhappy Leilah!"

End of Leilah's Story

A narrative so touching should have cut me to the heart; a confidence so misplaced should have brought a blush to my cheeks. But borne away as I was by an unbridled passion, nothing gave me pause. I had been much more attentive to the simplicity and grace with which Leilah expressed herself, than to the harrowing scenes she had placed before my eyes. In her innocence she misunderstood the cause of my agitation. She thanked me for the interest I had shown in her mother's misfortunes, and in her own, and returned to her apartment calling down blessings upon my head. But it was not Barkiarokh that she meant to bless, nor did any blessing come to him. On the contrary, the moment was imminent which would see him for ever accursed.

At last we started for the Miry Desert – my daughter and I in a palanquin,[1] the two women slaves on a camel, and twelve eunuchs on horseback as an escort. Our journey lasted only three weeks; but these seemed as long as three centuries, because of the war I had to wage continually between by criminal desires, and my fear of the fatal wand. I left Leilah, with the two women and the twelve eunuchs, in a caravanserai at a little distance from the Miry Desert – which I was in a hurry to reach. The slough, the swine, nothing stopped me. I came in a few moments to the Afrite, whom I found, as I had been told, seated at the entrance of his cave. He inclined his head, with civility, and asked me what I wanted. So I told him my story, without the least disguise, and finally besought him to show me the way to some place whither the Peri would be unable to follow me.

The Afrite, instead of replying, clapped his hands, with great glee, and cried, in a voice that made the very rocks tremble:

---

1 palanquin: a couch or litter borne by four or six men on their shoulders.

"Now Eblis be praised! Here is a man who is more vile and wicked than I!"

The compliment was scarcely flattering. Nevertheless, I smiled, and asked the Afrite to explain himself.

"Be it known to you," said he, "that your redoubtable father-in-law, Asfendarmod, who is as full of storms as the winter month to which he has given his name, condemned me, about forty years ago, to remain here, with my legs buried and fixed in the ground, saying, 'He alone whose crimes surpass thine own shall have power to deliver thee.' I have waited long; I have been prodigal of evil and pernicious advice to all who came to consult me; but in vain, I was speaking to little men, to men altogether devoid of resolution. The glory of being my liberator was reserved to thee, O unconquerable Barkiarokh! and thou shalt have thy reward; I will convey thee, and thy daughter, to the Palace of Subterranean Fire, where are gathered together all the riches of Soliman and the Preadamite Kings – and into that place Homaïouna can never enter. Rely upon my word, and lean both thy hands upon my knees."

No less pleased than the Afrite himself, I made haste to do as he wished, and immediately his long legs became disengaged from the earth. He rose, and walked thrice round the rock, crying with all his might: "let all here return to its accustomed order!" At these words a palace, adorned with a hundred shining cupolas, took the place of the rock; the quagmire became a clear and rapid stream; and the surrounding desert, a garden stretching to the horizon. The children emerged from the swine, and resumed their native beauty and grace. They all flocked around me, and, after caressing me in a thousand ways, led me to the bath. There I was rubbed and perfumed by powerful eunuchs, who afterwards clothed me in rich garments, and led me back to the Afrite.

He was waiting for me in a pavilion, where, under a dais ornamented with priceless pearls, a splendid banquet awaited us. "I am no longer reduced to clear, thin wine, and fruit, for my sole sustenance," said he; "I am going to feed thee right well. But," continued he, "thou dost not seem happy. Ha! Ha! I had forgotten. Nothing pleases unless thy daughter is near. Go and fetch her. Indeed it is necessary that she should grow accustomed to the sight of me, otherwise she might not consent to travel in my arms to the subterranean palace – and that palace none enters save voluntarily. She will play with my children while we are at table; and, when night comes, we will start for Istakhar."

I made short work of returning to the caravanserai through alleys now strewn with flowers, and soon came back again with Leilah, who opened large and astonished eyes at the sight of all that surrounded her.

"Where are we?" said she at last. "Is this the dwelling your friend has chosen for us?"

"No, no," I replied. "It is not here; here we should have no peace, for the place is known to Barkiarokh. This is the dwelling of the giant who loves me, and will bear us this very night to a place of even greater wealth and beauty."

"Is your friend then a giant?" she asked.

"Yes," I replied. "Does that alarm you?"

"I fear nothing, except Barkiarokh, when I am with you," said she, with an innocent affection that somewhat disconcerted me. Happily we were interrupted at this point by the attractive little girls and the pretty pages, who came to meet us, skipping and gambolling. Leilah was so pleased with these graceful creatures that, following the dictates of her age, she began to play with them and caress them, and run after them in the gardens, and manifested neither surprise nor terror when the Afrite appeared.

"She is very pretty," said that wicked Giaour to me. "Ere dawn to-morrow thou shalt be beyond the reach of the wand that would disturb thy pleasures."

He kept his word only too well. We left Leilah, with the children, in charge of the eunuchs, and remained alone, feasting on exquisite viands, and excellent wines. Our talk was free and gay. We laughed at all restraints, holding that they had not been invented for people of our condition. The Afrite related to me his atrocious adventures; but, notwithstanding the charm of listening to the details of a thousand crimes, each one blacker and more abominable than its predecessor, I felt eaten up with impatience: I yearned for the society of Leilah. I therefore thanked my redoubtable host, and reminded him that the hour of our departure was approaching.

Immediately he called Leilah. "Come hither, entrancing little one," said he, "will you let me take you to the subterranean palace of Istakhar?"

"I am willing to go anywhere with my generous protector," she replied.

"That is clear enough," he rejoined. "Come, get up, both of you, on my shoulders. Hold tight, and the journey, far as is the distance, will soon be accomplished."

We obeyed. Leilah trembled somewhat; but I upheld and reassured her, putting one of my arms round her slender waist.

The night was so dark that we could distinguish nothing in the vast spaces through which we flew. I was all the more struck by the vivid light emanating from the subterranean vault on whose brink the Afrite deposited us, crying: "Oh, oh! the vault has opened of itself! Doubtless they expected you down below, and knew whom they are about to receive."

Scarcely did I give heed to this exclamation, which ought to have made me hesitate, for I was too occupied in examining the magnificent flight of stairs that swept downwards before my eyes. It was very easy of descent, but there was a long space between the plane on which we stood and the first of the steps. To help Leilah, I sprang down to the first step, and held out my arms, into which she was about to spring, when the wicked Afrite called out, laughing: "Good-bye, Barkiarokh. I shall come shortly to inquire how you fare in your new abode, with your too credulous daughter!"

At these malicious words, Leilah uttered a great cry, and threw herself backwards so suddenly that it was impossible for me to catch hold of her. I tried to leap up again, but an invisible hand held me down, paralysed and motionless. At the same moment I heard myself called by a voice from the upper air, a voice I knew only too well. I raised my head and saw

Homaïouna, glorious, transfigured, and seated on a luminous cloud.

"Wretched Barkiarokh," she said; "thou hast nothing more to fear from the Wand of Remorse. Instead of profiting by its strokes, thou hast sought to evade them. Henceforward the rod that will beat upon thy heart is the rod of Despair, and thy heart, hardened as it is, will be broken and crushed throughout every moment of a frightful eternity. I have done all that was possible to save thee from the abyss into which thou hast now fallen. Thy crimes have merited their punishment only too fully; but Heaven would not suffer thy innocent child to follow thee in thy fall. Even if the Afrite had not treated thee as the wicked always treat one another, the same Power that now holds thee back, paralysed, would have prevented Leilah from following thy downward path. I bear away with me that dear child, so worthy of a different father. I shall place her on the throne of Daghestan, where, with the aid and counsels of the pious Kaioun, she will cause the horrors of thy reign to be forgotten. Then I shall myself return to my own happy land. I am recalled thither by my father, who considers that by the ills suffered at thy hand I have fulfilled the measure of my own punishment. He allows me henceforward to dwell with my sister Ganigul. I am about, in that loved companionship, to forget the interest I took in the human race, and to leave all to the care of Allah, who suffers indeed the ephemeral prosperity of the wicked, but chastises those whom He regards as worthy of his ultimate forgiveness."

Having spoken these words, The Peri came down to the earth, gathered up Leilah in her arms, and disappeared.

I uttered a fearful yell when I saw my prey thus snatched away from me; and words of horrible blasphemy were still upon my lips when I was hurled down into the crowd of the damned – with whom I am destined, like yourselves, O my wretched companions, to be whirled about for ever, bearing in my heart the fearful furnace of flame which I have myself prepared and ignited.

THE HISTORY OF THE PRINCESS
ZULKAÏS AND THE PRINCE KALILAH

translated by Sir Frank T. Marzials

My father, lord, can scarcely be unknown to you, insomuch as
the Caliph Motassem had entrusted to his care the fertile
province of Masre.[1] Nor would he have been unworthy of his
exalted position if, in view of man's ignorance and weakness, an
inordinate desire to control the future were not to be accounted an unpardonable error.

The Emir Abou Taher Achmed,[2] however – for such was
my father's name – was very far from recognising this truth.
Only too often did he seek to forestall Providence, and to direct
the course of events in despite of the decrees of Heaven. Ah!
terrible indeed are those decrees! Sooner or later their accomplishment is sure! Vainly do we seek to oppose them!

During a long course of years, everything flourished under
my father's rule, and among the Emirs who have successfully
administered that beautiful province, Abou Taher Achmed will
not be forgotten. Following his speculative bent, he enlisted the
services of certain experienced Nubians, born near the sources
of the Nile, who had studied the stream throughout its course,
and knew all its characteristics, and the properties of its waters;
and, with their aid, he carried out his impious design of regulating the overflow of the river. Thus he covered the country
with a too luxuriant vegetation which left it afterwards
exhausted. The people, always slaves to outward appearances,
applauded his enterprises, worked indefatigably at the unnumbered canals with which he intersected the land, and, blinded
by his successes, passed lightly over any unfortunate circumstances accompanying them. If, out of every ten ships that he
sent forth to traffic, according to his fancy, a single ship came

---

1 Masre, *Misr.* The Arab name for Egypt and Cairo in early Islamic times. [*Islam2* VII,
   146]
2 Abou Taher Achmed, *'Abd Allah b. Tahir.* Following the civil war occasioned by
   Harun al-Raschid's death, he returned Misr to Abbasid rule in 826. [*Islam2* VII,
   160]

back richly freighted, after a successful voyage, the wreck of the other nine was counted for nothing. Moreover, as, owing to his care and vigilance, commerce prospered under his rule, he was himself deceived as to his losses, and took to himself all the glory of his gains.

Soon Abou Taher Achmed came to be convinced that if he could recover the arts and sciences of the ancient Egyptians, his power would be unbounded. He believed that, in the remote ages of antiquity, men had appropriated to their own use some rays of the divine wisdom, and thus been enabled to work marvels, and he did not despair of bringing back once again that glorious time. For this purpose he caused search to be made, among the ruins abounding in the country, for the mysterious tablets which, according to the report of the sages who swarmed in his court, would show how the arts and sciences in question were to be acquired, and also indicate the means of discovering hidden treasures, and subduing the Intelligences by which those treasures are guarded. Never before his time had any Mussulman puzzled his brains over hieroglyphics. Now, however, search was made, on his behalf, for hieroglyphics of every kind, in all quarters, in the remotest provinces, the strange symbols being faithfully copied on linen cloths. I have seen these cloths a thousand times, stretched out on the roofs of our palace. Nor could bees be more busy and assiduous about a bed of flowers than were the sages about these painted sheets. But, as each sage entertained a different opinion as to the meaning of what was there depicted, arguments were frequent, and quarrels ensued. Not only did the sages spend the hours of daylight in prosecuting their researches, but the moon often shed its beams upon them while so occupied. They did not dare to light torches upon the terraced roofs, for fear of alarming the faithful Mussulmans, who were beginning to blame my father's veneration for an idolatrous antiquity, and regarded all these painted symbols, these figures, with a pious horror.

Meanwhile, the Emir, who would never have thought of neglecting any real matter of business, however unimportant, for the pursuit of his strange studies, was by no means so particular with regard to his religious observances, and often forgot to perform the ablutions ordained by the law. The women of his harem did not fail to perceive this, but were afraid to speak, as, for one reason and another, their influence had considerably waned. But, on a certain day, Shaban, the chief of the Eunuchs, who was old and very pious, presented himself before his master, holding a ewer and a golden basin, and said: "The waters of the Nile have been given for the cleansing of all our impurities; their source is in the clouds of heaven, not in the temple of idols; take and use those waters, for you stand in need of them!"

The Emir, duly impressed by the action and speech of Shaban, yielded to his just remonstrances, and, instead of unpacking a large bale of painted cloths, which had just arrived from a far distance, ordered the eunuch to serve the day's collation in the Hall of the Golden Trellises, and to assemble there all his slaves, and all his birds – of which he kept a very large number in aviaries of sandalwood.

Immediately the palace rang to the sound of instruments of music, and groups of slaves appeared, all dressed in their most attractive garments, and each leading in leash a peacock whiter than snow. One only of these slaves – whose slender and graceful form was a delight to the eye – had no bird in leash, and kept her veil down.

"Why this eclipse?" said the Emir to Shaban.

"Lord," answered he, with joyful mein, "I am better than all your astrologers, for it is I who have discovered this lovely star. But do not imagine that she is yet within your reach; her father, the holy and venerable Iman Abzenderoud, will never consent to make you happy in the possession of her charms unless you perform your ablutions with greater regularity, and give the go-by to sages and their hieroglyphics."

My father, without replying to Shaban, ran to snatch away the veil that hid the countenance of Ghulendi Begum[1] – for such was the name of Abzenderoud's daughter – and he did so with such violence that he nearly crushed two peacocks, and overturned several baskets of flower. To this sudden heat succeeded a kind of ecstatic stupor. At last he cried: "How beauti-

---

1 Begum: Indo-Persian honorific applied to ladies of high birth. [*Islam2* I 1161]

ful she is, how divine! Go, fetch at once the Iman of Soussouf – let the nuptial chamber be got ready, and all necessary preparations for our marriage be complete within one hour!"

"But, lord," replied Shaban, in consternation, "you have forgotten that Ghulendi Begum cannot marry you without the consent of her father, who makes it a condition that you should abandon..."

"What nonsense are you talking?" he interrupted the vizier. "Do you think I am fool enough not to prefer this young virgin, fresh as the dew of the morning, to cartloads of hieroglyphics, mouldy and of the colour of dead ashes? As to Abzenderoud, go and fetch him if you like – but quickly, for I shall certainly not wait a moment longer than I please."

"Hasten, Shaban," said Ghulendi Begum modestly, "hasten; you see that here I am unable to make any very effectual resistance."

"It's my fault," mumbled the eunuch, as he departed, "but I shall do what I can to rectify my error."

Accordingly he flew to find Abzenderoud. But that faithful servant of Allah had gone from home very early in the morning, and sought the open fields in order to pursue his pious investigations into the growth of plants and the life of insects. A death-like pallor overspread his countenance when he saw Shaban swooping upon him like a raven of evil omen, and heard him tell, in broken accents, how the Emir had promised nothing, and how he himself might well arrive too late to exact the pious conditions he had so deeply pondered. Nevertheless, the Iman did not lose courage, and reached my father's palace in a very few moments; but unfortunately he was by this time so out of breath that he sank on to a sofa, and remained for over an hour panting and speechless.

While all the eunuchs were doing their best to revive the holy man, Shaban had quickly gone up to the apartment assigned to Abou Taher Achmed's pleasures; but his zeal suffered some diminution when he saw the door guarded by two black eunuchs, who, brandishing their sabres, informed him that if he ventured to take one more step forward, his head would roll at his own feet. Therefore he had nothing better to do than to return to Abzenderoud, whose gaspings he regarded with wild and troubled eyes, lamenting the while over his own imprudence in bringing Ghulendi Begum within the Emir's power.

Notwithstanding the care my father was taking for the entertainment of the new sultana, he had heard something of the dispute between the black eunuchs and Shaban, and had a fair notion of what was going on. As soon, therefore, as he judged it convenient, he came to find Abzenderoud in the Hall of the Golden Trellises, and presenting Ghulendi Begum to the holy man assured him that, while awaiting his arrival, he, the Emir, had made her his wife.

At these words, the Iman uttered a lamentable and piercing cry, which relieved the pressure on his chest; and, rolling his eyes in a fearful manner, he said to the new sultana: "Wretched woman, dost thou not know that rash and ill-considered acts lead ever to a miserable end? Thy father would have made thy lot secure; but thou hast not awaited the result of his efforts, or rather it is Heaven itself that mocks all human previsions. I ask nothing more of the Emir; let him deal with thee, and with his hieroglyphics, as he deems best! I foresee untold evils in the future; but I shall not be there to witness them. Rejoice for a while, intoxicated with thy pleasures. As for me, I call to my aid the Angel of Death, and hope, within three days, to rest in peace in the bosom of our great Prophet!"

After saying these words, he rose to his feet, tottering. His daughter strove in vain to hold him back. He tore his robe from her trembling hands. She fell fainting to the ground, and while the distracted Emir was striving to bring her back to her senses, the obstinate Abzenderoud went muttering from the room.

At first it was thought that the holy man would not keep his vow quite literally, and would suffer himself to be comforted; but such was not the case. On reaching his own house, he began by stopping his ears with cotton wool, so as not to hear the clamour and adjurations of his friends; and then, having seated himself on the mats in his cell, with his legs crossed, and his head in his hands, he remained in that posture speechless, and taking no food; and finally, at the end of three days, expired according to his prayer. He was buried magnificently, and during the obsequies[1] Shaban did not fail to manifest his grief by slashing his own flesh without mercy, and soaking the earth with little rivulets of his blood; after which, having caused balm to be applied to his wounds, he returned to the duties of his office.

Meanwhile, the Emir had no small difficulty in assuaging the despair of Ghulendi Begum, and often cursed the hieroglyphics which had been its first efficient cause. At last his attentions touched the heart of the sultana. She regained her ordinary equability of spirits, and became pregnant; and everything returned to its accustomed order.

The Emir, his mind always dwelling in the magnificence of the ancient Pharaohs, built, after their manner, a palace with twelve pavilions – proposing, at an early date, to install in each pavilion a son. Unfortunately, his wives brought forth nothing but daughters. At each new birth he grumbled, gnashed his teeth, accused Mahomet of being the cause of his mishaps, and would have been altogether unbearable, if Ghulendi Begum had not found means to moderate his ill temper. She induced him to come every night into her apartment, where, by a thousand ingenious devices, she succeeded in introducing fresh air, while, in other parts of the palace, the atmosphere was stifling.

During her pregnancy my father never left the dais on which she reclined. This dais was set in a large and long gallery overlooking the Nile, and so disposed as to seem about on a level with the stream, – so close, too, that anyone reclining upon it could throw into the water the grains of the pomegranate he might be eating. The best dancers, the most excellent musicians, were always about the place. Every night pantomimes were performed to the light of a thousand golden lamps – lamps placed upon the floor so as to bring out the fineness and grace of the performers' feet. The dancers themselves cost my father immense sums in golden fringed slippers

---

1 obsequies: funeral ceremonies.

and sandals a-glitter with jewellery; and, indeed, when they were all in motion together the effect was dazzling.

But notwithstanding this accumulation of splendours, the sultana passed very unhappy days on her dais. With the same indifference that a poor wretch tormented by sleeplessness watches the scintillation of the stars, so did she see pass before her eyes all this whirl of performers in their brilliancy and charm. Anon, she would think of the wrath, that seemed almost prophetic, of her venerable father; anon she would deplore his strange and untimely end. A thousand times she would interrupt the choir of singers, crying: "Fate has decreed my ruin! Heaven will not vouchsafe me a son, and my husband will banish me from his sight." The torment of her mind intensified the pain and discomfort attendant on her condition. My father, thereupon, was so greatly perturbed that, for the first time in his life, he made appeal to Heaven, and ordered prayers to be offered up in every mosque. Nor did he omit the giving of alms, for he caused it to be publically announced that all beggars were to assemble in the largest court of the palace, and would be there served with rice, each according to his individual appetite. There followed such a crush every morning at the palace gates that the incomers were nearly suffocated. Mendicants[1] swarmed in from all parts, by land and by the river. Whole villages would come down the stream on rafts. And the appetites of all were enormous; for the buildings which my father erected, his costly pursuit of hieroglyphics, and the maintenance of his sages, had caused some scarcity throughout the land.

Among those who came from a very far distance was a man of extreme age, and great singularity, by name Abou Gabdolle Guehaman, the hermit of the Great Sandy Desert. He was eight feet high, so ill-proportioned, and of a leanness so extreme, that he looked like a skeleton, and hideous to behold. Nevertheless, this lugubrious and forbidden piece of human mechanism enshrined the most benevolent and religious spirit in the universe. With a voice of thunder he proclaimed the will

---

1 mendicants: beggars from religious orders.

of the Prophet, and said openly it was a pity that a prince who distributed rice to the poor, and in such great profusion, should be a determined lover of hieroglyphics. People crowded around him – the Imans, the Mullahs,[1] the Muezins[2] did nothing but sing his praises. His feet, though ingrained with the sand of his native desert, were freely kissed. Nay, the very grains of the sand from his feet were gathered up, and treasured in caskets of amber.

One day he proclaimed the truth and the horror of the sciences of evil, in a voice so loud and resonant that the great standards set before the palace trembled. The terrible sound penetrated into the interior of the harem. The women and the eunuchs fainted away in the Hall of the Golden Trellises; the dancers stood with one foot arrested in the air; the mummers had not the courage to pursue their antics; the musicians suffered their instruments to fall to the ground; and Ghulendi Begum thought to die of fright as she lay on her dais.

Abou Taher Achmed stood astounded. His conscience smote him for his idolatrous proclivities, and during a few remorseful moments he thought that the Avenging Angel[3] had come to turn him into stone – and not himself only but the people committed to his charge.

After standing for some time, upright, with arms uplifted, in the Gallery of the Daises, he called Shaban to him, and said: "The sun has not lost its brightness, the Nile flows peacefully in its bed, what means then this supernatural cry that has just resounded through my palace?"

"Lord," answered the pious eunuch, "this voice is the voice of Truth, and it is spoken to you through the mouth of the venerable Abou Gabdolle Guehaman, the Hermit of the Sandy Desert, the most faithful, the most zealous, of the servants of the Prophet, who has, in nine days, journeyed three hundred leagues to make proof of your hospitality, and to impart to you the knowledge with which he is inspired. Do not neglect the

---

1 mullah, *molla*: a general term of respect, normally applied to clergy and learned men.
2 Muezins, or criers, call the faithful to divine service.
3 Avenging Angel: Perhaps the angel of death, Asrael.

teachings of a man who in wisdom, in piety, and in stature, surpasses the most enlightened, the most devout, and the most gigantic of the inhabitants of the earth. All your people are in ecstasy. Trade is at a stand-still. The inhabitants of the city hasten to hear him, neglecting their wonted assemblies in the public gardens. The storytellers are without hearers at the margins of the public fountains. Jussouf [1] himself was not wiser than he, and had no greater knowledge of the future."

At these last words, the Emir was suddenly smitten with the desire of consulting Abou Gabdolle with regard to his family affairs, and particularly with regard to the great projects he entertained for the future. advantage of his sons, who were not yet born. He deemed himself happy in being thus able to consult a living prophet; for, so far, it was only in the form of mummies that he had been brought into relation with these inspired personages. He resolved, therefore, to summon into his presence, nay, into his very harem, the extraordinary being now in question. Would not the Pharaohs have so dealt with the necromancers [2] of their time, and was not he determined, in all circumstances, to follow the Pharaohs' examples? He therefore graciously directed Shaban to go and fetch the holy man.

Shaban, transported with joy, hastened to communicate this invitation to the hermit, who, however, did not appear to be as much charmed by the summons as were the people at large. These latter filled the air with their acclamations, while Abou Gabdolle stood still, with his hands clasped, and his eyes uplifted to heaven, in a prophetic trance. From time to time he uttered the deepest sighs, and, after remaining long rapt in holy contemplation, shouted out, in his voice of thunder: "Allah's will be done! I am but his creature. Eunuch, I am ready to follow thee. But let the doors of the palace be broken down. It is not meet for the servants of the Most High to bend their heads."

The people needed no second command. They all set hands

---

1 Jussouf, *Yusuf*: Arabic for Joseph, who foretold the future by interpreting dreams. See Genesis 40 and 41.

2 necromancer: sorcerer who conjures up spirits of the dead to predict the future.

to the work with a will, and in an instant the gateway, a piece of the most remarkable workmanship, was utterly ruined.

At the sound of the breaking in of the doors, piercing cries arose within the harem. Abou Taher Achmed began to repent of his curiosity. Nevertheless, he ordered, though somewhat reluctantly, that the passages into the harem should be laid open to the holy giant, for he feared lest the enthusiastic adherents of the prophet should penetrate into the apartments occupied by the women, and containing the princely treasures. These fears were, however, vain, for the holy man had sent back his devout admirers. I have been assured that on their all kneeling to receive his blessing he said to them, in tones of the deepest solemnity: "Retire, remain peacefully in your dwellings, and be assured that, whatever happens, Abou Gabdolle Guehaman is prepared for every emergency." Then, turning towards the palace, he cried: "O domes of dazzling brilliancy, receive me, and may nothing ensue to tarnish your splendour."

Meanwhile, everything had been made ready within the harem. Screens had been duly ordered, the door-curtains had been drawn, and ample draperies hung before the daises in the long gallery that ran round the interior of the building – thus concealing from view the sultanas, and the princesses, their daughters.

Such elaborate preparations had caused a general ferment; and curiosity was at its height, when the hermit, trampling under foot the ruined fragments of the doorways, entered majestically into the Hall of the Golden Trellises. The magnificence of the palace did not even win from him a passing glance, his eyes remained fixed, mournfully, on the pavement at his feet. At last he penetrated into the great gallery of the women. These latter, who were not at all accustomed to the sight of creatures so lean, gaunt, and gigantic, uttered piercing cries, and loudly asked for essences and cordials to enable them to bear up against the apparition of such a phantasm.[1]

The hermit paid not the smallest heed to the surrounding tumult. He was gravely pursuing his way, when the Emir came

---

1 phantasm: illusion; ghost.

forward, and, taking him by the skirt of his garment, led him, with much ceremony, to the dais of the gallery which looked out upon the Nile. Basins of comfits and orthodox liquors were at once served; but though Abou Gabdolle Guehaman seemed to be dying of hunger, he refused to partake of these refreshments, saying that for ninety years he had drunk nothing but the dew of Heaven, and eaten only the locusts of the desert. The Emir, who regarded this dietary as conformable to what might properly be expected of a prophet, did not press him further, but at once entered into the question he had at heart, saying how much it grieved him to be without an heir male, notwithstanding all the prayers offered up to that effect, and the flattering hopes which the Imans had given him. "But now," he continued, "I am assured that this happiness will at last be mine. The sages, the mediciners, predict it, and my own observations confirm their prognostications. It is not, therefore, for the purpose of consulting you with regard to the future that I have caused you to be summoned. It is for the purpose of obtaining your advice upon the education I should give to the son whose birth I am expecting – or rather to the two sons, for, without doubt, Heaven, in recognition of my alms, will accord to the Sultana Ghulendi Begum a double measure of fertility, seeing that she is twice as large as women usually are on such occasions."

Without answering a word, the hermit mournfully shook his head three times.

My father, greatly astonished, asked if his anticipated good fortune was in any wise displeasing to the holy man.

"Ah! too blind prince," replied the hermit, uttering a cavernous sigh that seemed to issue from the grave itself, "why importune Heaven with rash prayers? Respect its decrees! It knows what is best for all men better than they do themselves. Woe be to you, and woe be to your son whom you will doubtless compel to follow in the perverse ways of your own beliefs, instead of submitting himself humbly to the guidance of Providence. If the great of this world could only foresee all the misfortunes they bring upon themselves, they would tremble in the midst of their splendour. Pharaoh recognised this truth, but too late. He pursued the children of Moussa[1] in despite of the divine decrees, and died the death of the wicked. What can alms avail when the heart is in rebellion? Instead of asking the Prophet for an heir, to be led by you into the paths of destruction, those who have your welfare at heart should implore him to cause Ghulendi Begum to die – yes, to die, before she brings into the world presumptuous creatures, whom your conduct will precipitate into the abyss! Once again I call upon you to submit. If Allah's angel threatens to cut short the days of the sultana, do not make appeal to your magicians to ward off the fatal blow: let it fall, let her die! Tremble not with wrath, Emir; harden not your heart! once again call to mind the fate of Pharaoh and the waters that swallowed him up!"

"Call them to mind yourself!" cried my father, foaming with rage, and springing from the dais to run to the help of his sultana, who, having heard all, had fainted away behind the curtains. "Remember that the Nile flows beneath these windows, and that thou hast well deserved that thy odious carcass should be hurled into its waters!"

"I fear not," cried the gigantic hermit in turn; "the prophet of Allah fears naught but himself," and he rose on the tips of his toes, and touched with his hands the supports of the dome of the apartment.

"Ha! ha! thou fearest nothing," cried all the women and eunuchs, issuing forth like tigers out of their den.

"Accursed assassin, thou hast just brought our beloved mistress to death's door, and yet fearest nothing! Go. And become food for the monsters of the river!" Screaming these words they threw themselves, all at once, on Abou Gabdolle Guehaman, bore him down, strangled him without pity, and cast his body through a dark grating into the Nile, which there lost itself obscurely among the piers of iron.

The Emir, astonished by an act at once so sudden and so atrocious, remained with his eyes fixed on the waters; but the body did not again come to the surface; and Shaban, who now appeared upon the scene, bewildered him with his cries. At last

---

1 Moussa, *Musa*: Moses. The reference is to Pharaoh's pursuit of the Children of Israel in Exodus 14.

he turned to look upon the perpetrators of the crime; but they had scattered in every direction, and hidden behind the curtains of the gallery; each avoiding the other, they were overwhelmed with the thought of what they had done.

Ghulendi, who had only come to herself in time to witness this scene of horror, was now in mortal anguish. Her convulsions, her agonising cries, drew the Emir to her side. He bedewed her hand with tears. She opened her eyes wildly, and cried: "O Allah! Allah! put an end to a wretched creature who has already lived only to long, since she has been the cause of so terrible an outrage, and suffer not that she should bring into the world —" "Stop, stop," interrupted the Emir, holding her hands which she was about to turn against herself, "thou shalt not die, and my children shall yet live to give the lie to that demented skeleton, worthy only of contempt. Let my sages be summoned instantly. Let them use their art to keep thy soul from flitting hence and to save from harm the fruit of thy body."

The sages were convened accordingly. They demanded that one of the courts in the palace should be placed entirely at their disposal, and there began their operations, kindling a fire whose light penetrated into the gallery. The sultana rose from her couch, notwithstanding all the efforts made to restrain her, and ran to the balcony overlooking the Nile. The view from thence was lonely and drear. Not a single boat showed upon the surface of the stream. In the distance were discernable stretches of sand, which the wind, from time to time, sent whirling in the air. The rays of the setting sun dyed the waters blood-red. Scarcely had the deepening twilight stretched over the horizon, when a sudden and furious wind broke open the lattice-work of the gallery. The sultana, beside herself, her heart beating, tried to plunge back into the interior of the apartment, but an irresistible power held her where she was, and forced her, against her will, to contemplate the mournful scene before her eyes. A great silence now reigned. Darkness had insensibly covered the earth. Then suddenly a streak of blue light furrowed the clouds in the direction of the pyramids. The princess could distinguish their enormous mass against the horizon as clearly as if it had been noonday. The spectacle thus suddenly revealed, chilled her with fear. Several times did she try to call her slaves, but her voice refused its office. She endeavoured to clap her hands, but in vain.

While she remained thus – as if in the grip of some horrible dream – a lamentable voice broke the silence, and uttered these words: "My latest breath has just been exhaled into the waters of the river; vainly have thy servants striven to stifle the voice of truth; it rises now from the abysses of death. O wretched mother! see whence issues that fatal light, and tremble!"

Ghulendi Begum endured to hear no more. She fell back senseless. Her women, who had been anxious about her, hurried up at this moment, and uttered the most piercing cries. The sages approached, and placed into the hands of my father, who was in terrible perturbation, the powerful elixir they had prepared. Scarcely had a few drops fallen on the sultana's breast, when her soul, which had seemed about to follow the orders of Asrael, the Angel of Death, came back, as if in nature's despite, to reanimate her body. Her eyes reopened to see, still illuminating the pyramids, the fatal furrow of blue light which had not yet faded from the sky. She raised her arms, and, pointing out to the Emir with her finger that dread portent, was seized with the pains of childbirth, and, in the paroxysm of an unspeakable anguish, brought into the world a son and a daughter: the two wretched beings you see before you here.

The Emir's joy in the possession of a male child was greatly dashed when he saw my mother die before his eyes. Notwithstanding his excessive grief, however, he did not lose his head, and at once handed us over to the care of his sages. The nurses, who had been engaged in great number, wished to oppose this arrangement; but the ancient men, all muttering incantations simultaneously, compelled them to silence. The cabalistic lavers[1] in which we were to be immersed stood all ready prepared; the mixture of herbs exhaled a vapour that filled the whole palace. Shaban, whose very stomach was turned by the unspeakable odour of these infernal drugs, had all the trouble in the world to restrain himself from summoning the Imans,

---

1 cabalistic lavers: magical, occult liquids in which the babies are washed.

and doctors of the law, in order to oppose the impious rites now in contemplation. Would to Heaven he had had the courage to do so! Ah, how terrible has been the influence upon us of the pernicious immersions to which we were then subjected! In short, lord, we were plunged, both successively and together, into a hell-broth which was intended to impart to us a strength and intelligence more than human, but has only instilled into our veins the ardent elixir of a too exquisite sensibility, and the poison of an insatiable desire.

It was to the sound of brazen wands beating against the metal sides of the lavers, it was in the midst of thick fumes issuing from heaps of burning herbs, that invocations were addressed to the Jinns, and specially to those who preside over the pyramids, in order that we might be endowed with marvellous gifts. After this we were delivered over to the nurses, who scarcely could hold us in their arms, such was our liveliness and vivacity. The good women shed tears when they saw how our young blood boiled within us, and strove in vain to cool its effervescence, and to calm us by cleansing our bodies from the reeking mess with which they were still covered; but alas! the harm was already done! Nay, if even, as sometimes happened in after days, we wished to fall into the ordinary ways of childhood, my father, who was determined, at all hazards, to possess children of an extraordinary nature, would brisk us up with heating drugs and the milk of negresses.

We thus became unendurably headstrong and mettlesome. At the age of seven, we could not bear contradiction. At the slightest restraint, we uttered cries of rage, and bit those who had us in charge till the blood flowed. Shaban came in for a large share of our attentions in this kind; sighing over us, however, in silence, for the Emir only regarded our spitefulness as giving evidence of a genius equal to that of Saurid and Charobé. Ah! how little did anyone suspect the real cause of our frowardness! Those who look too long into the light are soonest afflicted with blindness. My father had not yet remarked that we were never arrogant and overbearing towards one another, that each was ready to yield to the other's wishes, that Kalilah, my brother, was never at peace save in my arms, and that, as for me, my only happiness lay in overwhelming him with caresses.

Up to this time, we had in all things been educated together: the same book was always placed before the eyes of both, each turned over the leaves alternately. Though my brother was subjected to a course of study rigorous and above his years, I insisted on sharing it with him. Abou Taher Achmed, who cared for nothing save the aggrandisement of his son, gave directions that in this I should be humoured, because he saw that his son would only fully exert himself when at my side.

We were taught not only the history of the most remote ages of antiquity, but also the geography of distant lands. The sages never ceased to indoctrinate us with the abstruse and ideal moral code, which, as they pretended, lurked hidden in the hieroglyphics. They filled our ears with a magnificent verbiage about wisdom and foreknowledge, and the treasure houses of the Pharaohs, whom sometimes they compared to ants, and sometimes to elephants. They inspired us with a most ardent curiosity as to those mountains of hewn stone beneath which the Egyptian kings lie sepulchred. They compelled us to learn by heart the long catalogue of architects and masons who had laboured at the building of them. They made us calculate the quantity of provisions that would be required by the workmen employed, and how many threads went to every ell of silk with which the Sultan Saurid had covered his pyramid. Together with all this rubbish, these most wearisome old dotards bewildered our brains with a pitiless grammar of the language spoken of old by the priests in their subterranean labyrinths.

The childish games in which we were allowed to indulge, during our playtime, had no charms for us unless we played them alone together. The princesses, our sisters, wearied us to death. Vainly did they embroider for my brother the most splendid vests; Kalilah disdained their gifts, and would only consent to bind his lovely hair with the muslin that had floated over the breast of his beloved Zulkaïs. Sometimes they invited us to visit them in the twelve pavilions which my father, no longer hoping to have that number of sons, had abandoned to their use – erecting another, and of greater magnificence, for my brother, and for myself. This latter building, crowned by five domes, and situated in a thick grove, was, every night, the scene of the most splendid revels in the harem. My father would come thither, escorted by the most beautiful slaves – each holding in her hand a candlestick with a white taper. How many times has the light of these tapers, appearing through the trees, caused our hearts to beat in sad anticipation? Everything that broke in upon our solitude was in the highest degree distasteful. To hide among the leafage, and listen to its murmur, seemed to us sweeter far than attending to the sound of the lute and the song of the musicians. But these soft luxurious reveries of ours were highly offensive to my father; he would force us back into the cupolaed saloons, and compel us to take part in the common amusements.

Every year the Emir treated us with greater sternness. He did not dare to separate us altogether for fear of the effect upon his son, but tried rather to win him from our languorous dalliance, by throwing him more and more into the company of young men of his own age. The game of reeds,[1] so famous among the Arabs, was introduced into the courts of the palace. Kalilah gave himself up to the sport with immense energy; but this was only so as to bring the games to a speedier end, and then fly back to my side. Once reunited we would read together, read of the loves of Jussouf and Zelica,[2] or some poem that spoke of love – or else, taking advantage of our moments of liberty, we would roam through the labyrinth of corridors looking out upon the Nile, always with our arms intertwined, always

---

1   the game of reeds: The game is called *djerid*, and is dangerous. It takes the form of a mock battle on horse. The participants take turns as pursuer and pursued and throw darts at one another. The game requires skill both in horsemanship and in aiming the darts. Kalilah's darts are likely palm branches stripped of their leaves; they are sharp. Beckford may have read the account in Cornelis de Bruyn. [*Islam2* II, 532]

2   Jussouf and Zelica: *Yusuf and Zulaikha,* a poem attributed to the Persian poet, Jami. An imaginative rendering of Genesis 39:7-20, it recounts the passion and temptation of the ravishing Zelica, wife of Potiphar, lingers on the exquisite agony of Joseph's desire, and concludes on Joseph's miraculous resistance.

with eyes looking into each other's eyes. It was almost impossible to track us in the mazy passages of the palace and the anxiety we inspired did but add to our happiness.

One evening when we were thus tenderly alone together, and running side by side in childish glee, my father appeared before us and shuddered. "Why," said he to Kalilah, "why are you here and not in the great courtyard, shooting with the bow, or else with the horse-trainers training the horses which are to bear you into battle? Must the sun, as it rises and sets, see you only bloom and fade like a weak narcissus flower? Vainly do the sages try to move you by the most eloquent discourses, and unveil before your eyes the learned mysteries of an older time; vainly do they tell you of warlike and magnanimous deeds. You are now nearly thirteen, and never have you evinced the smallest ambition to distinguish yourself among your fellow-men. It is not in the lurking haunts of effeminacy that great characters are formed; it is not by reading love poems that men are made fit to govern nations! Princes must act; they must show themselves to the world. Awake! Cease to abuse my patience which has too long allowed you to waste your hours by the side of Zulkaïs. Let her, tender creature that she is, continue to play among her flowers, but do you cease to haunt her company from dawn to eve. I see well enough that it is she who is perverting you."

Having spoken these words, which he emphasised by angry and threatening gestures, Abou Taher Achmed took my brother by the arm, and left me in a very abyss of bitterness. An icy numbness overcame me. Though the sun still shed its fullest rays upon the water, I felt as if it had disappeared below the horizon. Stretched at length upon the ground, I did nothing but kiss the sprays of orange flower that Kalilah had gathered. My sight fell upon the drawings he had traced, and my tears fell in greater abundance. "Alas!" said I, "all is over. Our blissful moments will return no more. Why accuse me of perverting Kalilah? What harm can I do him? How can our happiness offend my father? If it was a crime to be happy, the sages would surely have given us warning."

My nurse Shamelah found me in this condition of languor

and dejection. To dissipate my grief she immediately led me to the grove where the young girls of the harem were playing hide-and-seek amid the golden aviaries of which the place was full. I derived some little solace from the songs of the birds, and the murmur of the rillets of clear water that trickled round the roots of the trees, but when the hour came at which Kalilah was wont to appear these sounds did but add to my sufferings.

Shamelah noticed the heavings of my breast; she drew me aside, placed her hand upon my heart, and observed me attentively. I blushed, I turned pale, and that very visibly. "I see very well," said she, "that it is your brother's absence that so upsets you. This is the fruit of the strange education to which you have been subjected. The holy reading of the Koran, the due observance of the Prophet's laws, confidence in the known mercies of Allah, these are the milk to cool the fever heat of human passion. You know not the soft delight of lifting up your soul to Heaven, and submitting without a murmur to its decrees. The Emir, alas! would forestall the future; while, on the contrary, the future should be passively awaited. Dry your tears, perchance Kalilah is not unhappy though distant from your side."

"Ah!" I cried, interrupting her with a sinister look, "if I were not wholly convinced that he is unhappy, I should myself be far more miserable."

Shamelah trembled at hearing me speak thus. She cried: "Would to Heaven that they had listened to my advice, and the advice of Shaban, and instead of handing you over to the capricious teaching of the sages, had left you, like true believers, at peace in the arms of a blissful and quiet ignorance. The ardour of your feelings alarms me in the very highest degree. Nay it excites my indignation. Be more calm; abandon your soul to the innocent pleasures that surround you, and do so without troubling yourself whether Kalilah shares in those pleasures or not. His sex is made for toil and manly hardship. How should you be able to follow him in the chase, to handle a bow, and to dart reeds in the Arab game? He must look for companions manly and worthy of himself, and cease to fritter away his best days here at your side amid bowers and aviaries."

This sermon, far from producing its desired effect, made me altogether beside myself. I trembled with rage, and, rising to my feet like one bereft of reason, I rent my veil into ten thousand pieces, and, tearing my breast, cried with a loud voice, that my nurse had mishandled me.

The games ceased. Everyone crowded about me; and though the princesses did not love me overmuch, because I was Kalilah's favourite sister, yet my tears, and the blood that flowed from my self-inflicted wounds, excited their indignation against Shamelah. Unfortunately for the poor woman, she had just awarded a severe punishment to two young slaves who had been guilty of stealing pomegranates; and these two little vipers, in order to be revenged, bore testimony against her, and confirmed all I said. They ran, and retailed their lies to my father, who, not having Shaban at his side, and being, moreover, in a good temper because my brother had just thrown a javelin into a crocodile's eye, ordered Shamelah to be tied to a tree and whipped without mercy.

Her cries pierced my heart. She cried without ceasing: "O you, whom I have carried in my arms, whom I have fed from my breast, how can you cause me to suffer thus? Justify me! Declare the truth! It is only because I tried to save you from the black abyss, into which your wild and unruly desires cannot fail to precipitate you in the end, that you are thus causing this body of mine to be torn to shreds."

I was about to ask that she should be released and spared further punishment, when some demon put into my mind the thought that it was she, who conjointly with Shaban, had inspired my father with the desire of making a hero of Kalilah. Whereupon, I armed myself against every feeling of humanity, and cried that they should go on whipping her till she confessed her crime. Darkness at last put an end to this horrible scene. The victim was unloosed. Her friends, and she had many, endeavoured to close her wounds. They asked me, on their knees, to give them a sovereign balm which I possessed, a balm which the sages had prepared. I refused. Shamelah was placed before my eyes on a litter, and, of set purpose, kept for a moment in front of the place where I stood. That breast, on which I had so often slept, streamed with blood. At this spectacle, at the memory of the tender care she had taken of my infancy, my heart at last was moved — I burst into tears; I kissed the hand she feebly extended to the monster she had nourished in her bosom; I ran to fetch the balm; I applied it myself, begging her, at the same time, to forgive me, and declaring openly that she was innocent, and I alone guilty.

This confession caused a shudder to pass among all who surrounded us. They recoiled from me with horror. Shamelah, though half dead, perceived this, and stifled her groans with the skirt of her garment so as not to add to my despair and the baleful consequences of what I had done. But her efforts were in vain. All fled, casting upon me looks that were evil indeed.

The litter was removed, and I found myself alone. The night was very dark. Plaintive sounds seemed to issue from the cypresses that cast their shadow over the place. Seized with terror, I lost myself amid the black foliage, a prey to its most harrowing remorse. Delirium laid its hand on me. The earth seemed to yawn before my feet, and I to fall headlong into an abyss which had no bottom. My spirit was in this distraught condition when, through the thick underwood, I saw shine the torches of my father's attendants. I noticed that the cortège stopped suddenly. Someone issued from the crowd. A lively presentiment made my heart beat. The footsteps came nearer; and, by the light of a faint and doleful glimmer, such as prevails in the place where we now are, I saw Kalilah appear before me.

"Dear Zulkaïs," cried he, intermingling words and kisses, "I have passed an age without seeing you, but I have spent it in carrying out my father's wishes. I have fought with one of the most formidable monsters of the river. But what would I not do when, for recompense, I am afforded the bliss of spending a whole evening with you alone? Come! Let us enjoy the time to the full. Let us bury ourselves among these trees. Let us, from our retreat, listen, disdainful, to the tumultuous sound of music and dances. I will cause sherbet and cakes to be served on the moss that borders the little porphyry fountain. There I shall enjoy your sweet looks, and charming converse, till the first dawn of the new day. Then, alas! I must plunge once more into

the world's vortex, dart accursed reeds, and undergo the inter-
rogatories of sages."

Kalilah said all this with such volubility that I was unable to
put in a word. He drew me after him, scarce resisting. We made
our way through the leafage to the fountain. The memory of
what Shamelah had said concerning my excessive tenderness
for my brother, had, in my own despite, produced a strong
impression upon me. I was about to withdraw my hand from
his, when, by the light of the little lamps that had been lit on
the margin of the fountain, I saw his charming face reflected in
the waters, I saw his large eyes dewy with love, I felt his looks
pierce to the very bottom of my heart. All my projects of
reform, all my agony of remorse, made way for a ferment of
very different feelings. I dropped on to the ground by Kalilah's
side, and, leaning his head on my breast, gave a free course to
me tears. Kalilah, when he saw me thus crying passionately,
eagerly asked me why I wept. I told him all that had passed
between myself and Shamelah, without omitting a single particular. His heart was at first much moved by the picture I drew
of her sufferings; but, a moment after, he cried: "Let the
officious slave perish! Must the heart's soft yearnings ever meet
with opposition! How should we not love one another, Zulkaïs? Nature caused us to be born together. Has not nature, too,
implanted in us the same tastes, and a kindred ardour? Have not
my father and his sages made us partakers in the same magic
baths? Who could blame a sympathy all has conspired to cre-
ate? No, Zulkaïs, Shaban and our superstitious nurse may say
what they please. There is no crime in our loving one another.
The crime would rather be if we allowed ourselves, like cowards, to be separated. Let us swear – not by the Prophet, of
whom we have but little knowledge, but by the elements that
sustain man's existence – let us swear that, rather than consent
to live the one without the other, we will take into our veins
the soft distillation of the flowers of the stream which the sages
have so often vaunted in our hearing. That essence will lull us
painlessly to sleep in each other's arms, and so bear our souls
imperceptibly into that peace of another existence!"

These words quieted me. I resumed my ordinary gaiety, and

we sported and played together. "I shall be very valiant to-morrow," Kalilah would say, "so as to purchase such moments as these, for it is only by the promise of such a prize that my father can induce me to submit to his fantastic injunctions."

"Ha, ha!" cried Abou Taher Achmed, issuing from behind some bushes, where he had been listening, "is that your resolve! We will see if you keep to it! You are already fully paid this evening for the little you have done during the day. Hence! And as to you, Zulkaïs, go and weep over the terrible outrage you have committed against Shamelah."

In the greatest consternation we threw ourselves at his feet; but, turning his back upon us, he ordered the eunuchs to conduct us to our separate apartments.

It was no scruple with regard to the kind and quality of our love that exercised the Emir. His sole end was to see his son become a great warrior, and a potent prince, and with regard to the character of the means by which that end was to be obtained, he cared not one tittle. As for me, he regarded me only as an instrument that might have its use; nor would he have felt any scruples concerning the danger of inflaming our passion by the alternation of obstacles and concessions. On the other hand, he foresaw that indolence and pleasure, too constantly indulged in, must necessarily interfere with his designs. He deemed it necessary, therefore, to adopt with us a harsher and more decided line of conduct than he had hitherto done; and in an unhappy moment he carried that resolution into effect. Alas! without his precautions, his projects, his accursed foresight, we should have remained in innocence, and never been brought to the horror of this place of torment!

The Emir, having retired to his apartments, caused Shaban to be summoned, and imparted to him his fixed resolve to separate us during a certain time. The prudent eunuch prostrated himself immediately, with his face to the ground, and then, rising to his feet, said: "Let my lord forgive his slave if he ventures to be of a different opinion. Do not let loose upon this nascent flame the winds of opposition and absence, lest the final conflagration should be such as you are unable to master. You know the prince's impetuous disposition; his sister has to-day given proofs, only too signal, of hers. Suffer them to remain together without contradiction; leave them to their childish propensities. They will soon grow tired of one another; and Kalilah, disgusted with the monotony of the harem, will beg you on his knees to remove him from its precincts."

"Have you done talking your nonsense?" interrupted the Emir impatiently. "Ah, how little do you know the genius of Kalilah! I have carefully studied him, I have seen that the operations of the sages have not been void of their effect. He is incapable of pursuing any object with indifference. If I leave him with Zulkaïs, he will be utterly drowned in effeminacy. If I remove her from him, and make their reunion the price of the great things I require at his hands, there is nothing of which he will not prove himself capable. Let the doctors of our law dote as they please! What can their idle drivel matter so long as he becomes what I desire him to be? Know besides, O eunuch, that when he has once tasted the delights of ambition, the idea of Zulkaïs will evaporate in his mind as a light morning mist absorbed into the rays of the noonday sun – the sun of glory. Therefore enter to-morrow morning into the chamber of Zulkaïs, forestall her awakening, wrap her up in these robes, and convey her, with her slaves, and all that is necessary to make her life pleasant, to the borders of the Nile, where a boat will be ready to receive you. Follow the course of the stream for twenty-nine days. On the thirtieth you will disembark at the Isle of Ostriches. Lodge the princess in the palace which I have had built for the use of the sages who roam those deserts – deserts replete with ruins and with wisdom. One of these sages you will find there, called the Palm-tree-climber, because he pursues his course of contemplation upon the tops of palm-trees. This ancient man knows an infinite number of stories, and it will be his care to divert Zulkaïs, for I know very well that, next to Kalilah, stories are the chief object of her delight."

Shaban knew his master too well to venture any further opposition. He went, therefore, to give the necessary orders, but sighed heavily as he went. He had not the slightest desire to undertake a journey to the Isle of Ostriches, and had formed a very unfavourable opinion of the Palm-tree-climber. He was himself a faithful Mussulman, and held the sages and all their works in abomination.

Everything was made ready all too soon. The agitation of the previous day had greatly fatigued me, so that I slept very heavily. I was taken from my bed so quietly, and carried with such skill, that I never woke till I was at a distance of four leagues from Cairo. Then the noise of the water gurgling round the boat began to alarm me. It filled my ears strangely, and I half fancied I had drunk of the beverage spoken of by Kalilah, and been borne beyond the confines of our planet. I lay thus, bewildered with strange imaginings, and did not dare to open my eyes, but stretched out my arms to feel for Kalilah. I thought he was by my side. Judge of the feelings of hateful surprise to which I was doomed, when, instead of touching his delicate limbs, I seized hold of the horny hand of the eunuch who was steering the boat, and was even older, and more grotesquely ugly, than Shaban himself. I sat up and uttered piercing cries. I opened my eyes, and saw before me a waste stretch of sky, and of water bounded by bluish banks. The sun was shining in its fullness. The azure heavens caused all nature to rejoice. A thousand river birds played around amid the water-lilies, which the boat shore through at every moment, their large yellow flowers shining like gold, and exhaling a sweet perfume. But all these objects of delight were lost upon me, and, instead of rejoicing my heart, filled me with a sombre melancholy.

Looking about me, I saw my slaves in a state of desolation, and Shaban who, with an air at once of discontent and authority, was making them keep silence. The name Kalilah came at every moment to the tip of my tongue. At last I spoke it aloud, with tears in my eyes, and asked where he was, and what they intended to do with me. Shaban, instead of replying, ordered his eunuchs to redouble their exertions, and to strike up an Egyptian song, and sing in time to the cadence of their oars. Their accursed chorus rang out so potently that it brought an even worse bewilderment in my brain. We shot through the water like an arrow. It was in vain that I begged the rowers to stop, or at least to tell me where I was going. The barbarous wretches were deaf to my entreaties. The more insistent I was, the louder did they roar out their detestable song so as to drown my cries. Shaban, with his cracked voice, made more noise than the rest.

Nothing can express the torments I endured, and the horror I felt at finding myself so far from Kalilah, and on the waters of the fearful Nile. My terrors increased with nightfall. I saw, with an inexpressible anguish, the sun go losing itself in the waters – its light, in a thousand rays, trembling upon their surface. I brought to mind the quiet moments which, at that same hour, I had passed with Kalilah, and, hiding my head in my veil, I gave myself up to my despair.

Soon a soft rustling became audible. Our boat was shearing its way through banks of reeds. A great silence succeeded to the song of the rowers, for Shaban had landed. He came back in a few moments, and carried me to a tent, erected a few paces from the river's bank. I found there lights, mattresses stretched on the ground, a table covered with various kinds of food, and an immense copy of the Koran, unfolded. I hated the holy book. The sages, our instructors, had often turned it up to ridicule, and I had never read it with Kalilah. So I threw it contemptuously to the ground. Shaban took upon himself to scold me; but I flew at him, and endeavoured to reduce him to silence. In this I proved successful, and the same treatment retained its efficacy during the whole course of the long expedition. Our subsequent experiences were similar to those of the first day. Endlessly did we pass banks of water-lilies, and flocks of birds, and an infinite number of small boats that came and went with merchandise.

At last we began to leave behind us the plain country. Like all who are unhappy and thus led to look forward, I kept my eyes continually fixed on the horizon ahead of us, and one evening I saw, rising there, great masses of much greater height, and of a form infinitely more varied, than the pyramids. These masses proved to be mountains. Their aspect inspired me with fear. The terrible thought occurred to me that my father was sending me to the woeful land of the Negro king, so that I might be offered up as a sacrifice to the idols, who, as the sages pretended, were greedy of princesses. Shaban perceived my increasing distress, and at last took pity upon me. He revealed our ultimate destination; adding that though my father wished to separate me from Kalilah, it was not for ever, and that, in the meanwhile, I should make the acquaintance of a marvellous personage, called the Palm-tree-climber, who was the best story-teller in the universe.

This information quieted me to some extent. The hope, however distant, of seeing Kalilah again, poured balm into my soul, and I was not sorry to hear that I should have stories to my liking. Moreover, the idea of a realm of solitude, such as the Ostrich Isle, flattered my romantic spirit. If I must be separated from him whom I cherished more than life itself, I preferred to undergo my fate rather in some savage spot than amid the glitter and chatter of a harem. Far from all such impertinent frivolities, I purposed to abandon my whole soul to the sweet memories of the past, and give a free course to the languorous reveries in which I could see again the loved image of my Kalilah.

Fully occupied with these projects, it was with heedless eyes that I saw our boat approaching nearer and nearer the land of the mountains. The rocks encroached more and more upon the borders of the stream, and seemed soon about to deprive us of all sight of the sky. I saw trees of immeasurable height whose intertwisted roots hung down into the water. I heard the noise of cataracts, and saw the boiling eddies flash in foam and fill the air with a mist thin as silver gauze. Through this veil I perceived, at last, a green island of no great size, on which the ostriches were gravely promenading. Still further forward I discerned a domed edifice standing against a hill all covered with nests. This palace was utterly strange of aspect, and had, in truth, been built by a noted cabalist. The walls were of yellow marble, and shone like polished metal, and every object reflected in them assumed gigantic proportions. I trembled as I saw what a fantastic figure the ostriches presented as seen in that strange mirror; their necks seemed to go losing themselves in the clouds, and their eyes shone like enormous balls of iron heated red in a furnace. My terrors were observed by Shaban, who made me understand the magnifying qualities of the palace walls, and assured me that even if the birds were really as monstrous as they appeared, I might still trust, in all security, to their good manners, since the Palm-tree-climber had been labouring for over a hundred years to reduce their natural disposition to an exemplary mildness. Scarcely had he furnished me with this information, when I landed at a spot where the grass was green and fresh. A thousand unknown flowers, a thousand shells of fantastic shape, a thousand oddly fashioned snails, adorned the shore. The ardour of the sun was tempered by the perpetual dew distilled from the falling waters, whose monotonous sound inclined to slumber.

Feeling drowsy, I ordered a penthouse to be affixed to one of the palm-trees of which the place was full; for the palm-tree-climber, who always bore at his girdle the keys to the palace, was at that hour pursuing his meditations at the other end of the island.

While a soft drowsiness took possession of my senses, Shaban ran to present my father's letters to the man of wisdom. In order to do this he was compelled to attach the missives to the end of a long pole, as the Climber was at the top of a palm-tree, fifty cubits high, and refused to come down without knowing why he was summoned. So soon as he had perused the leaves of the scroll, he carried them respectfully to his forehead, and slipped down like a meteor; and indeed he had somewhat the appearance of a meteor, for his eyes were of flame, and his nose was a beautiful blood-red.

Shaban, amazed by the rapidity of the old man's descent, uninjured, from the tree, was somewhat outraged when asked to take him on his back; but the Climber declared that he never so far condescended as to walk. The eunuch, who loved neither sages not their caprices, and regarded both as the plagues of the Emir's family, hesitated for a moment; but, bearing in mind the positive order he had received, he conquered his aversion, and took the palm-tree-climber on his shoulders, saying: "Alas, the good hermit, Abou Gabdolle Guehaman, would not have behaved after this manner, and would, moreover, have been much more worthy of my assistance." The Climber heard these words in high dudgeon, for he had aforetime had pious squabbles with the hermit of the Sandy Desert; so he administered a mighty kick on to the small of Shaban's back, and thrust a fiery nose into the middle of his countenance. Shaban, on this, stumbled, but pursued his way without uttering a syllable.

I was still asleep. Shaban came up to my couch, and, throwing his burden at my feet, said, and his voice had a certain ring in it so that it awoke me without difficulty: "Here is the Climber! Much good may he do you!"

At the sight of such an object, I was quite unable, notwithstanding all my sorrows, to help bursting out into a fit of uncontrollable laughter. The old man did not change countenance, notwithstanding; he jingled his keys with an air of importance, and said to Shaban, in grave tones: "Take me again upon your back; let us go to the palace, and I will open its doors, which have never, hitherto, admitted any member of the female sex save my great egg-layer, the queen of the ostriches."

I followed. It was late. The great birds were coming down from the hills, and surrounded us in flocks, pecking at the grass and at the trees. The noise they made with their beaks was such that I seemed to be listening to the feet of an army on the march. At last I found myself before the shining walls of the palace. Though I knew the trick of them, my own distorted figure terrified me, as also the figure of the Climber on the shoulders of Shaban.

We entered into a vaulted apartment, lined with black marble starred with golden stars, which inspired a certain feeling of awe – a feeling to which, however, the old man's grotesque and amusing grimaces afforded some relief. The air was stifling, and nearly made me sick. The Climber, perceiving this, caused a great fire to be lit, and threw into it a small aromatic ball which he drew from his bosom. Immediately a vapour, rather pleasant to the smell, but very penetrating, diffused itself through the room. The eunuch fled, sneezing. As for me, I drew near to the fire, and sadly stirring the ashes, began to form in them the cipher of Kalilah.

The Climber did not interfere. He praised the education I had received, and approved greatly of our immersions, just after birth, by the ages, adding maliciously that nothing so sharpened the wits as a passion somewhat out of the common. "I see clearly," he continued, "that you are absorbed in reflections of an interesting nature; and I am well pleased that it should be so. I myself had five sisters; we made very light of Mahomet's teaching, and loved one another with some fervour. I still, after the lapse of a hundred years, bear this in my memory with pleasure, for we scarcely ever forget early impressions. This my constancy has greatly commended me to the Jinns whose favourite I am. If you are able, like myself, to persevere in your present sentiments, they will probably do something for you. In the meanwhile, place your confidence in me. I shall not prove surly or unsympathetic as a guardian or keeper. Don't get it into your head that I am dependent on the caprice of your father, who has a limited outlook, and prefers ambition to pleasure. I am happier amid my palms, and my ostriches, and in the enjoyment of the delights of meditation, than he in his divan, and in all his grandeur. I don't mean to say that you yourself cannot add to the pleasures of my life. The more gracious you are to me, the more shall I show civility to you, and make you the partaker in things of beauty. If you seem to be happy in this place of solitude, you will acquire a great reputation for wisdom, and I know, by my own experience, that under the cloak of a great reputation it is possible to hide whole treasures of folly. Your father in his letters has told me all your story. While people think that you are giving heed to my instructions, you can talk to me about your Kalilah, as much as you like, and without offending me in any way. On the contrary, nothing affords me greater pleasure than to observe the movements of a heart abandoning itself to its youthful inclinations, and I shall be glad to see the bright colours of a first love mantling on young cheeks.

While listening to this strange discourse, I kept my eyes on the ground; but the bird of hope fluttered in my bosom. At last I looked at the sage, and his great red nose, that shone like a luminous point in that room of black marble, seemed to me less disagreeable. The smile accompanying my glance was of such significance that the Climber easily perceived I had swallowed his bait. This pleased him so mightily that he forgot his learned indolence, and ran to prepare a repast of which I stood greatly in need.

Scarcely had he departed, when Shaban came in, holding in his hand a letter, sealed with my father's seal, which he had just opened. "Here," said he, "are the instructions I was only to read when I reached this place; and I have read them only too clearly. Alas! how wretched it is to be the slave of a prince whose head has been turned by much learning. Unhappy princess! I am compelled, much against my will, to abandon you here. I must re-embark with all who have followed me hither, and only leave in your service the lame Mouzaka, who is deaf and dumb. The wretched Climber will be your only helper. Heaven alone knows what you will gain from his companionship. The Emir regards him as a prodigy of learning and wisdom; but as to this he must suffer a faithful Mussulman to have his doubts." As he spoke these words, Shaban touched the letter three times to his forehead, and then, leaping backwards, disappeared from my sight.

The hideous manner in which the poor eunuch wept on leaving me, amused me much. I was far indeed from making any attempt to keep him back. His presence was odious to me, for he always avoided all conversation about the only subject that filled my heart. On the other hand, I was enchanted at the choice of Mouzaka as my attendant. With a deaf and dumb slave, I should enjoy full liberty in imparting my confidences to the obliging old man, and in following his advice, if so be that he gave me advice of which I approved.

All my thoughts were thus assuming a somewhat rosy hue, when the Climber returned, smothered up in carpets and cushions of silk, which he stretched out upon the ground; and he then proceeded, with a pleasant and contented air, to light torches, and to burn pastilles in braziers of gold. He had taken these sumptuous articles from the palace treasury, which, as he assured me, was well worthy of exciting my curiosity. I told him I was quite ready to take his word for it at that particular time, the smell of the excellent viands which had preceded him, having very agreeably whetted my appetite. These viands consisted chiefly of slices of deer spiced with fragrant herbs, of eggs prepared after divers recipes, and of cakes more dainty and delicate than the petals of a white rose. There was besides a ruddy liquor, made of date juice, and served in strange translucent shells, and sparkling like the eyes of the Climber himself. We lay down to our meal together in very friendly fashion. My amazing keeper greatly praised the quality of his wine, and made very good use of it, to the intense surprise of Mouzaka, who, huddled up in a corner, indulged in indescribable gestures, which the polished marble reflected on all sides. The fire burnt gaily, throwing out sparks, which as they darkened, exhaled an exquisite perfume. The torches gave a brilliant light, the braziers shone brightly, and the soft warmth that reigned in the apartment inclined to a voluptuous indolence.

The situation in which I found myself was so singular, the kind of prison in which I was confined was so different from anything I could have imagined, and the ways of my keeper were so grotesque, that from time to time I rubbed my eyes to make sure that the whole thing was not a dream. I should even have derived amusement from my surroundings, if the thought that I was so far from Kalilah had left me for a single moment. The Climber, to distract my thoughts, began the marvellous story of the Giant Gebir, and the artful Charodé,[1] but I interrupted him, and asked him to listen to the recital of my own real sorrows, promising that, afterwards, I should give ear to his tales. Alas, I never kept that promise. Vainly, at repeated intervals, did he try to excite my curiosity: I had none save with regard to Kalilah, and did not cease to repeat: "Where is he? What is he doing? When shall I see him again?"

The old man, seeing me so headstrong in my passion, and so well resolved to brave all remorse, became convinced that I was a fit object for his nefarious purposes, for, as my hearers will doubtless have already understood, he was a servant of the monarch who reigns in this place of torment. In the perversity of his soul, and that fatal blindness which makes men desire to find an entrance here, he had vowed to induce twenty wretches to serve Eblis, and he exactly wanted my brother and myself

---

1 Gebir and Charodé: I have not been able to locate the story [ed.].

to complete that number. Far indeed was he, therefore, from really trying to stifle the yearnings of my heart; and though, in order to fan the flame that consumed me, he seemed, from time to time, to be desirous of telling me stories, yet, in reality, his head was filled with quite other thoughts.

I spent a great part of the night in making my criminal avowals. Towards morning I fell asleep. The Climber did the same, at a few paces' distance, having first, without ceremony, applied to my forehead a kiss, that burned me like a red-hot iron. My dreams were of the saddest. They left but a confused impression on my mind; but, so far as I can recollect, they conveyed the warnings of Heaven, which still desired to open before me a door of escape and of safety.

So soon as the sun had risen, the Climber led me into his woods, introduced me to his ostriches, and gave me an exhibition of his supernatural ability. Not only did he climb to the tremulous tops of the tallest and most slender palms, bending them beneath his feet like ears of corn, but he would dart like an arrow from one tree to another. After the display of several of these gymnastic feats, he settled on a branch, told me he was about to indulge in his daily meditations, and advised me to go with Mouzaka and bathe by the border of the stream, on the other side of the hill.

The heat was excessive. I found the clear waters cool and delicious. Bathing pools, lined with precious marbles, had been hollowed out in the middle of a little level mead over which high rocks cast their shadow. Pale narcissi and gladioli grew on the margin, and, leaning towards the water, waved over my head. I loved these languid flowers, they seemed an emblem of my fortunes, and for several hours I allowed their perfume to intoxicate my soul.

On returning to the palace, I found that the Climber had made great preparations for my entertainment. The evening passed like the evening before; and from day to day, pretty nearly after the same manner, I spent four months. Nor can I say that the time passed unhappily. The romantic solitude, the old man's patient attention, and the complacency with which he listened to love's foolish repetitions, all seemed to unite in soothing my pain. I should perhaps have spent whole years in merely nursing those sweet illusions that are so rarely realised, have seen the ardour of my passion gradually dwindle and die, have become no more than the tender sister and friend of Kalilah, if my father had not, in pursuit of his wild schemes, delivered me over to the impious scoundrel who sat daily watching at my side to make me his prey. Ah! Shaban, ah ! Shamelah, you, my real friends, why was I torn from your arms? Why did you not, from the very first, perceive the germs of a too passionate tenderness exciting in our hearts, germs which ought then and there to have been extirpated, since the day would come when not fire and steel would be of any avail!

One morning when I was steeped in sad thoughts, and expressing in even more violent language than usual my despair at being separated from Kalilah, the old man fixed upon me his piercing eyes, and addressed me in these words: "Princess, you, who have been taught by the most enlightened of sages, cannot doubtless be ignorant of the fact that there are Intelligences, superior to the race of man, who take part in human affairs, and are able to extricate us from the greatest difficulties. I, who am telling you this, have had experience, more than once, of their power; for I had a right to their assistance, having been placed, as you yourself have been, under their protection from my birth. I quite see that you cannot live without your Kalilah. It is time, therefore, that you should apply for aid to such helpful spirits. But will you have the strength of mind, the courage to endure the approach of Beings so different from mankind! I know that their coming produces certain inevitable effects, as internal tremors, the revulsion of the blood from its ordinary course; but I also know that these terrors, these revulsions, painful as they undoubtedly are, must appear as nothing compared with the mortal pain of separation from an object loved greatly and exclusively. If you resolve to invoke the aid of the Jinn of the Great Pyramid, who, as I know, presided at your birth, if you are willing to abandon yourself to his care, I can, this very evening, give you speech of your brother, who is nearer than you imagine. The Being in question, so renowned among the sages, is called Omoultakos: he is, at present, in charge of the treasure which the ancient cabalist kings have placed in this desert. By means of the other spirits under his command, he is in close touch with his sister, whom, by the way, he loved in his time just as you now love Kalilah. He will, therefore, enter into your sorrows just as much as I do myself, and will, I make no doubt, do all he can to further your desires."

At these last words my heart beat with unspeakable violence. The possibility of seeing Kalilah once again excited transports in my breast. I rose hastily, and ran about the room like a mad creature. Then, coming back to the old man's side, I embraced him, called him my father, and, throwing myself at his knees, I implored him, with clasped hands, not to defer my happiness, but to conduct me, at whatever hazard, to the sanctuary of Omoultakos.

The crafty old scoundrel was well pleased, and saw with a malicious eye into what a state of delirium he had thrown me. His only thought was how to fan the flame thus kindled. For this purpose he resumed a cold and reserved aspect, and said, in tones of great solemnity; "Be it known to you, Zulkaïs, that I have my doubts, and cannot help hesitating, in a matter of such importance, great as is my desire to serve you. You evidently do not know how dangerous is the step you propose to take; or, at least, you do not fully appreciate its extreme rashness. I cannot tell how far you will be able to endure the fearful solitude of the immeasurable vaults that you must travers, and the strange magnificence of the place to which I must conduct you. Neither can I tell in what shape the Jinn will appear. I have often seen him in a form so fearful that my senses have long remained numbed; at other times he has shown himself under an aspect so grotesque that I have been scarcely able to refrain from choking laughter, for nothing can be more capricious than beings of that nature. Omoultakos mayhap, will spare your weakness; but it is right to warn you that the adventure on which you are bound is perilous, that the moment of the Jinn's apparition is uncertain, that while you are waiting in expectation you must show neither fear, nor horror, nor impatience, and that, at the sight of him, you must be very sure not to laugh, and not to cry. Observe, moreover, that you must wait in silence, and the stillness of death, and with your hands crossed over your breast, until he speaks to you, for a gesture, a smile, a groan, would involve not only your own destruction, but also that of Kalilah, and my own."

"All that you tell me," I replied, "carries terror into my bosom; but, impelled by such a fatal love as mine, what would one not venture!"

"I congratulate you on your sublime perseverance," rejoined the Climber, with a smile of which I did not then appreciate the full significance and wickedness. "Prepare yourself. As soon as darkness covers the earth, I will go and suspend Mouzaka from the top of one of my highest palm-trees, so that she may not be in our way. I will then lead you to the door of the gallery that leads to the retreat of Omoultakos. There I shall leave you, and myself, according to my custom, go and meditate at the top of one of the trees, and make vows for the success of your enterprise."

I spent the interval in anxiety and trepidation. I wandered aimlessly amid the valleys and hillocks on the island. I gazed fixedly into the depths of the waters. I watched the rays of the sun declining over their surface, and looked forward, half in fear, and half in hope, to the moment when the light should abandon our hemisphere. The holy calm of a serene night at last overspread the world.

I saw the Climber detach himself from a flock of ostriches that were gravely marching to drink at the river. He came to me with measured steps. Putting his finger to his lips, he said: "Follow me in silence." I obeyed. He opened a door, and made me enter, with him, into a narrow passage, not more than four feet high, so that I was compelled to walk half doubled up. The air I breathed was damp and stifling. At every step I caught my feet in viscous plants that issued from certain cracks and crevices in the gallery. Through these cracks the feeble light of the moon's rays found an entrance, shedding light, every here and there, upon little wells that had been dug to right and left of our path. Through the black waters in these wells I seemed to see reptiles with human faces. I turned away my eyes in horror. I burned with desire to ask the Climber what all this might mean, but the gloom and solemnity of his looks made me keep silence. He appeared to progress painfully, and to be pushing aside with his hands something to me invisible. Soon I was no longer able to see him at all. We were going, as it seemed, round and round in complete darkness; and, so as not to lose him altogether in that frightful labyrinth, I was compelled to lay hold upon his robe. At last we reached a place where I began to breath a freer and fresher air. A solitary taper of enormous size, fixed upright in a block of marble, lighted up a vast hall, and discovered to my eyes five staircases, whose banisters, made of different metals, faded upwards into the darkness. There we stopped, and the old man broke the silence, saying: "Choose between these staircases. One only leads to the treasury of Omoultakos. From the others, which go losing themselves in cavernous depths, you would never return. Where they lead you would find nothing but hunger, and the bones of those whom famine has aforetime destroyed." Having said these words, he disappeared, and I heard a door closing behind him.

Judge of my terror, you who have heard the ebony portals, which confine us for ever in this place of torment, grind upon their hinges! Indeed I dare to say that my position was, if possible, even more terrible than yours, for I was alone. I fell to the earth at the base of the block of marble. A sleep, such as that which ends our mortal existence, overcame my sense. Suddenly a voice, clear, sweet, insinuating like the voice of Kalilah, flattered my ears. I seemed, as in a dream, to see him on the staircase of which the banisters were of brass. A majestic warrior, whose pale front bore a diadem, held him by the hand. "Zulkaïs," said Kalilah, with an afflicted air, "Allah forbids our union. But Eblis, whom you see here, extends to us his protection. Implore his aid, and follow the path to which he points you."

I awoke in a transport of courage and resolution, seized the taper, and began, without hesitation, to ascend the stairway with the brazen banister. The steps seemed to multiply beneath my feet; but my resolution never faltered; and, at last, I reached a chamber, square and immensely spacious, and paved with a marble that was of flesh colour, and marked as with the veins and arteries of the human body. The walls of this place of terror were hidden by huge piles of carpets of a thousand kinds, and a thousand hues, and these moved slowly to and fro, as if painfully stirred by human creatures stifling beneath their weight. All around were ranged black chests, whose steel padlocks seemed encrusted with blood ...[1]

---

1   Samuel Rogers reported that the story continues with a meeting of brother and sister: "[Kalilah] had carnal connections with this sister, in the centre of the great Pyramid." While their presence in the Hall of Eblis is evidence of such a consummation of their passion, no continuation has been found among the manuscripts in the Beckford Papers.

Appendix A: The History of Prince Alasi and the Princess Firouzkah (translated by Sir Frank T. Marzials)

I reigned in Kharezme,[1] and would not have exchanged my kingdom, however small, for the Caliph Vathek's immense empire. No, it is not ambition that has brought me to this fatal place. My heart, so soon to burn in the fires of the divine vengeance, was armed against every unruly passion; only the calm and equable feelings of friendship could have found entrance there; but Love, which in its own shape would have been repelled, took Friendship's shape, and in that shape effected my ruin.

I was twenty years of age when my father died; and I regretted his loss sincerely, not only from natural affection, but also because I regarded kingship as a burden very heavy to be borne.

The soft delights of the harem had little charm for me; the idea of marriage's more formal bonds attracted me even less. I had been solemnly betrothed to Rondabah,[2] Princess of Ghilan,[3] and this contract, entered into by my father on my behalf, for the good of the two countries, was one which I could not lightly venture to cancel. All I could dare to allow myself was delay.

With this almost misanthropic repulsion from the ordinary ways of men, I had to ascend a throne, to govern a numerous people, to endure the ineptitude of the great, and the folly of the meaner folk, to do justice to all, and, in a word, to live among my subjects. But in those days generosity and virtue

---

1 Kharezme, *Kharazm*: A province of the Khalifate on the Oxus River and extending to the Aral Sea; present-day Turkmenistan makes up much of the province. [*Islam2* IV, 1060]

2 The "Firouzkah" version published by Lewis Melville in 1912 presents a misreading of Rondabah for Roudabah and Lalzer for Zalzar that this appendix reflects.

3 Ghilan, *Gilan*: A province of the Khalifate extending along the shore of the Caspian Sea. It had only two considerable cities: Rasht or Rachut, on the sea, and Lakshan, also known as Ghilan, situated inland. [*D'Herbelot, Islam2* II, 1111]

were not in me mere vague and empty words. I fulfilled all my duties exactly, and only from time to time indulged in the delights of solitude. A tent, disposed after the Persian manner, and situated in a dense forest, was the place where I spent these moments of retirement, moments that always seemed to pass too quickly. I had caused a considerable number of trees to be cut down so as to leave an open clearing of fair size, and had filled this clearing with gay flowers, while round it coiled a moat whose waters were as clear as those of Rucnabad. Near this bright spot, which I used to liken to the moon shining full-- orbed in the dark blue of the firmament, I often admired the gloomy depths of the enfolding woods, and strayed in their recesses, to dream!

One day, when, stretched at length upon the moss, I was caressing a young deer that would come tame to my hand, I heard the sound of a horse galloping – not far distant; and soon after a rider came in view, who was unknown to me. His dress was outlandish, his countenance fierce, his eye haggard. But he did not long keep my attention. An angelic form, in a boy's dress, soon riveted my gaze. The stranger held this lad, who seemed most graceful, most delicately fashioned, straitly clasped to his breast, and seemed anxious, as I thought, to prevent him calling for help. Outraged by what I took to be an act of lawless violence, I rose, I barred the stranger's way, I flashed my sword in his eyes, and cried: "Stop, wretch! Do you dare commit this wrong in the sight of the King of Kharezme?"

Scarcely had I uttered these words, when the stranger sprang to the ground, without releasing his precious charge, and said, saluting me with every mark of respect, "Prince Alasi, you are the very object of my search. I wish to entrust to you a treasure beyond all price. Filanshaw,[1] King of Shirvan,[2] the intimate friend of the king your late father, is reduced to dire extremity. His rebellious subjects hold him besieged in the citadel of Samakhié.[3] The troops of the Caliph Vathek are upholding

---

1 Filanshaw, *Filanshow*: ruler of Shirwan during the reign of Vathek.
2 Shirvan, *Shirwan*: province in Persia extending to the western shore of the Caspian Sea, to the north and west of Ghilan. It includes present-day Azerbaijan. Vathek added the province to his empire. [D'Herbelot, *Islam2* VII, 382]
3 Samakhié, *Schamakie*: the capital of *Shirwan*; present day Shemakha in Dagestan.

them in their revolt. They have sworn the utter ruin of their sovereign. Filanshaw accepts undaunted the decrees of Fate so far as he himself is concerned, but anxious, if that be yet possible, to save alive his only son, the lovely child whom you see here, he has commanded me to place him in your hands. Hide this pearl of incomparable price in your bosom; suffer its origin, the shell in which it was formed, to remain unknown, until such time as the years bring security. And so farewell. I fear pursuit. Prince Firouz[1] will himself tell you all else that you may wish to know."

I had, while he was speaking, opened my arms to Firouz, and Firouz had sprung into them. We held one another embraced with a tenderness that seemed to fill the stranger with satisfaction. He mounted his horse and was gone in a moment.

"Oh, take me hence," then said Firouz; "now indeed do I fear to fall into the hands of my persecutors. Ah! would they tear me from the side of the friend Heaven has given me – the friend towards whom my whole heart gives one bound?"

"No, dear child," cried I; "nothing shall tear you from my side. My treasures, my army, all I have, shall be used for your protection. But why hide your birth here in my dominions, where no harm can come to you?"

"Nay, it must be so, my most generous defender," rejoined Firouz; "my father's foes have sworn to extirpate his race. They would brave death itself in obedience to their oath; they would stab me in your very presence if I were recognized. The man who brought me here, and has guarded me through my infancy, will do all he can to persuade them I am no longer alive. Find some one to father me – it matters not whom – I shall have no other pride save that of loving you, and deserving that you should love me in return."

Thus speaking, we came to the tapestried enclosure that surrounded my Persian pavilion, and I ordered refreshments to be brought – but neither of us did more than taste of them. The sound of Firouz's voice, his words, his looks, seemed to confuse my reason, and made my speech come low and haltingly. He

---

1 Firouz, *Firuz*: Persian word for the third day of the five added at the end of the solar year. It signifies *victorious* and *triumphant*. [*D'Herbelot*]

perceived the tumult raging in my breast, and, to appease it, abandoned a certain languor and tenderness of demeanour that he had so far affected, and assumed the childish gaiety and vivacity natural to his years, for he did not appear to be much more than thirteen.

"How," said he, "have you nothing here except books? No instruments of music?"

I smiled, and ordered a lute to be brought. Firouz's playing was that of a master. He sang and accompanied himself with so much feeling, with such grace, that he raised in my breast another storm of emotion, which he again was careful to dispel by innocent mirth.

Night came on, and we separated. Though happy beyond what I conceived possible, I yet desired to be alone. I felt the need of introspection. This was not at first easy: all my thoughts were in confusion! I could not account to my own self for the agitation of feeling that I had experienced. "At last," said I, "Heaven has hearkened to my dearest wish. It has sent me the true heart's-friend I should never have found in my court; it has sent him to me adorned with all the charms of innocence – charms that will be followed at a maturer age, by those good qualities that make of friendship man's highest blessing – and, above all, the highest blessing of a prince, since disinterested friendship is a blessing that a prince can scarcely hope to enjoy."

I had already extended beyond its customary term the time I devoted to seclusion and solitude. My absence, so short to myself, seemed long to my people, and a return to Zerbend became imperative. Some days before we left our retreat, I caused a shepherd living in the neighbourhood to be brought before me, and commanded him, on pain of death if he divulged our secret, to acknowledge Firouz his son. The precaution seemed to reassure the young prince. He multiplied his marks of affection for me, and took more pains than ever to give me pleasure.

Friendship, as one may say, exercised upon me a humanising influence. I no longer shunned diversions and entertainments. Firouz shone in them, and was universally admired. His amenity and grace won golden opinions, in which I fully shared, so that I was not a little surprised to see him coming to me, one day, wild and furious. "King of Kharezme," said he, "why have you deceived me? If you were not prepared to love me, and me alone, you ought not to have accepted me as your friend. Send me back to the Mage, since the Princess Rondabah, who is instantly expected here, must, in the nature of things, take full possession of your heart!"

This extraordinary outburst seemed so out of place and unreasonable, that I assumed a very stern tone, and replied: "What excess of folly is this, Prince of Shirvan? How can my union with Princess Rondabah in any wise concern you? What is there in common between the affection I shall owe to my wife, and the affection I shall ever entertain for yourself?"

"Oh! it concerns me greatly," rejoined he. "It concerns me much that a woman, lovely and lovable, should also become your staunch friend! Is it not said that the Princess of Ghilan unites to the fortitude, the courage of a man, all the charms of her sex? What more will you want when you possess her? Where shall I stand then? Perhaps you imagine you will have done all I am entitled to expect at your hands when you have reinstated me in my dominions; but I tell you beforehand that, if you placed the world's empire at my feet in exchange for your tenderest friendship, I could only regard you as my deadliest enemy!"

Firouz knew me better than I knew myself. He played upon me as he listed. Besides, he had himself well in hand, knew how to act so as to excite my sympathy, and to seem yielding and amenable, as it served his purpose. He quieted down after this outburst and resumed his ordinary playfulness.

Though he passed for the son of a shepherd, Firouz, as being the son of the King of Shirvan, had a claim to my fullest consideration; and I would rather have been accused of a ridiculous partiality than that he should be treated without the deference due to his real rank. He occupied the pleasantest quarters in my palace. He had chosen his own attendants, in addition to two eunuchs, sent to him by the Mage, on the very day of his arrival at my Persian pavilion. I had provided him with instructors in every kind of knowledge – whom he exasperated; with superb horses – which he rode to death; and with slaves – whom he ill-treated without mercy. But all this was hidden from me. My boundless partiality gave rise to some murmurs, no doubt, but it prevented any direct accusation from reaching my ears.

A venerable Mullah, highly esteemed for learning and piety, was commissioned to expound, for his benefit, the salutary moral teachings of the Koran, and caused him to read and learn by heart a variety of its sacred texts; and of all my young friend's tasks this was the most irksome. But I attributed his distaste to any cause but the real one. Far indeed was I from suspecting that his mind had already been saturated with doctrines altogether opposed to those of Islam.

One day that I had passed several hours without seeing my amiable pupil, I went to look for him, and found him in one of the large halls, capering and dancing about with a strange figure grotesquely huddled up in an ass's skin. "Ah, my dear prince," cried he, running up to me open-armed; "you have before you the very strangest spectacle in the world. My Mullah is transformed into an ass – the king of asses, since he talks even as he talked before!"

"What do you mean?" cried I; "what game are you playing now?"

"It's not a game," replied the Mullah, waving two false ears of an immeasurable length; "I am trying in all good nature, to fully realise the character I am now personating, and I entreat your Majesty not to be scandalised and take my so doing in evil part."

At these words I stood confounded. I misdoubted whether I was listening to the voice of the Mullah, or whether I really had before me a donkey, which, by some miracle, had been endowed with the gift of speech. Vainly did I ask Firouz for an explanation. He only laughed immoderately and replied, "Ask the donkey."

Finally, my patience quite exhausted, I was about to order this disgusting buffoonery to be brought forcibly to an end, when Firouz assumed his most serious air, and said: "Sire, you will, I hope, forgive the innocent artifice by which I have endeavoured to demonstrate how much you, and other princes, are deceived as to the character of the people about them. This Mullah has, doubtless, been presented to you as a man of very superior merit; and, as such, you have appointed him to act as teacher to your friend and pupil. Well! be it known to you that, in order to obtain one of my most hideous negresses, with whom he is madly in love, he has consented to remain three days thus ridiculously accoutred, and so to be a universal laughing-stock. And, indeed, you must agree that he presents the form and figure of an ass in a highly satisfactory manner, and that his speech does no discredit to his outward seeming."

I asked the Mullah if what Firouz said was true.

"Not quite," he replied, stammering and stuttering in a pitifully absurd way; "the girl he is to give me, though black as night, is beautiful as day; the oil with which she makes her charms lustrous is scented like the orange-flower; her voice has the bitter-sweet of the pomegranate; when she toys with my beard, her fingers which are prickly as the thistle, titillate my very heart! Ah! so that she may be mine, suffer me, suffer me to remain for three days in the form and figure of an ass!"

"Wretch, in that form and figure thou shalt die!" I cried, with an indignation I could not contain; "and let me never hear speak of thee again!"

I retired as I spoke those words, casting at Firouz looks of a kind to which he was in no way accustomed.

The rest of the day I spent in reflecting on Firouz's ill-nature, and the infamous conduct of the Mullah; but, when evening came, I thought only of again seeing my friend. I caused him to be summoned. He came at once, timidly and affectionately. "Dear prince," said he, "you don't know what grief I have felt all day at the thought that you seemed angry with me. In order to obtain forgiveness, I have lost not a moment in executing your commands. The ass is dead and is buried. You will never hear speak of him again."

"This is another of your ill-timed jests," I exclaimed. "Do you ask me to believe that the Mullah, who spoke with such vigour this morning, is dead to-night?"

"He is, and by your command," replied Firouz. "One of my negro slaves, whose mistress he wished to appropriate, despatched him, and he was buried incontinently and without ceremony, like the donkey he was."

"This is really too much!" cried I. "What! do you think you can, with impunity, assassinate a man whose head you yourself had turned?"

"I executed your orders," he rejoined. "I executed them literally. Surely the loss of so vile a creature is not to be regretted. Farewell, I go to weep over my own imprudence, and the fragile nature of your affection – which any slightest jar can shatter."

He was about to retire. I stopped him. The most exquisite viands, delicately served in plates of enamel, were placed before us; we began to eat together, and I was again weak enough, during our repast, to laugh at all his jokes and jibes upon the subject of the ass.

The public did not take the Mullah's death with quite so much equanimity. It was said that Firouz, in derision of the faith of the true believers, had administered some philtre to the holy man, causing him to lose his wits. An act so atrocious was naturally regarded with abhorrence, and I was accused of culpable partiality for a child of low birth and vile instincts. The queen, my mother, felt herself bound to bring these mutterings of discontent to my knowledge. She spoke of them openly, and in no ambiguous terms, before Firouz himself, so as to moderate his arrogance, if that were possible. For myself, I recognised the justice of her reproofs, which were at once affectionately expressed and reasonable; but my friend never forgave her.

He was specially outraged by the contempt heaped upon him because of his humble birth, and told me it was absolutely necessary his true parentage should be disclosed. I represented the dangers involved, a danger that he had himself set before me in such strong terms, and entreated him to wait at least for the return of the envoys I had sent to Shirvan. But he was too impatient to wait, and, in order to overcome my objections, bethought himself of a device which I could certainly never have foreseen.

One morning when I was about to start on a hunting expedition, the Prince of Shirvan, who always gladly accompanied me on such occasions, feigned sickness. I wished to remain by him; but he urged me not to stay, assuring me that, with a little rest, I should find him, on my return, in a fit condition to share with me in such amusements as would be a pleasant relaxation after the fatigues of the day – amusements that he would himself devise.

Accordingly I did find, on my return, a superb collation, prepared and served in a little grove of trees, forming part of my gardens, and decked and illumined after a fashion all the prince's own – in other words, with the utmost taste and refinement. We sat under a kind of dais formed of the intertwining branches of pomegranates and oleanders. A thousand flowers, shed at our feet, formed a rich carpet, and filled the sense with their intoxicating fragrance. Unnumbered crystal vases, containing fruits perfumed with ambergrise, and floating on snow, reflected the light of small tapers daintily set on the margin of a succession of fountains. Choirs of young musicians were so disposed as to charm the ear without interrupting the discourse. Never was eve more delicious; never had Firouz shown himself more gay, mare amiable, more enchanting. His pleasant mirth, his wit, enlivened me even more than the wine, which he poured out freely. When the wily son of Filanshaw perceived that my head was in a whirl of pleasant excitement, he knelt before me on one knee, and, taking both my hands in his said: "Dear Alasi, I had forgotten to ask you to forgive a wretch who has deserved death."

"Speak," I replied. "You know that from me you should have but to ask in order to obtain it; and, besides, I should be pleased indeed to find your heart sensible to pity."

"The matter stands thus," rejoined Firouz. "I was to-day in my apartment, surrounded by your flatterers, who at once hate me and seek to win my favour, when the shepherd, my supposed father, came in to kiss me, open-armed. At that moment the blood of Filanshaw surged rebellion in my heart. 'Hence, churl,' said I to the shepherd, 'go and stifle thy misbegotten brats with thy clumsy caresses! Wouldst thou have the unblushing effrontery to maintain that I am thy son?' 'That I am bound to do so, you very well know,' he replied firmly. "I will maintain it with my life.' This reply of his was, no doubt, in strict accordance with his duty; but, curious to see how far we can really depend on those to whom we entrust our secrets, I ordered the man, who seemed so resolute, to receive the bastinado.[1] He endured it but a short time – he revealed all. After your express orders, and the punishment with which you threatened him, he is no doubt worthy of death; but I pray you forgive him."

"The ordeal was severe," said I. "Will you ever be cruel? What irresistible power compels me to love you? Assuredly not the sympathy of fellow-feeling."

"It is most true," he rejoined, "that I do not endure mankind as patiently as you do. To me men seem as ravenous as wolves, as perfidious as the foxes in Loqmans's Fables,[2] and so flighty of feeling, so false to their promises, that it is impossible not to hold them in abhorrence! Why are we two not alone in the world? Then the earth, now swarming with the vile and wicked, might boast itself inhabited by two faithful and happy friends."

By such exalted and romantic outbursts of sentiment, Firouz brought me to tolerate this new proof of the essential badness of his heart. He had, indeed, not told me the whole story, as I learned on the morrow. It was by his own orders, and at his suggestion, indirectly conveyed, that the shepherd had come into his presence, and accosted him as he had done; and, moreover, the poor wretch had the fortitude to endure his punishment almost unto death before infringing my commands. I sent the unhappy creature a sum of money, and held myself most to blame for his condition.

As this transaction had filled all Zerbend with indignation, and seemed to reflect more blame on Firouz than he actually

---

1 bastinado: To beat the soles of the feet with a stick.
2 Loqman, *Lukman*: A writer of legendary wisdom, mentioned with respect in the Koran for his book of proverbs and maxims. [*Sale* 335-36n]. Both D'Herbelot and Chardin connect Loqman and Aesop. D'Herbelot especially argues that they are the same person, that "the manner of instructing by fables conforms more to the genius of the orientals than to the peoples of the occident" [*D'Herbelot*] Loqman's reputation as a writer of fables comes from the late middle ages. [*Islam2* V, 811]

deserved, I publicly, and with some pomp, declared his real birth, and the reasons why it had been hidden. I also thenceforward surrounded him with regal state; and was not a little surprised to see that those who had hitherto been most bitter against him were now all eagerness to do him service. This made me somewhat mistrust their real intentions. But the Prince of Shirvan reassured me. "Don't be afraid," said he laughing; "you can trust the care of my person to these people just as safely as to their fellows; there is nothing that really savours of treachery in their bearing; their affection has only changed with the change in my fortunes. I am now no longer the sly and cruel little shepherd lad, who, for his evil pranks, was sure sooner or later to be sent back to his hovel. I am a great prince, good and humane of disposition, from whom a thousand benefits may be expected. I am ready to wager that I could have the heads of five or six of them cut off daily by lot, and that the rest, trusting to be more fortunate than their companions, would continue to sing my praises."

Such speeches – and I knew only too well how true they were! – served insensibly to harden my heart. It is a great evil to look upon mankind with a too clear vision. You seem to be living among wild beasts, and you become a wild beast yourself.

I had thought at first that, in his new position, the Prince of Shirvan would yield, even more freely than he had done before, to his evil bent; but in this I was mistaken. He showed himself noble in manner and sensible in conduct, and his bearing towards great and small was affable and obliging. In short, he completely obliterated the bad impression produced by his former practices.

These days of quiet lasted till the arrival of Rondabah. I happened to be in Firouz's apartments when news was brought that that princess, attended by a retinue suitable to her rank, was only at a few parasangs'[1] distance from Zerbend. Startled, I scarce knew why, I turned my eyes on my friend. His condition

---

1 parasang, *farsakh*: measurement of distance based on how far troops can march in an hour. To D'Herbelot, it equals two French leagues, or 8 km, or 5 miles. The modern equivalent of one parasang is 6 km. [*Islam2* II, 812]

makes me tremble even yet, as I think of it. A deathly pallor overspread his countenance, his movements became convulsive, and at last he fell to the ground, senseless. I was about to bear him to his couch, when the Mage's two eunuchs took him from my arms, saying: "Leave him to our care, lord – and deign to retire. If, on recovering his senses, he were to see you by his side, he would instantly expire."

These words, and the tone in which they were uttered, impressed me so much that I could scarcely drag myself through the portal of the apartment. Once outside, I awaited the issue with anguish unspeakable. At last one of the eunuchs came out and begged me to re-enter. Firouz, leaning on the arm of the other eunuch, advanced to meet me with halt and trembling steps. I made him sit down by the divan, and, seating myself by his side, I said: "Friend of my soul, fate alone can be answerable for the strange and unaccountable feelings of our hearts. You are, against all comprehension, jealous of Rond-abah; and I, notwithstanding the engagements into which my ambassadors have entered, am ready to risk all rather than plunge you into a sea of sorrows!"

"Nay, let us go and see this redoubtable heroine," replied Firouz; "suffer me only to accompany you in this your first interview; at my age my presence cannot be open to objection. If you leave me here alone, I shall die before you return."

To this I had nothing to reply. The fascination he exercised upon me was extraordinary, to myself quite inexplicable. And I could but agree to his every wish. He resumed his ordinary spirits, and continued to repeat, as we went along: "Ah! if only this accursed princess should prove not to be beautiful!"

She was beautiful, however; but of a beauty that inspired awe rather than excited desire; very tall, of majestic port, her whole aspect proud and austere. Her hair, black as ebony, enhanced the whiteness of her complexion, and her eyes, of the same dark hue, looked command but did not softly allure. Her mouth, though graceful in its lines, had no inviting smile, and when her coral lips opened, the words were words of sense indeed, but very rarely moving and persuasive.

Stung, as it seemed, by my want of a lover's ardour, and offended because, contrary to all use and custom, I had come accompanied by my friend, Rondabah no sooner perceived us advancing than she turned to my Mother and said; "Which of these two princes is the one to whom I am destined?"

"To both, if you please," replied Firouz unhesitatingly and mockingly, so that I almost burst out laughing. I restrained myself, however, with an effort, and was preparing to find some excuse for my friend's ill manners, when the Princess of Ghilan, after looking me over attentively from head to foot, and casting a disdainful look at Firouz, remarked – always addressing herself to the queen: "Those who allow an insult to pass unnoticed deserve to be insulted; farewell, madam. And you Kali," continued she, turning to the chief of her eunuchs, "make all the necessary preparations for my return to Ghilan this very night." Saying these words she retired, and the queen was not slow to follow her, only stopping to threaten us with all the calamities that must ensue from the offence given to Rondabah. But we were at that moment in no humour to listen. As soon as we found ourselves alone, we burst out laughing at the scene which had just taken place. "Is that a woman?" asked Firouz. "No, it is the ghost of Roostum,[1] or of Lalzar[2] – or may we not rather say that the spirit of some famous warrior, Rondabah's ancestor, has taken possession of that tall and stately form, which we are asked to look upon as hers? Ah! my dear Alasi, sharpen your sword, prepare to defend your life if you do not in all things exactly conform to the ceremonial enjoined by the all-powerful Kali, with his voice of silver."

We remained in this mood till the queen interrupted us. She had nearly appeased Rondabah, and wished me to complete her task. Her representations, dictated by all a mother's love, were strong and urgent, and I yielded to them.

On the day preceding that fixed for the marriage ceremonies, I rose earlier than usual. Anxious, agitated, I went down alone into the large gardens, containing the funereal

---

1   Roostum, *Rustam*: A great Persian hero and general, celebrated as a model of strength and courage. He killed the dive Argenk, or *Arzang*. [*Richardson* 132, 146].

2   Lewis Melville misreads the manuscript as *Lalzer*. Zalzar is the father of Rustam.

monuments of my ancestors. I wandered through the most sombre alleys, and entered at last into a grotto, through which ran a stream of water. The darkness was such in the grotto's deeper recesses that scarce a feeble ray of light could be discerned. I penetrated into the blackest shade, so as to be able to dream unseen and undisturbed. Soon, to my surprise, I saw a figure approaching that bore, in form and attire, a close resemblance to Amru, the son of my vizier. He went and seated himself in a part of the grotto where a little light was shining, so that I could see him while he could not see me. I spoke not a word, but saw with surprise another mysterious personage approaching, out of the very heart of the darkness; and this figure bore the likeness of Rondabah's chief eunuch. The second personage accosted the first, and I seemed to hear him say: "Son of Ilbars, too charming Amru, let your heart rejoice; it shall possess the object of its desire! Rondabah, my mistress, will come here this very night. The first of her love-vows will be yours. Only the aftermath will be given to the King of Kharezme to-morrow." Amru kissed the ground in token of submission, and murmured a few words whose meaning was lost in the sound of the running water. They then left the grotto.

I was about to follow, and wash out the affront in blood; but a moment's reflection arrested this first impulse. I had no love for Rondabah. I was only marrying her for reasons of state, and out of pity. That there should be anything in what had passed to make me really unhappy was out of the question. I had only to bring her criminal perfidy into full light, and I should be quit of her, and recover my own freedom with all honour. These thoughts passed swiftly through my brain. I thanked whatever lucky star had led me in time to this important discovery, and ran to impart it to Firouz. What was my dismay when, on entering his apartment, I found him in the arms of his two eunuchs, who were holding his hands and weeping and crying: "O master, loved master! What harm had your beautiful locks done? Why have you ruthlessly cut them off? And now you would gash your lovely white forehead! No, not if we die to stay your hands!"

This sight so moved me that I could not utter a single word. My speechless anguish seemed to quiet Firouz. He tore himself from the arms of his eunuchs, and, running to me and embracing me, exclaimed: "Calm yourself, generous Alasi! It is my condition that troubles you? Surely it should cause you no surprise; but forget that you have seen me thus; notwithstanding these tears, this hair that I have given to the flames, notwithstanding the despair to which you saw me reduced, I wish you every happiness with Rondabah – yes, though it should cost me my life!"

"Ah," cried I, "perish a thousand Rondabahs if your nerves, so delicately strung, could thus be spared these terrible shocks and jars – yes, perish a thousand Rondabahs, one and all, even if they were as true as our Rondabah is false!"

"What!" cried Firouz in turn, "Have I heard aright? Are you speaking of the Princess of Ghilan? For pity's sake explain yourself?"

I then told him all that had happened in the grotto, and my determination to blaze abroad to all men the shame of Rondabah. He fully approved my design, and made no effort to hide his joy at the course things were taking. "I congratulate you," said he, adding in a whisper: "It has cost me my hair, but you have had a lucky escape."

We resolved not to reveal our secret to the queen, my mother, until the time came for taking her with us to surprise Rondabah.

The queen seemed more astonished than grieved when we went to her apartment and told her what had brought us thither so late. The affection she had at first shown for Rondabah had gradually cooled as mine had appeared to increase. Nevertheless, she had not been able to help respecting her, and never ceased, while following us, to express amazement at her shameless conduct. Firouz, on his part, laughed, and for more reasons than one.

We went down into the garden. A faithful slave, whom I had set to watch the place, came and told us that the two culprits had been in the grotto for some minutes. Immediately we entered, with torches, and in such numbers that those whom we thus surprised must, as one would have thought, fall dead for very shame. They seemed, however, in no wise disconcerted. I drew my sword in a fury and thought, with one blow, to send their two wretched heads rolling on to the ground; but my sword clove the empty air alone: they vanished from my sight!

At this moment of confusion a cry arose: "The Princess of Ghilan has forced the guard at the entrance to the grotto!" And she appeared before us. "King of Kharezme," she said in clear tones, modest but unabashed, "I am advised that a plot is being hatched in this place against my honour; and I am come to confound my enemies. What is going on here?"

"Fly, wretched creature," said the queen, "or my son will repeat the blow you have just evaded by your magic arts."

"I do not fear death," replied Rondabah quietly. "Alasi has made no attempt on my life. If you have been misled by some seeming prodigy, I ask you to tell me what was its nature. I rely on the help that Heaven always extends to innocence, and have no doubt as to my ability to undeceive you."

Rondabah's proud and noble bearing, her looks, that commanded respect, all served to confound me. I almost doubted the evidence of my eyes and ears, when Firouz exclaimed: "Oh! we must indeed confess that the Princess of Ghilan's memory is of the shortest! We find her in the arms of her beloved Amru; she disappears with her favourite, and when, within a moment, it pleases her to reappear on the scene, she has entirely forgotten all that has taken place."

At these words Rondabah changed colour. The flush died on her cheeks, and left them deadly pale. She turned upon me eyes that were full of tears. "Oh, most unhappy prince!" she said, "I now see the full depth of the abyss yawning at thy feet. The monster dragging thee thitherward will not fail of his prey! The spirits of darkness are at his beck and call. I cannot save thee, and yet I shudder at abandoning thee to thy fate. Thou hast covered me with infamy, but it is thy ruin only that wrings my heart!" Having thus spoken, Rondabah retired with majestic steps, none daring to stay her.

We stood as if turned to stone, and looked fixedly at one another, unable to speak. "Surely we must all have lost our wits," cried the queen at last. "What! the cool effrontery of an unworthy magician would make us disbelieve the evidence of our eyes and ears! Let her go, and deliver us for ever from her hateful presence! Nothing could happen better!" I agreed. And Firouz, who seemed confused and frightened, most assuredly was of no other opinion. We each went towards our own apartments.

I left the place so troubled that I did not see Firouz was following close at my heels, nor could I altogether repress a feeling of horror when I found we were alone together. But ah! when the heart is evil, all presentiments are sent to us in vain!

Firouz threw himself impetuously at my feet, and said, sobbing: "Why, why, O King of Kharezme, did you give me shelter? Why did you not leave me to die with my father? I was then but a child; no one could have accused me of being a magician. Is it at this court of yours, and here by your side, that I have learned the art of conjuring up the Dives? And yet Rondabah, the wicked Rondabah, has almost persuaded you. Will she not also say I have gained your friendship by some evil charm? Alas! you know well enough that the only charm I have used is to cherish you a hundred times more than my own life!"

But why dwell upon this scene? All of you must foresee its inevitable end. Firouz succeeded in dissipating my suspicions. Like the Caliph Vathek, I had heard the voice of a beneficent spirit, and, like him, I had hardened my heart against its saving influence. Rondabah's words were forgotten; I disregarded the confused doubts they had aroused in my mind. The Prince of Shirvan became more dear to me than ever. That moment was the turning-point in my life. It sealed my ruin.

We heard on the following morning that Rondabah had departed during the night, with all her retinue. I ordered public rejoicings.

A few days afterwards Firouz said to me, before the queen, my mother: "You must see, King of Kharezme, that war with the King of Ghilan is now inevitable. His daughter, with her wiles, will easily persuade him that she is innocent, and he will want to avenge her wrongs. Forestall him; raise an army; invade Ghilan, and ravage the country: you are the aggrieved party!"

The queen agreed with Firouz, and I assented. Nevertheless, I watched the war preparations with regret. I thought the war a just war, and yet was troubled in conscience as though it had been unjust. Moreover, the qualms I felt with regard to my extreme attachment to Firouz grew stronger day by day. The son of Filanshaw had learned to read in my heart very clearly, and was in no wise deceived by the pretexts I put forward for my misgivings, and involuntary fits of perplexity; but he made as though he accepted my explanations, and took occasion of my perturbed state to devise new pleasures and forms of distraction.

One morning, as we were starting on a great hunting expedition, we found, in the palace yard, a man who bore a heavy chest, and was disputing with the guards. I inquired what was the matter. "It is a jeweller from Mossul,"[1] replied the chief of the eunuchs. "He says he has certain gems of the utmost rarity; but he is importunate, and refuses to await your majesty's leisure."

"He is quite right," said Firouz; "nothing that pleases and amuses can ever come amiss; let us go back and examine these wonders. The beasts of the forest are doubtless prepared to await our pleasure."

We retraced our steps accordingly, and the jeweller unclasped his chest. Nothing in it seemed worthy of our curiosity, till my eyes fell on a golden casket, round which were engraved these words: "PORTRAIT OF THE FAIREST AND MOST UNHAPPY PRINCESS IN THE WORLD."

"Let us look at her," exclaimed Firouz. "The portrait of this beauty, doubtless in tears, will appeal to our hearts. It is good, now and again, to be moved to pity."

I opened the casket and was struck mute with astonishment. "What are you looking at in that way?" asked my friend. He looked in turn, was moved to indignation, and, turning to the

---

1 Mossul, al Mawsil: A city on the west bank of the Tigris, opposite ancient Ninevah. [Islam2 VI, 899]

eunuchs, exclaimed: "Lay hands upon this insolent merchant, and throw him, his chest, and all his wares into the river! What! Shall a wretch like this disclose to the whole world the face of Filanshaw's daughter – the rosebud that I pictured to myself sheltered from every evil wind beneath the humble roof of adversity?"

"Heavens!" I exclaimed in turn; "what do I behold? What do I hear? Let no one touch this man! And thou, friend of my soul, speak! Is this indeed thy sister – thy sister, featured like thyself?"

"Yes, King of Kharezme," replied the Prince of Shirvan; "you have here indeed the portrait of my twin sister, Firouzkah. The queen, my mother, saved her, with myself, from the fury of the rebels. When they separated us, and handed me over to the charge of the Mage, I was told that she would be hidden in some place of safety. But I now see only too clearly that I was deceived."

"My lord," then said the merchant, "the queen, your mother, has taken refuge with her daughter in a house of mine, near Mossul. It is by her orders that I carry this portrait through divers countries of Asia, in the hope that Firouzkah's beauty will rouse the beholders to avenge the wrongs done to the king, your father. I have already travelled through various lands, and not without success; but the queen never told me I should find you here."

"Doubtless she knew it not," said Firouz, "and thought I was still with the Mage. But," he continued, turning towards me, "you are pale, dear friend; let us regain our apartments, and put off our hunting to another day."

I let him lead me in, and, having first cast myself down on the divan, did not cease to look at the portrait. "Oh, my dear Firouz," I cried, "these eyes, this mouth, all these features are thine. The hair, indeed, is not quite like thine, and I would it were; but this has taken the colour of camphire, while thine has the colour of musk."

"What!" said Firouz laughing, "a pale cold picture can thus inflame with love a heart that resisted all the fire of Rondabah's charms! But calm yourself, my dear Alasi," continued he, more seriously; "the wife of Filanshaw will yet call you her son. I purpose sending the jewel-merchant back to her. He will tell her, from me, to accept no help of any prince save yourself – that it is you, my benefactor, my friend, who are the destined avenger of her wrongs. But let us first make haste to punish the Princess of Ghilan for the indignities she has heaped upon you. Let us anticipate the fury of her attack. How can you reconquer my kingdom while your own is in jeopardy?"

From the moment that my passion seemed to myself intelligible and normal, my heart regained its calm. Peace reigned in my breast. I gave strict orders that the preparations for our enterprise should be hastened, and very soon, with a numerous host, we were marching against the enemy.

The frontiers of Ghilan were undefended. We ravaged the march country without mercy. But Firouz's strength did not equal his courage. I spared him as much as possible, even at risk of giving the enemy time to complete the full equipment of his forces.

One day that I called a halt, in a valley clothed with fresh moss, and watered by a clear stream, we saw tripping by, not far from us, a doe whiter than milk. Immediately Firouz caught up his bow, and sent an arrow flying after the innocent creature. The shaft went home; the doe fell; we ran to the spot. A peasant, perceiving us, cried: "What have you done? You have killed the holy woman's doe!" This exclamation seemed to amuse Firouz. But his mirth was of short duration. An enormous dog, the doe's companion, leapt upon him, dragged him to the ground, held him pinned down with heavy paws, and seemed to be only waiting some master's orders before putting its fangs through his throat. I dared neither to speak nor attack the dog, for fear of enraging it the more; nor could I attempt to shear off its head: the heads were too close to one another. At last, when I own I was almost terrified to death, I saw approaching a woman, veiled, who forced the dog to relinquish its hold, and then, turning to me, said: "I did not think, King of Kharezme, to find you here, in a place where I had come to bury myself alive. I have just, according to the divine precept, returned good for evil, in saving the life of Firouz. Do not you, on your part, return evil for good by destroying this people, who, far from seeking to avenge my wrongs, are quite ignorant of the indignities heaped upon me."

As she finished speaking these words she lifted her veil, and disclosed the majestic countenance of Rondabah. Then she turned on her heel, and retired with quick steps, leaving us in a state of inexpressible surprise.

Firouz was the first to recover. "Well," said he, "do you still entertain any doubt as to Rondabah's dealing in magic? What shall we do to protect ourselves against her arts? I know but one remedy: let us surprise her this very night; let us take a band of our trusty followers, and burn her alive in her retreat – which we can easily discover by skilful inquiry; or else we may resign ourselves to being torn to pieces by the Afrites, who serve her in the shape of savage beasts."

"Shame!" cried I. "Would you thus repay the service she has just done us? What ever she may be, she has this moment saved you from a cruel death."

"Too credulous prince," rejoined Firouz, "do you not see that the infamous sorceress defers her vengeance, that she is only fearful of losing its full fruition by undue haste? But what am I saying? I only am the object of her malignity; nor would I wish it otherwise. I only hope that, after my death, she will spare your life and be satisfied with making you her slave!"

This speech produced its desired effect. I was not master of my own judgement when Firouz opened out a glimpse of danger to himself. I became as eager as even he could wish, in the execution of his black and horrible design. The flames that consumed Rondabah's rustic dwelling were kindled by my hands as well as his; and, notwithstanding the resistance of the peasantry – whom we slaughtered without mercy as a reward for their generous efforts on her behalf – we did not leave the spot till we had left Rondabah buried as we believed, beneath a heap of smoking ashes.

A few days afterwards I wished to advance, with my army, into the interior of the country; but soon found my way blacked by the enemy's forces, under the command of the King of Ghilan and his son. It became necessary to offer battle.

Firouz, not notwithstanding all I could urge, insisted on fighting by my side. This did not add to the effectiveness of my arms. I thought less of attacking the foe than of parrying the blows aimed at my friend. He, on his side, threw himself in the way of those directed against myself. Neither suffered his sight to be diverted from the other. No one could doubt, seeing us, that each, in defending the other's life, was defending a life dearer than his own.

The prince of Ghilan had sought me out everywhere. We met at last, and, swooping on me with uplifted sword, he cried: "King of Kharezme, thy life shall pay forfeit for the atrocious wrongs done to my sister; had I known of them before, I should have sought thee out in thy very palace, and maugre all the spirits of darkness that dwell there!"

Scarcely had he spoken these words than the hand that held the avenging sword fell to the ground, struck off at the wrist by the a back-handed blow from the blade of Firouz. The King of Ghilan hastened up, foaming with rage, and aimed at us two crashing blows. I avoided the one; and the other went home on Firouz's shoulder. I saw him reel in the saddle. To send the old king's head flying in the air, to take Firouz on to my own horse, to spur out of the battle – all this was but the work of a moment.

The son of Filanshaw had lost consciousness. I was scarcely in better plight. Instead of returning to my camp, I plunged into a forest, deep and gloomy, where I did nothing but wander, almost aimlessly, like one bereft of reason. Fortunately a woodman saw us. He approached and said: "If you have not altogether lost your wits, and have no wish to see this young man die in your arms, follow me to my father's cabin, where you can get help."

I suffered him to lead me. The old man received us kindly. He caused Firouz to be placed on a bed, ran to fetch an elixir, and made him drink of it; and then said: "But a moment more, and this young man would have been dead. He has nearly lost all his blood. The first thing to be done was to repair that loss. Now we will examine his wound; and, while my son goes into the forest to find some simples that I will require, you must help me to undress your friend."

I was doing this mechanically, and with a trembling hand; but came to myself with a start when, on opening Firouz's vest, I saw a breast which the houris might have envied. "Why it's a woman!" said the old man.

"Now Allah be praised!" cried I, in a delirium of surprise and joy: "but what of her wound?"

"That is of no consequence," replied the good man, examining it, "and when I have bound up the gash, she will soon come to her senses. Compose yourself, therefore, young man," continued he, "and be specially careful not to disturb the rest of one to whom, as I well perceive, you are passionately attached. Any emotion, at the present moment, would cause her to die before your eyes."

The transport of love and joy that filled my soul here gave place to the apprehension caused by the old man's words. I helped him in silence to perform his kindly offices; and then, having enveloped the inanimate form of Firouzkah – for she it was – in a coverlet of leopard-skin, I waited, in mortal anxiety, till she should open her eyes.

The hope held out to me by the old man was soon realised. My well-beloved gave a sigh, turned her languishing eyes upon me, and said: "Where are we, friend? Is the battle lost, and are we...?"

"No, no!" I interrupted, placing my hand on her mouth; "all is gained since your precious life is safe! But keep still; you don't know how much depends upon your silence."

Firouzkah did not fail to understand the full meaning of my words. She spoke no more, and soon, from very weakness, fell into a deep sleep.

The old man watched her, well pleased; while my own breathing seemed to repeat every rise and fall of her breast, on which I had softly laid my hand. She slept for two hours, and never woke till the woodman entered abruptly into the hut. He did not bring with him the herbs for which his father had sent him, at which I expressed surprise. But Firouzkah, now restored by her slumbers, interrupted me, and said: "Thou hast news to tell us, hast thou not?"

"Yes, yes," said he, "and the very best of news. The army of the Kharezmians has been cut to pieces, and their camp pillaged. The victory would be complete if they could only catch those wicked princes, Alasi and Firouz, who have escaped, after killing the king and his son. But the princess Rondabah has ascended the throne, and is causing search to be made for them everywhere. She offers such great rewards that they must soon be captured."

"I am delighted at what you tell me," cried Firouzkah, without suffering any change to appear in her countenance; "we had been assured that Rondabah was burned to death in her woodland dwelling; and I had been most grieved to hear it, as I knew she was a most excellent princess."

"She is even better than you think," replied the woodman, with a cunning look; "and that is why Heaven has kept her from harm. The prince, her brother, chanced upon her retreat, and took her away some hours before the perpetration of that wicked crime – a crime which, please God, will not long remain unpunished."

The clod's tone sufficiently showed that he took us for what we really were; and he made signs to his father to follow him out of the room. They went out together. Afar we heard the trampling of many horses. Firouzkah immediately rose to a sitting posture, and, presenting me with a razor, which she took from under her dress, said in a whisper: "You see, dear Alasi, the danger we are in; cut off my hair, which, as you see, is growing again, and throw it into those flames. Don't answer a word. If you lose a moment it is all up with us!"

I could but comply with such a pressing command; and I did so. A few seconds later, a Dive, shaped like an Ethiopian, appeared before our eyes, and asked Firouzkah what she wanted with him. "I desire thee," she replied, "to carry me this instant, with my friend, to the cavern of the Mage, thy master, and as thou passest, to crush the worthless wretches who are bargaining for our lives!"

The Dive needed no second orders. He took us both in his arms, sprang from the hut – causing it, with one kick, to fall on our late hosts, and then shot through the air so rapidly that I lost consciousness.

When I came to myself I was in the arms of Firouzkah, and saw only her charming face, lovingly near my own. I softly closed my eyelids again, as one does when wishing to prolong a pleasant dream; but soon I felt my happiness was real. "O wicked Firouz, O cruel Firouz!" I cried. "What needless torments have you caused me to endure!" Uttering these words, I pressed again and yet again, with burning kisses, those sweet and beautiful lips, that had themselves pressed mine while I lay entranced, and that now seemed to elude my own; when, suddenly recollecting my well-beloved's wound, I gave her time – at once to breathe, and to answer my anxious questions.

"There is no need for anxiety, dear Alasi," she answered, "I am perfectly healed, and all will shortly be explained to you. But lift up your head, and look around."

I obeyed, and thought myself transported beneath a new firmament, encrusted with stars a thousand times more brilliant and nearer to us than the stars in the natural world. I looked round on every side, and it seemed to me I was in a vast plain, and that round it were transparent clouds, which held enfolded, not only ourselves, but all the most beautiful and delicious products of earth. "Ah!' cried I, after a moment of surprise, and embracing Firouzkah, "what is it to us if we have been carried into Cheheristan[1] itself? The true realms of bliss are in thine arms!"

"This is not Cheheristan," replied the daughter of Filanshaw. "It is only the Mage's cave, which an infinite number of beings, superior to our race, take pleasure in decorating with a varied beauty. But such as it is, and whatever may be its inhabitants, everything will be done here to anticipate your wishes. Is it not so, my Father?" continued she, raising her voice.

"Undoubtedly," replied the Mage, appearing suddenly

---

1   Cheheristan: perhaps *Shehrizur*, a fertile plain in Kurdistan; its southern boundary is the River Sirwan.

before our eyes, and advancing towards me with a smile. "Prince Alasi will be treated here as he has treated my dear Firouzkah; and, moreover, the priceless jewel I confided to his care – Firouzkah herself – shall be his to possess forever, if such be his desire. Come, let the marriage feast be at once prepared, and all things made ready for so great an event!"

He had no sooner spoken these words, than the cavern again changed its aspect. It assumed an oval shape, and diminished proportions, and appeared all encrusted with pale sapphires. Round us, on divans, were ranged boy and girl musicians, who charmed our ears with melodious strains, while from their heads, light-encircled, shone rays more pure and soft than would be shed by a thousand tapers.

We were placed at a table covered with excellent dainties and the most exquisite wines, and were served delightfully by Persian boys and by Georgian girls – all as white and graceful as the jasmine sprays engarlanding their fair heads. With their every motion the gauze robes, that half clothed, half revealed them, exhaled the sweetest perfumes of Araby the Blest.[1] Firouzkah, who could not at once forget her part as Firouz, sported with these children as they filled our cups, and indulged in a thousand pleasant pranks.

When the repast was ended, the Mage, first ordering the most profound silence, and addressing himself to me, spoke as follows: –

"You are doubtless surprised, King of Kharezme, that, with the power I possess, I should have taken the trouble to seek you out and obtain your protection for the girl-treasure committed to my charge. You must understand just a little why Firouzkah should have gone to you disguised, and have left you to the mercy of love-feelings, incomprehensible to yourself, which she might so easily have explained.

"Be it known to you, then, that the people of Shirvan, always a rebellious race, and inclined to murmur against their rulers, had begun to grumble because Filanshaw had no children. But when at last the queen, his wife, bid fair to become a mother,

---

1 Araby the Blest: *Arabia Felix* is the Latin name for Yemen.

their insolence passed all bounds. 'She must have a son!' they cried round the royal dwelling; 'we will have no princess to place us under the yoke of some stranger prince. She must have a son!'

"The poor queen suffered quite enough discomfort from her condition without the disquiet of such alarming cries. She pined visibly. Filanshaw came to consult me. 'You must deceive these blockheads,' said I. 'Even that is much more than they deserve. If the queen has a daughter, pretend the daughter is a boy, and, in order that you may not be compelled to entrust the secret to her nurses, send the child here. My wife Soudabe, will bring her up with a mother's care and affection, and, when the time comes, I myself will spare no pains in her education.' My proposal saved the queen's life. Firouzkah came into the world, and we called her Firouz. Under that name her birth was hailed with public rejoicings; and Soudabe, who received her from the king's hands, brought her to my cavern – from whence she was taken, from time to time, to show herself at court.

"We gave her the double education, which in view of all eventualities, it seemed desirable that she should have.

"She accepted Soudabe's instructions and mine, with an equal zest, and would seek relaxation, after her studies, in the company of the Dives, of every form, who haunt my cavern.

"These active spirits were so attached to Firouzkah that there was no whim of hers that they were not ready to gratify. Some taught her such exercises as are common to either sex. Others kept her amused with pleasant games, or told her marvellous stories. A great number went the world over to find her rare and curious things, or interesting news. She never found time hang at all heavy on her hands, and always came back to my cavern with transports of delight whenever she had been obliged to pass a few days at Samakhié.

"The Princess of Shirvan had just reached the age of fourteen, when the Dive Ghulfaquair, being maliciously inclined, brought her your portrait. From that moment she seemed to lose her natural gaiety of spirits, did nothing but dream and sigh, and, as may be supposed, gave us great anxiety. The cause of her pain she carefully concealed, and the Dive took care to keep us in like ignorance. He was, moreover, pretty busy in following your movements, so as to be able to give her a report of all your doings. What he told her of your shyness, your insensibility to love, only served to further excite her passion. She burned with the desire of taming your mood, and bringing you under the sway of her charms; and soon the course of events was such as to add, to that desire, hope. The open rebellion of the people of Shirvan, Filanshaw's entreaties that I should so dispose of his daughter as to protect her from their fury, all conspired to embolden Firouzkah, and she spoke to me with entire freedom.

"'You, who have been a father to me,' she said; 'you, who have taught me not to be ashamed of the passions Nature has implanted in us, you will understand when I say that I love the Prince Alasi, King of Kharezme, and that I intend – however hard the task – to win his love in return. It is now no longer a question of hiding my sex so that I may reign over a people who have destroyed all my family, and whom I must ever hold in abhorrence. I shall now use my disguise in order to insinuate myself into a heart which soon, I hope, will be altogether mine. Alasi is insensible to woman's charm. It is in the guise of friendship that I must make him feel woman's power. Take me to him; ask him to protect me as the son of the King of Shirvan. He is too generous to refuse; and I shall owe to you a happiness without which life would be hateful!'

"I felt no surprise on hearing Firouzkah speak in this way. She was a woman; she wanted a husband; what could be more natural? I contented myself, therefore, with questioning her as to how she had become acquainted with you. She told me all, and spoke of you in such terms that I soon perceived any opposition would only make her unhappy. So I said, 'I will take you to the King of Kharezme, under the name Firouz, because I feel I can rely on your prudence, and the strength of mind I know you possess. You will need both; for by my magic arts I have discovered that you have a powerful rival, whose triumph would be your eternal despair. When, however, you are so pressed as to stand in need of supernatural help, burn your hair, and my Dives will instantly attend to receive your commands.' The rest, King of Kharezme, is known to you," continued the Mage. "Firouz has laboured hard in the cause of Firouzkah: *he* has won your heart by his gaiety, his light sportiveness; *she* must keep it by her love, and the prudence from which she has never deviated, even amidst dangers that would have daunted the courage of most women."

"Oh!" cried the Princess of Shirvan, "I ran great risk of losing the heart it had cost me so much to gain and I should have lost at least a part of it if I had not, at the sacrifice of my beautiful locks, called up the helpful Dives who so effectually impersonated Rondabah, Amru, and Kali! What do you say, Alasi?"

"That I shall ever cherish the motives that induced you to commit that act of injustice," I replied, with diplomacy, and some misgiving.

My daughter," said the Mage, "the word 'injustice,' which Prince Alasi has just uttered, can only apply to your suggested doubt as to his constancy. For he must be aware that every being has the right, by all possible means, to remove hurtful objects from its path, and that the motives of anger and fear which impel us so to act are born of the living and self-preserving forces of Nature. But the hours are fleeting fast. It is time you should enjoy the happier fruits of your frequent sorrows. Receive, King of Kharezme, the Princess Firouzkah at my hand; lead her to the nuptial chamber, and may you there be endowed with a full share of the life-giving fire which the earth contains in her bosom, the same fire that nightly rekindles the starry torches of the sky!"

We stood in no need of the Mage's good wishes; the feelings that glowed in our hearts were all-sufficient for our happiness. Friendship, love – their transports were alternate, and commingled in an unutterable ecstasy.

Firouzkah had no desire for sleep, and related to me how, in a moment, the Mage had healed her wound. She vaunted his power, and advised that I should ask him to show me his Hall of Fire, confessing that she herself had been brought up in the religion of Zoroaster,[1] and considered it the most natural and rational of all religions. "Think, then," she added, "if I could ever have taken delight in the absurdities of the Koran. Would that all your Mussulman doctors had shared the fate of the Mullah whose discourses wearied me to death! That moment was indeed delicious when I induced him to put on the outward seeming of an ass. I should have taken a like pleasure in plucking out all the feathers from the wings of the Angel Gabriel,[2] and thus punishing him for having furnished a pen to the man who wrote therewith so much nonsense, – if indeed I had been simpleton enough to believe that absurd story."

There was a time when such words would have seemed to me unspeakable for very wickedness; and in good sooth I did not like them much then. But any remaining scruples formed but a weak defence against the alluring caresses with which Firouzkah accompanied her every word.

A voluptuous sleep enveloped us at last; and we did not wake till the lively song of birds proclaimed broad day.

Surprised by sounds which I had no reason to expect in such a place, I ran to the grotto's entrance, and found it led to a garden containing all that is most delightful in nature, while the encircling sea enhanced the beauties which the earth exhibited to our gaze.

"Is this another illusion?" I asked, "for this, at least, cannot be part of the Mage's cavern?"

"It is one of its issues," replied Firouzkah; "but it would take you more than one day to explore all the beauties of the place. The Mage says that everything has been made for man's use, and that man must possess himself of everything he wants whenever the opportunity offers. He has spent part of his life in acquiring his power, and is spending the remainder in enjoying its fruits."

---

1 Zoroaster, *Zarathushtra* (c. 650 BC): Founder of Zoroastrianism, an ancient pre-Islamic religion of Persia. Beckford can safely ascribe a variety of beliefs and practices to the religion since little was and is known about it.
2 The Angel Gabriel is reputed to have inspired Muhammad to write the Koran, even, in some accounts, supplying a feather from his own wing for him to write with.

I did not fail to express to the Mage a very strong desire to see his Hall of Fire. "It will please you," said he, with a satisfied air; "but I cannot conduct you thither until you have visited my baths, and been invested with robes suitable to the majesty of the place."

To please Firouzkah I consented to everything that was demanded of me; and, for fear of offending her, I even refrained from laughter at the grotesque robes in which we were both ridiculously accoutred. But what were my feelings on entering the Hall of Fire? Never has spectacle so filled me with surprise and terror – never, until overwhelmed by the sight that met my eyes on entering the fatal place in which we now are!

The fire that the Mage worshipped seemed to issue from the bowels of the earth and to soar above the clouds. The flames sometimes shone with an unendurable brightness; sometimes they shed a blue and lurid light, making all surrounding objects appear even more hideous than they actually were. The rails of glowing brass that separated us from this dread deity did no more than partially reassure me. From time to time we were enveloped in a whirlwind of sparks, which the Mage regarded as graciously emitted in our honour – an honour with which I would very gladly have dispensed. In the portion of the temple where we stood, the walls were hung with human hair of every colour; and, from space to space, human hair also hung in festoons from pyramids of Skulls chased in gold and ebony. Besides all this, the place was filled with the fumes of sulphur and bitumen, oppressing the brain and taking away the breath. I trembled; my legs seemed to give way; Firouzkah supported me. "Take me hence," I whispered; "take me from the sight of thy god. Nothing save thine own presence has enabled me to endure *his* presence for a moment!"

It was sometime before I fully recovered. In order to effect my restoration, the Dives introduced a fresher air through orifices in the vault of the cavern where we had supped the night before. They also redecorated the cavern itself in a novel manner, and prepared for us an exquisite repast. I was thus enabled to listen to the Mage with renewed patience. What my terrible host told me about his religion did not indeed possess the charms of novelty: I knew most of it before, and I paid small heed to this part of his discourse. But his moral teachings pleased me hugely, since they flattered passion and abolished remorse. He greatly vaunted his Hall of Fire – told us that the Dives had built it, but that he himself has supplied the decorations at the risk of his life. I asked him for no explanations on this point; I was even afraid lest he should give them unasked. I could not think of those skulls, of that human hair, of what he called "decorations" without trembling. I should have feared the worst in that dreadful place if I had not been so sure of the heart of Firouzkah.

Fortunately I was not called upon to listen to the Mage's discourses more than once a day. The rest of our time was spent in amusements and pleasures of every kind. These the Dives never failed to supply; and Firouzkah caused them to gratify my every taste by an infinite variety. Her assiduous care, her ingenuity of tenderness, made my every moment hurry by in such voluptuous enjoyment that I was in no case to measure the flight of time; and the present had so far obliterated the past that I never once thought of my kingdom. But the Mage put an end all too soon, alas! to this period of delirium and enchantment. One day, one fatal day, he said to us: "We are about to separate, my dear children; the hour of bliss, for which I have sighed for such long years, is approaching; I am expected in the Palace of Subterranean Fire, where I shall bathe in joys untold, and possess treasures passing man's imagination. Ah! why has this moment of supreme felicity been so long delayed? The inexorable hand of death would not then have torn from my side my dear Soudabe, whose charms had never suffered from the ravages of Time! We should then have partaken together of that perfect happiness which neither accident, nor the vicissitudes of life, can ever mar in the place to which I am bound."

"Ah!" I cried, "where is that divine sojourn in which a happy eternity of mutual love and tenderness may be enjoyed? Let us follow you thither."

"You may do so, if you worship my god," replied the Mage; "if you will do homage to the powers that serve him, if you will win his favour by such sacrifices as he ordains."

"I will worship any god you like," said I, "if he will suffer me to live for ever with Firouzkah, and free from the horrible fear of seeing pale disease or bloody steel threaten her beauteous life. What must I do besides?"

"You must," replied the Mage, "cause the religion of Zoroaster to be received in your dominions, raze the mosques to the ground, erect Halls of Fire in their stead, and, finally, sacrifice, without pity, all whom you cannot convert to the true faith. This is what I have myself done, though not so openly as you can do it; and, as a sign of what I have been able to accomplish, see all these locks of hair that ornament my Hall of Fire – dear evidences that I am about to enter the gates of the only place where lasting joys are to be found."

"Quick, quick! let us go and cause heads to be cut off," said Firouzkah, "and so amass a treasure of human hair! You will agree, my dear Alasi, that the sacrifice of a whole tribe of crazy wretches who will not accept our belief, is as nothing if we can obtain thereby the supreme felicity of loving each other to all time!"

By these flattering words Firouzkah obtained my complete assent, and the Mage, having reached the height of his wishes, resumed: "I esteem myself happy, King of Kharezme, in seeing you, at last, convinced of the truth of my faith. Several times have I despaired, and I should certainly not have taken so much trouble about you if you had not been the husband of the daughter of Filanshaw – my friend and my disciple. Ah! what honour will be mine when your conversion is known in the Palace of Subterranean Fire! Hence, therefore! Depart at once. A ship, ready equipped, awaits you upon the shore. Your subjects will receive you with acclamation. Do all the good you can. Remember that to destroy those who are obstinate in error is accounted a great merit by the stern god you have promised to serve. When you deem that your reward is fully earned, go to Istakhar, and there, on the Terrace of the Beacon Lights, make a holocaust of the hair of those whom you have immolated in so good a cause. The nostrils of the Dives will be gratified by that sweet-smelling sacrifice. They will discover to you the steep and secret stairway, and open the ebony portals: I shall receive you in my arms, and see that you are received with fitting honours."

Thus did I yield to the last seductions of the Mage. I should have laughed his exhortations to scorn if my heart had not been so interested in the truth of his promises. For a moment indeed I did misdoubt them, and thought they might be false; but, nothing venture, nothing have, and soon I decided that, in view of the predicted reward, every hazard must be risked.

No doubt the Mage, urged on by ambition and an evil covetousness, had made a similar calculation, – to find himself ultimately deceived and cozened, as are all the miserable wretches who find their way to this place!

The Mage wished to see us embark. He embraced us affectionately at parting, and advised that we should keep in our service, as followers on whom we could always rely, the twenty negroes appointed to navigate our ship. Scarcely had we set sail when we heard a terrible sound – a sound like that of thunder as the lightning goes crashing among the mountains and heaping up the valley with ruin. Turning, we saw the rock we had just left crumble into the sea. We heard the cries of joy with which the exultant Dives then filled the air; and we judged that the Mage was already on his way to Istakhar.

Our twenty negroes were such good sailors, so adroit and alert, that we should have taken them to form part of the Mage's supernatural following if they had not assured us that they were simple Fire-worshippers, and no more. As their chief, Zouloulou by name, seemed very well acquainted with all the mysteries of the cavern, we asked him what had become of the pages and the little Georgian girls, for whom we had conceived a liking. He replied that the Intelligences, who first gave them to the Mage, had disposed of them, doubtless for the best, and that we could not do better than leave them in their hands.

My subjects celebrated my return, and my marriage, with such transports of joy that I quite blushed at the designs I entertained against them. They had found Firouz amiable as a boy; they found Firouzkah divine in the habiliments of her sex. My mother, in particular, overwhelmed her with caresses. But she changed her tone when we discovered that Motaleb, whom she had just established as her first minister, had thrown all the affairs with which he was charged into great disorder. She nourished a fancy for that ignorant vizier, and took it in very ill part that we should be angry with him. Firouzkah, who cared very little what she thought, would whisper in my ear: "Motaleb has a very good head of hair; let us cut off his head." But I was satisfied with deposing him from his office, and appointed, in his stead, a feeble old man who did everything as he was told, and never hesitated to cause the Great Mosque at Zerbend to be razed to the ground so soon as I ordered its demolition.

This revolutionary measure excited universal surprise. The queen, my mother, came in haste to ask what I meant by an act so impious and sacrilegious. "We mean," answered Firouzkah quietly, "never again to hear mention of Mahomet, and his crazy dreams, and to establish, in Kharezme, the religion of Zoroaster, as being the only religion worthy of credence." At this reply the good princess could not contain herself. She overwhelmed me with angry words. She heaped upon us imprecations – which have been only too terribly effectual. I listened to her without resentment; but Firouzkah induced me to commit her to her apartments – where, not long afterwards, she ended her life in bitterness of spirit, and cursed the hour when she had brought me into the world.

Iniquity had now no terrors for me. I was resolved to stop at nothing if so I might allay the fear of an ultimate separation from Firouzkah – which fear an inordinate affection had implanted in my breast.

At first I met with so little resistance that Firouzkah, who saw how easily the courtiers and the army yielded to my wishes, would say: "Where can we get hair? How many locks I see would be of admirable use to us if only the heads that bear them were a little more obdurate! It is to be hoped there may be a change, or we stand in danger of never getting to Istakhar."

At last there came a change indeed! Most of those who frequented the Halls of Fire I had erected were only waiting for a favourable moment to rise in rebellion. Several plots were discovered, and then executions became frequent. Firouzkah, who wished to proceed with order and method, was fully acquainted with the zeal and qualifications of Zouloulou, and established him as her head missioner. She caused him to get up, every day, on to a tall stage, erected in the midst of the city square, to which the people most resorted – and there the brazen negro, vested in a robe of vermilion, his countenance assured, his voice piercing, would pour forth his orations, while his nineteen compeers stood ready, with drawn swords, at the bottom of the steps leading to the stage, and cut off the heads of all who refused to accept the preacher's teaching; nor, as I need scarcely add, did they forget to secure the hair of their victims.

Mine was still the stronger side. I was beloved by the soldiery, who generally care very little what god they serve so long as they are caressed by their king.

Persecution produced its ordinary effect. The people courted martyrdom. They came from all parts to deride Zouloulou – whom nothing disconcerted – and to get their heads cut off.

The number of deaths became at last so great that the army itself was scandalised. Motaleb incited them to rebellion. He sent secretly, in the name of the soldiers, of the nobles, and of the people generally, to offer the crown of Kharezme to Rondabah – inviting her to come and avenge the death of her father, and of her brother, and her own wrongs.

We were not without information regarding these secret machinations – for parasites seldom altogether abandon a monarch so long as the crown still glitters on his head; but we felt no serious alarm till we perceived that we were becoming the weaker party. My guards had already, on more than one occasion, suffered the negroes to be maltreated – at a cost, to Zouloulou, of his two ears. He was the first to advise us not to lose the fruit of our labours.

By the care and vigilance of this zealous follower, everything was soon made ready for our departure. In the middle of the night I left my kingdom, which was by this time in almost full rebellion against my rule – left it with a heart as triumphant as if I had been a conqueror instead of a fugitive.

Firouzkah persuaded me to allow her to resume male attire; and that is why the Caliph Vathek mistook her sex. We were mounted, she and I, on two steeds, as swift, as superb, as Shebdid and Bariz, the ever-memorable coursers of Khosrou.[1] The twenty negroes each led a camel. Ten of the camels were laden with human hair.

Though anxious to reach our journey's end, yet, in sooth, we did not hurry overmuch. It was, no doubt, by some true presentiment that we could not bring ourselves to finally abandon our present pleasures for those we had been led to anticipate. We used to encamp at night, and often stayed, for days together, at the places of delight that lay in our way. For half-a-moon we had been enjoying the beauty of the vale of Maravanahar when, one night, I awoke suddenly, under the oppression of a confused and fearful dream. What was my horror at not finding Firouzkah by my side! I rose, half beside myself, and quickly left our tent to seek her. She was coming towards me – distracted. "Let us fly, dear Alasi," she said. "Let us to horse instantly, and gain the desert, which is but at a few parasangs distance; Zouloulou knows all its hiding-places, and will lead us to some spot where we may find shelter from the danger that threatens us."

"I fear nothing, beloved," I replied, "now that thou art found again; and will follow thee withersoever thou listest."

At the point of day we entered a wood so thick that the sun's rays scarce penetrated into its dark recesses. "Let us stop here," said Firouzkah, "and I will tell you of the strange adventure that befell me last night. I was sleeping by your side when Zouloulou woke me cautiously, and whispered in my ear that Rondabah was only about a hundred paces away, that she had wandered some little distance from the army she was leading into Kharezme, and that she was at that moment resting in her

---

1 Khosrou, *Key Khosrow, Chosroes*: Emperor Khosrow was a great warrior general who established himself on the throne of Persia through battles with rivals and wars with the Turks. Roostum was his champion. During peace, he was renowned for his justice. *Shah-nama*: "He spread justice abroad in the world and tore out of the ground the roots of tyranny."

pavilion, with no other following than a few of her guards and some of her women; and, moreover, that these were all sound asleep. At these words I was seized simultaneously with fear and fury. I remembered the prediction of the Mage, and, dressing myself in haste, I felt the edge of my sword. 'What do you mean to do?' asked the eunuch. 'Moderate yourself. Be warned. You can accomplish nothing against the life of Rondabah. The Mage ordered me to tell you so, if occasion required, and to tell you further that you would yourself perish in the attempt. A Power against whom nothing can prevail, protects the Princess of Ghilan. But if you will be calm, and listen to my advice, we can do much worse to her than cut off her head.' While he was thus speaking we had left your tent and reached our destination. Zouloulou, who saw that I kept perfect silence, said, 'You are quite right to rely on me. I will cause all Rondabah's people to inhale certain fumes, and sleep for a long time without waking. We shall easily make our way, undetected, as far as her pavilion, and can then, as our fancy dictates, bedaub the face of your enemy with this unguent, which possesses the power of making the most beautiful countenance ugly and repulsive.'

"So said, so done. But Rondabah, whose slumbers were natural and undrugged, nearly prevented me from accomplishing more than half my purpose: I rubbed her face so hard that she awoke with a cry of pain and terror. Hastily did I finish my work, and then, having detached a mirror that hung from the girdle of one of her women. I presented it to her, and said: 'Acknowledge, majestic princess, that that little monster of a Firouz is a model of courtesy; he flatters himself that this beautifying unguent, which he has just applied to your countenance, will cause you to remember him – always!' Whether the masculine courage of Rondabah was daunted by my presence, or whether she was filled with despair at finding herself the most loathsome object in the world, I know not; but she fainted away. We left her to come to herself again at her leisure.

"I was naturally pleased at having prevented my rival from repeating the triumph predicted by the Mage; but that feeling soon gave way to fear lest we should be pursued. Now, however, we are in a place of safety. Let us rest here. This breast, which is still a-flutter with its late alarms, will serve you as a pillow. Alas! Firouzkah and Firouz may have been guilty of acts of cruelty, but only when others have attempted to dispute with her the empire of your heart!"

The seductive turn which Firouzkah thus gave to her story did not altogether blind me to the atrocity of the crime she had just committed; and I was surprised that, with a heart so tender and full of feeling where I was concerned, she could yet be capable of frenzied hate and the most horrible cruelty. What struck me most, however, in her story was the argument used by Zouloulou to prevent her from carrying her criminal designs on Rondabah to even greater lengths. "The Power that protects Rondabah," said I to myself, "must love the good, for she is good. That Power, which is pure and supreme, cannot then be the same Power which is about to receive into its palace beings such as Firouzkah and myself, for we are wicked. But if it reigns supreme over all other Powers, what is to become of us? O Mahomet! O Prophet beloved of the world's Creator, thou hast forsaken me utterly and without hope! What refuge have I, save with thine enemies?"

With this despairing thought came the last feelings of remorse I was destined to experience. Such feelings I always owed to the Princess of Ghilan; but, alas! they always came in vain!

I willingly allowed Firouzkah to lure me from such melancholy reflections – reflections that seemed to make her anxious. I could not recall the past – probably I should not have recalled it if I could. No course was open to me save to leap, with eyes self-bound, into the yawning abyss of the future.

The cloud passed away in a soft rain of tender kisses. But Firouzkah, by intoxicating me with love, redoubled my fear of losing her by some unexpected danger as we had just avoided. She, on her side, was assailed with doubts as to Rondabah's permanent disfigurement. She regretted the time we had lost on the journey – a journey which, as she believed, and as I strove to believe, was to end in the abode of an even greater felicity.

Thus, with a common consent, and to the great joy of our twenty black eunuchs, we now used the utmost diligence to reach Istakhar.

It was already night when we came to the Terrace of the Beacon Lights; and, notwithstanding all that we could say to one another of endearment and encouragement, we were filled with a kind of horror as we walked it from end to end. There was no moon in the firmament to shed upon us its soft rays. The stars alone were shining there; but their trembling light only seemed to intensify the sombre grandeur of all that met our gaze. We regretted, indeed, none of the beauties, none of the riches of the world we were about to leave. We thought only of living in a world where we should be for ever inseparable; and yet invisible ties seemed still to draw us back and hold us to the earth.

We could not repress a shudder when we saw that the negroes had done piling up our enormous heap of human locks. With trembling hands we approached our torches to set it on fire; and we thought to die for very fear when the earth opened before our feet, the rock shattering into a thousand pieces. At the sight of the stairway that seemed so easy of descent, and the tapers illuminating it, we were somewhat reassured. We embraced in a transport, and, each taking the other's hand, began cautiously to descend – when the twenty negroes, whom we had forgotten, hurled themselves upon us so impetuously that we fell, headlong, against the ebony portal at the bottom.

I will not describe the dread impression produced upon us by the aspect of the place in which we now are – all who are here have had that fearful experience – but one object of terror peculiar to ourselves was the sight of the Mage. He was pacing to and fro amid the restless, miserable crowd, with his right hand on his breast. He saw us. The flames devouring his heart leapt out through his eyelids. He darted upon us a fearful glance, and hurried away. A moment after, a malevolent Dive accosted Firouzkah. "Rondabah," said he, "has recovered her beauty. She has just ascended the throne of Kharezme; the hour of her triumph is that of your unending despair!"

At last Eblis declared all the horror of our fates. What a god have we served! What fearful doom has he pronounced upon us! What! we who had loved one another so well, must our love be turned to hate? We, who had come hither to enjoy an eternity of love, must we hate each other to all time? O dire, O accursed thought! O for instant annihilation!

Sobbing, sobbing, as they uttered these words, Alasi and Firouzkah threw themselves into each other's arms; and for a long space a mournful silence reigned in that unhappy company.

But at last this silence was broken by Vathek, who asked the third prince to relate his story. For Vathek's curiosity was still intact. He had yet to suffer the last punishment those criminal souls were destined to endure: the final extinction of every feeling save hatred and despair.

Appendix B:

1. The Explanatory Footnotes and Beckford's Orientalism

Jorge Luis Borges and Edward W. Said represent contrasting attitudes toward Orientalism in Western literatures. Said sees the very word, *Orientalism*, and the complex connotations informing it, as contributing to a "political vision of reality whose structure promoted the difference between the familiar (Europe, the West, "us") and the strange (the Orient, the East, "them")."[1] He sees in Orientalism a subtle justification for imperial expansion beginning with Napoleon's invasion of Egypt in 1798. To Borges, *"Orient* and *Occident, East* and *West"* are words "which we cannot define, but which are true."[2] To Borges another such term is *Latin America*. Borges turns Said's imperialism on its head when he calls the *Arabian Nights* a "splendid Oriental invasion" that utterly undermined Boileau's "cult of reason." Beckford would probably agree with Borges, but then his interests in the Orient pre-date Napoleon's. Borges reminds us that the German for Orient is *Morgenland*, the place where the sun originates. The word evokes both the worlds of wonder of the *Arabian Nights* and the world of learning at the cradle of Western culture and civilization. It is worth remembering that Beckford combined both interests.

Literary Orientalism became prominent in 1704 when the first volumes of Antoine Galland's translation, the *Arabian Nights Entertainments,* exploded upon western Europe. The wild imaginings of the *Arabian Nights* undermined the rational realism insisted upon by the fashion for neoclassicism nurtured by Boileau and, instead, encouraged an untrammeled creativity in settings where anything can and does happen, settings in which the supernatural invades the natural. Galland's translation was quickly re-translated from the French into most

---

1 Edward W. Said, *Orientalism* (New York: Pantheon Books, 1978) 42–43.
2 Jorge Luis Borges, "The Thousand and One Nights," in *Seven Nights*. Trans. Eliot Weinberger (New York: New Directions Books, 1984) 42–51.

European languages and spawned a tribe of imitators. Beckford's forebear, Antoine Hamilton, mocks the genre – and his society's enthusiasm for it – in *Les Quatres Facardins*,[1] a series of tales narrated with the utmost solemnity arising from the chance encounter of four men with the unlikely name of "Facardin." Joseph Addison included among the entertaining variety of his *Spectator* papers a parable set near Baghdad called "Vision of Mirza," a moral fable on the vanity of human wishes. The Oriental mode was attractively adaptable to a variety of literary and artistic purposes: for social satire (Montesquieu's *Lettres Persanes*, 1721), for moral, cultural, and philosophical commentary (Samuel Johnson's *Rasselas*, 1759), for opera (Mozart's *Die Entführung aus dem Serail*, 1782), and for a multitude of thrilling stories like *Mogul Tales* (1736) or *The Adventures of Abdalla* (1729)[2] that caught the fascinated attention of readers of all ages and developed respect for the teeming imagination. Richard Holmes tells of Coleridge as a little boy of six waiting anxiously for the rising sun to touch the book on the window seat, giving him renewed light and courage to dare return to spectre-haunted adventures from the *Arabian Nights*.[3] Wordsworth recalls in his *Prelude* his own childhood passion for "The tales that charm away the wakeful night/ In Araby ..." (V, 496–97).[4]

European interest in the Middle East resulted also in works of serious scholarship. Knowledge of Turkey, Persia, Arabia, and India increased with the researches of scholars and the detailed accounts of travellers. Barthélémy d'Herbelot's *Bibliothèque Orientale* (1697) is a reference book organized alphabetically to give full and detailed accounts of historic figures, geographical sites,

---

1   Hamilton writes in French with a mordant wit that Beckford seems to have taken as a model. He died in 1719, without publishing any of his Oriental tales, but they were in print by 1749. See André Parreaux *William Beckford Auteur de "Vathek"* (Paris: A.G. Nizet, 1960) 303–07.

2   Thomas Simon Gueullette, *Mogul Tales* (English translation, 1736); J.P. Bignon, *Adventures of Abdalla, son of Hanif* (English translation, 1729).

3   Richard Holmes, *Coleridge: Early Visions* (New York: Viking, 1990) 11.

4   William Wordsworth, *The Prelude: A Parallel Text*, ed. J.C. Maxwell (Harmondsworth, Penguin Books, 1971; rpt 1976) 197.

and social and cultural customs. The travel works of Jean Chardin and Cornelis le Brun[1] contain vivid accounts of encounters with various cities of Islam and, of special significance to this work, detailed descriptions and drawings of the ruin at Persepolis near Istakhar. In 1734 George Sale published his translation of *The Koran*: he accompanied it with a Preliminary Discourse, giving, with considerable sympathy, details of history, customs, and mythology. John Richardson's *Dissertation on the Languages, Literature and Manners of Eastern Nations* is both rich in detail and succinct. His views of Zoroaster, his assessment of the effects on the occidental mind of Greek and Christian bias, his accounts of judicial astrology, and details of Persian and Arabian mythologies, colour, and customs have a direct bearing on the cultural tensions that Beckford built into *Vathek* and *The Episodes*.

For the young William Beckford, tutored at home and constantly in the company of adults, the Orient of stories and scholars satisfied a profound need and set his imagination into reckless motion. His reading, writing, and drawing on Oriental subjects counteracted his sense of being hemmed in by attitudes and values with which he seemed by youth and nature to have little in common. But his studies became increasingly scholarly. While in Italy, he studied Arabic and prepared himself to translate the manuscripts brought from Turkey by Edward Wortley-Montagu.[2] His friendship with Samuel Henley was founded on a deep and intelligent grasp of the scholarly materials both were familiar with at Christmas 1781 when they first met. Their conversations inspired a good deal of Beckford's study and writing between 1781 and 1786, including *Vathek* and *The Episodes*.

The 1823 catalogue of the books he offered at auction when he sold his gothic mansion, Fonthill Abbey, reflects the depth of Beckford's Oriental interests; it includes over 100 years of the most authoritative works available in Europe on geography,

---

1   Details of these three works and others read by Beckford are listed at the end of this introduction under "Abbreviations."

2   Boyd Alexander, *England's Wealthiest Son* (London, Centaur Press, 1962) 100-01.

culture, and language of Persia, Arabia, and the Indian sub-continent.[1] These were the books he was willing to part with for his move to a smaller (but still ample) house in Bath; many other books went with him. The auction catalogue reflects only part of his commitment to Oriental studies. The Beckford Papers contain pages of Beckford's translations from the Arabic.[2] His various stories reflect a detailed knowledge of religion, customs, historic and mythological figures, and literature. *The Episodes* displays a remarkable knowledge of the *Shahnama*, Ferdowsi's great epic of legendary Persian kings – remarkable in view of the fact that a full translation was not available until the nineteenth century.[3] Beckford was a serious Orientalist.[4]

Henley's 1786 translation of *Vathek* includes an array of notes that requires almost as many words as the story and made an early reviewer think that the tale was written to supply a text for the notes.[5] Henley, it appears, had his own agenda. He was willing to provide an effective translation, but he made use of Beckford's little story for scholarly display. In their letters back and forth, Beckford protested what Henley was doing, but he may not have realized the extent of Henley's venture. While Beckford was in Switzerland, waiting in vain for the Powderham scandal to take its course and then fade, Henley completed

---

1 Fonthill Abbey. *A Catalogue of the Magnificent, Rare, and Valuable Library (of 20,000 volumes). Which will be Sold by Auction, by Mr. Phillips, at the Abbey, on Tuesday, the 9th of September, 1823.*

2 T.D. Rogers, *Catalogue of the papers of William Beckford (1760-1844)* (Oxford: Bodleian Library, 1987) 35-38.

3 The note explaining the name, *Roudabah*, in the first *Episode* suggests a considerable familiarity with *Shah-nama*. The first complete English translation was published in Calcutta in 1811; the first French translation was published between 1838 and 1855. Beckford's source, whether in English, French, or Arabic, remains unknown.

4 Boyd Alexander argues convincingly for attributing to Beckford *The story of Al Raoui, a tale from the Arabic.* (London: C. Geisweiler, 1799). See "The Authorship of Al Raoui" in Howard B. Gotlieb, *William Beckford of Fonthill, A Brief Narrative and Catalogue of an Exhibition* (New Haven: Yale University Library, 1960) 83-85.

5 "These verses [from Virgil] are quoted and commented upon in a late publication, under the name of Vathek, p. 269, which, it should seem, has been composed as a text, for the purpose of giving to the publick the information contained in the notes." *Gentleman's Magazine* 57 (January 1787) 55.

his project by publishing the English *Vathek*. He resumed the career interrupted by the heady experience with the wealthy young Beckford: his responsibilities as a teacher at Harrow, as a clergyman at his church in Suffolk, and as an antiquarian with publications on Virgil, Tibullus, and Babylonian inscription. His industry was rewarded with the appointment in 1805 as principal of the new East India College in Haileybury.[1]

Until 1816, only Henley's English version of *Vathek* (re-issued in 1809) was available to English-speaking readers. Its extensive notes coloured its reception: the story and the notes shared admiration at a time when Oriental tales were exciting but not demonstrably indebted to genuine Oriental research. Lord Byron was a highly influential case in point. *Vathek*'s fame owed much to the praise of Byron, the most popular and exciting writer of the second decade of the nineteenth century. He commends *Vathek* and its notes in his early success, *The Giaour* (1813):

> For the contents of some of the notes I am indebted part-
> ly to D'Herbelot, and partly to that most eastern and, as
> Mr. Weber justly entitles it, 'sublime tale,' the 'Caliph
> Vathek.' I do not know from what source the author of
> that singular volume may have drawn his materials, but
> for correctness of costume, beauty of description, and
> power of imagination, it far surpasses all European imita-
> tions; and bears such marks of originality, that those who
> have visited the East will find some difficulty in believing
> it to be more than a translation.[2]

Beckford seems far less interested in writing notes to his Oriental tales. The first French-language edition published under his auspices in Lausanne in late 1786 has only four sketchy notes. The edition published in the summer of 1787 in

---

1 Henley merits an entry in the *Dictionary of National Biography* to which my account of his later life is indebted.
2 Lord Byron, *The Complete Poetical Works*, ed. Jerome J. McGann (Oxford: Claren-don Press, 1981) III, 423.

Paris, after Beckford had seen Henley's English edition, translates abbreviated versions of Henley's notes, but they extend over only 23 pages of a 190 page work, while in Henley's edition the notes occupy 121 pages and the text, in a larger font, occupies only 211 pages. After Byron's acknowledgment, the very existence of the notes demanded that they be published. When Beckford brought out corrected versions of *Vathek* in French and English in 1815 and 1816, it was with a revised, edited, pared, but still substantial, display of Henley's notes. Thus, Henley's industrious note-writing have had their effect: they have left the impression that Beckford's work is as much a work of scholarship as it is a work of fiction.

When we put *Vathek* together with *The Episodes* we begin to see the notes in a more appropriate perspective. Beckford tries to be accurate and rich in his allusions, but he uses his materials and lore for his own purposes and his own inspirations. To Mahmoud Mansalaoui, he creates "almost a private mythology."[1] Although Beckford contributed to the notes and demonstrates an impressive command of detail in the correspondence concerning them, the notes, for the most part, are Henley's.[2] The footnotes to this combined edition are not concerned with recording Henley's industry, since the content of many of his notes are more engaged with parading his own scholarship than explaining Beckford's fiction. The notes to this edition are concerned with Beckford's adaptation of his sources to his fiction: with revealing Beckford's allusions, disclosing his sources, and suggesting some of his purposes, particularly in references that connect the frame tale, *Vathek*, with *The Episodes*, such as Beckford's imaginative construction of Zoroastrianism. Other notes simply explain some of the terms Beckford uses to readers lacking backgrounds in the early Islamic world. Rather than perpetrate the limitations of the scholarship available to Beckford and Henley, I have chosen to

---

1 Mahmoud Mansalaoui, "Pseudo-Orientalism in Transition: The Age of *Vathek*," in *Fatma Moussa Mahmoud, ed. William Beckford of Fonthill, 1760-1844: Bicentenary Essays* (Cairo: Cairo Studies in English, 1960) 148.
2 Morrison, *Collection of Autograph Letters*, 196-97.

draw many explanations from modern encyclopedias, turning to Beckford's sources when they reveal something of Beckford's art and to Roger Lonsdale's perceptive commentary on Henley's notes in his fine edition of *Vathek*[1] when no other clarifications are satisfactory. Sadly, none of his manuscripts of *The Episodes* is provided with explanatory notes; all the notes there originate from the editorial process.

Abbreviations

The following abbreviations are used in the explanatory footnotes:

Islam2   *The Encyclopaedia of Islam*. Eds. E. van Donzel, B. Lewis, and Ch. Pellat. Leiden: E.J. Brill, 1986-97. The terms in italics are in modern Islamic usage and drawn from this or the following work.

Islam1   *First Encyclopaedia of Islam, 1913-36*. Eds. M.Th. Houtsma, A.J. Wensinck, H.A.R. Gibb, et al. Leiden: E.J.Brill, rpt.1993.

Lonsdale   Roger Lonsdale's notes in William Beckford. *Vathek*. Oxford: Oxford University Press, 1970; rpt. 1983.

Arabian Nights   Arabian Nights Entertainments ... Translated ... from the Arabian MSS. by M. Galland, 4 vols., London: 1798.

Anecdotes   Anecdotes Arabes. Paris: chez Vincent, 1772.

le Brun   Voyages de Corneille le Brun par la Moscovie, en Perse, et aux Indes Orientales. 2 vols. Amsterdam: 1718.

---

1   In William Beckford. *Vathek*. ed. Roger Lonsdale. (Oxford: Oxford University Press, 1970; rpt. 1983).

Chardin   *Voyages de Monsieur Le Chevalier Chardin en Perse, at Autres Lieux de l'Orient.* 3 vols. Amsterdam: 1711.

Habesci   Elias Habesci. *The Present State of the Ottoman Empire.* London: R. Baldwin, 1784.

d'Herbelot   Barthélémy d'Herbelot de Molainville. *Bibliothèque Orientale, Ou Dictionnaire Universel Contenant Généralement Tout ce qui regarde la conoissance des Peuples de l'Orient.* Paris, 1697.

Inatulla   *Tales translated from the Persian of Inatulla of Delhi.* Trans. Col. Dowe, 2 vols. London:1768.

Morrison Papers   Alfred Morrison, ed. *Collection of Autograph Letters and Historical Documents,* Second Series 1882–1893, Vol. I (A-B). Printed for Private Circulation, 1893.

Richardson   John Richardson, Esq., F.S.A. *A Dissertation on the Languages, Literature and Manners of Eastern Nations.* Oxford: 1777.

Sale   George Sale. *The Koran ... to which is prefixed A Preliminary Discourse.* London: Wilcox, 1734.

2. Notes on the Choice of Texts

Vathek:

The text of *Vathek* is not a duplication of any single documentary form, but rather a reconstruction based on the critical examination of all authoritative editions of *Vathek* and upon research into the circumstances surrounding the publication of these relevant editions. A machine collation of copies of every edition published in Beckford's lifetime determined the true editions representing new type settings. These were then hand collated against one another and substantive variants recorded.

Three editions showed unusual activity in revision and external evidence pointed to Beckford as the source of the revision. These editions are:

1. *An Arabian Tale.* From an Unpublished Manuscript with Notes Critical and Explanatory. London: J. Johnson, 1786.

2. *Vathek.* Translated from the Original French. London: W. Clarke, 1816.

3. *Vathek.* Translated from the Original French. London: W. Clarke, 1823.

Two other editions published in Beckford's lifetime contain no authoritative emendations.

4. *Vathek.* London: Bentley's Standard Novels, 1834.

5. *Vathek.* Paris: Baudry, 1834.

The machine collation of copies of the 1816 edition reveals an extraordinary and portentous revision. During the press run, Reading B was substituted for Reading A.

Reading A:

When the afflicting narrative was closed, the young man, who first addressed him, began in the following manner: — "The history of the princes and friends, Alasi and Firouz, confined in the palace of subterraneous fire." The next was: — "The history of Prince Barkiarokh, confined to the palace of subterraneous fire." Then: "The history of Prince Kalilah and Princess Zulkais, confined in the palace of subterraneous fire." The third prince had reached the midst of his adventures, when a sudden noise interrupted him, which caused the vault to tremble and to open. (p. 220)

Reading B:

When the afflicting narrative was closed, the young man entered on his own. Each person proceeded in order; and when the third prince had reached the midst of his adventures, a sudden noise interrupted him, which caused the vault to tremble and to open. (p. 220)

The two variant states of the 1816 London edition of *Vathek* define the precise moment during the press run when Beckford gave up the enterprise of producing an edition uniting *Vathek* and *The Episodes* in the English language. This edition supplies a united edition as conceived by Beckford before that fateful moment in 1816 when he changed his mind.

The 1816 edition shows evidence of painstaking revision of substantives and accidentals as well as the substitution of Reading B for Reading A; such close attention indicates the author's intervention. The 1816 edition best fulfills the characteristics of Beckford's first edition and is the copy-text on which the text of *Vathek* in this edition is based. Unless indicated otherwise, spellings and punctuation are drawn from this edition.

The Episodes

The publication history of *The Episodes of Vathek* is simpler than that of *Vathek*. Lewis Melville published in French *Episode* One (the "Firouzkah" version) and *Episode* Three in *The English Review* in 1909 and 1910.[1] In 1912 he published in a single volume three *Episodes* in French – "Firouzkah," "Barkiarokh," and "Zulkais" – with English translations of the three stories by Sir Frank T. Marzials.[2] This edition begins a chain of publications of French and English texts more or less copied directly from it.

1. Guy Chapman, ed. *Vathek with the Episodes of Vathek*. 2 vols. London: Constable, 1929. [This edition is entirely in

---

1 *The English Review* 4 (1909): 163-84, and 6 (1910): 137-47, 309-22.
2 Lewis Melville, ed., *The Episodes of Vathek*. Published in French with an English translation by Sir Frank T. Marzials. (London: Stephen Swift and Co., 1912).

French. It normalizes the eighteenth-century French of Melville's *Episodes* and combines that work with the Paris 1787 edition of *Vathek*, ignoring Beckford's revisions of the Londres 1815 edition. It omits all the notes.]

2. J.B. Brunius, ed. *Vathek et les Episodes*. Paris: Edition Stock, [1948?]. [This edition seems to derive from the Chapman edition; it "purifies" the text from errors in idiom, but does not list or justify the alterations.]

3. Ernest Giddey, ed. *Vathek et les Episodes*. Lausanne: Editions Rencontre, 1962. [The editor is explicit about derivations: his *Vathek* is based on the Paris 1787 edition; his *Episodes* are taken from Chapman's 1929 edition.]

4. Maurice Lévy, ed. *Vathek et les Episodes*. Paris: Flammarion, 1981. [The editor derives his *Vathek* from Paris 1787 and his *Episodes* from Melville's 1912 edition, modernized and corrected of the most obvious faults; it omits entirely the last, but fragmentary, *Episode*, "L'Histoire de la Princesse Zulkaïs et du Prince Kalilah."]

5. Lin Carter, ed. *Vathek and The Episodes*. New York: Ballantine, 1971. [This edition unites Henley's unauthorized 1786 edition (ignoring Beckford's 1816 revision) with the Marzials translation.]

6. Robert J. Gemmett, ed. *The Episodes of Vathek*. London: Associated University Presses, 1975. [This edition offers only the Marzials translation with a few, unspecified, corrections.]

7. Malcolm Jack, ed. *The Episodes of Vathek*. London: Dedalus, 1994. [The Marzials translation with numerous, but unspecified, corrections.]

Episode One in this edition is drawn from a fair-copy manuscript of a version of the first *Episode of Vathek* that has never been published (MS. Beckford d.13). Internal evidence shows that it was written between 1782 and 1785 while Beckford was polishing *Vathek* in French, writing *Episodes* in French, supervising an English translation of *Vathek*, and contemplating a single work with *Vathek* as a frame tale introducing a suite of three or four *Episodes*. This *Episode* was translated from Beckford's French and located in this edition as the true first *Episode*. Its translation was intended to harmonize with the style of the Marzials translations and, indeed, to use their phrasings when that was possible. *Episodes* Two and Three are drawn from Marzials' translation (with a few recorded corrections). The Marzials translation of the Firouzkah version, that Beckford prepared late in his life, is supplied as Appendix A.

3. Emendation Notes: *Vathek*

Emendations to the copy-text, the first state of the 1816 edition, are not commented on if they simply normalize or clarify matters of spelling and punctuation. These notes indicate more substantive changes. The amended reading is given first, followed by the reading in the copy-text, both in italics. An explanation for the change is offered after the square bracket.

41:10 *me, adore* replaces *me? adore* in the 1816 edition] The 1786 version reads: "'Wouldest thou devote thyself to me? Adore then the terrestrial influences . . ..'" In his revision it seems likely that Beckford, intending to tighten the structure of the sentence, changed the question mark to a comma, began *adore* with the lower case, and marked out *then*. The compositor included all revisions but the substitution of a comma for a question mark. The editorial emendation brings the text into agreement with the Lausanne version which, in a similar structure, uses a comma rather than a question mark.

42:22 *thee?* – *Come* replaces *thee;* — *Come* in the 1816 edition] According to Beckford's fairly consistent usage, an interrogative statement is followed by a question mark. In this case the capitalized "Come" would indicate that Beckford intended to use a question mark rather than a semicolon, since he never follows a semicolon with a new sentence beginning with a capital letter. Beckford altered this passage in the 1786 edition to conform with his French-language edition of 1815. In that version a question mark was used.

48:18 *contests* replaces the 1816 *contest*] The 1823 revision accords with all French-language versions in using the plural.

79:19 *hath* replaces *had*] The 1786 reading is adopted; it corresponds in tense to all French-language versions.

209:6 *round* replaces *around*] The 1823 reading is adopted.

Emendation Notes: *Episodes*

Titles: *History* replaces *Story* throughout to accord with Beckford's usage in State 1 of the 1816 edition of *Vathek*. Quotation marks are normalized as well.

Episode One: "Firouz"

29] The manuscript reads: "~~Un voluptueux~~ Le sommeil ~~s'empara~~ enfin" but no alternative phrasing is provided. The editor amended the passage, "*Un voluptueux sommeil s'empara enfin.* "and translated it: "*A voluptuous sleep took possession of us at last.*"

30] The manuscript reads: "Nous descendîmes [~~dans le jardin, où, sous une treille de laquelle pendaient des grappes très appétissantes, nous trouvâmes le mage qui, aussi bien que nous, fit honneur à un excellent déjeuner qu'on nous servit.~~]." To supply missing continuity this passage was restored to the French text and translated as: "*We descended into the garden where, under a trellis from which hung most appetizing grapes, we found the*

Magus who, just as we, did justice to the excellent breakfast served to us."

Episode Two: "Barkiarokh"

45] *Shiraz* replaces *Chiraz* to accord with usage in *Vathek*.

56] *I am the true daughter of ...* replaces Marzials' awkward translation, *I am own daughter to ...* The text in French reads, *"Je suis le propre fille de ..."*

58] *Kaf* replaces *Caf* to accord with usage in *Vathek*.

74] *proferring* replaces the mistranslation *preferring*.

108] *in my attendance at"* replaces *at my attendance at.*

109] *Deggial* replaces *Degial* to be consistent with usage in *Vathek*.

114] *Farukrouz* replaces *Farukrouz* to keep the spellings consistent.

133] *harrowing* replaces *horrowing*.

134] *Soliman* replaces *Solieman* to be consistent with *Vathek*.

Episode Three: "Zulkaïs"

141] *Here I am unable to make* replaces Marzials' *I am not here in case to make*; the French reads: *je ne puis faire ici ...*

143] *sight.* replaces *sight?* to accord with reason and the punctuation of the French version.

145] *Pharaohs' examples* replaces *Pharaoh's example* for reasons of logic and accuracy.

159] *precincts.* replaces *precincts?* for reasons of logic and accuracy.

168] *so far as I* replaces *so far I* for reasons of logic.

Appendix A: Firouzkah version

Lewis Melville's misreadings of *Rondabah* for *Roudabah*, *Lalzer* for *Zalzar*, and *Amru* for *Amni* are allowed to stand in this version.

Appendix C: Geography and Maps

The geography of *Vathek with The Episodes* moves from the centre to the periphery of the Islamic empire of Vathek's time. The map provides a rough representation of that world. The action of *Vathek* keeps to the centre of the empire, moving from Arabia to Persia, from Samarra near Baghdad to Istakhar, near Persepolis, following routes past Shiraz and Rocnabad as described by Chardin and le Brun, Beckford's principal sources. The movement from Arabia to Persia may have been intended to express a moral movement away from a strict fundamentalism of Islamic Arabia to a more negligent and sophisticated Persian civilization still containing a lurking Zoroastrianism. *The Episodes* extend the geography northward to lands bordering on the Caspian and Aral Seas in the first two *Episodes*, and westward to Egypt in the third *Episode*.

The map supplied draws heavily on eighteenth-century sources as well as modern ones. Indicated borders between states and provinces are not intended to be authoritative.

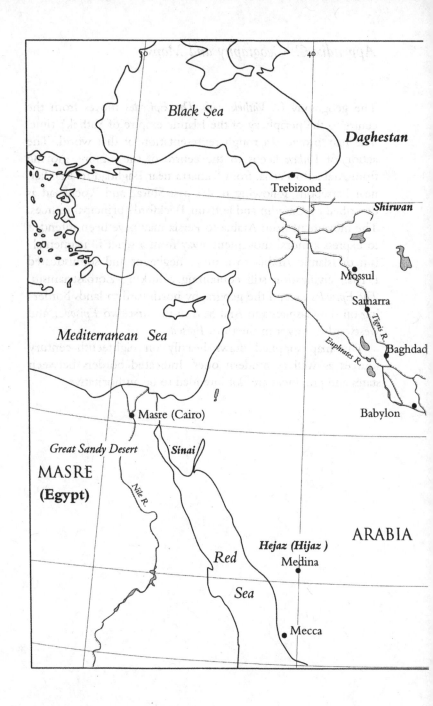

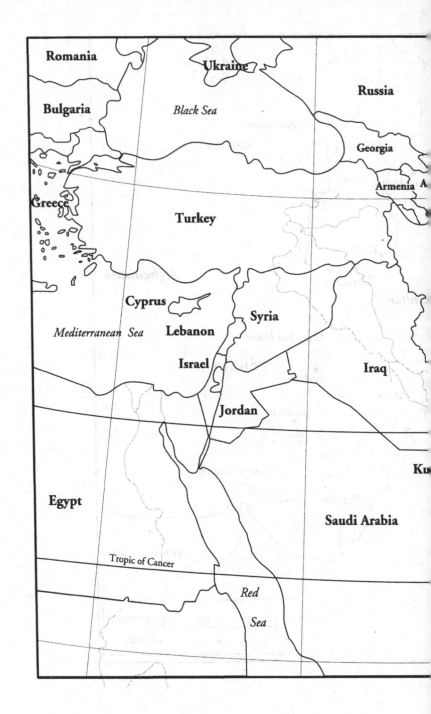

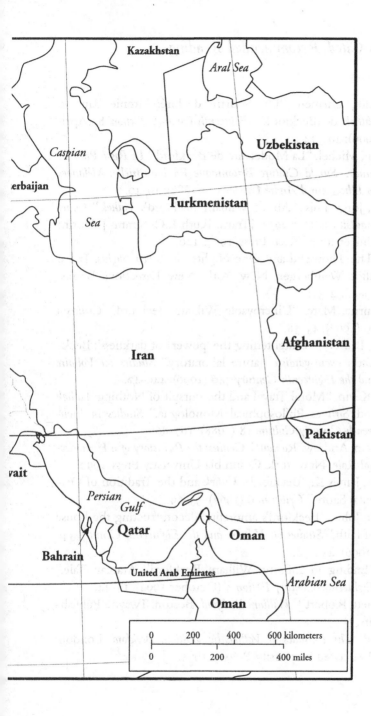

Works Cited/Recommended Reading

Alamoudi, Carmen. "Un Sourire déchiré: l'ironie dans le *Vathek* de Beckford." *Eighteenth-Century Fiction* 8 (April 1996): 401-14.

Baridon, Michel. "La Modernité de Beckford." *Le Passé Present: Études Sur la Culture Britannique Pre-industrielle: Mélanges en L'honneur d'André Parreaux* 9 (1988): 19-40.

Borges, Jorge Luis. "About William Beckford's *Vathek*," *Other Inquisitions 1937-1952.* [Trans. Ruth L.C. Simms.] Austin: University of Texas Press, 1964. 140.

——. "The Thousand and One Nights," in *Seven Nights.* Trans. Eliot Weinberger. New York: New Directions Books, 1984. 42-51.

Chadourne, Marc. "L'incroyable William Beckford." *Criticism* 69 (1962): 43-58.

Chatel, Laurent. "Enlightening the 'powers of darkness': Beckford's *avant-gardiste* nature laboratory." *Studies on Voltaire and the Eighteenth Century* 346 (1996): 440-42.

Cope, Kevin. "Moral Travel and the Pursuit of Nothing: *Vathek* and *Siris* as Philosophical Monologue." *Studies in Eighteenth-Century Culture* 18 (1988): 167-86.

Elfenbein, Andrew. *Romantic Genius: the Prehistory of a Homosexual Role.* New York: Columbia University Press, 1999.

Folsom, James K. "Beckford's *Vathek* and the Tradition of Oriental Satire." *Criticism* 6 (1964): 53-69.

Garrett, John. "Beckford's amorality: deconstructing the house of faith." *Studies on Voltaire and the Eighteenth Century* 346 (1996): 455-58.

——. "Ending in Infinity: William Beckford's Arabian Tale." *Eighteenth-Century Fiction* 5 (October 1992): 15-34.

Gemmett, Robert J. *William Beckford.* Boston: Twayne Publishers, 1977.

——, ed. *The Episodes of Vathek by William Beckford.* London: Associated University Presses, 1975.

Giddey, Ernest. "La Vision Créatrice de *Vathek* de Beckford." *Lausanne University Faculté des Lettres Publication* 18 (1966): 43-56.

Gotlieb, Howard B. *William Beckford of Fonthill, A Brief Narrative and Catalogue of an Exhibition.* New Haven: Yale University Library, 1960.

Graham, Kenneth W. "Beckford's Design for *The Episodes*: A History and a Review." *Papers of the Bibliographical Society of America* 71 (1977): 336-43.

——,ed. *Vathek and the Escape from Time: Bicentenary Revaluations.* New York: AMS Press, 1990.

Hachicho, Mohamad Ali. "English Travel Books About the Arab Near East." *Welt des Islams* 9 (1964): 134-205.

Haggerty, George E. "Literature and Homosexuality in the Late Eighteenth Century: Walpole, Beckford, and Lewis." *Studies in the Novel* 18 (Winter 1986): 341-52.

——. *Men in Love: Masculinity and Sexuality in the Eighteenth Century.* New York: Columbia University Press, 1999.

Holmes, Richard. *Coleridge: Early Visions.* New York: Viking, 1990.

Jack, Malcolm. "William Beckford: the poor Arabian storyteller." *Studies on Voltaire and the Eighteenth Century* 346 (1996): 451-53.

——. "Introduction," *The Episodes of Vathek.* London: Dedalus, 1994.

Le Yaouanc, Collette. "Le thème sexuel dans *Vathek.*" *Études Anglaises* 76 (1977): 257-64.

Liu, Alan. "Toward a Theory of Common Sense: Beckford's *Vathek* and Johnson's *Rasselas.*" *Texas Studies in Literature and Language* 26 (1984): 183-217.

Lonsdale, Roger, ed. Introduction and Notes. William Beckford. *Vathek.* Oxford: Oxford University Press, 1970; rpt. 1983.

Mansalaoui, Mahmoud. "Pseudo-Orientalism in Transition: The Age of *Vathek.*" Fatma Moussa-Mahmoud, ed. *William Beckford of Fonthill, 1760-1844: Bicentenary Essays.* Cairo, Egypt: Cairo Studies in English, 1960.

Mayoux, Jean-Jacques. "La Damnation de Beckford." *English Miscellany* 12 (1961): 41-77.

Maynard, Temple J. "Depictions of Persepolis and William Beckford's Istakar." *Eighteenth-Century Life* 3 (1977): 119-22.

——. "Eschewing present pleasure for an eternity of bliss: the irreligious motivation of Beckford's protagonists in *Vathek*." *Studies on Voltaire and the Eighteenth Century* 265 (1989): 1676-79.

——. "The Landscape of *Vathek*." *Transactions of the Samuel Johnson Society of the Northwest* 7 (1974): 79-98. With a reply by David McCracken, 99-103.

——. " The Movement Underground and the Escape from Time in Beckford's Fiction." In Kenneth W. Graham, ed. *Vathek and the Escape from Time: Bicentenary Revaluations.* New York: AMS, 1990. 9-31.

Melville, Lewis, ed. *The Episodes of Vathek.* [Trans. Sir Frank T. Marzials.] London: Stephen Swift and Co., 1912.

Morrison, Alfred. *Collection of Autograph Letters and Historical Documents,* Second Series, 1882-93. London: Printed for Private Circulation, 1893.

Moussa-Mahmoud, Fatma. "A Monument of the Author of *Vathek*." *Études anglaises* 15 (1962): 138-47.

——. "Oriental in Picaresque: A Chapter in the History of the Oriental Tale in England." In *Oriental Tales and Influences in 19th Century.* Cairo: Cairo Studies in English, 1961-62. 145-88.

——. ed. *William Beckford of Fonthill, 1760-1844: Bicentenary Essays.* Cairo, Egypt: Cairo Studies in English, 1960.

Parreaux, André. "Beckford et Byron." *Études Anglaises* 8 (1955): 11-31, 113-32.

——. *William Beckford Auteur de "Vathek."* Paris: A.G. Nizet, 1960.

Potkay, Adam. "Beckford's Heaven of Boys." *Raritan* 13 (Summer 1993): 73-86.

Richardson, John. Esq. F.S.A., *A Dissertation on the Languages, Literature and Manners of Eastern Nations.* Oxford: Clarendon Press, 1777.

Rieger, James Henry. "Au Pied de la Lettre." *Criticism* 4 (1962): 302-12.

Said, Edward W. *Orientalism*. New York: Pantheon Books, 1978.

Shaffer, E.S. *"Kubla Khan" and The Fall of Jerusalem: The Mythological School in Biblical Criticism and Secular Literature 1770-1880*. Cambridge: CUP, 1975. See Chapter 3, The Oriental Idyll: 96-144, 325-34.

——. *"Vathek* and *The Episodes of Vathek* – separately, but not together." *Beckford Journal* (Spring 1995): 23-27, 45-47.

Svilpis, J. E.. "Orientalism, Fantasy, and *Vathek.*" In Kenneth W. Graham, ed. *Vathek and the Escape from Time: Bicentenary Revaluations*. New York: AMS Press, 1990. 49-72.

Taylor, W.S., and J.H. Pringle. *Correspondence of William Pitt, Earl of Chatham*, 4 vols. London: J. Murray, 1838-40.

From the Publisher

A name never says it all, but the word "Broadview" expresses a good deal of the philosophy behind our company. We are open to a broad range of academic approaches and political viewpoints. We pay attention to the broad impact book publishing and book printing has in the wider world; for some years now we have used 100% recycled paper for most titles. Our publishing program is internationally oriented and broad-ranging. Our individual titles often appeal to a broad readership too; many are of interest as much to general readers as to academics and students.

Founded in 1985, Broadview remains a fully independent company owned by its shareholders—not an imprint or subsidiary of a larger multinational.

For the most accurate information on our books (including information on pricing, editions, and formats) please visit our website at www.broadviewpress.com. Our print books and ebooks are also available for sale on our site.

broadview press
www.broadviewpress.com